Acclaim for *Nashville*

"Thoroughly down-home delightful."

—Stephanie Grace Whitson, bestselling author

"Move over Jennifer Weiner—a new voice has just hit town! *Nashville Dreams* gives us a fun peek at what it might be like to be a struggling songwriter in the heart of the south. Hauck's storytelling is a rare and luminous gift. I'm her number one fan."

—Colleen Coble, bestselling author

"*Nashville Dreams* strums the heart strings with humor and a girl's search for purpose. For Robin McAfee, finding the spotlight isn't easy, but always fun."

—DiAnn Mills, author of *Lanterns and Lace*

"Fun, funny and full of good ol' country charm, *Nashville Dreams* grabbed me on the first page and didn't let go. Pour yourself a tall glass of sweet tea, sit back in a comfortable chair, and get ready to meet one of the sassiest Southern chicks in Christian fiction. You won't be sorry!"

—Virginia Smith, author of *Just As I Am*

"Thanks to Hauck's masterful storytelling and characterization, aspiring songwriter Robin Rae McAfee from Freedom, Alabama lingers in my mind like a lifelong friend. *Nashville Dreams* breaks through genre lines so smoothly that anyone with a heart and a sense of humor will love this story."

—Christine Lynxwiler, author of *Arkansas*
and the Pinky Promise Sisterhood series

"Perfect! Beautifully written with perfect Southern charm, Rachel Hauck superbly captures the world of NashVegas—the fears, the hopes, the people, and the aspirations of a wanna-be songwriter. I found myself cheering for Robin Rae: a brave, spunky, good ol' country gal shouldering not only her dreams, but the dreams of the people she loves. Encore, Encore!"

—Susan May Warren, award-winning author
of *Everything's Coming up Josey*

"With a lively cast of characters and a Southern setting so real I feel like I've just returned from a visit, *Nashville Dreams* grips the reader from start to finish, offering a fun glimpse into the world of songwriting and a storyline that's as good as warm apple pie on a lazy afternoon."

—Diann Hunt, author of *RV There Yet?*

Nashville DREAMS

RACHEL HAUCK

THOMAS NELSON
Since 1798

Dedicated to my dear friend, Stuart Greaves.
I'm inspired and challenged by you—that you
spend your talents, your ambitions, your time on
a radical pursuit of Jesus. Without your touch
my life would be incomplete. I love you, bro.

© 2006, 2019 by Rachel Hayes Hauck

Originally published as *Lost in NashVegas*. *Nashville Dreams* was first published as an e-book.

Published in Nashville, Tennessee, by Thomas Nelson. Thomas Nelson is a registered trademark of Thomas Nelson, Inc.

Thomas Nelson, Inc., titles may be purchased in bulk for educational, business, fund-raising, or sales promotional use. For information, please e-mail SpecialMarkets@ThomasNelson.com.

Publisher's Note: This novel is a work of fiction. Names, characters, places, and incidents are either products of the author's imagination or used fictitiously. All characters are fictional, and any similarity to people living or dead is purely coincidental.

ISBN: 978-0-7852-5897-1 (trade paper)
ISBN: 978-0-7180-1557-2 (e-book)

Library of Congress Cataloging-in-Publication Data

Hauck, Rachel, 1960-
    Lost in NashVegas / Rachel Hauck.
        p. cm.
    ISBN-13: 978-1-59554-190-1 (pbk.)
    ISBN-10: 1-59554-190-X (pbk.)
    1. Women country musicians--Fiction. 2. Musical fiction.   I. Title.
    PS3608.A866L67 2006
    813'.6—dc22

                                                                    2006026231

20 21 22 23 24 25 LSC 9 8 7 6 5 4 3 2 1

How I let Daddy and Granddaddy Lukeman talk me into singing a "couple" of my songs at the Spring Sing, *again*, is beyond me. I can't do it. I can barely breathe, let alone sing.

Blood thumps from my heart up to my ears, over my scalp, and down to my toes. Cold sweat beads on the back of my neck and under my arms. My feet burn as if I'm standing on Florida sand in mid-July.

"Gonna chicken out again, Robin?" Smiley Canyon nudges me with his pointy elbow.

"Nooo," I lie, gripping my old Taylor guitar for security.

Smiley laughs at me. "Let's see—last year you broke out in hives the night before the show, didn't ya?"

"I had a rash from stem to stern. You saw me the next morning."

"And the year before that you couldn't find the keys to your truck . . ." He plucks the strings of his beat-up Gibson, trying to tune. Smart aleck. No wonder Nashville kicked him back home to Alabama.

"And didn't you get lost driving across town once?"

I ball my fist. One pop, right in the kisser. Come on, Lord, look the other way, just for a second.

But when I look Smiley in the eye, I see what I don't care to see: the truth. I relax my fingers and attempt to deflect attention. "Your song was real good. Was it a new one?"

"Naw, wrote it a few years back."

I nod. "Good for you."

He tips the brim of his cowboy hat my way. "Better go get my seat. Don't want to miss your debut." He says *debut* like "de-butt"—as if I'm going to fall flat on mine—and walks off snickering.

With a tiny step forward, I peer around the stage curtain. Freedom Music Hall is packed. An electric twinge constricts my middle, and I take two giant steps back. Let Smiley be right. Let him laugh at me again. It's better than public humiliation.

Turning to flee, I bump smack dab into Jeeter Perkins, the Hall's emcee.

"Get ready, Robin Rae. You're up next." He grins and adjusts his bolo tie.

Hello, Robin. What'll it be? Anxiety attack in front of a thousand of your closest friends and family? Yes? Right this way.

"Jeeter, I changed my mind. I'm not singing."

He rolls his eyes. "Now, Robin Rae—"

"How about you let old Paul Whitestone go on with his Dixie Dos?" Behind Jeeter, the former bluegrass icon waits with his round-faced, rosy-cheeked granddaughters—Elvira, Elmira, and Eldora. (Identical triplets. Tall, big girls.)

"Listen, girl, I've heard your songs a hundred times on your granddaddy's porch. You got a gift. A gift." Jeeter pinches my arms in his bony grip and bugs out his eyes. "Sometimes you have to face your fears."

I squint. "And sometimes ya don't."

This isn't like the first day of school or one of Momma's Saturday night dinners. Nope. Singing in the Hall is optional. And I'm opting out.

Jeeter shakes his head and brushes past me as the Blues Street Boys finish and exit stage left to mild applause. "Thank you, boys," he says into the mike. "I don't think I've ever heard such unique, *ahem*, harmonies." He glances over at me and raises one bushy brow.

Shaking my head, I step backward and poke Paul Whitestone, who's nodded off. "You and the girls are on, Paul."

The old man sputters to life. "Huh? Oh, we're on?" He waves his long arm at the triplets. "Girls, come on. We're up."

Jeeter rouses the crowd with a big call into the microphone, waving his hat in the air. "How y'all doing?" They give Jeeter what he wants—hoots and hollers, whistles and cheers.

"The hills are alive with the sound of music!" Jeeter cuts a glance at me. "We got a real treat for you folks tonight . . ."

Hand on my guitar, I tip my head in the direction of the ladies' room and mouth, "Got to go."

"Next up," Jeeter's voice trails after me, "Paul Whitestone and the Dixie Dos."

Ducking into the ladies' room, I push the lock and fall against the door. My stomach feels like a firecracker just exploded in it. My heart is racing at top NASCAR speed, and my legs are trembling like Granddaddy's old hound, Bruno, when it thunders.

Go out there . . . Sing in front of folks . . . Who'm I kidding? Freedom, Alabama, and their *Nashville* tradition have haunted me for the last time.

I shift my guitar so it hangs down my back and dampen a wad of paper towels. Patting the sweat beads from my forehead, I wonder if I'll make it out of the Hall alive. Blue spots flicker before my eyes.

"Should've stayed home where you belong," I scold my reflection in the mirror. "At twenty-five, you should know better."

Grandpa McAfee is right: if you can't run with the big

dogs, stay on the porch. Drawing a shaky breath, I adjust my guitar strap so that it's not cutting into my shoulder and unlock the door. But before I can jerk on the knob, the door flies open, bonking me on the head.

"Ouch!" My hand goes to my forehead as Arizona Parish shoves her way inside.

"What're you doing?" She tilts her soft blond head to one side and props her hands on her skinny waist.

I pop her on the shoulder. "What are *you* doing? There's only room for one in here."

"I came to find out what *you're* doing." She looks down at me with her eyebrows pinched and her lips tight. "So, what are you doing?"

"Hiding. My palms are sweating, my heart's racing, and my stomach feels like the finale of the Fourth of July show."

"Robin, it's just performance anxiety. Stage fright." She grabs me by the arms. "Take a deep breath, say 'Help me, Jesus,' and get on out there." She gives me a quick shove toward the stage entrance. "Wow 'em."

"Your sympathy is overwhelming."

"I'm not here to be sympathetic, Robin. I'm here to tell you the time has come to face your fears. You sing like an angel, and your sappy lyrics have ruined my mascara more times than I can count."

"Well, hot diggity dog for me. I don't care what my lyrics have done to your mascara, I'm not going out there." I jab my finger toward the stage door. "I'm going home."

My boot heels thud across Freedom Music Hall's ancient wood floor. The floor that has borne the soles of Garth Brooks, Tammy Wynette, Lionel Richie, and the great Billy Graham. Center stage, old Paul is plunking his banjo while the triplets clog on top of a three-tiered platform, shaking their ruffled skirts, shaking the entire Hall.

Arizona follows me to my guitar case. "How three pudgy girls move their feet so fast is beyond me."

"They've been clogging and eating since they were born." I settle my guitar in its case.

She sighs. "Got to admit, they have the best legs in Freedom."

This makes me laugh. "Can't argue there."

"Robin, don't lock up your guitar. Get out there. Beat this stage fright. If those triplets have the best legs in Freedom, you have the best voice and the best songs. Please. For me." Arizona clasps her hands under her chin and bats her eyes.

I stop buckling up my guitar case. Arizona Parish has a way of getting under my skin, forcing me to dig deep and dream big. She introduced herself to me a few years ago as "the girl from Miami." Her journey to Freedom is still a mystery.

"There was a situation," she said.

"Promise me the law ain't after you."

"Promise." She crossed her heart and flashed the Girl Scout salute.

Now, backstage at the Hall, Arizona kneels beside me. "Please. Go out there."

Standing, I look toward the stage with a shake of my head. "Why I let Daddy and Granddaddy talk me into this every year is crazy. Plumb crazy."

"You know why." She pokes me in the chest with her bony finger. "Deep inside, you know."

Before I can rouse up a crushing reply, a loud crack comes from center stage. Followed by three very distinct thuds.

Elvira.

Elmira.

Eldora.

"What in the world . . ." My first glimpse of three white-ruffled bottoms shaking in the spotlight takes my breath away.

It's followed by a *sppptt* as I choke back a laugh. "Holy clogging platform, Batman."

The girls' three-tiered clogging platform has broken clean
through.

For about ten seconds, there's a heavy hush over the auditorium and a collective holding of breaths. Are they all right?
Then, a snort. A muffled guffaw. A fading tee-hee behind
someone's hand.

But when Elvira—or is it Elmira—sticks her round hand
in the air and says in a high-pitched voice, "We're all right,
Papa," it's over. Laughter explodes like water balloons and
douses every one of us.

Arizona hides her face behind her hand. "This is terrible.
Oh, the humiliation." She ducks behind the stage curtain, pressing her face against the cold wall, honking and gasping for air.

"See?" I say, pointing. "This is what I'm talking about.
What if that happens to me?"

She just shakes her head. Can't even get it together
enough to chew me out or give me ten reasons why I'm wrong.

Paul is trying to pull the triplets out of the rubble. He's so
shaken he forgets to set down his banjo. His weathered hand
grasps one of the girls', but his grip breaks, and he stumbles
backward.

His look of panic sobers me. "Somebody help them," I
mutter.

Jeeter strides into view from stage left and, without making a big to-do of it, motions for a couple of the stagehands to
hop up and help out.

This isn't right. Poor Elvira, Elmira, and Eldora. I can't
just let them be embarrassed like this. I can't.

Something in me snaps. Jumping back to my case, I grab
my guitar and strap it on. "Okay, Lord, here I go. Guess it's
time to cowgirl up." And if He doesn't go with me, I'm done for.

Against their will, my legs carry me out to center stage. The lights are bright. And hot. More cold sweat beads up under my arms. Shivering and half praying for the tornado siren to go off—that'd get me out of this pickle while saving face—I pull my pick from my hip pocket, squinting in the light, and step up to the mike.

"Hi, everybody. I'm Robin McAfee." My voice is weak and squeaky. "I'm, uh, gonna, er . . ." I tune my guitar for the hundredth time, distracting myself from the fact my feet are telling my brain to *ruunnnn.* "I'm gonna, ahem, uh, sing a few songs. No, a song. One song."

Breathe. Breathe. Breathe. I'm sitting on Granddaddy's back porch singing "Jesus Loves Me." I'm on Granddaddy's porch . . .

But when I finally strum my first chord, I realize there's no sound coming out of the monitor. I'm playing to myself. My heart starts jitterbugging, and my brain tells my feet to run. Run *now!* No. Steady, Robin. Steady. Can't let the girls' tragedy, as funny as it is, be the highlight of the evening. Let it be my humiliation instead. I take a step back to gather myself and calm down.

"Yow! Watch it, Robin." Joe Boynton looks up at me, shaking his hand. It's red with my boot print.

"Sorry." Heat creeps across my cheeks. "What're you doing down there?"

Joe holds up a cable. "Plugging you in."

"Oh. I've never . . . well . . . never done this before."

"Yep, I know." He hands me the cable, which I hastily plug into my guitar hookup, then taps my leg. "You're good to go. Knock 'em into next week." He winks and clicks his tongue.

Yeah, knock 'em into next week. That's my secret plan. All this quaking in my boots is to throw 'em off. I close my eyes and step back up to the mike. Since I'm not looking, I bonk my chin and send a loud *thunk* reverberating into the auditorium, followed by a very high-pitched squeal. Snickers ripple from the crowd.

Run, Robin, run!

Joe *pssts* me from the wings. "Don't point your guitar at the monitor," he mouths, motioning with his hands.

Every cell of my five-four frame is trembling. Are the triplets upright yet? I glance back. They are but look rather stunned. Two of the men move broken boards from the stage. I hope Jude Perry from *Freedom Rings!* isn't here. He prides himself in displaying other people's tragedies on page one of our local paper, above the fold.

"Go on, Robin," Jeeter urges from the wings.

Cough, clear throat, bonk my chin on the mike, *again.* Dern it all. All this stalling is only dragging out the nightmare.

"I wrote this song about a friend of mine." My voice sounds like a cassette tape on fast forward. I try to slow it down. "She was born with a cleft palate and hated to smile or have people see her face. But, uh—" I strum a chord and a little bit of courage creeps in. "My friend is beautiful. I hope someday she sees herself as others do. This is for you, Rosalie."

As I start the song, my heart thumps to the rhythm as if it's the bass drum. It's hard to sing when I can't breathe. But somehow, by the time I finally hit the chorus, the words are flowing from some deep place where the music dwells. I feel like I did when I was ten, swinging on the old tire swing, stretching my toes to touch the fallen leaves.

> *Smile for me, Rosalie,*
> *Let your heart dance, let it be free.*

Then it washes over me as if I were standing under a mountain waterfall on a hot day: God's pleasure. My insides go all mushy.

I sing through the chorus two or three times, feeling the moment, and then realize I'm not sure how to end and exit. Except for my voice and guitar, the auditorium is silent. I wonder if everyone figured the show was over once the triplets were upright and went home. I open one eye.

The crowd is staring at me. In an instant, my knees buckle like weak wood, and I lose the peaceful sensation of God's pleasure. Shoot. I play the last chord and let my vocal fade away as chills replace the warmth. Will there be a snort, a muffled guffaw, and fading *tee-hee* just like with the triplets?

Coming up behind me, Jeeter catches me around my shoulders so I can't leave. He grabs the microphone, wearing a big cheesy grin on his leathery face. "Freedom, Alabama's own Robin Rae McAfee, everyone. Let's hear it!"

The auditorium explodes with applause. Whistles. Cheering. Some people even jump to their feet.

Bumbling a bow, I whisper to Jeeter, "Can I go now?"

"I told you, Robin Rae," he slaps my back. "They love you. Sing another song."

He can't be serious? "Isn't one enough?"

His face crinkles into an even wider grin. "If you're a coward, I suppose so." He sweeps his arm toward the crowd. They're settling down as if waiting for more. "You have them eating out of your hand. Might as well go for it."

My sweaty little hand?

Jeeter shoves me toward the mike and heads off, calling over his shoulder, "Sing."

My smile feels rather shaky as I stand there, rubbing my hands down the sides of my jeans, riffling through my mental song catalog.

"Sing something fun," Jeeter hollers from the wings, his hands cupped around his mouth.

"Okay, this is a song I wrote a few weeks ago. 'Your Country Princess.'"

The beat is chompy and fast as I hit the E string then belt out the lyrics with a strong and clear voice.

You say you're working late, again.
To earn an extra fifty bucks.
You say we're gonna have a better life.
Buy me a diamond ring and you a big Ford truck.

As the song builds to the chorus, the energy of the crowd gets me going, and I stomp out the rhythm with the heel of my boot.

Ooo, let me be your Country Princess.
Plain and beautiful, that's what life is . . .
Merry-go-rounds and Christmas lights . . .

Rocking through the chorus and into the second verse, I relax a little, bravely peeking at the crowd beyond the first row. They're clapping and swaying, and when I loop back into the chorus, a choir of female voices raises the rafters.

Ooo, let me be your Country Princess . . .

A banjo starts plucking, and Paul Whitestone saunters up beside me. Next, a fiddle whines as Granddaddy Lukeman walks my way, his blue eyes snapping as he does a little Pa Ingalls jig. Behind him, Jeeter comes out with his steel guitar, and the triplets, fully recovered, stomp and swirl across the stage.

We let the music go a round without the words, the players circling and leaning together. My heart soars with the music, rising above the thousand pairs of eyes watching.

Now this I could do the rest of my life.

2

"You did it, Robbie!" Daddy picks me up and swirls me around. "I'm so proud of you."

Ricky Holden, my man of six months, tucks his arm around my waist and kisses me on the cheek. "How's it feel?"

"I did it for the triplets. But . . ." I grin. "It feels great." I hope he doesn't think "Country Princess" is about him. Because it's not. Really, it's not.

Momma's off to my right, pressing her lips into a straight line. "The Lord knows Robin don't need encouragement to waste time playing music." She clucks and fluffs like a mad hen.

"Simmer down, Bit," Daddy says, his big hand resting gently on her shoulder.

I glance up at Ricky. He's seen Momma, on a few occasions, aflame with moral and/or social injustice, but this is his first opportunity to see steam coming out of her ears.

"Ten minutes in the Hall don't make you a star, Robin Rae." She steams all over me.

"What? Who said—"

"We're going home, Bit." Daddy gently takes Momma by the arm, an indication her last comment was his last straw. "'Night, Robin. 'Night, Ricky."

"'Night, Daddy." I watch them go.

"Hey, do you want to grab a bite before the diner closes?" Ricky weaves his fingers through mine. Innocent as it is, it makes me feel like a possession. But I don't pull away.

"Not tonight. We have to work early." I tug on his hand. "So, did I really do okay?"

He shrugs. "Yeah, you were all right."

"Just all right?" I shuffle around him in a little Cowgirl Boogie 'N Strut.

He grins. "Maybe even pretty good. Didn't know you had it in you."

"Me, neither. But, I did it for the triplets." I peel my hand away from his. "Better get my guitar."

He follows me to where I left my guitar by the stage curtain. "What's with your momma and you singing?"

"I have no idea." I glance out to the emptying auditorium. "She's acted funny about me and music ever since Granddaddy Lukeman gave me a guitar for my tenth birthday. Momma exploded like Mount St. Helens, spewing and spitting, changing the whole atmosphere of the room. Me and five other ten-year-olds ran for cover under the trampoline."

Ricky laughs. "Sweet Bit, exploding?"

"Sweet Bit, nothing. You saw a little of Sour Bit just now, and believe me, there's plenty more."

Just then, Momma runs back across the stage and stops right in front of me. "You'll be at dinner tomorrow night, right?"

Daddy ambles up behind her and gently drags her away again, hollering hellos and waving across the auditorium to Bill Hamilton and Mike Greaves.

"Robin? Dinner?" Momma calls.

"Yes, dinner," I say with a sigh.

Saturday night dinner at Bit McAfee's is the eleventh commandment. My sister, Eliza, and little brother, Steve, are pardoned from the commandment since they live and breathe out of town, but for me it's a requirement. I'm suspicious that the eleventh commandment is why Eliza left for college, and Steve got married and joined the Marine Corps.

"Bring Ricky," Momma calls from halfway up the aisle.

Everyone looks around at us. "All right, Momma," I mumble, snapping the buckles on my case.

Ricky lifts my face with a touch of his finger. "You okay?"

"Yeah, just worn out."

His very sexy blue eyes survey mine for the truth. "I guess facing your fears and your Momma in one night has to be tough." He chuckles and bends down for a kiss.

He thinks he's joking, but he's right. I walk with him toward the stage door. "If I didn't know better, I'd think they were one and the same."

"What do you mean?"

I shove my hair behind my ears. "Me afraid to sing on stage, Momma afraid for me to sing on stage . . . I don't know, but something's not right . . . or missing."

He waves to his friend, Mitch Pearce, who's leaving the Hall. "You'll figure it out."

"Yeah, sure." Typical Ricky. I try to take the conversation deep, discuss the intimate issues of my heart, and he opts for the baby pool.

At his truck, he falls against the door and wraps me up. "See you in the morning?" He kisses me like he's not thinking about work in the morning.

I rub my hand over his short blond hair. "Bright and early."

I bolt upright to the high-pitched beeping of my alarm, my hair flopping over my eyes. Parting the strands, I stare bleary-eyed. Three a.m.

If the good Lord meant for folks to get up before the crack of dawn, He would've made us all roosters and been done with it.

But, truth be told, it's not waking at three a.m. that bothers me. It's the reality of the job itself—stocking shelves at Willaby's Market & Grocery. Is this the culmination of my twenty-five years? Shelving food for the masses?

The other day Mrs. Farmington came into the store, saw me blocking down the sardine section, and said in her shrill voice, "Well, Robin McAfee. What in the world?"

Yeah, that's what I'd like to know. What in the world?

After showering, I find that my Willaby's uniform is on the bedroom floor, wrinkled and soiled. Should've done a load of washing last night. I left in such a jittery rush to get to the Music Hall, half hoping for an earthquake or flash flood (regardless of dry skies) to stop the show, I forgot all about my pile of laundry. Gathering an armful of clothes from the floor and making sure it contains two uniform pants and two shirts, I hurry to the stacked washer and dryer tucked into a kitchen corner.

The washer hesitates when I click the dial to *Normal* and push *Start*. Come on, Betsy. I bang the side and the machine lurches.

"Good going, girl. You'll be worth my fifty bucks yet."

The set came from my landlord, Boon Crawford Jr. "Hate to see you toting your stuff to the Laundromat," he'd said the afternoon he and Daddy helped me move in.

"I can always do laundry at Momma and Daddy's," I answered.

That's when Daddy raised his eyebrows and stuck out his chin. "If you're gonna move out and be independent, might as well go all the way."

Who'd have thought a washer and dryer would symbolize my emancipation?

Standing at the time clock at Willaby's, I punch in and follow my nose to the coffee machine. French vanilla. Ricky and the rest of the stock crew are waiting for me as my nose leads me around the back hall corner. They whoop and holler when they see me, scaring me right into the box baler.

"Way to go, Robin!"

"You were hotter than bare feet on blacktop last night."

"Girl, you can sing."

"Did you write those songs? They were good."

"Stop, y'all. Stop," I demand, stirring too much sugar into my coffee.

They chatter about the Freedom Sing while refilling their cups, snickering a little about Elvira, Elmira, and Eldora until I tell them to hush up.

We have a lot of stock to work up today, so the crew starts hauling pallets of groceries out to the main floor. When the last crew member disappears, Ricky lures me behind the baler and with a wicked grin nuzzles my neck. "So, maybe you've got a little bit of fame after all." His breath is hot on my neck.

"How-do, now you get it?" I press my hands on his chest. "Too little, too late."

"Robin!" Mr. Chancy's voice booms down the hall.

My heart catapults into my throat. "Here, sir." Ricky grabs at me with his octopus hands as I pop out from behind the baler with a whispered, "*Stop!*"

Mr. Chancy's right there. He narrows his eyes and stands with his hands on his hips, his belly dangling over his belt like a soft wad of dough. "Just because you were a hit last night doesn't give you cause to goof off today."

"No, sir. Wasn't planning on it."

He turns on his heel. "Holden, get to work," he says without looking back.

Ricky sticks his head out, waits until the coast is clear, then grabs me for a little more necking.

"Ricky, come on! We're on the clock." I squirm, trying to get away, trying not to giggle. His kisses tickle.

He brushes my hair away from my shoulders. "Hair like the fall leaves—red, gold, and brown." He holds me tight and props his chin on my head.

I can't breathe. "Rick, please, we have work to do," I mutter into his chest. "Chancy's already been on my case several times this month. I'm, like, the worst Willaby's employee ever."

Ricky laughs low. "You're not. Remember Wes Duvall? Lazy son of a gun."

"Wes Duvall?" I break away from Ricky. "I'm one rung above Wes Duvall? How hideous. I don't want to bumble around on the job, meandering through life."

He walks toward the swinging doors. "Then do something about it."

Sure, Robin, just do something about it. Simple, right? Ricky is swimming in the shallow end of my emotional pool again. If he really thought about what he said . . .

He watches as I slip my green apron over my head. "I love you, Robin."

Now he wants to get deep. "I know."

His blue eyes snap. "That's it? Would it kill you to say you love me too?"

"Yeah, probably." I grin and shove through the doors so that Ricky tumbles forward. He swerves to the left as I go right, pausing to pull my little black song notebook and pen from my apron pocket. What was it he said earlier? *Hair the color of fall leaves*? I jot it down, thinking it might make a great first line to a chorus.

"Robin, let's go." Chancy bellows at me from the end of the aisle.

"Yes sir." Tucking my notebook away, I head for my aisle. Over the PA system, the country radio station is playing a Sugarland hit. I belt out the lyrics with Jennifer Nettles. "Gotta be more than this . . ."

Late in the afternoon, I park beside my trailer in the shade of the elm. Bone tired, I cut the engine and sit for a second. Mr. Chancy caught up with me as I clocked out and spent an hour giving me the stockperson's pep talk, reminding me that if I want a Willaby's career, I gotta step it up.

After a Chancy talking-to, a girl needs an RC Cola and a Moon Pie, maybe some fried chicken, and a little guitar picking outside under the tree. Though I've missed most of the early May day, what remains is still lovely and perfumed with the sweet scent of budding corn and freshly mown grass.

The trailer's front door sticks again, so I hip-butt it open and step inside. My foot squishes into the worn shag carpet, and water floods my shoe.

"What in the world—"

Glistening water covers the trailer floor, and I can hear a gushing noise coming from the kitchen.

Splash. Squish. Splash. Squish. I make my way across the small pond on my trailer floor. What the Sam Hill happened? Then, "My songs!"

Splish-splashing down the hall to my room, I pray for dry carpet. Oh, relief. The flood waters haven't spread this far . . . yet. Dropping to my knees, I fish around for my cardboard box of song notebooks. Finding it tucked up against the wall, I pull it out and toss it on my bed, then splish-splash back to the kitchen and snatch up the portable phone.

"Crawford Realty."

"I'm flooded, Boon."

"What happened?"

"The washer, I think." I shove the washer-dryer stack aside. Sure enough, a broken hose spurts water in my face. "Hurry."

"I'm on my way, Robin."

I cut off the valve and dial Daddy next. "Help."

When Boon walks in with his toolbox a few minutes later, he splashes through the puddles, grinning like a kid after a good thunderstorm. Meanwhile, I'm on my hands and knees mopping up the mess with towels.

"Robin, I didn't know you could sing like that." He drops his toolbox on the kitchen counter. "That song about Rosalie was something. I haven't thought of her in a long time."

"Well, we all have our little hidden talents."

Boon laughs. "Not me. What you see is what you get."

Wringing the towels out in the sink, I glance over my shoulder at him. "Something to be said for 'what you see is what you get.'"

"Do you like what you see, Robin?"

"What?" I drop the towel to the floor.

"Do you like what you see?" Boon props himself against the counter, crossing his arms.

Is he teasing or fishing? Lean and wiry, Boon's a decent-looking fellow, though his backside can't hold up his breeches. His dark hair is always clean and trimmed, his round brown eyes always laughing, and his smile reflects the sweetness in his heart. But he's more like a brother than a lover.

"Yeah, I like what I see, Boon. You're going to make some girl very happy."

His cheeks glow. "Can't blame a guy for trying, Robin." He fusses with the toolbox latches.

"No, guess not."

I go back to mopping with towels while Boon assesses the

damage to the trailer with a hammer in his right hand. Yeah, a hammer. I don't know why.

"I don't think this place is worth fixing up," he says.

"What?" I wring out another water-soaked towel in the sink. "Boon, you got to be kidding."

He shakes his head and props his hands on his narrow hips. "The water damage is too much, Robin. Look at this." He hops up and down, and the old floor sways underneath him. A musty odor rises from the carpet.

"Well, stop jumping. I don't go around jumping."

He waves the hammer at me. "Look here, girl, you can't spray perfume on a skunk and call it a kitty." He lifts his nose, sniffing. "Yep, Dad will want to junk the place, count on it."

"Junk the place? Boon, where am I suppose to live?"

"Home, I guess."

"I can't move home." He's plumb off his rocker. "Don't y'all have another trailer I can rent?" After all, Boon is partly responsible for this problem. He sold me that no-good washer-dryer combo. I should've been suspicious when he said, "Only costs fifty bucks. Runs like a top too."

Boon tosses the hammer into the toolbox with a clank. "Naw, Dad keeps all our properties rented out and making money."

"Robin Rae . . ." Daddy calls from the front door. "What's going on?"

"Noah's flood," I answer. Boon laughs.

"Look at all this water." Daddy strolls into the kitchen. The hem of his blue work pants are stuck into the top of his laced boots.

Boon gives him the lowdown, and when he says "move out," Daddy looks at me.

"I just painted your old room and polished the floor. It'd make your momma's day." His gray eyes scrunch up when he smiles. Laugh lines run from the corners of his eyes down the sides of his cheeks.

"By all means, let's make Momma's day." I cross my arms and fall back against the refrigerator.

"Only temporarily, Robin."

"Temporarily," Boon echoes absently, then adds, "I *believe* Marie Blackwell is getting married in six months, and her place will be open."

"Six months!"

"Marie's getting married?" Daddy settles against the sink as if he's ready for an afternoon of chewing the fat. "I hadn't heard. Good for her. What's she pushin', thirty-five?"

"I reckon so, Mr. McAfee."

Great day in the morning. I'm in crisis, and they're calculating the age of Freedom's oldest spinster. "She's thirty-six," I fire into their conversation. "Boon, are you sure there're no other rentals?"

"I'm sure, Robin."

Defeat. I slap my arms down my sides. "If I'm moving home, let's get to it." My eyes well up. I'm gonna miss my little trailer and the stupid washer and dryer.

Boon Jr. slams his toolbox shut. "Let's get 'er done."

3

Get a root canal.

Dive into Black Snake Quarry, scraping my toes against the granite wall all the way down.

Learn to sew.

Three things I'd rather do than move back to the McAfee homestead, into Momma's domain.

Isn't twenty-five too old to move back into my old room? The first of three kids born into the Dean McAfee family, I was the last to leave. My sister, Eliza, went to Auburn three years ago, and baby brother Steve married his junior high school sweetheart, Dawnie, then went Semper Fi. He's twenty, overseas, and recently found out he's going to be a dad.

When Daddy, Boon, and I pull up, Momma comes out on to the porch, her apron pulled tight around her full figure. The dogs bay at Boon when he says, "Hey, Mrs. McAfee."

Momma hushes the dogs while shoving an errant, dark curl from her forehead. "What's all this?"

"Washing machine flooded the trailer, Mrs. McAfee," Boon says as he hauls the first load of hanging clothes through the kitchen door.

"Upstairs, last room on the right, Boon," I call after him, toting in the laundry basket of wet clothes. "Hi, Momma."

She holds out her hands for the basket. "Might as well let me."

I wrangle open the kitchen screen door and inhale the warm aroma of baking bread. "No thanks, Momma. I can do my own washing."

"Just offering to help."

Hesitating, I gather my courage and turn toward her. "I love you, Momma, but I don't need you babying me. Don't get up at three a.m. and put on a pot of coffee or pack me a lunch or call Mr. Chancy to let him know I'm on my way, okay?"

"Will you be eating dinner here this evening, your highness?"

With a sigh, I let the screen door slam behind me. "Most likely."

After dinner, Mo and Curly walk with Ricky and me out to his truck. Though it's only May, the night is warm and humid. A chuck-will's-widow calls from somewhere in the dark trees.

"Your mom seems happy tonight." Ricky scoops my hand into his.

"One of her little chicks has come home."

"Her *favorite* chick has come home." He angles up against the tailgate and pulls me to him, planting a kiss on my forehead.

"Favorite? What are you smoking?" I straighten his shirt collar as a pretend laugh gurgles in my throat. "We don't understand each other at all."

"Maybe it's because you're so much alike."

"Bite your tongue."

"Robin," he laughs, "you are."

"I am *not* like Momma. She's wound tighter than a top. One of these days she might just spin out of control."

Ricky brushes my hair away from my shoulder. "So, are you okay with moving home?"

I drop my cheek against his rocklike chest. "Do I have a choice?"

"I think you do."

His tone makes me shiver. I can feel the thumping of his heart beneath my hand. Don't ask, Robin. Don't ask. But, I do. "What would that choice be?"

"Marry me."

I had to ask.

"W-w-what?" He knows I heard.

"Marry me, Robin. Next week."

"Next week? Over Bit McAfee's dead body." For the first time, I'm grateful to have a slightly obsessive, opinionated mother. "Her oldest daughter married in a rush? She'd never let us live it down. Besides, she'd need at least three months to fuss and fret." I break out of his arms and walk around to the side of his truck, scuffing my boots over the driveway gravel.

"Okay, three months. July? August?"

"Too hot."

"September?"

"Even hotter." I'm stalling. He knows it. I try to rest my arm on top of the truck bed, but I'm too short.

Ricky unlatches the tailgate and motions for me to come sit. "October? It's not too hot, and don't you dare say it's too cold."

"Well, I wasn't, but now that you mention it . . ." With a sigh, I peer into his eyes. "I can't, Ricky."

"What do you mean you can't?" He leans forward, propping his broad hands on his thighs.

I stare up at the house. The tall windows watch me with pale yellow eyes. "I'm not ready." I try to look him in the eye again, but when a flicker of anger, or maybe hurt, darkens his expression, I glance back to the windows.

"Oh, I think you are ready." He wraps his arm around my shoulders. "Remember last Saturday night, down by the river?"

I knock him away with my elbow. "Hush. You got me all worked up, kissing me and saying sweet things."

His warm lips brush my neck, and he mutters something like, "Um-hum."

I squirm free and hop off the tailgate, certain Ricky is gearing up for a repeat of last Saturday night. "You're not wearing me down this time."

He rests his elbows on his knees. "Robin, you're twenty-five. Isn't it about time a healthy, beautiful girl like you settles down? Besides, you hate your job; you said it ain't the person you want to be. Marry me and you can quit."

Settle down? I haven't settled up yet. "Quit and do what?" I slap at his leg. "Hang around the house all day waiting for you to show up? Nothing doing. What redneck rule says a girl has to be married by twenty-five or twenty-six? Marie Blackwell is just now getting married, and she's thirty-five."

"Marie Blackwell? That's who you're aiming to be like?"

For a moment, I picture the lean and mean Marie, who's scared off three fiancés and four dogs. I get Ricky's point.

"Okay, forget Marie Blackwell. But, Ricky, I—" This is hard. How can I express my feelings in a way he understands? "When I was about ten or eleven I remember thinking I want to do something with my life. Something important."

"Marrying me is doing something with your life." His frustration sharpens each word. "Something important."

I jam my hands in the front pockets of my jeans and study the ground. "I'm not saying it's not, but I don't want to get married yet." I look at his face. "I haven't figured out God's purpose for me yet. I can't be Mrs. Ricky Holden or Mrs. Anybody until I discover who He made me to be. Can you understand?"

The next seconds last for an eternity. Then he utters, "Guess so," pouting like a benched Little Leaguer. Without another word, he slides off the tailgate and slams it shut.

"Where're you going?" I scoot behind him as he gets into his truck.

"I got something to do." He revs the engine and shifts into reverse.

"Like what?"

"Ain't your concern now, is it?"

"Hey, you were the one who said I should do something about my life if I'm not happy."

"I didn't mean dump me."

"Dump you? Rick, I never said 'dump.' I said I didn't want to—"

He guns out of the driveway, spraying dust over me, and careens off into the night.

With my old Taylor in hand, I make my way up the attic steps and out to the summer porch. Though the night air is cool, the porch is still warm from the southern sun. It feels good. Carefully, I prop my guitar against the screened wall and fumble in the moon's glow for the old lawn chairs.

The conversation with Ricky echoes across my mind, and my stomach feels like I swallowed a rock. What a terrible way to end the evening. But at the same time, I'm glad we slew that dragon. The marriage question has always lurked beneath the surface. Sooner or later, it had to rear its ugly head.

Ah, one of Daddy's old chairs. Rain has rusted the joints, so I wrangle it open, but when I sit, the rubber straps give way like warm silly putty. I sink down, holding my breath, hoping they don't snap.

Settling my guitar on my knee, I strum softly, listening for the song of the crickets or the hum of the cicadas, but the night is solemn. So am I.

I play until I finally realize the chair is just too uncomfortable. Slipping the guitar strap over my head, I wriggle to my feet and stand by the screen, looking out over McAfee land.

Daddy, the uncles, Grandpa, Great-Grandpa McAfee, and, I believe, the grandpa before him, were all born right here in Freedom. Born free, Daddy likes to say. But for me, Freedom born isn't free. Other than the freedom Jesus gives my soul, my life feels more like a lost marble, hidden under the bed, waiting to be found.

But deep down, in the secret place, I know what I want to do with my life. Or try to do.

Write songs.

I have no idea if I'm as good as Jeeter and all say, but I'm getting a little tired of doing the two-step with fear and anxiety. A little tired of waiting around for "some day."

All I know is when I'm old, I don't want to sip from the cup of regret, wondering what could've been. Too many people doing that already. Momma, for one. Whatever she's sipping from her I-wish-I'd-done-different cup makes her whole face pucker.

With those thoughts rattling around my soul, I sit on the old picnic bench and work out my burden with a song.

Lord, You are my wise Counselor,
My Prince of Peace,
My very best Friend,
So here I am at Your feet.
I need the wisdom of the Ancient of Days,
Enlightened eyes with a deeper faith,

I hide myself in You, O Lord
So here I am, seeking Your face.

The familiar feeling of God's pleasure shines a spotlight on the monster of worry, and it shrivels. It's in moments like these I have a sense of destiny.

"I've been looking all over for you." With a bang, the porch door opens and the light from the bare bulb overpowers the darkness.

I twist around to see Eliza walking toward me and close my little black notebook, clicking off my pen. "Well, well, look what the tiger dragged home. Did you flunk out of Auburn?"

"Bite your tongue." My sister grabs a rusty lawn chair. Rather than warn her, I watch as she pops it open with a squeak and sits on the sun-baked rubber straps. Her bottom sinks below the metal frame.

"Comfy?" I grin at her.

She rests her brown head against the top of the chair. "Quite, as a matter of fact."

"I hope you are, because your butt is stuck forever. Why do you think I'm sitting on the bench?"

She waves me off with a flick of her long fingers. "Daddy has a blow torch if I need it."

"Sure enough. And he loves firing it up." Come to think of it, there's not much around here that needs torching. So burning Eliza out of that old chair just might make his night. Sorta like finding a quarter between the couch cushions when you're twenty cents shy of an ice cream cone down at the Dairy Queen. It's the little things that make life worthwhile.

Eliza points at my guitar. "I liked the song you were playing. Is it new?"

"Sorta," I say, not willing to expose my private thoughts

to her. They are between me and Jesus, for now. "You missed Saturday night dinner."

"Ah, shucks." She snaps her fingers.

"You can forage the fridge for all the leftovers."

"I imagine so." She grins. "Momma's got to do something with all that Tupperware."

I laugh. "Daddy said she bought more at a show last week." Still strumming the same three chords over and over, I inform Eliza of the latest. "The washing machine flooded the trailer. I had to move home."

She lifts her head. "Really?" Her chair creaks and cracks and leans a little to the left.

"Boon and Daddy helped me move back."

"Where's Ricky?" She wiggles around to bend the chair back to the right while tugging her jeans straight at the knees.

"Took off after dinner." The raw light from the overhead bulb shines on Eliza's sweet oval face, and suddenly I crave my sister's wisdom. "He asked me to marry him."

"What?" She tries to jump up, but the chair refuses to let go. Her arms fly in the air over her head as the rust-ruined legs buckle, and she crashes to the floor. With her legs kicking, she tries to wrangle free while looking up at me. "What did you say?"

Grinning, I yank on the bent frame, and Eliza pops onto her feet. "I said no. I'm not ready."

"Oh, man, did Momma have a cow or what?" She squares away her jeans and straightens her blouse.

"Shhh, she doesn't know."

Eliza pops her hand to her forehead. "What? You know she's gonna find out. Oh, man, we're gonna have to visit her in the hospital."

"So Momma has a history of overreacting. I don't think rejecting Ricky will send her to the ER. At least I hope not."

With a sigh, Eliza kneels in front of me and looks me in the eye intently. "Do you love him? Do you want to marry him?"

I can't help it. Tears flood my eyes as I shrug and mutter, "I'm not ready to get married, Eliza. I don't want to marry Ricky, or any man, because I'm twenty-five and it's the next thing on a girl's to-do list."

I prop my guitar against the bench and wander back over to the old, worn screen. "There's stuff I might like to do . . . maybe."

"Like what?"

"I don't know. Write songs . . . maybe."

At that, Eliza claps her hands. "Hallelujah, it's about time. Do it, Robin. Move to Nashville. Write songs."

I glance back at her. "I don't know, I'm just thinking. I've still got this whole stage fright thing."

She laughs. "I grew up in the same house with you, Robin. You're about the bravest person I know. You just have this one little thing."

"One little thing? It's huge. The idea of singing in front of strangers terrifies me." I square off in front of her. "And except for last night, I never sang anywhere but Granddaddy and Grandma's porch."

"You sang in the church choir."

"Sure, hiding in the back."

Eliza crosses her arms with a smirk. "I'm going to England for the summer."

"W-what? Really?" Smiling, I wrap my sister in a hug. "You've always wanted to go to England. Good for you. What will you be doing? How long will you be gone?"

"Four months. I won a fellowship to study English lit at Cambridge, all expenses paid."

"Cambridge. Well, la-de-da." How'd she inherit courage while I inherited fear? I take a seat on the bench again, thinking.

"Let's make this our summer, Robin." Eliza joins me on the bench. "I'm living my dream—well, one of them. Live yours too." She nudges me with her shoulder. "I'll go to Cambridge, you go to Nashville. Why should Steve and I be the only ones who venture out? He's married, a soldier, and a daddy-to-be. *You're* the big sister, the one we looked up to, the one who fought our battles until we could take care of ourselves."

"Took your whuppings for you."

Eliza sticks out her tongue. "Only once, and I've never forgiven myself for it."

I slip my arm around her, and she rests her head against my shoulder. "I could've ratted you out, but I knew Daddy would take it easy on me. He suspected you for that mess anyway."

"Should I confess now?"

I tug a strand of her thick, curly hair. "A little late, don't you think?"

"I suppose," Eliza says with a grin, propping her chin in her hand. "How many songs do you have written?"

"A few." I pick up my guitar and begin to strum softly.

"A few? Right, you had a few when you were sixteen."

I bump my shoulder against hers. "Don't think I don't see what you're doing. Provoking me to go to Nashville."

"Can't blame me for wanting a famous songwriting sister."

I laugh. "Do you know how many wanna-be songwriters are waiting tables in that city, or perking coffee for some Music Row execs?"

"They aren't you."

"Forget it, Eliza."

"Look, just call Skyler. See if you can stay with her."

"Ah, cousin Skyler." I shake my head. "Last time I talked to her, she was busy with her new job. Plus, she has a roommate."

"So, you know Skyler, Robin; she'd love to help. You two were thick as thieves growing up. And—" Eliza wags her finger at me. "—she's an entertainment lawyer, for crying out loud. Connections, my sister. Connections."

"You want to give Momma a heart attack? You flying over the Big Pond to live for the summer and me moving to Nashville. And Steve in harm's way overseas."

Eliza hops off the bench. "Forget about Momma, will you?" She grabs my hand, so I stop playing. "She had her day with the Lukeman Sisters, but she gave it up to marry Daddy. If she doesn't want you to try because she didn't, then too bad."

"All right, Miss Cambridge, what if I don't make it? Then what? Come home with my guitar tucked between my legs?"

"What if you *do* make it? What if you deal with the restlessness in your soul and *be* who God made you to be? Robin, you've had four jobs since you graduated high school—a vet tech, a cashier, a clerk at the courthouse, and a stocker at Willaby's. You liked them when you started, but six months later you talked of doing something else. You tried two semesters of college and hated it too."

"What's your point?" There's a twang of truth in her words. But isn't it easier to see when looking from the outside in?

She shakes her fist with a growl. "My point? You want to be a songwriter. Stop wasting your time searching for something else."

"Maybe."

I'm being a little stubborn, I admit. But if I'm going to dive off the high dive, I want to know the pool is full of water. Preferably heated.

It's after eleven when we finally flick off the porch light and go to bed. Eliza's words echo in my soul as I close my eyes.

I'm moving to Nashville to become a published songwriter. A hit songwriter. I let the notion sink down deep in my soul like Momma's tulip bulbs in rich soil. Maybe one day after a little sunshine and rain, they will bloom.

4

Sunday after dinner everyone gathers out on Grandma and Granddaddy's porch—all the family plus Paul Whitestone and Jeeter Perkins. We're fat and happy from a lunch of chicken and dumplings and sweet tea.

Granddaddy picks up his fiddle and Paul his scuffed banjo. "Run in and pull a guitar, Robin," Granddaddy says. "How's that song go that you were singing the other night? 'Ooo, let me be your Country Princess'?"

"You're the ugliest princess I ever did see, Burch," says Granddaddy's brother, Uncle Chet, as he angles against a porch post, chomping on his toothpick. Laughter ripples under the eaves, riding along with the breeze.

"Wrong key," I call through an open window. "Take it down to D." Finding Granddaddy's new Gibson, I decide that today's as good a day as any for poking the bear, raising the dead, and in general, walking on water.

Hi, everybody, I'm moving to Nashville. A nervous twinge makes my heart beat a little faster.

But Momma's in good humor, happy there ain't so much as a spoonful of her dumplings left over. She bustles between

Grandma's kitchen and the porch. "Here's a jug of Mother's sweet tea," she says. "Ice is in the cooler."

Grandma Lukeman's iced tea is the best in Freedom. Maybe the best in all of Alabama. Ask anyone. She makes a ton of it every morning for Harold's Diner, a little meat and three on the edge of town. Arizona is the head waitress. She tells me they run out of Grandma's tea every day, right in the middle of lunch.

"Can't keep it around," she says. "If Harold asks her to make an extra couple of gallons, we run out even faster."

I hurry to get a glass of tea before it's all gone and before Granddaddy completely butchers "Your Country Princess." He's encouraging Eliza to sing with him. Of course, Eliza sings in the key of Q. There's a reason the girl went off to college to study literature.

Meanwhile, Granddaddy, Jeeter, and Paul wail like love-sick bulls. "'Merry-go-round and something, something lights . . . Ooo, I want to be your Country Princess.'"

Granddaddy's hound, Bruno, rises up on his front paws, sticks his nose in the air, and howls at the porch ceiling. On key.

I laugh so hard I can't play. "Bruno sings better than you, Liza." Never have I seen Bruno, in all his ten years, lift his nose and join the singing.

"Oh, hush up."

"Right catchy tune, Robin." Granddaddy says. "Got the makings of a hit."

Hint, hint. He's always hinting, prodding, and pushing me to take my pill-box size talent to Nashville. He's convinced I've got something special.

"What else you been working on?" Uncle Dave, daddy's brother, leans against the porch rail. He and his wife, Aunt Ginger, never had kids, so they love on me, Eliza, and Steve as their own.

"Well," I strum an F minor, then move to C. "The reverend

mentioned how Mary poured oil on Jesus' feet. Got me thinking about her. She was always running to Jesus." I glanced
around. "Y'all don't really wanna hear this, do you?"

"Just sing," Eliza says.

I close my eyes, blocking out the dozen pair of eyes staring
back at me, and let the melody wash down.

> *Here she comes again,*
> *Kneeling at his feet.*
> *She breaks open the box,*
> *The perfume it is so sweet.*
> *And not knowing that he'll die,*
> *She anointed him for life.*

I play it through a few times, fiddling with new words and
extra chords. "That's about all," I finally say, opening my eyes.

Uncle Dave croaks, "Down right moving, Robbie Rae." He
clears his throat and looks left over the lawn.

Granddaddy taps his heart and says in a husky whisper,
"You got it right here, girl, right here."

The afternoon moves into evening, and I still haven't made my
announcement. Fireflies dart around the porch, flashing
green, urging me to go, go, go.

Arizona stops by to visit with her new beau, Ty Ledbetter,
then Steve's wife, Dawnie, and last but not least, two more of
Granddaddy's old bluegrass buddies, Earl and Grip.

Jeeter, Grip, and Earl sing backup for Granddaddy on
"Just As I Am." Jeeter's high harmony is raspy but sweet. I
play the lead notes.

Reverend Miller and his wife, Jenny, pull up, waving as
they take to the porch. "We heard the music."

"Come, sit, Preacher, Miss Jenny," Grandma says, motioning to the spare chairs. "The peach cobbler is about to come out of the oven."

The reverend steps up to the porch. "Looks like you got the whole crew out, Burch."

"We do, Eli," Granddaddy says. "Come on up and take a seat."

Reverend Miller takes the wicker rocker by Granddaddy, holding Jenny on his lap.

"Here you go, Reverend. Jenny." Grandma hands them each a tall tumbler of iced tea.

"Loralee's tea. What a treat."

Reverend Miller enjoys the tiniest details of life, finding beauty in simplicity. His eyes always twinkle like he's 100 percent sure Jesus loves him. He's in his midfifties, I reckon, and has spent a fair amount of his life as a missionary in South America. During his last few years, he enjoyed the hospitality of a guerilla group.

Kidnapped and held prisoner, he got the tar beat out of him for believing Jesus is the Christ. When he shared his testimony with the board of elders at Freedom Bible Church, they hired him on the spot. On his first Sunday in the pulpit, good ole boys from all over the county packed the pews, wanting to see a man who endured suffering for his convictions.

I wrote a few lyrics about him and worked up a melody, but I found it hard to do justice to his trial when I'd barely begun the fight myself. I tucked it away for another day.

"Piping hot cobbler." Grandma and Momma bring out the warm, sweet smell of peaches and vanilla. "Who wants ice cream on theirs?"

Every hand goes up.

"Let me help," Jenny says, hopping up. "Dawnie, how's that baby?"

"Not making me sick anymore," Dawnie says grinning, hand resting on her slightly round belly.

Grip taps the reverend on the knee. "Did you ever think you wouldn't make it out of prison alive?" He wrinkles his face as if anticipating pain.

I see a shadow of something pass across the reverend's composed expression. Is it pain? Devotion? Faith?

"Don't we all ask that question when times get hard?" He puts a pastoral hand on Grip's shoulder. "When the bills are more than the paycheck? When our kids lose their way? When our weak heart feels cold toward Jesus?"

"Oh, no, Preacher," I protest. "What you went through . . . None of us have been beaten or locked away in a cold dark cell for what we believe. A rogue kid or overdue bill hardly compares."

"I don't know if I can claim that my trial surpasses the heartache of the abandoned spouse or an abused child."

"Here you go, Eli." Grandma hands him a plate of cobbler covered with ice cream.

"Thank you." The reverend picks up his fork. "But, I tell you folks, I had to pray hard to love my captors."

Love? Can we just canonize him now? How do you even want to love people who beat the crap out of you? Yet isn't love like that a required ingredient for all Christians? Isn't it what Jesus did?

The reverend cuts off a bite of cobbler and continues his story. "But every time I so much as breathed, 'Jesús Cristo,' they'd starve me for a few days. I considered it fasting." He actually chuckles. "Or they'd lock me in solitary, put a fist to my face or a rod to my back."

A bolt of terror runs down my spine. And I'm chicken to sing in front of folks.

Grandma passes me a plate of warm and cold sweetness.

Doesn't seem right to enjoy cobbler while the reverend talks about his suffering. The porch congregation is mesmerized, picking at their food, pondering.

"It's funny," he continues, "when you're in a place where only God can sustain you, something happens to your soul. You find your destiny." He spears a chunk of cobbler and looks right at me. "You find out what you're really made of."

I flinch as if a sharp puff of air has hit my face. Is he talking to me? It feels like he's talking to me. *Should* I move to Nashville? Discover my destiny and find out what I'm made of—clay or steel?

Steel. Please let it be steel.

"Well, I didn't come here to talk about me." The reverend points his fork at the banjo and guitars. "How about some singing, Burch?"

"Happy to oblige, Eli." Granddaddy, the boys, and I pick up our instruments. Granddaddy starts a song he likes, "Grace Like Rain," and Reverend Miller sings with more heart than any of us.

It's not long before the sun yawns and disappears behind the treetops. Daddy lights the porch lamps, and Grandma flicks on all the house lights. We are bathed in a warm, yellow glow.

Eliza strolls out of the house with a second bowl of ice cream. "Did you tell them yet, Robin?"

"Ah, shoot, eat your ice cream, Eliza."

"Tell us what?"

"You got news?"

"Come on, Robin Rae, out with it."

"Well," I lean Granddaddy's guitar against the porch rail and wipe my hand down the side of my jeans. A firefly blinks its green bottom under my nose.

"You're engaged!" Momma lifts her hands overhead and claps as if she were praising the Lord.

Arizona leans from her chair, her expression doubtful. Next to her Dawnie's eyes are wide, her cheeks puffed with ice cream and cobbler.

Grandma echoes, "Engaged?"

"Well, now, ain't that something?" Grip says with a big, toothy smile.

"Congratulations," Granddaddy says, half-hearted, gripping my arm.

"No, y'all. She's not engaged." Eliza wields her spoonful of ice cream like Zorro's sword. "Settle down." To me she says, "Hurry up before Momma has you pregnant."

"Pregnant?" The word launches Momma from her chair. "Robin Rae."

"No, Momma." Again, Eliza slashes the air with her spoon. "Sit down. Gee whiz. I was kidding. Go on, Robin. Your news can't be worse than all this speculation." She scoops another bite of ice cream and waits for me to speak.

She is having way too much fun with this.

I cross my arms. "Well, everyone, actually, Eliza has news." I smirk at her. "Why don't you tell us, Cambridge?"

She huffs and wrinkles her nose. "Fine, Chicken Little." She takes center stage. "Momma, Daddy, everyone . . . I received a fellowship."

"What'd she get? A fellow?" Paul's a little hard of hearing. No wonder the girls clog like they're stomping out world hunger.

"No, she got a *fel-low-ship*," Grip yells in his ear. He's on his third plate of cobbler and ice cream. An old bachelor, anything that doesn't taste like frozen tinfoil is gourmet to him.

Eliza pats Paul on the shoulder. "A fellowship at Cambridge University to study English lit."

"Oh, mercy, ain't that something."

"My daughter the scholar." Momma presses her cheek to Eliza's, smiling as if my sister just handed her an Eliza

McAfee original—*Kindergartener Finger Painting,* 1990. "I'm so proud of you."

Daddy kisses her forehead. "I always knew you could do whatever you put your mind to, Eliza."

Grandma swings through the door, her blue eyes snapping. She's carrying two tins of leftovers and hands one to Grip, another to Jenny Morris. "What's all the excitement?"

"I'm studying English lit at Cambridge this summer, Grandma."

"Well, now, we'll have to drive up to see you."

"Yeah, we could all go," Earl says. "They like bluegrass up there in Massachusetts, don't they?"

I slap my leg, laughing. "She's going to England, not Massachusetts."

"England!" echoes around the porch.

"England!" Momma says with a gasp. "That's a lot farther than Massachusetts, Eliza."

"I've been working for this all year, Momma," Eliza says. "You know I've always wanted to study at Cambridge. And I'll only be gone a few months."

"Don't worry, Bit." Daddy swings Momma around in a two-step. "She'll be fine. We could fly over and visit. Stop in on the queen."

Momma squeals. "Dean, stop. You're being silly." She laughs through her protest.

Grip jabs his finger in the air. "Now you're talking, Dean. We could visit the queen. They like bluegrass over the Big Pond, don't they?"

A snort escapes my nose. Rednecks in London. This, I got to see.

After a moment or two more of banter and congratulations, Granddaddy holds up his hands. "Okay, what's Robin's news?"

"Yeah, we haven't heard from Robin Rae." Jeeter folds his arms, smiling like he suspects what I'm going to say.

Might as well strike while the cobbler is hot. Miss Cambridge warmed the porch congregation for me. "Well . . ." I swallow hard. "I'm moving to Nashville."

5

"*Robin, that's fantastic! Momma, Daddy, isn't that great? About*
time." Cambridge stirs up the crowd.

Arizona joins her. "Robin, you're going to be a smash."

"Congratulations!" Dawnie throws her arms around me.
"Steve will be proud."

Jeeter props his elbow on the porch post. "Finally tackling
ole NashVegas. Good for you. I'll give you the number of an old
friend, Birdie Griffin. She has a big house with a third-floor
apartment right near Music Row."

"Nothing doing." Momma thunders over to me, her footsteps resounding against the porch boards. She's short like me,
and powerful. "Jeeter, I'll thank you and your . . . friend . . . to
stay out of this."

"Free country, Bit."

I pinch my lips so as not to laugh. Jeeter doesn't swallow
sass. Not even Momma's.

She ignores him and turns to me. "Land a-mighty, Robin,
you haven't sung in front of anyone other than this crowd here
until last Friday. It took those tubby Whitestone girls—"

"Hey now," Paul pipes up. *That* he hears.

"Sorry, Paul, but it's true. You should tell their momma

to put them on a diet. All that clogging . . . They ought to be sticks."

I pick up the guitar. What was the tune I played last night up in the attic?

"You can't stop her, Bit," Granddaddy says.

"You should know, shouldn't you?" Momma's words are harsh, but Granddaddy's mild expression remains unchanged.

"Different time, different girl."

I glance up. "Different time, different girl? Granddaddy, what—"

"What about Ricky?" Momma fires at me. "You're going to break that boy's heart." She fusses with the same wild curl that never does what she wants.

"Ricky's a big boy, Momma," I say. Although he wasn't in church this morning, which means he's fishing in the Tennessee River, which means he's not acting like a big boy but a pouting baby.

"I think we ought to be getting home." Grip stands. "Let you folks sort this out."

Take me with you, Grip.

Jeeter whispers to me. "Stick to your guns." He presses a napkin into my hand with a telephone number scrawled on it.

"Jeeter," Momma hollers after him. "I'll thank you to mind your own business."

Something inside snaps. "Same to you, Momma."

She steadies herself by gripping the porch post. "Do you think you're going to waltz into Nashville and magically find the courage to sing before a crowd of strangers? To talk to important people about your songs?" Momma's cheeks are flushed and her jaw is tight.

"Bit, simmer down," Daddy says in a low tone.

"Don't tell me to simmer down, Dean." She looks at him with pleading eyes. "Robin . . . Nashville . . ."

Wearing her debate face, Eliza says, "It's Robin's life. She should do what she wants. You seem fine with me going to England. Why can't you—"

"It's not the same—" Momma clams up and starts stacking dirty dishes.

With my head down, I echo my resolve. "I'm going, Momma." Once decided, the idea of staying in Freedom cuts off my air and suffocates my dreams.

With her arms loaded down, Momma goes inside. Seems I've won the battle but not the war.

The tension on the porch evaporates as Granddaddy follows Grandma in the house, their heads bent together, muttering, and Daddy talks NASCAR with Uncle Dave and Ty. I bend over the guitar, playing, half listening to Eliza, Arizona, and Dawnie talk about the English summer, half wondering what's going on inside Momma's head.

Eliza is saying, "My real goal is to meet a Greek tycoon, fall madly in love, marry impetuously, and sail around the world on his yacht."

I lift my head. "Don't you need to be in Greece to find a Greek tycoon, Liza?"

Arizona laughs. "I was thinking the same thing."

"Semantics, ladies, semantics. What you don't know is that I plan to meet him in Paris."

"Paris?" Truth is, if anyone can sweep a Greek tycoon off his feet, it's my lovely southern sister. Her blue-diamond eyes and innocent smile make the boys go gaga over her as if they've found a rare treasure. But they always get their heart broken no matter how gentle Eliza lets them down. I'm already worried for the Greek tycoon.

The screen door creaks open as Granddaddy returns. "It's not much, Robin Rae, but Grandma and I want to help out." He holds out a check.

"What's this?" I read the amount. "A hundred dollars?" I gape at him. "Granddaddy, no, I don't want your money."

"You're giving her money?" Momma steps through the screen door. The garbage bag she's holding shakes and crackles. "Daddy?"

"It's just a little egg money, Bit. A hundred dollars. Don't get all rattled over it."

Daddy slips his arm around Momma and holds her real close. She is shaking. "I'm not rattled about the money, Daddy, and you know it."

Grandma leans away from Granddaddy's shoulder. "Bit, certainly you knew this day would come. She's gifted."

Momma buttons her lips. I'm not sure she's breathing. I shove the check back at Granddaddy. "Here, I don't need this." Anything to get Momma to stop shaking. "I have a small savings."

He pushes my hand away. "Take it. Keep you in gas for a month."

Momma's expression is tighter than bailing wire, then she drops the trash bag and stumbles down the porch steps and into the night.

"I'll see to her," Daddy says.

I grab his hand as he passes by. "Daddy, am I doing the right thing? Why is she so upset about this?"

He smiles and covers my hand with his. "Ancient history, baby, and yes, you're doing the right thing."

Leafy green spring trees line Route 72 as I head south Monday afternoon to find Ricky. Slow-moving, cottony clouds float across a clear blue sky. Nevertheless, my mood is black.

Turning off the main road and onto a red dirt trail, my truck bounces and sways over rain-washed potholes. I spot

Ricky's F250 under a canopy of branches and hear Alan Jackson's "Drive" blasting from the stereo.

I cut the engine and take the footpath down to the shore. Ricky's waded out thigh deep, casting his line.

"Are they biting?" I wave, smiling as if all is well.

He reels in his line. "No," he says, with not so much as a glance over his shoulder or a by-your-leave.

"You got a second?"

"Do I look like I got a second?"

"Yes." Smart aleck. The gloves are off. No, the gloves are on. Which is it? Gloves off? Gloves on? No matter, the *fight* is on.

"Nope, don't think I do." Ricky zips the line through the air. The silverfish lure grabs a ray of light just before breaking the water's surface.

"I thought the fish weren't biting." I slip my hands into my hip pockets and cock my head to one side.

"They aren't. Just like my girlfriend."

Ah, yes, the gloves are off. "Can we talk about this?"

Before he can answer, Ricky's rod bows to the zip of a reeling line. His arm muscles flex as he works to bring his catch in. "Well, looky here, you brought me luck." But as quickly as it began, it's over. The tip of the rod whips toward the heavens, and the taut line goes limp. Ricky's shoulders droop, then he swears.

"Sorry," I say, for lack of anything better.

He wades out of the water and brushes past me. "Must not be my weekend for landing the Big One."

Wincing, I realize this conversation is not going to be easy. But, I'm tired of running, tired of choosing the easy road. "Missed you in church yesterday."

"Surprised you even noticed."

"I noticed." My eyes follow him as he walks to the back of his truck, tossing his rod into the bed. He steps out of his waders and jerks his T-shirt over his head. I whirl around to face the other way.

I don't want to marry Ricky, but mercy me, sometimes he makes me wish I did. Just for a night or two. He's lean and muscled, like a wrangler. His abs are well defined. The only six pack I've ever touched.

Shirtless, Ricky slips up behind me, brushing my hair away from my neck, sending chills down my spine. "Marry me, Robin. Come on, it'll be fun."

"I'm moving to Nashville." The confession sounds soft and weak, but the words sink down and grab hold.

"Nashville?" He turns my shoulders to face him. "Since when? To do what?" A red tint outlines his narrowed eyes.

"Be a songwriter."

"Be a songwriter?" At that he backs away from me and hooks his arms over the bed of his truck, crossing his legs at the ankles. He stares at me like I'm a cyclops—or worse, Millie Miner the day she wore so much makeup for our senior picture it looked like we actually had a class clown.

"Why are you looking at me like that?" Hands on my hips, I pretend to be brave, pretend this is the best idea since the Colonel invented Kentucky Fried Chicken.

"Because I'm wondering if you've lost your mind. Do you even know what it takes to make it as a songwriter?"

"Yes, well, a little."

"You're going to get lost in the sea of wanna-be Nashville songwriters. For every one that makes it, there's a million more trying."

"I'm not one in a million?"

He points his finger at me and laughs low. "Ah, clever girl. I'm not falling for that one-in-a-million bait. I'll live to regret it."

"Clever boy." As I'm talking, I retrieve my little black notebook and a pen from my hip pocket.

"Look, baby, all I'm saying . . . What are you doing?"

"Just jotting some thoughts."

"We're in the middle of a discussion."

"Hold on a sec." I scribble *one-in-a-million, clever girl, clever boy.*

"Robin—" He reaches for my arm, knocking my book and pen to the ground.

"Ricky!" I jerk away, stooping to pick them up. "Thin ice, bud. Very thin."

"You weren't listening." He stares at me for a second. "Until Friday night, the only singing you ever did was on your grandpa's porch. Songwriting is a long shot."

"Oh my stars, you sound like Momma." I tuck my notebook and pen in my hip pocket.

Ricky gently tugs me close. The scent of stale cologne mingled with sweat and river water stings my nose. He brushes my lips with the tip of his thumb, then lowers his lips to mine. "Let's get married, make a few babies."

His words electrify the hairs on the back of my neck. "You just want to have sex."

His grin is impish. "Do you blame me? Look at you. Cuddlier than a passel of pups and sexier than Shania."

"Shania? You're crazy."

"Ask any man in Freedom, Robin."

"What? You've talked to other men about me?" My entire body burns with embarrassment.

"No, but get your head out of the sand, Robin. Men know what other men are thinking."

I narrow my eyes and make a fist. "Look, I'm not marrying you just so you can sleep with me. Shoot, Ricky, what kind of woman would I be?"

"Very happy." He snickers.

My protesting fades with a laugh. "You're sure of yourself."

"I love you. I want to marry you. I want to sleep with you under the stars on the bank of the Tennessee River. I want twelve kids that look just like us."

"Twelve kids? What're you thinking?" Sex on a muddy river-bank and having more kids than I got fingers. Ha! "Ricky, it's taken me a long time to work up the guts to admit my dream, and you're asking me to cash it in for a roll in the hay."

"Not one roll. Many rolls." He tries to sound sultry, but it's more like a tacky used-car salesman telling me, "She runs like a top."

"Besides," he continues, "you can write all the songs you want right here in Freedom."

"No one in Freedom is going to buy my songs."

"Probably no one in Nashville will either."

I stare toward the river. I hate that he's half right. But more, I hate his argument against me.

"Life's too short to be chasing rainbows," he says.

I bristle back at him. "Life's too short not to chase a rainbow or two."

"Come on, forget about Nashville." In one deft move, he swings his leg around, knocking my feet out from under me. We tumble to the ground amid the tall grass as I hoot with laughter. I can't help it. This is the irresistible part of Ricky Holden. The next second we're rolling around, laughing and giggling, wrestling against each other, each trying to come out on top. Until . . . We slow down. He peers into my eyes.

"Robin."

I peer back. "Ricky."

Next thing I know, we're making out like a couple of junior high kids, slobbering all over each other. See, the boy does things to me.

But when he grabs for my T-shirt, I shove him off and jump to my feet. "No you don't, Ricky."

He falls over on his back, hand on his chest, breathing deep. The rascal knows he can't get to second base with me.

"You're driving me wild."

I tug my shirt straight. "You're doing it to yourself, dude."

He rises up on his elbows. "No, you're doing it to me."

He's impossible. I start for my truck before he wears me down.

Just beyond the thicket, dust billows, and car tires crunch against the rocks and dead tree limbs. A car door opens then slams shut.

"Ricky? Sugar? You here? You left your jacket at my place Saturday night."

Through golden ribbons of sunlight, Mary Lu Curtain rounds a clump of blooming honeysuckle.

Ricky scrambles to his feet. "Mary Lu." He lets loose with an obviously nervous chuckle. I notice he doesn't look my way. "How'd you find me?"

"You said you'd be fishing . . ." She glances at him, then me.

I motion to Mary Lu. "This is what you had to take care of Saturday night?"

"Robin, he told me you two broke up. Really." Ricky's leather jacket, the one I bought for him, dangles from Mary Lu's fingers.

"Guess we did, Mary Lu." The hinges of my truck door moan when I jerk it open.

Mary Lu flicks her wrist. "By the way, you did good the other night, girl. Never knew you could sing."

"Shut up, Mary Lu," Ricky growls.

I slam my door with a huff and a puff. Keys. Where are my keys? I look in the ignition, patting my pockets. I can't find my keys.

Ricky storms over. "Robin, it ain't what you think."

"Oh, really? What do I think?"

He drops his head against the doorframe. "I was upset—"

My eyes start to burn. "Ricky, find my keys, please." It galls me to ask, but I'm not hunting around in the weeds while Mary Lu stands by.

He sighs and wanders off, leaving me to wait and *not* cry.

Then he's back. "Here." He dangles my keys in front of my face. "I ran into her at Dottie's after I left your place."

"Dottie's? What did you have to take care of at Dottie's on a Saturday night? You're such a liar, Rick."

Cranking the engine, I shift into gear. "You know—" What am I doing? There's nothing more to say. "See you, Ricky." I pop the clutch and careen over the meadow toward the highway.

6

Tuesday morning, my Willaby's uniforms aren't on the floor
where I left them, crumpled and wrinkled, so I go searching.

In the kitchen, Momma's sitting at the table drinking coffee.

"Morning, Momma. You're up early." I shove open the
laundry-room door to find my uniforms washed and pressed,
hanging from a dowel rod.

"Couldn't sleep," she says.

"You didn't have to wash my uniforms, Momma. I've gone
to work wrinkled before."

She raises her mug to her lips. "So I've heard."

Good grief. Town gossips at it again. They could drive a
mad woman mad. I duck behind the laundry room door and
change.

When I come out, Momma says, "Coffee's ready if you want."

I smile. It's killing her not to pour me a cup. "Smells good."
Flopping my robe over the back of a chair, I twist my wet hair
up with a scrunchy.

"I can make eggs." Momma motions to the black iron skillet on the stove top.

"Thanks, but I'll grab a donut from the bakery." I pick a
mug from the mug tree and sweeten my Maxwell House with

sugar and cream. When I put the cream back in the fridge, an old note stuck to the door with a magnet catches my eye.

Lose 25 lbs.

The letters are faded by the years of afternoon sun streaming through the kitchen window. I touch it lightly with my fingertips. *I wonder if . . .*

Momma breaks into my thoughts. "You can't move to Nashville, Robin."

Here we go. At three-thirty in the morning, no less. "And why not?"

"Your home is here. Freedom." She gets up to freshen her coffee, stomping the kitchen chair against the hardwood floor.

"That's not a reason."

"You'll get your heart broke."

"By who?"

"Music Row. The business. Do you know how many people move to Nashville to write songs, or to become somebody the good Lord never meant for them to be?"

"What'd you do? Powwow with Ricky?"

"And by the way, were you going to tell me you turned down his marriage proposal?"

I glance out the sink window. Twilight has not yet disturbed the darkness. "Seems the town gossips beat me to it."

"You know I volunteer at the library on Mondays."

I face her. "Ah, yes, the epicenter of town lore."

"How do you think it made me feel to hear the news from Elaine McDougal?"

"Then stop listening to Elaine McDougal." I take a sip of coffee, thinking how the spiky aroma will always remind me of this kitchen.

"Don't you want to stay here and marry Ricky? Do you know how many girls would love to have what you have?" Forced cheer drives Momma's words.

I lift my chin and meet her gaze. "Perhaps songwriting is what the Lord created me to do."

She returns to her seat at the table. "I don't think you have any idea of the Lord's will for you."

Those are bodacious fighting words. "And you do?"

"I'm a mite older and wiser than you, Robin, so yes, I think I have the Lord's mind on the matter."

I walk over to the fridge and yank off the crusty note. "How long has this been up there?"

Momma snatches at the edge, tearing the corner. "Don't be smart."

"I'm serious, Momma, how long? Ten years? Twenty?"

"What's your point, Robin Rae?" She drops the torn edge onto the table. Her long fingers are brown from working in the spring garden, but her young face is old with worry.

"Momma." I kneel beside her. "Maybe some day you'll tell me the truth about why you're against me moving to Nashville, but I'm going. Accept it. I don't want my kids finding a sticky note on the fridge that says 'Be a songwriter.'"

Mr. Chancy attempts a cartwheel down the back hall when I give my notice. Seriously, he tries, but he can't manage to get his feet wheeling in the right direction. I watch him jig and jive toward the swinging doors with my face squished, my shoulders hunched, and my chin tucked to my chest. When he starts clapping and singing, I get a little offended. Was I that bad?

His final act of celebration is to whip out his tube of Tums and plop it into the trash. Is he serious? I caused *all* his heartburn? Good gravy. The market value of Tums will plummet today.

"You still mad at me?" Ricky asks, leaning against the wall, his arms folded.

"I reckon not."

The man is an ornery cuss, but he's sweet and tender underneath. I do care for him, and there's no use writing songs about life and how people should give up their grudges if I'm gonna hold on to one.

He steps toward me with his blue gazed fixed on my face. "The thing with Mary Lu . . . It was nothing, Robin. You have to believe me. Mitch called on my way home, said he and some others were going to Dottie's for her new dessert special. Somehow we all wound up at Mary Lu's . . . I was upset . . . She asked about you . . . I said we broke up . . ."

"Don't grovel. You're too good for that. I believe you. This time."

He exhales. "So, you're really leaving?"

"I'm really leaving." The confession feels right. Worthy of a true cartwheel.

Ricky raises his chin. "So, then."

"So, then," I echo, hoping there's more. Will he finally say he's happy for me?

"Better get to work."

"Right."

Hard to imagine a few days ago we were necking behind the stairs.

As I walk to my aisle, Martina is belting "Independence Day" over the PA, and my confidence kicks up a little. I'm sure I'm doing the right thing—I think.

From the end of the upstairs hall, the attic calls me to visit. I stare at the attic door with my hand wrapped around the handle of Daddy's old leather suitcase.

Leaving home stirs a longing to roam and reminisce, so I sit the luggage inside my bedroom door and creep across the moaning hardwood floor to the attic door. The attic is not off limits—no room in the McAfee house is off limits—but the attic has always contained secrets. Momma's. So, I feel a little devious sneaking up the stairs.

At the top of the steps, the musty fragrance reminds me of rainy Saturday afternoons, playing up here with Eliza and Steve, turning the attic into a wilderness fort or a Star Wars space station.

Remembering Great-Grandma Lukeman's authentic Tiffany lamp is in the far corner next to her worn rocker, I fumble in the dark until my fingers touch the lamp's faded gold chain. With one click, a rosy glow angles across the room.

The attic is cozy and warm, stuffed to the gills with things Momma calls memories.

First, there's the wall of Momma's ribbons. Hundreds of them. Each one embossed with a gold-lettered "First Place." Great day in the morning. Bit McAfee, Queen of Canning. Queen of First Place. She *should* visit Eliza this summer and stop in on the queen. Jude Perry can write a headline: "Queen of Canning to Visit Queen of England."

In the corner opposite of the ribbons is Momma's cedar chest. I try the lid. Locked. Still locked. Always locked. We used to asked her about it when we were kids—not because we cared, but because she told us, "Never you mind," gave us cookies, and turned on the TV.

But today I notice something sticking out from under the chest's lid. I lightly tug on the corner of a picture and carry it over to the light.

In faded Kodak color, there's Momma, her face framed with Farrah Fawcett hair. She's smiling and her expression is one I've never seen before. So carefree.

There are four others in the picture with Momma. Two men and two women. I study their faces. They're young, about

my age, but captured in time twenty-five years ago. The guys'
long hair flows into their wide, open collars, and one of them
sports Elvis-like sideburns. I run my finger over the snapshot's smooth surface.

*Who are these people, Momma? What are you doing? Why
have I never seen this before?*

I flip the photo over to see if Momma wrote anything on
the back. She didn't. At the bottom of the picture, there's a
sign or something. But the image is torn, and I can't make out
the words. I try to match the photo's tattered edges, but they
are too frayed.

"Robin?" A muffled call floats up the stairs.

I jerk my head up.

"Robin, where are you? Eliza's on the phone."

I hurry to the trunk and try to slip the photo in, but it
won't go. Trying a different angle, I only manage to get the
picture stuck. Now what? I tug lightly to free the picture, and
then *rrrrrip*.

Crap. Perfect. Just perfect.

Another muffled, "Robin Rae! Mercy, did you fall in the
toilet? Eliza's waiting. Long distance still costs money."

Leaning against the trunk lid and thumping it with the
heel of my hand, I work the stuck half of the picture free
and hurry down the attic stairs, hiding the picture in my hip
pocket. Surely there's a place in Nashville that fixes photos.
But the original is torn. Forever.

"Where've you been?" Momma asks, handing me the phone.
"Eliza's getting ready to go to England, and you're dilly-dallying."

"I do *not* dillydally." I hop up on the counter. Savory smells
drift from Momma's oven. "Hey, Liza."

"How's Momma behaving?" she asks.

I mutter into the receiver, "She's not on board, but she's
accepting it."

"That's something. I can't get why she's so boiled over you moving to Nashville but so accepting of me going to England."

"Story of our lives, I reckon."

"Are you going to e-mail me when I'm in England?"

"Did I e-mail you at Auburn?"

"No."

"There you have it."

"You're a horrible big sister."

"Oh, really?" I cup my hand over the phone. "Say, Daddy, remember when Granddaddy's valuable coin collection was stolen?"

Eliza's laugh floats down the line. "Okay, you win best big sister *ever*! You did take my punishment for me."

"What's that, Robin Rae?" Daddy cranes around his easy chair, a red licorice whip dangling from his lips. He quit smoking twenty-five years ago and took up licorice.

I smile. "Nothing, Daddy."

Eliza tells me a letting agent (translation: *realtor*) found her a flat (translation: *apartment*) in Cambridge near the university. She can walk or bike to most places or take the buses.

Then, too soon, she says, "I'd better go. I still have a lot to do."

My heart lurches. It's hard to say good-bye. I ward off my tears by picking at the small hole in the knee of my jeans. "Be careful, you."

My baby sister, thousands of miles away. It was one thing when she was only a few hours south in War Eagle country. One small plea for help and we'd send down the cavalry. But all the way over in England? I suppose Eliza has to find out what she's made of too. Steel or clay.

"You know I will."

"Eliza, I tease you about being all brains, but you're very beautiful. Be smart about it."

She sniffs. "Same to you, Robin. Don't let no sweet-talking cowboy get in your way, because once they hear your songs, they'll fall in love with your soul."

"Sure they will. As soon as I work up the nerve to sing to them."

"Let me talk to Momma again. I want to say good-bye."

Handing the phone back to Momma, I realize how soon my own life will change. I'm leaving home. Leaving the comforts and sounds of Freedom for a life and a city I don't know. And that doesn't know me.

Will Nashville welcome me?

I meander into the living room where Daddy's dozing off. Sitting on the floor, I press my cheek against his knee, defenseless against the tears that form when his hand rests gently on my head.

"Last day?"

I look up as Ricky approaches me Friday afternoon with his work apron wadded in his hand. His cowlick sweeps his thick blond hair off his forehead.

I smile though the sad shimmer in his eyes, and it stings my heart. "This is it. Just finishing up next week's order for Lil. She's taking over my aisle."

"I need your truck," he says.

"My truck? Why?"

"Because."

"Because? You can't have my truck on a 'because.' I still remember what you and Mitch did to Reed Larson's car."

His jaw drops as if he's completely innocent of painting the man's car pink and green. "Robin, please, I never touched Reed's car."

"Right. But the paint did, didn't it?" I wink at him. He

and Mitch, who owns Pearce Paint & Body Shop, are kings of innuendo and double-talk. They've planned and executed more secret missions than the CIA.

"I'm not going to hurt your truck. Please, give me the keys."

"You're not going to put tractor tires on it, are you? Or paint angry, hood-eating flames across the front?"

He narrows his eyes. "No, but I still think flames are a great idea."

"No flames." We had this argument at Christmas. He wanted to paint flames on my hood as a present. I refused. Got a year's worth of guitar strings instead. Good man.

"Let me have your truck." He leans down to my ear. "Please."

His warm breath melts every "No" in my body. "O-okay." Is it hot in here?

He slips his arm around my waist and pulls me tight to kiss me. "I'll come by tonight and pick it up." The man has the best lips. "And just to clarify, I did not touch Reed's car."

I laugh as he releases me. "Liar." A mental picture of Reed's pink car pops into my head. Got to be a song in there somewhere. Right up there with a boy named Sue. I pull my black notebook and pen from my apron pocket and flip to a blank page. "By the way," I say to Ricky, "I leave Monday at eight."

He turns to leave. "She'll be ready."

Monday morning the sun burns away the first layers of fog as I wait for Daddy on the back porch. A low rumble of fear has me thinking I might change my mind, but I grapple it down.

I've rented the third-floor apartment from Jeeter's friend, a Nashville artist named Birdie Griffin who had a pretty good run as a star in the '70s and '80s. I also called cousin Skyler Banks. Her momma is Daddy's sister, Louise. "About time," Skyler said when I told her my plan.

Yesterday I sat with Ricky in church. "How's my truck?" I asked before worship started.

"Not pink."

"Good." I elbowed him in the ribs.

"So, what about us?" he asked, resting his arm around my shoulders on the back of the pew.

I wave at Mrs. Stebbins. "What about us?"

Ricky turns my chin so we're eye to eye. "Are we broken up?"

"Can we just wait and see?" I couldn't bring myself to say something final like "It's over." Especially with Mary Lu on the prowl. Is that horrible?

"For now," he agreed.

So here it is Monday morning, and I'm about to take flight. On the porch next to me, Daddy's big leather suitcase is stuffed to the gills, along with the Wal-Mart tote Arizona insisted on buying me. Plus a box of bedding and such, and my guitar. Birdie called Sunday evening to remind me that the apartment is furnished, so no need to bring anything but clothes and trinkets.

After I hung up with her, Momma warned, "Be careful, Robin Rae—check for fleas and lice when you get there."

"Fleas and lice? Momma, she's a respectable lady, not a bordello madam."

"Don't be snippy. I'm just saying . . . if you need anything, call and we'll run it up to you." She bonked a head of lettuce against the counter and pulled it apart.

Grandma gave me a basket of goodies. Two jugs of her tea, a tin of ginger cookies, and my favorite coffee mug of hers. "Gotta have something of the old home."

Momma handed me two goose-down pillows and the quilt from my old bed. "You'll need these."

I felt like it was 1880, and I was going West on a wagon train never to be heard from again. Goose-down pillows, a quilt, and "something of the old home"? Nashville is two hours away.

"Ready?" Daddy steps onto the porch and hands me a bag of licorice.

"Wow," I whisper. "This is a huge sacrifice for you. I don't know what to say."

"All right, all right. So I like licorice." He jerks my suitcase from the porch floor, chuckling.

We load up and drive in silence to Mitch's, where Ricky stowed my truck for the weekend, the only sound the click of Daddy's tongue as he chews on his toothpick. I'm homesick already. By the time we turn in to Pearce Paint & Body Shop, my eyes are battling tears.

Daddy cuts the engine and says, "I'm gonna miss you."

"Same here, Daddy." A few tears escape and slip down my cheeks.

He reaches for my hand. "My firstborn. You're the most special, but I'll deny it if Eliza or Steve catch wind."

"It's our little secret."

"I know you're scared, but I'm proud of you." He squeezes my hand as if to give me a shot of confidence. "Courage isn't the absence of fear but the ability to confront it. You're showing courage here, Robin Rae."

"Thank you," I whisper, wiping the edge of my face where the tears drop off.

"You have a bit to overcome, but learning to fly with your own wings will make you strong. Listen to your old daddy—you are a great songwriter. The Lord is with you."

Old daddy? At forty-eight, his hair is still thick and black, and his crisp brown eyes look at Momma with youthful love. He's the steady, ever-present man. A man of his word. A man of the Word.

I lunge across the seat into his arms. "How did I get so blessed to have a daddy like you?"

He coughs and sputters, patting my shoulder. "I think I'm

the lucky one. Now, we'd better see what Ricky and Mitch have done to your truck." He kisses my forehead before letting me go.

Outside, Daddy pounds the heavy, sliding doors with his fist. "Hello, it's Dean and Robin."

Ricky answers through a crack. "Not quite ready."

"Fine, son, but let us in. We can get a cup of coffee while we wait." Daddy shrugs at me with a glance at his watch.

"Ricky, what's going on?" I holler. "There better not be one flame . . . Or antlers. No bull or deer antlers. Or moose." One set of antlers or yellow flames, and I promise, *pow*, right in the kisser.

The garage doors open. There, in the bright shop lights, is my '69 Chevy, it's midnight-blue body polished to a mirrorlike shine.

"Holy cow." I walk beside the truck. "Ricky, it's beautiful." Inside the cab, my white seats are whiter than fresh snow, and the small tear on the driver's side is gone. "You fixed my seat and detailed the interior . . . Is that a new roof lining?"

"Yeah, couldn't let you—" A cough chokes off his thought.

Daddy props one arm over the door. "You must have worked all weekend. This is mighty nice of you and Mitch, son."

Ricky waves off Daddy's comment with a sigh. And his eyes are on me. "Couldn't send Robin off to Nashville looking like a country bumpkin."

I laugh. "But I am a country bumpkin. And proud of it."

"Robin," Daddy calls from the other side of the truck. "Look here."

I walk around. There on the driver's side of the truck bed is the most beautiful red bird, wings spread, soaring above a white, fleecy cloud. Underneath, Ricky has airbrushed the words *Freedom's Song*.

I fly into his arms, bury my face in his chest, and bawl like a baby.

7

A steady rain pelts my windshield as I cruise north on I-65
just past the Cool Springs exits. The truck's wipers grunt
and groan, and despite blasting the defrost, a thin layer of
fog creeps up the inside of the glass. Wiping it down with an
Arby's napkin, I glimpse the road signs. Nashville's up ahead.

My insides quiver and my leg shakes a little. "Getting
closer—"

Holy cow! I slam on the brakes.

Freedom's Song fishtails and hydroplanes into the next
lane. My heart bucks as I brace for the crunch of metal against
metal. But by God's grace, I miss two passing cars by a hog's
hair and manage to get control before spinning into the guard-
rail.

With my heart thundering and my head throbbing, I drop
my forehead against the wheel and gasp for air. Was there
really a woman standing in the middle of the right lane?

Tap, tap, tap.

I roll down my window. A little wisp of a woman stands
beside my truck. "Thank you for stopping," she says, rain drip-
ping from her short, brown hair onto her heart-shaped face.

"Don't mention it." It dawns on me I'm facing south in a

northbound lane, and headlights are closing in. At a quarter to ten, there's still a good bit of going-to-work traffic. I clutch and shift. "Let me get out of the road."

I whip the truck across the lanes and park behind her car on the berm. All those Saturdays doing donuts in wet fields around Freedom? Priceless.

With my shoulders hunched up against the cold May rain, I get out and walk toward the little woman's car. "What's the trouble?"

"I don't know." She kicks the car door. "Stupid piece of junk."

"Can you pop the hood?" I've looked over Daddy's shoulder enough times to know my way around an engine. I can find obvious problems.

Steam rolls from the radiator as I lift the lid. "You know, you gotta water these things." The putrid odor of a dry radiator stings my nose.

"I just get in and drive." She fans the steam away from her face.

"This is what gives girls a bad name. Car ignorance."

She laughs. "Guilty."

The rain thickens, and I drop the hood. It's a nice vehicle—a Saturn. I know people who'd give their eyeteeth for a piece of *junk* like this.

"I have radiator fluid in my truck," I say, "but we need to wait for the engine to cool." I motion for her to follow me.

She jogs alongside, shivering. "What woman drives around with radiator fluid?"

"One who doesn't break down on the highway and almost gets herself killed."

"I like you." She shovels her wet bangs out of her face and goes around to the passenger side door. Inside the truck cab, water drips from the ends of our hair and puddles on my clean seats.

"When the engine cools, I'll pour in some Prestone. Hope you're not in a hurry." I reach in the glove box for my stash of napkins and pass half of them to my passenger.

She looks at me with really blue eyes. "Nope, no hurry. I'm free as a bird."

I'm not surprised. "What's your name?"

"Mallory Clark." She rubs her wet hair with a napkin. "Thanks for stopping."

"Robin McAfee, and you gave me no choice." I glance at her from the corner of my eye. She's reapplying mascara. I grin. Bet her story is a doozy.

Putting her makeup away, she settles back in the seat, propping her wet Reeboks on my dash. I know it's an old Chevy, but it's my old Chevy, and Ricky just cleaned it. "You mind?" I flick at her dangling shoestrings.

"Sorry." She drops her feet to the floor.

"Are you on your way to Nashville?" I squeeze the last of the water from my hair with a soggy, shredding napkin.

"Yeah, going home." Mallory fluffs her short hair, making the ends stand up. "Just getting back from a vacation in hell."

I make a face. "How was it?"

She laughs. "I knew I liked you." But her merriment quickly fades. "I chased my boyfriend to Florida where he promptly introduced me to his new girlfriend." She collapses against the seat with a heavy sigh. "I'm twenty-two and still chasing boys like a stupid schoolgirl."

"No accounting for love, I suppose."

Mallory props her elbow on the door's arm and stares out. "My family was livid with me, but—" her shoulders rise and fall. "—I had to try."

"Nothing wrong with trying." The rain makes the day dreary, and I'm trembling from almost running someone over. "I'm terri-fied to sing in front of people." The words come before I can think about them. "Yet I'm moving to Nashville to be a songwriter. What a hoot, huh? My momma and boyfriend think I'm crazy."

Mallory picks up my black notebook lying on the seat between us. "Ah, but it's those mommas and boyfriends who inspire hit songs." She flips through the pages without asking but without reading. For some reason, I don't mind that she has invaded my private world. "My boyfriend—" She stops. "My *ex*-boyfriend was a songwriter. I do a little singing myself. At least I did."

"What happened?"

"Mr. Two-timer ran off with Miss Fake Boobs. Matt and I were in a cover band together. I paid the bills while he worked on his own stuff. Oh, we had big dreams."

I grin. By Mallory's tone, I know she's going to survive just fine. "How'd you meet this Mr. Two-Timer?"

"He wanted a backup singer for Songwriter's Night at the Bluebird Café. A mutual friend suggested me, and next thing I know, I'm in love." She laughs. "I was so whacked to fall for him."

"Mallory . . ." I stop. What can I say to ease her pain? She just has to go through it and hopefully come out stronger. "At least you found out before you married him."

She cuts a sideways glance at me. "I suppose so."

"Do you have family in Nashville?"

She nods. "Born and raised. Parents, aunts, uncles, grandparents, cousins."

The ring in her voice is familiar. "I have all that in Freedom, Alabama."

"My mom hated Matt. She thought I was the one with all the talent and that he was using me."

"Was he?"

She sighs. "Probably. It's hard to admit."

"Love, for all it's merits, can be confusing."

Mallory chuckles. "Sweet nothings make me weak."

A picture of Ricky flashes over my heart "Me too."

Raindrops still pelt the windshield, but I figure her engine is cooled by now. "Ready to water your car?"

"Let's do it." Mallory dashes ahead while I grab the coolant from the toolbox in the truck bed.

She ducks behind the wheel while I fill the radiator.

"Start the engine," I holler. Cold rain is running down my hair, into my jacket collar, and down my neck.

The engine roars to life, and Mallory hops out of the driver's seat. "Oh, yay! My hero. Thank you, thank you."

I twist the cap back on the Prestone. "No problem. Glad to help."

"See you around Nash*Vegas*." She pistols her fingers at me with a wink. "Hey, maybe I'll catch you at the Bluebird Café. You're gonna sing there, of course. I mean, if you want to be a songwriter, you have to do the 'Bird." She scribbles her phone number on a ripped gas station receipt. "Call me when you're going to be there. I'll come and see you."

"Sure." Hope you're not married with five kids by then.

By the time I get back to my truck, Mallory's little blue car has vanished behind the veil of rain. I shiver and reach for the last of the napkins. *If you want to be a songwriter, you have to do the 'Bird.*

Mallory's right. So focused on moving to Nashville, and not losing my nerve, I hadn't planned beyond today.

Anxiety and fear—evil twins, the two of them—buckle up in the seat next to me as I picture myself walking into an open-mike night or trying out for a songwriter's night. As a member of Nashville Songwriter's Association, I can sign up to audition for the Bluebird's Sunday night Songwriter's Night as early as tomorrow if I want.

I think I'm getting hives.

So, I make a Robin McAfee decision. And it's forbidden to go

back on one of my decisions. It's my own weird rule, and somehow it works.

Here it is: I'm going to kick fear in the patoot, dig up a
mustard seed of courage, and sing at an open-mike night
within the month.

Besides, we don't know when Jesus plans on coming back,
and I sure-as-shooting don't want to be caught holding my one
dinky talent over a hole in the ground.

"Oops. Hey, Jesus, I've been meaning to do something with
this . . ."

On the napkin Jeeter gave me, scrawled in black ink, is Birdie
Griffin's address: 2120 Ashwood Avenue. It's a boxy-looking
three-story brick with a wide stone porch and tall windows. I turn
into the drive and glance up at the third floor. Welcome home.

I park behind an old blue Mercedes and step out. The
rain has stopped, but my clothes are still wet from rescuing
Mallory. I adjust my jeans, loathing the icky feeling of my
skivvies sticking to me. I hadn't figured on meeting my new
landlady looking like a wet pup.

To hide my wet hair, I reach behind the seat for the Auburn
cap Eliza gave me for Christmas her freshman year. Mallory's
hair looked cute, my hair looks like a ragged mop. For the first
time, I consider doing something with my hair. New town,
new 'do?

A car horn toots wildly down the street, and a hand waves
out the window. I grin and wave back. Skyler. She whips in
behind my truck and hops out of her . . . BMW? Wow, Music
Row lawyering pays.

"Robin! You made it." She runs toward me with her arms
spread wide, looking like a snapshot from *Vogue*. Then says,
"You're . . . wet." She stops short, lowering her arms.

"Nice to see you too." I tug on the Auburn cap. "What are you doing here?"

Skyler's one of those instant-connect cousins. No matter how much times passes between conversations, we always pick up where we left off.

"I couldn't miss your move-in day. Besides, Aunt Bit called Mom who called me. Yadda, yadda."

I shake my head. "Figures."

Skyler motions behind her. "My office is right over there off Music Row on 17th Avenue South."

"You're on Music Row?" I hoist my suitcase from the truck bed. Water sloshes in my shoes.

"Yep, well, not technically, but Music Rowish. A few doors down." She poses with her hands on her hips. "How do you like me now?"

Grinning, I hand Skyler the tote bag. "Toby Keith would be proud. Maybe if I can't make it on Music Row as a song-writer, I'll slim my way in as a lawyer."

Skyler laughs, following me toward Birdie's front steps. "I always wondered why you never went to college. You're the smartest of all the cousins."

"Don't know about being the smartest," I say over my shoulder, setting the suitcase down to ring the front bell. "But I couldn't take another four years of sitting in a desk, facing forward. But next thing I know, I'm blowing out twenty-five candles and stacking shelves at Willaby's."

Skyler adjusts the strap of my hanging bag on her shoulder. "Well, it's all going to change now. I'm glad you're here, Robin. We're going to have fun."

"I have a lot to learn, a long way to go."

"So, you can still have fun." Skyler kicks me with her sword-toe shoes. "Now tell me, whose place is this again?"

"Birdie Griffin."

Her eyes pop. "You're kidding. Mom would die. She loved Birdie Griffin back in the day." Skyler sings, "'Are you gonna keep talking boy? Just kiss . . . me . . . now . . .'"

"Shhh, she'll hear you." Footsteps resound from the other side of the door.

"So? She'll be happy to know someone my age remembers one of her songs. Especially since she was a hit in the eight-track era."

I swallow a laugh. "Maybe. But let's not push it."

The paned-window front door swings open. "Well, well, Robin McAfee." Birdie Griffin stands in the doorway wearing a pair of tight blue jeans and a white top. In her mid fifties, she's attractive, tall and slender, with big blonde hair and long, red nails.

I meet her brown, snappy gaze and offer my hand. "Birdie Griffin, it's a pleasure to meet you."

She laughs and pulls me in for a hug. "Any friend of Jeeter's is a friend of mine." My face is buried in her pillowy bosom. I hear Skyler's snicker. "Your apartment is all ready. You called me just in time. I just sent my last tenant packing."

"Oh?" I follow her up a wide oak staircase.

"Tried to make it as a songwriter, but—" Birdie's poofy hair bounces as she walks "—she couldn't pay the rent, so I told her to go on home and stop wasting everybody's time. Especially her own." She stops at the top of the landing. "Then you called."

"Lucky me." An eerie feeling shimmies down my legs. No fooling around with this woman.

"Tough business, songwriting," Skyler offers.

"It ain't for the weakhearted." Birdie starts up the second flight of stairs, her backless high-heeled shoes slapping against her heels. "And you are?" She looks back at Skyler.

"The weakhearted," Skyler says.

"Is she going to be around here much?" Birdie asks with a smirk.

I nod. "Birdie, meet my cousin, Skyler Banks."

"I suppose I'll get used to it," Birdie says with a huff, handing me my apartment key.

Skyler sticks her tongue out behind Birdie's back. I warn her with a sharp glance to shape up as I unlock the door to my new place and step inside.

"Wow. Birdie, this is great."

"It's cozy," she says.

The three of us enter into the living room, furnished with a rusty brown-leather sofa, club chair, coffee table, and beige area rug. The bedroom is to the right, behind a divider, and the dining area, complete with a kitchenette, is to the left. The slanted ceiling and angled walls are painted a pale yellow with a soft blue trim.

Birdie taps the wall with her fingernail. "I picked the trim color, Robin's-egg blue, the day before you called."

"It's a sign," Skyler says, walking over to the long row of front-facing windows. "Robin, you've got a great deck out here." She swings open one of the hinged windows. A gust of spring air rushes in.

"The porch is great for catching the moonlight on a clear night," Birdie offers.

Skyler steps through the window. "You can see the rooftops of Music Row from here. Another sign."

"Stop with the 'It's a sign' stuff, will you?" I join Skyler on the deck. "Isn't it enough of a sign that I'm here?"

I peer through the thick branches of Birdie's front maple to see the rooftops of Music Row. Well, well. My new home watches over the land of the legends. It makes me feel small and unworthy. Who am I to try to join them?

"Let me show you a few more things." Birdie draws us

back inside. "Here's your kitchenette." She runs her hand along the forest-green Formica counter, then reaches for a pocket door. "You can pull this door and close off the kitchen in case you're messy."

I stand in the middle of the tiny kitchen and hold out my arms so the tips of my fingers almost touch the stove and the refrigerator.

"Your bathroom," Birdie says with a clap of her hands, "is through the closet. Did you girls ever see *The Mary Tyler Moore Show?*" She flicks her hand at us. "Reckon not—too young."

"I've seen reruns." I go with Birdie into the broad, deep closet. The floor is covered with orange and green shag carpet.

"I love Mary Tyler Moore," Skyler says.

"Now, here's your bathroom." Birdie shoves the door open . . . and a man pops out.

I scream and jump back. "Great day in the morning." My heart is thumping and my knees knock.

"What? What is it?" Skyler crashes into me. "Oh. Wow."

Birdie glowers at us over her shoulder. "Oh, for Pete's sake."

The handsome man winks as he maneuvers his broad shoulders through the doorway. My face burns, and Skyler exhales hot air on the back of my neck. I shove her aside. I saw him first.

Birdie pats his muscled arm. "This is Lee Rivers. He's a big-time contractor and a good friend of mine. He humors me by occasionally doing an odd job or two around here."

"You're one of my first and best customers." Lee puts his arm around Birdie. "The drywall behind the toilet was warped. I replaced it, but it still needs paint. I'll send one of the men over to finish up. Or—" he peers down at me "—I might see to the job myself."

My knocking knees buckle at the same time Skyler falls against me. We almost topple onto him. "I need some painting done at my place," she says.

For crying out loud. "Skyler." I swear she's salivating.

Lee grins as if Skyler's comment tickles. "I only do jobs for Birdie. But I can give you the name of a good painter."

"So, Robin, this is your bathroom." Birdie sidesteps Lee. "It's small, but sufficient."

I squish around Lee—dern, he smells good—and peek into the bathroom. It is small, but I don't plan on living in there.

By the time I come out, Skyler is in the living room making third-degree goo-goo eyes at Lee. I'm about to hip butt her out of the way when I catch sight of myself in the closet door mirror.

My hair is sticking out from under the Auburn hat like I'm the Scarecrow's bride. And please, is that a grease stain streaking across my right boob?

I try to wipe the grease away, but I only smear it. Oh, geez. I look up. Lee is watching me.

"Grease," I say, pointing to the stain.

He nods. "I see."

Land a-mighty. Did I just point the man to my chest?

Skyler grabs my arm and pulls me to her. "What are you doing?"

I whine, "I don't know."

"Stop. He'll think you're addled or something."

"I am addled."

Lee packs up his tools while Birdie talks to him about renovating her kitchen. His triceps bulge under his shirt sleeves when he picks up the heavy metal box.

"See you girls later." Birdie stops at the door with a gander at my head. "We just met, sugar, but you best do something about your hair. Don't want to scare anyone on Music Row."

Skyler throws her arm around my shoulders. "I'll see to it, Birdie."

Birdie winks at Skyler. "You're all right. Did you tell me your name?"

"Skyler. Skyler Banks. Robin's cousin and an attorney. In case you need one."

Birdie rolls her eyes and closes my door, leaving with Lee, who I swear lets his final gaze linger on my face for a good long second.

Skyler is about to rave over him when Birdie pops in again. "Robin, I forgot. A friend of mine, a songwriter, Marc Lewis, runs a cleaning service. He said he could use an extra hand if you don't mind scrubbing toilets for a living."

"No, I don't mind."

"He's got a few clients downtown and on Music Row, so you'll enjoy that part of it. Even if the Clorox gets to you after awhile."

I smile. "Thanks, Birdie."

"Got his number down in my place. Oh, need your first month's rent today. Come down to the kitchen when you get settled." She pauses before closing the door. "Welcome to your new place, shug."

8

While I unpack, Skyler makes an appointment for me at her new hair salon.

"I don't have a lot of money, Sky," I remind her while she talks.

She smiles and nods, waving me off. "Great, yeah, something chic . . . Color?" Skyler glances at me. "No, she's got plenty of color. But a deep conditioning treatment would be good."

"I don't have a lot of money, Sky."

She plugs her ear and turns her back. The nerve.

When's she's finished talking, she flips her phone shut and says to me, "Wednesday at four."

"Did you hear me?" I set the torn picture of Momma and her friends on the top shelf of the bookcase, clear of the open window breeze. "I don't have a lot of money, Sky."

"You're going to love Bishop's. It's a few minutes away but it's worth the drive. Come by my office, and I'll go with you."

I lean toward her and shout, "How much?"

She picks up her purse and walks toward the door. "For a shearing? Like . . . two dollars." She laughs.

I toss my suitcase on the bed. "Funny. What a funny girl.

I *get* the county cousin bit. Don't think I'm not on to you." I note Birdie made the bed with new sheets and a fat new pillow. I can store Momma's pillows and quilt in the closet.

"Right, you're on to me," Skyler calls from the door. "I have to get back to work, but what are you doing tonight? Nothing? Great. Meet me at the Frothy Monkey at seven."

"Frothy Monkey?" I poke my head out the closet door. "What's a Frothy Monkey?"

The Frothy Monkey is a coffee shop over on 12th Avenue South. I arrive late after getting turned around on all the one-way streets and stopping briefly in a strip mall parking lot to fight an icky alone-in-a-crowd feeling.

I admit I'm a little homesick for Freedom. Right now, Momma and Daddy are cleaning up after dinner. The smell of roasted meat and potatoes lingers in the air. In a few minutes, they'll go upstairs to change their clothes for the Monday night prayer meeting at Ramon and Marsha's, chatting the whole time about their day.

Skyler waves at me. "Robin, over here." She's standing on the deck with a raven-haired woman.

I wave back, bumping into a handsome man on my way to where Skyler is standing. "Oh, I'm so sorry."

"Not at all," he replies in a rich, melodic voice.

Skyler watches me with her hand over her mouth. When I get to her she says, "You just ran over Gerry House."

I look back at him. "Who's Gerry House?"

"Mr. Controversy-pants," offers the dark-haired woman.

"Mr. Controversy-pants?"

Skyler smiles. "He's a big on-air personality for The Big 98 WSIX. Also a songwriter and song publisher." She tips her head down. "And *you* just ran him over."

"Oh, man," I look again to where we collided. "Sorry Mr. House."

"Robin," Skyler says. "I'd like you to meet my roommate, Blaire Kirby. Blaire, my cousin, Robin McAfee."

"Nice to meet you." I step up, holding out my hand.

"Same here." Blaire's gaze flickers over my face but doesn't land there. She looks around me, behind me, but not at me. Who is she looking for? Mr. Controversy-pants?

I tug my Auburn cap lower on my forehead, feeling like a bloated tick next to the statuesque Blaire. She's the kind of woman classified as "out of my league" by 90 percent of the earth's male population. The other 10 percent simply lie to themselves.

Should've showered before I came, but after unpacking, leaving a quick message on the folks' answering machine, paying Birdie my first month's rent, and picking up Marc Lewis' phone number, I fell asleep face first on my new bed. When I woke up, it was time to find the Frothy Monkey.

"Come on, let's order," Skyler says, walking toward the front door.

Inside the intimately lit Frothy Monkey, a low hum rises from the crowded tables. We wait in line next to the spiral staircase.

Blaire is first to order. "Café mocha. No, wait, skinny latté. Wait, do you have chai tea?"

The girl behind the counter grimaces and points her pencil toward the menu.

"Gee whiz, Blaire, you act like you've never been here before," Skyler moans.

"Don't rush me."

I hide my grin behind my hand. Blaire's the kind of woman whose beauty could command a thousand ships, but she can't decide between tea or coffee. Finally, she decides on tea, then Skyler orders a café mocha while I try one of the skinny lattés.

"Blaire," Skyler launches the conversation as she leads the way to a table on the outside deck. "Robin's a songwriter." We sit at the last vacant table. The cool night is hosted by an array of stars twinkling down from a clear Nashville sky.

Blaire tips her head at me. "In Nashville? How unique."

"Blaire." Skyler pops her lightly on her hand, tossing me an I'm-sorry look.

Blaire offers no apology.

I sink down into my chair. Blaire and I size each other up while Skyler does most of the talking. A table of guys across the way are watching us like dogs on the hunt. Their fat textbooks are cracked open under their noses, but something or someone at our table is way more interesting.

And it ain't me.

Skyler rises halfway out of her chair and hollers across three tables. "Hey, dudes, tongues back in your mouth, noses back in your books."

The boys jerk their faces back to their books, as amused by Skyler as they were captivated by Blaire.

I, the bloated tick, slide further under the table. "What do you do, Blaire?" I cuddle my cup to my chest for security and warmth.

She swings her long black hair over her shoulder. "I'm a freelance photographer."

"She's fabulous, too, Robin. One of the best in Nashville."

"My knowledge of photography starts with *point* and ends with *click*," I say with a lilt. No one laughs. Tough crowd.

Skyler turns to Blaire. "You can shoot Robin's publicity photos when she needs them, right?"

Blaire responds in monotone. "If she'd like."

Very chilly Blaire breeze. What's her problem?

"She used to be a model," Skyler informs me.

Blaire regards Skyler with her chin in her hand as if she enjoys letting my energetic lawyer cousin talk for her.

"What made you move behind the camera?" I ask, pushing myself up in the chair.

"She got saved," Skyler answers.

"I'm not sure the God thing took very well, but—" Blaire looks away "—I try."

At last, common ground. "It's a journey, like everything else. We're not perfect, but love the One who is."

Skyler whams the table with her hand. "See, I told you she was cool. Don't you just love her?"

Blaire shrugs. Skyler apparently kicks her under the table or something because she winces. "I'm sure we'll become good friends." She offers me a half smile.

I see. She's nervous I'll use cousin privilege to squeeze her out. "I'm sure we will," I say, giving her a whole, wide smile.

Skyler launches into a tale about one of her artist-clients, "Who shall be nameless but her initials are L. Y. Nothing, I mean nothing, makes her happy."

Blaire laughs at Skyler's imitation of the high-maintenance artist, peeks at me, and exhales a little.

In the next breath, Skyler shifts the conversation. "We should do movie night at your new apartment." She turns to me with big eyes. "Break it in with a few chick flicks."

"Chick flicks?" Guess my cousin doesn't know me as well as we'd like to pretend. "I hate chick flicks. Give me Clint Eastwood, John Wayne, Mel Gibson, but no chicks, please."

Skyler flicks her hand at me. "Blaire, meet my redneck cousin."

Just then, a skinny dude with floppy hair and baggy jeans stumbles into the middle of the deck, his arms spread.

"She said yes! I'm engaged. Me!" He dashes from table to table. "I'm getting married!"

I peek around to see who said yes. A blushing blonde on the upper deck. Her left hand sparkles as she covers her shy laugh.

Her fiancé runs inside. "I'm engaged!" seeps through the open windows.

Blaire sighs. "Can we clone him? At least *this* part of him?"

He runs back out, hands on both sides of his head like he's holding the "freak" together. "I need a song. A song. Does anyone have a song?"

Skyler bolts out of her chair. "Over here." She dances her finger over my head.

"No, no, no, no. Skyler, what are you doing?" I grab her hand. "Sit down. I don't have a song. I don't even have a guitar."

Skyler jerks her hand from mine and cups it around her mouth. "Does anyone have a guitar?"

Oh my gosh! We're in freakin' Nashville. Of course, someone has a guitar. If you spit into the wind, you'll hit someone who owns a guitar.

I slide down in the chair so only my hat is showing. Surely where there's a guitar, there's a singer or a songwriter. Lord, please, get me off the hook. Just this once. I promise to face my fear another day. Tomorrow. I promise.

"Here," a scruffy voice says beside me.

I peek out from under my cap to see who's talking. It's a wide-brim cowboy hat with a square chin.

"No, thanks. You go ahead," I manage to whisper, though my tongue is clinging to the roof of my mouth.

The voice under the black hat croaks, "Can't. Laryngitis."

Of all the rotten luck. I wonder if now would be a good time to exercise my faith for healing and pray for this guy.

"Come on, cuz." Skyler pulls me from my chair by the crook of my arm. "The lovers are waiting."

"Graham Young," the guitar player says, handing me a nice Yamaha. "It's tuned."

"Yippee." I take the guitar. Please, Lord, right quick send a tornado or a bolt of lightning.

"Strap it on. Let's go." Skyler shoves me to the center of the outdoor deck.

"You always were the bossy cousin," I mutter.

"And you were always the one with a guitar."

Every limb trembles. Fear whispers for me to run. The deck is filling up, closing in around me, as people move out from the inside.

"Ladies and gentlemen," Skyler steps into the center of the outside deck. Blaire whistles through her fingers. *Now* she comes alive. "I'm happy to present to you a wonderful new songwriter in town, Robin McAfee."

Small applause. More folks wander out. I'm sweating, profusely. And an anchor has fallen on my chest and collapsed both lungs. I'm drowning. Jesus, help. What am I doing here? I'm insane. Moving to Nashville on a whim with a gallon or two of fear, following the yellow brick road that's haunted by my very own lions, tigers, and bears. Oh, my.

Skyler drapes her arm over my shoulder and addresses the young couple. "What's your song?"

I pretend to do something akin to tuning, but my hands are shaking so bad I think I untuned it. Graham shoots me a scornful look.

Did I ask for this?

People are getting comfy for the show, leaning against the railing, packing every inch of free space. Terror prickles across my chest and down my arms. Another anchor drops, forcing out the last bit of my air.

"Honey," the groom-to-be says, bending to one knee, "we don't have a song."

"How about 'Love Me Tender'?" the bride-to-be suggests, gripping her hands with his.

Elvis? They want Elvis? I gaze around for the nearest escape route.

Skyler whispers, "You got any original love songs. Might as well launch your career tonight."

I shake my head. The word "no" is trapped somewhere in my nether regions.

"What? No love songs?" She pats me on the back. "We'll work on that."

Help me!

Someone shouts, "'Making Memories of Us.'"

Another: "How 'bout 'Breathe'?"

Elvis? Keith Urban? Faith Hill? They want a cover show. They're sadists. All of them. Cruel, cruel sadists. My hands are sweating, rusting the strings.

Skyler sticks me with her elbow. "Sing. Everyone's waiting."

Purple dots. I see purple dots. A third anchor slams down on me. Suddenly, there it is. A light. A thin line between a hippy and a blue-haired Goth girl. I thrust the guitar at Skyler.

And run.

Skyler barges into my apartment with sultry Blaire in tow. "What's the matter with you?" She points behind her at nothing.

Birdie pops her head in the door. "Robin, are you okay?"

"I'm fine," I fib with a dramatic flop down to the couch.

"You are *not* fine. What happened?" Skyler stares at me with her hands on her hips, tapping her toe. Birdie listens by the door, and Blaire picks at her manicured nails.

"I just didn't feel like singing, that's all."

Skyler drops her hands to her side. "What? Since when? Last time I was in Freedom, your Granddaddy Lukeman shut off the porch light and locked the door to get you to end the show. Only ones listening were the dogs."

I press my hand over my eyes. "It's not the same thing." I lift my head, peeking at Skyler through my fingers. From the corner of my eye, I see Birdie quietly slipping away.

"I'm terrified to sing in front of people."

Skyler screeches, "What? Kick-butt-and-take-names Robin McAfee? Does the family know this? How can a Lukeman be scared to sing in front of people?"

"Stage fright."

Skyler and I crane around at the sound of Blaire's voice. "Stage fright. Happens all the time. Barbara Streisand. Donny Osmond. Judy Garland."

"Yes, stage fright." I waggle my finger at Blaire. "She's right."

"I dealt with it when I started modeling."

"Please." I sit forward. "How'd you get over it?"

"Picture people in their underwear," Skyler offers.

"Good grief, no." Blaire rolls her eyes.

Skyler bites the tip of her thumbnail, thinking. "Picture them all facing the back of the room?"

Blaire responds, "What? No. Stop guessing."

I agree. "Right, no underwear. Blaire, what can I do?"

She sits in the club chair and crosses her long legs. "Get plenty of sleep before a performance, cut caffeine, listen to soothing music, meditate."

"Like transcendental meditation?" Skyler wrinkles her nose.

"Well, if you're into TM." Blaire picks a piece of lint from her slacks.

"I'm not. What else?" I ask.

"Therapy and medication for really severe stage fright." She studies me for a moment. "Seems you've got a severe case."

"Yes," Skyler answers for me.

Without a word, Blaire reaches down for her purse and dumps the contents. "I got herbs, vitamins, Lexapro, Zoloft . . ."

"You take all of these?" I ask, examining the pill bottles as she hands them to me. "This can't be good, Blaire."

Skyler takes one of the bottles. "Her last boyfriend said it'd be like raising the *Titanic* to find the real Blaire Kirby."

I laugh but I stop the moment my gaze meet Blaire's. "I'm sorry. Do you still have stage fright now that you don't model?"

She repacks her purse. "Now I just have fright in general."

"Oh." I want to tell her I'll pray for her, but the words seem inadequate. Not on Jesus' part, but mine.

More and more, I realize fear wins when folks run and hide—or cover it with excuses. I'll be the first to admit, it ain't easy to press though, but dern it, I'm shining the Light on this monster under my bed.

Besides, I can't go back on a Robin McAfee decision

Skyler faces Blaire with her hands on her hips. She's still wearing her fancy lawyer suit. "So, are you saying all Robin needs to do is meditate and drink decaf?"

Blaire smiles. Skyler is the bright balloon tied to the end of Blaire's lifeline. "You make it sound so simple. I'm saying she needs to find tools to help her overcome. Prayer, meditation, whatever." She looks at me with smoky gray eyes.

I slip the Auburn hat from my head. "But mostly, I just need to get out there and sing. Face my fears."

Skyler snatches up her purse. "Great idea. Let's go."

9

Skyler navigates the Music Row roundabout and swerves onto Demonbreun. She whips her Beemer into a parking slot and gets out. "Let's go."

"Where?" I lean over the seat.

"On the Rocks Bar & Grill." Skyler points toward the row of red-brick restaurants and cafés.

"Why?" I want to know. "Drinking won't solve anything."

Skyler opens my door. "Not drinking, goof. Karaoke."

"Oh no, nothing doing." Sitting back, I cross my arms.

Skyler reaches in to unbuckle me. "You just admitted you need to get out there and sing. So, let's go."

"I didn't mean karaoke." I shove her hand away from the seatbelt buckle.

Blaire crawls in beside me. Now she likes me; now she wants to be my friend. "This is a good way to go, Robin. A lot of singers wanting to be artists do a little karaoke. I think Mindy McCready got her start in karaoke."

"Nothing doing. I'm not going in there."

"Robin, how the heck do you expect to sing at The Bluebird, the Douglas Corner Café, or The French Quarter if you can't sing karaoke On the Rocks?"

I drop my forehead on Skyler's headrest. "Hadn't planned that far."

"Time to declare war on terror."

"But karaoke? It's so stupid."

"Yes, and stage fright is so smart and classy."

I stick my tongue out at her. Snooty lawyer. I slip out of the seat belt, square my shoulders, and puff out my chest. "Let's do it."

Skyler, Blaire, and I stride toward On the Rocks like Charlie's Angels, but just as we reach the door, I swoop around, head straight back to the car, and buckle myself in.

The remaining Angels scurry after me. "Robin, come on."

"I can't sing to a track. And look." I point to my hat head. "I don't have my hat. Don't have my guitar for security . . . I can't."

Skyler slams my door shut and gets behind the wheel. "Come on, Blaire."

"Where we going?" I slink down in the seat.

"Freedom."

I lurch forward. "Alabama?"

From Skyler's stereo, Martina sings to me that "this one's for the girls." "Yep. Might as well take you home since you can't do what you came to Nashville to do."

"You're kidnapping me?"

"If you can't run with the big dogs, Robin, stay on the porch. Make room for somebody else. You heard what Birdie said to her old tenant."

"Turn around, Skyler. Take me home."

"Freedom, here we come." She merges on to the highway.

"No, home to Ashwood Avenue. Birdie's."

Skyler looks at me in the rearview mirror. "Sing karaoke."

She ain't the boss of me. I reach up and grab her by the hair.

"Ack! Robin, what are you doing?" Her car swerves against the white center line.

"Take me home." I tug a little tighter while Blaire hovers against the passenger door, clutching her purse.

"No." Skyler grips the wheel with both hands, watching the road down the slope of her nose.

"Do it." I twist and yank again.

Skyler winces. "No."

Blaire's white as cotton. "Robin, she's going to wreck. Let her go."

"Tell her to take me home."

Speeding down I-65, we argue. Blaire digs in her purse. "I'll give up Zoloft if you sing at karaoke."

I let go of Skyler. "What? Are you serious?" Finally, something interesting on the bargaining table. "Can you do that?"

Skyler rubs the back of her neck. "You pulled out all my little hairs. You're so gonna pay for this."

Blaire hesitates to answer, then nods. Once. "Yes."

I'm bamboozled. "How?"

"A little at a time, yes. My doctor's been advising me to wean myself off—"

"And me," Skyler interjects.

"He wants me to take a milder med for awhile."

I slouch against the Beemer's leather seat. "I don't know . . ."

"Good grief, Robin, what's it gonna take? Do you realize what Blaire's put on the table?"

"All right." I sigh. "I'll do it."

Here's the inherent problems with singing karaoke, in my humble opinion. People. Smoke-filled room. People. No rehearsal. People.

Even for porch singing, sometimes Granddaddy would rehearse us a little before the evening started.

By the time we walk into On the Rocks, I'm scareder than

the devil at a revival meeting. My mind is frantic for an excuse
to run. Blaire and her high-price offer. Shoot fire.

Skyler drops her arm over my shoulder. "We're going to
walk through those doors to a new, braver you."

My brain tells my lips to grin, but they refuse. Isn't it
funny how God put people like Arizona and Skyler in my life
for the proverbial kick in the pants?

"You know what I used to do?" Blaire says softly. "I used
to pretend I was queen of the world and everyone in the room
was my loyal, doting subject."

"There you go," Skyler says. "Think beautiful Robin McAfee."

"Right," I snort and finger the tangled ends of my hair.

Blaire taps her watch. "We're wasting time. If we don't get
Robin signed up, she won't have time to sing. The regulars will
have all the spots."

"There are regulars?" I walk with Blaire to the door, Skyler's
hand gentle on my back.

"Oh, yeah."

On the Rocks is a wide-open place with a high, exposed
beam ceiling where track lighting shoots blue and greens hues
across the karaoke stage. The spacious ambiance gives me
room to breathe, and I relax a little.

Blaire flashes a smile over her shoulder. "You're going to
have fun, Robin. Really. And . . . sorry I was so cold before.
You know—at the Frothy Monkey."

I smile. "No problem."

"Really, there's no excuse."

I touch her arm. "We all have our moments. So, how do I
go about picking a song?"

Blaire flashes me her beautiful smile and shows me how to
pick a song, which I do, and jot it on a piece of paper. I hand
it to the DJ, Mandy.

She looks at my choice. "LeAnn Rimes?"

"'I Need You.'" I point to the paper.

"Ever sing karaoke before?"

"Nope," I choke.

She nods. "Okay, then. When you're up, I'll walk around, calling your name. Take the mike and sing. The lyrics display on the monitors." She waves the cordless microphone at a couple of dozen monitors around the room.

"All righty." I spin on my heel and go back to the table. "Water," I croak to Skyler.

She buys me a bottle and pats my shoulder as I gulp it down. "Are you going to be okay?"

I slam the water bottle on the tabletop. "Do I have a choice?"

"Not really. This is good for you. Another step toward your dream."

I turn to Blaire. "Do they boo if you're bad?"

She shakes her head. "I've never seen anyone booed."

"What if the person is good?"

"They bring down the house."

Skyler presses her fingers into my arm. "Bring the house down, Robin."

"Sky, I just want to make it to the stage and sing the entire song."

Blaire winces at me. "I don't mean to second-guess you, but is a LeAnn Rimes song going to work for you? She's all diva, big voice, you know."

I slide up onto my stool. "It works in my truck."

"There you go," Skyler says, fist to the table.

So we wait. I'm infused with confidence when a good singer takes the stage, struck with fear over the bad one. I try to concentrate on the table conversation. Blaire's telling a story about a photo shoot she had in the afternoon, but I keep getting lost in a jungle of anxiety.

"Think you can cowgirl up?" Skyler asks after awhile, nudging me with her shoulder.

I manage a smile and whip my hand in a circle like I'm roping a calf. "Yee-haw."

Blaire winces as the current singer falls flat on why Ruby took her love to town. "Can't say as I blame her for leaving," she says with a snicker.

I don't laugh. "The man is doing the best he can."

Blaire's smile fades. "Sure he is. Sorry."

"How do, ladies?" asks a voice under a Stetson hat.

Skyler gives him the once over before answering "Fine."

"Waiting to sing?" he asks.

Blaire points to me. "She is."

I give him a nod. He's about to introduce himself when DJ Mandy gears up with the mike, walking the room, stirring the crowd, calling, "Tom Jenkins, you're up next at On the Rocks karaoke."

The Stetson bows. "That'd be me." He swaggers to the stage like he's been on a long cattle drive.

"You think he'll be any good?" I ask the girls.

Skyler studies him for a second. "Maybe, but I bet he's a suit by day and a frustrated singer by night."

"Definitely," Blaire agrees.

Onstage, Tom stiffly moves the mike to his lips as the music starts. I wince and suck air through my teeth, hunching my shoulders and clasping my hands between my knees. "Keep the day job, Tom," I whisper.

The crowd indulges him as he butchers a George Straight tune. They applaud politely when he's done. Tom strides offstage grinning like a kid who's hit his first home run. Then it dawns on me: Tom conquered *his* fear.

"Next up, we have a new singer. Robin McAfee." I freeze as Mandy strolls my way, playing to the crowd.

Skyler gently shoves me off my stool. "Go get 'em."

"Don't rush me." Somehow I move forward without seeing, without thinking, without breathing. Mandy hands me the mike, and I face the crowd like a '60s robot. *I'm on Granddaddy's porch.* No problem.

My right leg quivers, and my stomach argues with the remains of my dinner. The music starts, but I don't.

Mandy stops the song. "Time to sing, darlin'." She gives me the eye like, "Wake up, girl, you're on." Her finger is poised over the start button. "Ready?"

I nod slightly, maybe wince, but whichever, she starts the music. Closing my eyes, I concentrate on the rhythm and melody. Please Lord . . .

As I start to sing, I open my eyes to catch the lyrics as they scroll up the monitor. "Stop." I glance at Mandy. "Please. I'm sorry." The mike trembles in my hand.

"What now?" She cocks her head to one side.

"The song's too low. Can you take it up one key, please?" I shoot the crowd an apologetic look, but I can't gaze at them too long.

"All righty." Mandy makes the adjustment and the music starts. I hum along with the intro to make sure I'm in the right key. When the lyrics roll again, I sing as if I'm strolling through a rose garden on a spring afternoon with the sun warming my shoulders. My voice has extra vibrato from my quivering leg. Not my favorite vocal accent, but it's working. I love the soul of this song, and let words speak from my heart.

Then, it's there. The sensation of God's pleasure. I smile, lift my free arm, and belt the chorus, letting love emote out of me instead of terror.

I need you like water, like breath, like rain.

The crowd stirs. I peek to see a few people rising to their feet, joining in as I sing the second verse. By the time I round back to the chorus, On The Rocks is rocking. Just like the night in the Hall.

When the song ends, the crowd's applause and whistles explode over me. I hand the mike back to Mandy and shove against the noise back to my table.

"Cousin, you rock." Skyler grabs me in a country-girl hug.

Blaire squeezes my arm. "How can such a little body have such a big voice?"

I wring my hands. "Did I really do all right? I missed a few words on the last chorus."

"Oh my gosh, you had them on their feet. How can you doubt?" Skyler grips my face with her hands.

Blaire holds up her pill bottle and twists off the lid. "Tonight, I'm throwing out a whole pill since you were such a gutsy smash."

"Blaire, you're the bravest person I know."

"I'm in good company," she says in a low, sincere tone.

Mandy is standing in front of me, her face pinched into a question mark. "What's with the scared-girl thing? You're a tough act to follow." She jerks her thumb toward the singer bumbling her way through "Breathe."

"I'm new in town, not really comfortable singing—"

She laughs low with an easy shake of her head. "There are folks who've been coming here for years trying to do what you just did."

"I like to sing that song." I don't know what else to say.

She turns to leave, but pauses. "Well, whatever you're doing, keep doing it. By the way, nice hair."

10

"Morning, Birdie," I say, standing in the doorway of her kitchen.
She's humming and buttering toast.

"Robin. Come in, come in. Sleep well?" She hands me the piece of toast.

"I did, thank you." I bite the corner. My first breakfast in my new place, in my new town, in my new life. Best piece of toasted bread I ever had.

"Sometimes it's hard to adjust in a new town, new place. When I first came to Nashville, I couldn't sleep for a month." Birdie drops two more pieces of bread into the toaster. "Hard to believe it's been thirty-five years. I came in nineteen seventy-one. Just turned twenty."

I perch on the kitchen stool. "Jeeter says you had a pretty good decade from the mid-seventies to the mid-eighties."

She keeps her eyes on the toaster. "I had a few moments in the spotlight."

I swallow my toast. Birdie's tone is not defensive, but I feel as if I touched a tender issue. "Sorry, Birdie. It's none of my business."

"It's not like the matter is private. Read any country music history book, and you'll find a line or two dedicated to my short career." Birdie taps the butter knife against the kitchen island. "You want some good advice?" The soft lines of her smooth cheeks deepen.

"Sure."

"Work hard, don't give up, keep your nose clean, and hold on to your self respect."

"You speaking from experience?"

She laughs. "I can't deny it. Nashville, for all its charm and beauty, is a hard town. Some call it a nine-year town. Takes about that long to break in. There'll be a lot of disappointments between now and then."

Her words suck all the spit out of my mouth. "Nine years?" I choke. "I'll be thirty-four." Toast crumbs stick to my lips.

"You all right?" Birdie asks as her toast pops up.

It takes all my effort to swallow. "Water? Please."

Birdie grabs a glass from the cupboard and offers me orange juice instead, to which I nod vigorously. Quick. Anything. Crumbs are collecting in my windpipe.

"The girl who lived in the apartment before you took a hard hit about three years ago. She had a song on hold with Clint Black—"

"Really?"

"But a hold doesn't guarantee anything. An artist may have a hundred songs on hold when they're getting ready to go in the studio. Anyway, one day she ran in here, squealing and carrying on. Clint had recorded her song. She'd made it."

Birdie pauses to read my face. I gaze back at her without so much as a blink. She's gonna drop a bomb here, I know it.

"A month later, she found out her song didn't even make the album."

"Why?" My heart starts pounding.

"Lots of reasons. It happens to songwriters every day. Clint and his producers probably found a song they liked better. Or, they may have recorded twenty or so songs, but only ten or twelve made it on the CD. Like I said, this business ain't for the weakhearted."

I gulp my juice. Nine years . . . weakhearted . . .

"And you need to build relationships, network, get to know folks. Don't sit around upstairs daydreaming and wishing. Get out there. You need to sing your first open-mike night by next week, no later."

With the crumbs washed away, I mutter, "Open-mike night."

She grins. "You're eyes are bugging out. Too much info?"

"No, no," I say, shaking my head.

Birdie pours another cup of coffee. "So, you got the fright?"

I brush crumbs from my lap. "Yeah."

"All the more reason you need to get out there and sing at open-mike nights."

"You're not going to kick me out, are you?"

Birdie's round brown eyes narrow with humor. "No, not yet, anyway." She chuckles. "Listen, some friends of mine are singing in the round at the Bluebird tonight. Be ready to go with me at eight-thirty."

"A-all right."

"Might as well start meeting people. My friend, Walt Henry, is singing. He just got a cut with Trisha Yearwood."

I stuff the last of my toast in my mouth and help myself to more OJ. "I love Trisha. Is his song making it to the album?"

Birdie chuckles. "You're getting it. Yes, his song made it. The CD will be in stores next month." She looks at the stove clock. "Mercy, I need to get going." She grabs her purse, pausing at the back door. "Are you a member of the songwriter's associations? NSAI or ASCAP."

I nod. "Yes to NSAI. No to ASCAP."

She points at me. "ASCAP has a great pro staff to help

with your songwriting. They're the big building at the end of Music Row West."

"Couldn't miss it when I drove in yesterday."

She smiles. "Guess not. See you later, shug."

I ring Marc Lewis and accept a job for which I do not interview.
I don't know if that's good for me and bad for him, or bad for me and good for him, but I'm gainfully employed. Hopefully, neither one of us is a creep.

"I'm hiring you on Birdie's recommendation," Marc says.

"I accept on Birdie's recommendation," I counter.

He chuckles. "Birdie said you were feisty. You'll start tomorrow at five in the morning. Eight bucks an hour. Twenty-five, thirty hours a week, depending.

Okay on the money and the hours, but five a.m.? So, I'm back in the land of the roosters. Marc rattles off directions to Lewis Cleaning Co. and asks me to meet him at his downtown office at four this afternoon.

Hanging up with him, I take stock of my bare fridge and call Skyler.

"Where can I buy groceries?"

"Harris Teeter."

I jot down her directions and hop in my truck, making a mental list of what I need (everything) and calculating how much money I'll have when I'm done (none). Granddaddy's hundred is as good as gone. And half my savings went to Birdie for rent.

Still calculating, I stride toward the entrance and run smack dab into . . . great guns, Billy Currington.

"Ssssorry." I freeze on the spot, mesmerized by his blue eyes.

"No problem." He pauses for a second. "Can I help you with something?"

I can't take my eyes off him. "N-no."

"You're sure?"

"N-no."

He steps away, flashing me an electrifying smile. "Well, have a nice day."

"N-no, um, yes. Thank you. Hey," I holler. "Must be doing something right."

He looks back at me, sort of frowning, then tips his chin. "Right. Thanks."

I conk my forehead against the glass door and fish my cell phone from my purse. "Arizona, Billy Currington. I just ran into Billy Currington. Literally."

"You did not."

"I quoted his own song to him. 'Must be doing something right.'"

Arizona's laugh is loud. "You did not."

I walk over to the buggies and yank one free. "I did."

"Oh my gosh." Dishes clink in the background. "You're going to have to work on your cool if you're going to live in Nashville."

I slam my purse into the buggy seat. "Thanks for pointing it out."

"Don't get defensive. You know what I mean. So, other than colliding with Billy Currington, how's Nashville?"

"I sang karaoke last night."

"Get out. How'd it go?"

"Good. I sang a LeeAnn Rimes tune."

"Behold, the butterfly . . ."

Over the phone, I hear a loud crash followed by robust, rapid swearing. "Arizona?"

"Holy cow, Harold, what were you doing? Robin, call you later."

The call goes dead, so I flip the phone closed, but it rings again before I wheel down the first aisle.

"Robin, it's Momma. Why didn't you call back last night?"

"Hi, Momma. I went out with Skyler."

"I couldn't sleep a wink. I just knew something awful happened."

"Great day in the morning, Momma. I'm just up the road in Nashville, not Siberia." No wonder I got the fright. "Why didn't you call me if you were so worried?"

"You didn't answer."

"Ah."

"Well, how is it?"

"Fine." I stop at a Pop-Tarts display and toss a box of cherry Pop-Tarts into the cart. And, oooh, chocolate-covered mini donuts.

"And how's your new place?"

"Fine." I need bread, jelly, peanut butter, milk. And a twelve-pack of Pepsi.

"Fine? You're a songwriter and all you can say is *fine*?"

I maneuver down the first aisle. "No, but I need a guarantee you're not going to criticize me."

"Fine."

And she wonders where I get it. While I shop, I tell Momma about my third-floor apartment using descriptive words like "eggshell-blue" and "spacious."

"No lice or fleas?"

"Nope, it's cleaner than spring hay."

"Just be careful, Robin Rae. Smiling people carry knives."

"Terrific attitude, Momma. Thanks. But everyone I've met has been really nice." Salad dressing, cucumbers. Apples, oranges, tomatoes, bag-o-lettuce.

"I didn't fall off the turnip truck yesterday, girl."

"So I've noticed."

"Don't be smart."

I sigh. "So how are things there?"

She launches into an update on life in Freedom and her best friends, Henna Bliss and Sissy Workman, though not much has changed in the day and a half I've been gone. She ends with, "I'll have your Daddy call you when he gets home."

"Thanks, Momma." Hamburger, chicken . . . oh, I should get some spices. "I sang in front of people last night."

Big pause. "You did? Where?"

"On the Rocks Bar & Grill. They have Monday night karaoke."

"Land's sakes, girl. That's not singing-*singing*."

"Land sakes, Momma, it is singing. Trust me."

"Well, how'd you do?"

"I brought the house down, if you must know."

"I'm not surprised."

"Listen, I'm at the checkout counter. Better go." I start unloading my cart.

"Robin. I-I love you," Momma says tenderly.

I set the ice cream down on the conveyor belt. Her confession smoothes the sting of her criticism and creates a warm spot smack-dab in the middle of my heart.

"I love you too."

Before I meet with Marc Lewis, I swing by the Nashville Songwriters Association office on the corner of 18th Avenue South and Roy Acuff Place. A tingle of excitement runs through me as I take the steps of the Old Mill Music building.

"Can I help you?" The curly haired NSAI receptionist smiles at me.

"I just moved to town."

"Welcome to Nashville."

"Can I schedule a critique with a pro or the membership manager?"

"You sure can. I'm Ella, by the way. I assume you're a NSAI member?"

"I am, proud to—"

"Well, if it isn't the runaway singer." A raspy voice breaks between Ella and me.

"Hey, Graham." Ella flutters.

It's big-cowboy-hat-and-square-chin guy from the Frothy Monkey.

"Ella." He smiles at her with a nod, then props his elbow on the desk and turns his back to her so he can stare at me. "Why'd you run?"

"Nervous habit."

"Better break it. Is this a new problem, a life-long problem, the result of watching *The Wizard Of Oz* when you were a kid?" He talks like he has permission to dig into my soul. "By the way, nice escape between the hippy and the Goth girl."

"Did you get your guitar?" I ask to avoid his probing.

"Your friend gave it to me." He shoves aside his long black duster and sets his hand on his belt.

"How's the laryngitis?" Something about him makes my stomach swirly. He's nice enough, though his cockiness is a little over the top for me.

Graham scratches his throat. "Better."

"So," Ella butts in, stepping around the reception desk, "you want a song critique?" Her gaze falls on Graham's face.

"If I could, that'd be great."

Graham tugs his hat lower on his forehead. "You actually wrote something?"

"I've written a lot of somethings."

"Great, let me hear one." He picks up his guitar and heads across the foyer. "Ella, I'll be her pro appointment. We'll be downstairs in one of the writing rooms." He looks at me. "What's your name?"

"Robin McAfee. I wasn't ready to meet with a pro right now, today." My voice cracks.

He smiles a white, even smile. "No time like the present, Robin McAfee. Get your guitar and sing me a song."

The white-walled Writing Room number one is small but cozy, with a love seat and chair, a Baldwin piano, and Graham.

"I have to leave in about an hour," I say, pulling my guitar from the case.

He laughs. "Well, I wasn't planning on being here all afternoon."

"This was your idea."

He pushes back his hat a little. "A sassy one, eh, short stuff?"

Short stuff? He acts like we're best buds. If he keeps this up, I might start to like him.

He props his guitar on his knee. "Do you have a work tape or lyric sheet?"

I shake my head.

"You're going to need those. A tape of your song, and the lyrics and chords."

I nod, feeling like a first-grader on the first day of school.

"Well, go ahead and play one of your great songs for me."

My fingers stumble through the first few chords of "Your Country Princess." I'm not so thrilled with his sarcasm. *Play one of your great songs.*

Graham listens, hiding his eyes underneath that ridiculous hat. Below it, his clean-shaven face is good looking, and smiling.

But in the middle of singing the second-round chorus, he stops me. "Is this your best song?"

"Huh?

"Is this your best song?"

"I'd like to think so."

"Really? Seems sorta sophomoric. Like a couple of teeny-bopper newlyweds."

The back of my neck burns. "Sophomoric? What's wrong with teen newlyweds. My brother, the *marine*, was a teen newlywed."

He taps my hand with his. "Don't get all mad. But, seriously, can you see Reba or Faith singing this song?"

"No, but maybe Carrie Underwood." I feel my face redden.

Graham laughs. "Okay, yeah, Carrie Underwood. Look, Robin." He peers into my eyes. "You're going to have to step it up if you want to make it in Nashville."

I rise to my feet. "I didn't ask for your critique."

"You ask for a NSAI pro, and I'm a NSAI pro. Sit down. I'm trying to help you. I know what I'm doing."

"Do you now? What have you done?"

"Had a cut a few years ago with Bryan White."

"Oh." I sit down, settling my guitar on my knee. This is the hard part of Nashville Birdie talked about. I didn't expect to run into it so soon.

"Brighten up, green eyes. Your song has potential." His gray eyes linger on me too long. I squirm. He clears his throat. "L-let's work on it."

"I need to go." I reach for my guitar case.

"So, Your Country Princess. It's not autobiographical, is it?"

"Nope."

"Boyfriend back home?"

"None of your business."

Under his black hat, I see Graham smile. "Fine, but you don't need to go yet, do you? Sit down, let's beef this baby up."

With a quick glance at my watch, I cave and sit. "All right, let's hear what you got. How can we beef this *baby* up?"

"The chorus needs more energy. How's the song go?"

For forty-five minutes, we play through "Your Country Princess," examining chord and lyric. We argue. We play through the song and argue some more. Graham is one arrogant dude, but I'm already starting to like him.

In the end, we change a line of the first verse, rewrite the second, add a few stops in the chorus to jazz up the melody, and Graham comes up with one rocking guitar lick between the second verse and the chorus.

I have to admit, his touch elevated the song to a new level. "Now *that* I can hear Reba or Faith singing," he says.

"Thanks for your help. I learned a lot today."

"Let's record a work tape." Graham walks over to the cassette dubbing deck. "It's good to have tapes of your songs. Never know who you're going to meet."

"Maybe another time," I say. Since I'm not sure where Marc's office is located, I need time to get lost. Besides, I planned a stop-off before meeting up with my new boss.

Graham looks up from the dubbing deck. "We can make an appointment to get together. Do some cowriting."

I nod while settling my guitar in its case. "I'd like that."

He walks me to the stairs. "See you Monday night?"

"Monday night?"

"Open-mike night at the Bluebird Café. You need to get over your fear."

"So I've heard." I start up the stairs.

"Get there early, short stuff. Five o'clock."

"Right, early."

11

Maneuvering down Broadway in midday traffic, the Nashville skyline looms around me. Stopped at the 7th Avenue light, I angle around my steering wheel for a better look at the BellSouth building. Twin towers jut skyward from the roof line, reminding me of the Batman logo.

I love this city.

The light changes, and I head for 4th Avenue and the Ryman Auditorium, the mother church of country music. When I was a kid, Granddaddy talked a lot about the grand old landmark, and I've always wanted to see inside.

At the ticket window, I purchase a single, private-tour entrance, preferring to take my time and wander the hundred-and-fourteen-year-old sanctuary alone and imagine history.

In the concession area, the buttery smell of popcorn makes my stomach rumble. After all my grocery shopping, I forgot to fix lunch. I ask the girls behind the counter, "Can I buy a bag?"

The girl to my right shakes her head. "No, sorry. It's for tonight's show."

"Oh, okay." The gift shop is across the way, so I peek inside to see if they have candy bars, but what's the use? My nose riled up my taste buds for hot, buttery popcorn.

Popcornless, I step inside the Ryman sanctuary, listening for sounds from the past—old Sam Jones preaching the gospel, the laughter and music of the Grand Ole Opry, or Minnie Pearl's "How-dee!" The scarred, ancient wood floor creaks under my feet as I make my way down the center aisle toward the stage.

A woman dressed in a uniform motions to me. "Stand up there and I'll take your picture."

I step over to her. "How much?"

"Five dollars."

I pull a few bills from my pocket. Five dollars is a small price to pay for a "before" picture. The round steps wobble as I make my way to the top.

"You can hold one of the guitars if you want," the photographer tells me.

Perfect. I pick one of the two display guitars and slip the strap over my head. This feels amazing. I start to play.

"You're pretty good with that thing. Smile, now."

One bright flash and I'm captured in history with an instant camera. Robin McAfee on the Ryman stage—almost.

The sanctity of the moment is lost when a touring couple passes through, and the photographer offers, "Do you want your picture? Stand up on the steps and hold one of the guitars."

The couple stands on the steps, and the camera flashes. They chat with their Ryman tour guide while I secretly wish they'd leave. I want to do something, and I don't have all day. A glance at my watch tells me it's three-thirty already.

Oh, forget the people, Robin. Go for it. "Y'all mind if I sing a song?"

"Oh, no, go ahead. Go ahead."

Quivering, I stand in the center of the top step, close my eyes, and sing my all-time favorite song. Simple. Sweet. And true.

Jesus loves me this I know.

The tour guide interrupts. "I know that song. I'll join you." He steps up next to me and clears his throat.

Grinning, I start the song over. "Jesus loves me this I know . . ." The guide sings the low harmony.

The touring couple applauds when we're done. My hands tremble as I set the guitar back on the stand. But I did it—sang at the Ryman Auditorium. Noted or not, I just joined history.

Waiting for me in the front hall, Birdie is decked out in suede fringe and leather.

"If you're Tonto, am I Kemo Sabe?" I ask, jogging down the steps.

Her lips curl into a slow grin. "Are you always this sassy?"

"Mostly."

We walk out the door toward her Explorer. "When's your hair appointment?"

"Tomorrow. Why?" I touch the ends of my hair. I did the best I could without resorting to a ponytail.

"Can't come soon enough."

And I'm sassy?

The Bluebird is a small, cozy place nestled between a dry cleaning business and Helen's Children's Shop on Hillsboro Road. I love the family atmosphere immediately. It seems fitting that such a humble place launches such great careers. Folks like Garth Brooks. How can I not love a place that embraces people like me?

Birdie weaves through the thick crowd, saying hello and kissing cheeks like it's old home week. She introduces me as Robin McAfee, a friend of ole Jeeter Perkins.

While she pauses to catch up with someone—"We have to write together," I hear Birdie say. "Let's get something on the books."—my gaze wanders the room. The clean but close-walled café is so opposite from last night's venture into On the Rocks. Blowups of country legends like Dolly, Willy, and Don Schlitz line the wall, and opposite the bar, above the pew seats, are dozens of photos of Nashville songwriting greats like Victoria Shaw, Suzy Bogguss, and Richard Leigh.

Is there room on the wall for me? Shoot, first I've got to make it to the Bluebird stage. I glance at the door as more folks flood inside and stand along the walls. A knife of anxiety cuts my breath.

"Come on, shug, let's get to our table." Birdie presses her hand against my shoulder. Her buoyant voice shines light on my dark moment. As I turn to follow, my eye catches a vacant little corner on the bottom of the songwriter's wall. There's room.

Squeezing between the tables, Birdie leads me to the center of the room where bright lights shine down on three circled chairs. "This is called singing in the round."

I grin. "Got that much down, Birdie."

"Well, then, you're all set. What'd you need me for?" She takes the table behind one of the songwriters' chairs.

"Are you always this sassy?" I ask, laughing to create my own antianxiety medicine. The small room is closing in on me. I can't sing in here. There's no air.

"Mostly." Birdie laughs with a wink.

As we sit, a giant of a man with dark squinty eyes and a skunk-striped pompadour bends to hug Birdie. "How's my favorite songwriter?" He's wearing a fringed jacket, like Birdie, and holey jeans.

Birdie chortles like a flitting bird. "She's fine, Walt."

"Good, good." He slips through his guitar strap. The guitar's tan wood body is scarred from years of hard strumming. "Who's this little lady?"

"Robin McAfee. My new tenant."

Walt shakes my hand. "A songwriter, I take it?"

"Trying to be," I say, smiling, realizing for the first time Walt Henry is *the* Walt Henry I listened to growing up. Granddaddy always noted the songwriter of our favorite tunes: "The writer's as important as the singer."

Walt takes his seat. "You'll learn a lot from Birdie. Listen to her. Are you planning to sing the 'Bird, Robin?" He leans over his guitar to tune.

"Y-yes, sir."

Birdie pats the back of my hand. "Remember Jeeter Perkins, Walt?"

"Why sure. Best steel guitar player I've ever heard."

"He's a friend of Robin's. Says she can really belt out a tune. And write too."

I flush under her praise. "Jeeter's partial." How do I know? The impartial Graham Young didn't think my song had all that much going on.

Walt shakes his head. "Jeeter knows his stuff. I'd like to hear you sometime."

"Any time," my mouth says without my brain's permission.

The other songwriters arrive. Eric Exley and James Dean Hicks.

I lean over to Birdie. "James Dean Hicks? I *looove* his music. He's one of my, you know, heroes."

"James Dean!" Birdie pops out of her chair and waves the handsome man over. "Come meet Robin."

"Birdie—" I growl.

James Dean smiles and takes my hand. "Good to meet you."

"Good to meet you," I echo.

"She's the next hit songwriter, James, so you better stay sharp," Birdie teases.

I gawk at her. What's she thinking? Stay sharp? Holy cow. James Dean is so far out of my league that I can't even see the ballpark. But, I want to be him when I grow up. Write the songs of my soul and turn them into hits.

"I look forward to hearing your songs," James says.

"Hopefully before the Second Coming." I will my eyes to smile like James Dean's.

"Are we ready to get started?" Walt steps up and slaps James Dean on the shoulder.

"Let's do it."

By now, the Bluebird is standing-room only. *In the round* is literally surrounded. *I. Can't. Breathe.* The door is obscured. I'm pinned in by people, tables, and chairs. There's no escape without a scene. *Breathe deep. Listen to the music* I tell myself.

"Take it away, Walt," James says. "We'll be here all night singing your hits."

The room laughs, but once the music starts, there's no sound but the writers' clear, rich voices and astounding guitar playing. Their lyrics and melodies are clever and heartwarming, funny and witty. I'm amazed, discouraged, and challenged all at once.

While Birdie orders a brie and bread dip plate, I slurp down Cokes, calculating my future in Nashville. Hell might freeze over before I gather the courage to sing in this place, much less write like these guys and have my photo stapled to the wall. Wonder if Chancy will let me go back to tossing up stock at Willaby's.

But I made a Robin McAfee decision. It can't be revoked. Besides, if I chicken out, Ricky will never let me live it down.

And Momma. Forget it.

When it's Walt's turn to sing again, he looks over his shoulder at our table. "I'm gonna pull a surprise."

Birdie smiles and leans forward, touching my arm. My head snaps around. Surprise? What surprise?

"We got a gal in here tonight and—"

Is Walt going to call me out? He can't. My heart stops beating. Literally. *Nooooo.*

Walt unhooks his guitar strap. "I'd love for her to come sit and sing a song or two in my place. Y'all mind?"

The Bluebird applauds.

But I'm not prepared. I've never even sung at the Bluebird. Is this legal? Don't I have to try out first? My nerves launch fiery missiles and fry half my brain cells. I get up, shaking my head.

"Birdie Griffin, what'd you say?" Walt offers his hand to my tablemate, and the crowd applauds again. "Y'all remember 'Take Me Home' and 'Once More for Love'?"

More applause.

Birdie. Of course, he meant Birdie. Embarrassment burns across my nose and down my neck to the tips of my fingers. I sit slowly, ducking my head. What a doofus.

Birdie straightens her fringed leather skirt. "Guess I could do a song or two."

Eric and James banter with Walt, entertaining the crowd while gracious Birdie takes a chair. "Ain't she something?" Walt says when he joins me at our table. His eyes are plastered on her face.

I'll be. Walt Henry's got a crush. "She sure is."

"What key, Birdie? We'll play with you," James says, nodding at the former icon.

"Let's try one in G, James. Eric, man, you're a looker. You still married?" Birdie starts strumming.

"My wife says I am."

Laughter ping-pongs around the room. So, this is how it's done. My hands stop trembling, and I study Birdie's polished, easygoing performance. She wins every heart in the room with her clear voice and gutsy lyrics. Including mine.

12

"Ready for a treat?" Skyler asks, climbing into my truck when I pick her up Wednesday for my hair appointment.

"Treat? It's a haircut." I tug on the bill of my cap. I'm sorta getting attached to it.

"Time for a new you."

I bristle. "What's wrong with the old me?"

"Frizzy hair."

I smack her arm. She's right, but I can't let her get too cocky. At the light on 17th Avenue South, I ask, "Which way? Keep in mind I need to stop at Wal-Mart for a laundry basket."

"Wal-Mart?" Skyler says, pointing to the left turn lane while also changing the station on my radio. "Let me introduce you to Bed, Bath, & Beyond."

I curl my lip. "Hello, I'm cousin Robin McAfee, Freedom, Alabama. Wal-Mart queen, K-Mart princess, avoider of stores with silly alliterations like Bed, Bath, and Beyond."

"Fine, spoilsport." She huffs and turns up the volume of Big 98. "Head down Broadway to I-40.

"Where are we going?" I picture Supercuts or Fantastic Sams.

"You'll see."

Skyler hauls me way south of town, by way of Starbucks for a grande caffé mocha, to a swank place called Bishop's Salon & Day Spa. When we walk in, Blaire is waiting for us, reading the newspaper. "I was starting to think I had the wrong day."

"Traffic," Skyler says in her lawyer voice as she approaches the reception desk. "Hi, Deanna, how are you?"

"Skyler, great to see you. Did you bring us another one of your clients?" Deanna smiles at me.

"No, this is my cousin, Robin McAfee. We have an ap*point*ment."

I do *not* like the way she says "appointment"—like it involves bodily harm.

Deanna's smile is downright evil. "Yes, right. The Rejuvenation package." Her pointy red fingernail taps the appointment book.

"Why do I feel like I'm going to hate this?" I whisper to Skyler.

She bumps me. "You won't."

Deanna tells us to take a seat, *they'll* be right with us.

I plop down in one of the chairs. Bishop's is far and above any hair cuttery place I've been to before. It's a beautiful, big room with mood lighting, a shiny wood floor, and rows of products, with styling stations to one side and a spa center to the other.

When my eye catches the massage sign, a cold, nervous shiver makes me sweat. "Skyler, what's a Rejuvenation package, and why am I getting one?"

"You'll love it. Promise."

"I'm not taking my clothes off."

She stares at her magazine. "We'll see."

Next to me, Blaire sighs and swings her dangling, crossed leg. "I am so looking forward to a massage and manicure."

I hop to my feet. "I'm here for a haircut." I point to the hat covering my frayed locks. "Haircut. Nothing else."

Blaire chuckles and leans over to Skyler, the newspaper crinkling in her hands. "I thought she was going to say, 'I'm here for the party.' I've been singing that song all day."

Skyler tugs on my arm. "Sit down and relax, will you?"

I sit on the edge of the seat with my back straight.

Blaire's newspaper crackles in my ear as she flips the pages. "Ah, good, the latest 'Brad About You' column."

"Ooo, read aloud," Skyler says. "Any scoops?"

"Keith Urban was spotted at Bread & Co. last week."

"We're so going there."

"Keith Urban?" I whistle low. "Dang. Where is this Keith Urban Bread & Co?"

Skyler grins. "Green Hills. Across from the Bluebird."

"Robin?" Deanna interrupts. "Are you ready?"

With a sideways glance at Skyler, I mutter, "Sure." I stand and lean over, whispering into my dear, darling, blonde cousin's ear, "Be afraid. Be very afraid."

She laughs, but I see a flicker of concern. As there should be. The summer we were twelve, she visited Freedom for a month. Spent the whole time telling me Bobby Jacoby wanted to be my boyfriend. I never believed her, but I caved one July day when I saw him at the pool. "I'd like to be your girlfriend, if you still want."

He guffawed in my face.

Yeah, Skyler knows what it means to be afraid, very afraid.

Deanna introduces me to Natalie, a pretty brunette with saucerlike brown eyes. "The first part of your Rejuvenation package begins with a pedicure and manicure."

"Thank you." I smile because there's no use grousing. I'm here. This is Nashville. Might as well try it. I suppose I could use a little rejuvenation. Wouldn't it be nice to have pretty, trimmed nails for playing my guitar around town? A new hairdo, shiny nails . . . That's all the courage I need.

I recline in a comfy leather chair while Natalie asks, "How are you this afternoon? Aren't the spring days in Nashville gorgeous?" She starts rolling up my pant legs.

I haven't shaved in a week. "I'm fine, thanks."

"Is this your first time at Bishop's?" Her voice is high and lively as if she actually enjoys rubbing soap between other folks' toes for a living.

"Yes."

"Oh, you're going to love it."

"So I hear . . ." Suddenly my feet are dunked into bubbling, warm, silky water. Oh, my.

"We'll let your little piggies soak for a few minutes." She wrinkles her nose at me.

This is sort of nice. I close my eyes and rest my head against the back of the seat. Then, without warning, Natalie dunks my right hand in another bucket of warm, soapy water.

My eyes fly open.

"I see you have a hair styling appointment with Zack. He's really fabulous." She dunks my other hand in warm, wonderful water.

I bolt upright. Tell me it isn't so. Oh, brother. I can't believe this. But after five cups of coffee this morning and the café mocha Skyler insisted on buying, I gotta *go*. Now.

"Are you okay?" Natalie gently tries to push me down.

"I need to go." My gaze darts around for the ladies' room.

She tips her pretty little head. "What do you need? Let me get it for you."

"Don't think you can help with this, Natalie." I lift my feet out of the water and shove off the chair. The floor is cold and slippery.

"Where are you going?"

"Which way to the ladies'?" I slip and slide, turning and looking.

"Over here." Natalie leads the way. "They're unisex so just take the first available."

She gets my sudden plight. I fall once. Man, wood flooring can be hard on the derriere. "Skyler and her rejuvenation ideas," I mutter. "Who puts a woman's hands in warm water without warning?"

My wet hands slip as I try the bathroom door. I reach for a second try and the door swings open.

As I live and breathe. Lee Rivers.

"Well, hello." He looks down at me, a slow smile on his lips.

My legs quiver. "Hello to you too." I breathe, then laugh low. "You're like a genie in a bottle. Popping in and out of bathrooms."

He props his hands on his hips. "Only when you're around."

"What are you doing here?"

"Remodeling specs for the owner, Misty. I came to look around, write up some estimates."

He reaches for a towel from the pile by the door. "Here. Dry your hands."

"Thank you." Our fingers touch, and an army of goose bumps marches over my scalp and down to my toes.

"So, what's your big hurry?" He wads the towel in his big hands when I'm done.

"Just heading for the latrine, as my marine brother would say." I cannot imagine how I look. My hair in the same hat as two days ago, pant legs rolled up.

He stares at me with his deep-set, corn-silk blue eyes. "It's good to see you again."

His loping grin makes my insides puddle. "You too."

We stand there assessing each other for a thick moment. Then he steps aside, tipping his head toward the bathroom door. "Guess I'll let you go."

This is nice, isn't it? Chiseled-faced Lee clearing the way for my bodily functions. I'm so going to kill Skyler.

"See you around." I back toward the door.

"I hope so."

He winks.

I blush.

At least I didn't have a grease stain running across my chest this time. Do I? I glance down. No, no stain.

Natalie is right. Zach, the hair stylist is the best. In all things pertaining to himself.

He jerks my hat off and tosses it aside while rattling on and on about styling Miranda Lambert's hair for some photo shoot and how he chatted with Faith Hill and Tim McGraw at Barnes & Noble last weekend.

How lucky am I to be in his chair?

He shampoos my hair, then whirls me around to face the mirror. "You should go *short*. What do you think?" He gathers my wet hair on top of my head.

"I'm already short."

He shoves my shoulder with a snort. "I mean short hair. You have such the face for it. Look at those cheeks."

Yeah, look, at those freckled cheeks.

"Let's do it." He whips out his shears and waves them over my head.

"Well, I am in a state of trying new things . . ."

He whirls me around again so my back is to the mirror.

Snip. Snip.

"But, Zach, not too short."

Snip. Snip.

"Did you hear me?"

Snip. Snip.

I can't bring myself to look down at the floor. I'm sure it's covered with my autumn-colored hair.

Then, oh, hallelujah, my phone rings, and Zach steps back from his frenzy.

"Excuse me, Zach."

"No problem," he says, sizing up my hair for a second round of snipping. "Coffee?"

"Noooo. Thanks." I flip open the phone.

"Hey," says a smooth, familiar voice.

I grin and fiddle with the edge of the neck drape. "Ricky, hey. What're you doing?"

"Missing you like crazy."

I glance down. The floor is covered with my red hair. "Holy cow. I'm practically sheared."

"Sheared? Robin, what's going on?"

"Skyler hijacked my hair appointment for a fancy, shmancy spa day, and some stylist has just cut off all my hair."

"What? How'd you let them cut your hair?" His tone is intense, as if my shearing is a personal affront.

"I don't know. He was yakking about all his famous friends, and next thing I know . . ." I start to laugh.

"What?" Ricky demands.

"I like it." I run my fingers through the short, wet ends.

"So, come home. Let me inspect this new hair of yours."

I sigh. "Maybe for the Fourth."

"Can I come up there?"

Hesitating, I see his face in my mind's eye. It would be nice to see him, I reckon. But I catch my new reflection in the mirror. In the background, Lee Rivers strolls across the salon. "Ricky, just wait, please. Give me a little space."

"How much space?"

"I don't know. Space. Call you later?" I wish I could be more definite, but the words won't come.

"Robin, I won't be patient long."

"I'm not asking for you to be patient." Zach is coming my way.

"What are you asking?"

"Ricky, can we have this conversation later?"

"You know the number."

My phone goes silent.

Letting your cousin sign you up for a spa day?

$180.

"Do I look like I have lawyer money?"

"Shush, keep your voice down. You're not in a barn." Sklyer pats the air with her hands, smiling over her shoulder at Deanna. "Be right there."

"Okay, fine," I whisper. "Is this better? And I still don't have $180 for a spa treatment."

In the middle of this, Blaire snickers. "This is Skyler's payback for pulling out her hair." Blair adds a little triumphant "Ha!"

"What?" I glare at Skyler. "But you'd made the appointment before karaoke."

She screws up her face. "We planned it while you were signing up. Then I called them back."

"You did not." I ruffle up some good old-fashioned ire. "You forced me to sing karaoke, and while I'm busting my fear, you and this Zeta-Jones look-alike planned to punk me?"

"Hey," belts Blaire.

"Well, when you put it like that, of course it sounds hideous," Skyler says, twisting her lips.

"I'm telling Aunt Louise on you," I fire off. Though I don't know why. She never had much sway over Skyler.

"Oh, please."

"She's right, Skyler."

I turn to Blaire. "I like you more every day."

Skyler huffs and glances from me to Blaire, back to me again. "Dang. Okay, Blaire, you pay $90 and I'll pay $90."

"Oh, now, wait a minute." I pull two tens from my front pocket. "I can toss in twenty bucks for my haircut."

Skyler snatches the bills, giving one to Blaire. "This'll buy dinner."

Blaire tucks the money in her purse. "Country cousin, one." She leans toward Skyler. "City cousin, zippo."

"Robin," *Lee calls, striding out of Bishop's across the parking* lot. "You forgot your hat." He jogs toward us, waving my precious Auburn cap in the honeyed light of the setting sun. His chest muscles roll under his T-shirt, and the breeze brushes his brown bangs across his forehead.

Skyler mutters, "Sakes alive. It's him."

"Wow," Blaire breathes.

He hands me my hat, and my eyes are fixed on him.

"I like your hair," he says.

I squirm under his intense blue gaze. "Thanks." I hold up the hat. "I'd be lost without it."

"You forgot this, too." Lee hands me a business card, then greets Skyler. "How are you?"

"Fine," she squeaks. Gone is her deep, commanding lawyer voice. "This is our friend, Blaire."

"Nice to meet you, Blaire." Lee shakes her hand.

"Pleasure's all mine." Blaire's voice is silky and low as she slips her manicured, slender hand into his.

I wince. Even with my cute, new 'do, I can't compete with Blaire in the beauty arena. She's going to have to tone it down a tad.

"See you ladies later." Lee pulls away from Blaire's handshake with a quick glance at me. "I hope."

All three of us watch him walk away. He knows it too. When his broad back and narrow hips disappear inside Bishop's, Skyler turns to me, her lips pressed into a thin line. "If you don't marry him, I will."

I shake my head and jerk open my truck door. "Marry him? I just met him. Besides, there's the small matter of what to do with Ricky Holden."

Skyler climbs in the passenger seat and slaps her door shut. "I'd have two words for him if I were you: bye-bye."

I hear Ricky's terse words. *You know the number.*

"Easier said than done, Sky." Slipping behind the wheel, I crank the engine.

Blaire leans in my window. "Don't drive off yet. What does Lee's card say?"

"I don't know." The card is still in my hand, gripping the wheel. The front is his business information, but on the back is a handwritten note. "Meet me at Faith Community Church, Hillsboro Drive, Sunday morning, 10:30, don't be late. Lee."

They had to hear us squealing down in Freedom, Alabama.

13

Thursday morning before the rooster crows, I drive down Demonbreun. Five a.m. is an insane hour to think of cleaning toilets and mopping floors.

Half asleep and new to downtown, I turn onto 4th Avenue North going the wrong way. So I cut down another street—Printer's Alley, I think—and end up going the wrong way on 3rd.

Headlights flash. A car horn blares. I swerve left and careen over the sidewalk. Holy smokes. Downtown Nashville is dangerous at five a.m.

I'm awake now. The car horn continues to blow as it passes. A little vehicular swearing. "Yeah, I hear you. I'm new in town. Cut me some slack."

Tossing up a few flare prayers, I manage to get on the right street in the right direction, and it's *only* five-fifteen when I arrive at First Bank, my first job for Lewis Cleaning Co.

My trainer waits for me outside The Plaza office complex. "Glad you could make it," she says, sizing me up.

"Got lost." It's too early to say more, and I'm still a little shaken from being cussed out by a driver.

She grins. "Guess downtown is kind of confusing. Marty Schultz."

"Robin McAfee."

Marty unlocks the front door and punches in the security code. "Marc says you're a songwriter."

"Yep."

She motions to a cleaning cart and a portable vac pack. "Just what this town needs—another songwriter."

Just what I need—another skeptic.

She leads me toward the reception area, rattling off the rules of cleaning and how Marc likes things done. "He's a bit anal, so beware." Marty plops down on a crushed suede chair. "But before we get started—" she reaches down for a Starbucks bag "—coffee and a danish."

"Oh, bless you." I grip the tall cup with both hands.

"I figured you'd forget to eat breakfast on your first day."

She figured right. I wolf down my danish while Marty nibbles at hers.

"I was a songwriter," she says without looking at me. She picks icing bits from her danish with the well-worn tip of her thumbnail. "And the front woman for the little-known Delaney Brown Band."

The last bite of my danish is stuck on my teeth as I repeat, "Delaney Brown Band?"

"Yep, and today I sniff Clorox." Marty drops her barely eaten danish into the Starbucks bag. "I spent two years putting the band together, and we were this close to signing a deal . . ." She pinches her thumb and finger together. "But my dad died unexpectedly, and my mom fell apart. I went home to take care of her."

"I'm sorry." Her true confession is doing more to combat my sleepiness than the caffeine.

She shrugs as if it doesn't matter. "I spent a year in Arkansas taking care of Mom and all the loose ends that go with an old-fashioned couple where *he* took care of everything and *she* took care of him. Selling Dad's business took twice as long as I planned, so the band found a new label and a new lead singer. Marty Schultz became a, 'Huh? Who?'"

She peers right into my eyes as if willing me to share the load of her disappointment. "They recorded my songs, since they were technically—" she air quotes "technically"—"Delaney Brown songs. Last year they won a Grammy for best new country group and the CMA Horizon Award."

I modulate my tone so I sound like it's no big deal the band moved on without her. "Yeah, I read something about them winning a few awards."

"A few?" She swigs from her coffee cup. "Never mind. Let's get to work."

I fumble with my vac pack. "So you gave up?"

She stops at the first office. "Yep."

"Why? You must know people. Surely they know you wrote the lion's share of the band's hits."

She slaps her hand over her heart and tips back her head. "Ah, the innocence of a new hopeful."

"At least I'm determined and trying." I crash the vac pack against the door frame as we go in the first office.

Marty whirls around, her expression fierce. "I owned 'determined' for fifteen years. Don't—" She stops. "Here's the cleaning routine."

Sunday morning, I sit in the back of Faith Community Church, alone, jotting notes in my little black notebook.

Song about being new to a town. Lonely, homesick feelings. Missing my family and friends. Can't go home again. Made the break, can't undo my freedom.

"Hum. Maybe."

Song about crazy cousin.

Song about waiting. Will he come? Is he the one I'll love?
The one with eyes the color of shallow southern seas?

The worship leader is on stage with her guitar, and the folks milling around in the aisles slide into their seats. "Welcome," she says, beginning to play, "to the Faith Community. For those of you who don't know, I'm Rebekah Gunter."

With the rest of the congregation, I stand, craning over my shoulder for a shot of Lee. Still no sign. Where is he?

The opening song is about the beauty of God, so I close my eyes and enter into the truth of the lyrics, loosening my grip on my notebook.

"Sorry I'm late." Lee's baritone voice whispers in my ear. His woodsy cologne scents the air around me.

Without opening my eyes, I say, "You had me thinking I was stood up."

"Stood up? Who do you think I am?"

John Wayne.

As he brushes past me, his hand touches mine, and electric tingles shoot up my arm. My notebook slips from my fingers. As it tumbles forward, Lee snatches it in midair.

"I think this belongs to you."

Shawn Bolz, the pastor, preaches with passion about God's love, then calls us to stand for the closing prayer. Lee takes my hand as if he's done it a thousand times before, and I let him.

When Shawn says amen, Lee smiles down at me. "You thought I stood you up?"

"You were late." I relax my fingers so he can let go of my hand if he wants. He doesn't.

"My clock stopped in the middle of the night," Lee explains, waving to Shawn as we join the herd heading for the door.

"'My clocked stopped'? That's your best excuse?"

He squeezes my fingers. "It's the truth. Good morning, Mrs. Ferguson, this is Robin McAfee." Lee introduces me like it's a privilege.

"Lee, sugar, wait up." An older woman with flaming red hair and tight gray slacks shuffles our way.

"Oops, it's Miss Millie." Lee shoves me out the door. "Sorry, but I have to run. I'll call you tomorrow about the remodel."

He drags me down the front steps.

"Whoa, where's the fire?"

He holds onto my arm. "Miss Millie wants me to date her niece."

"I see." I laugh and hurry to keep up with his long, quick stride.

"Here we are." He stops by my truck. "*Freedom's Song.*" He smoothes his hand over Ricky's airbrushed inscription.

"Yep, here we are at *Freedom's Song.*" Is this it? Please don't say good-bye.

"Do you have lunch plans?" Lee crosses his arms and falls against the tailgate.

"What do you have in mind?" I grin up at him. Being in church makes me feel bold.

He steps around and opens my truck door. "You game?"

"For what?" I slip in behind the wheel.

"Follow me."

Lee takes me to Centennial Park.

"That's an exact replica of the Parthenon," he says, pointing to a large stone building looming on the green lawn.

"How amazing." A replica of ancient Greece right here in Nashville. I smooth my hand along the thick stone column and imagine Greek philosophers pacing the portico.

Lee grabs my hand. "Come on. This isn't why we came

here." He leads me down a grassy knoll and stops under the shade of a seasoned oak, where he pops a blanket open and spreads it over the grass. We sit. The spring air is sweet and weighted with shouting and laughter. Across the way, two guys and two girls with Greek letters on their T-shirts toss a Frisbee.

"What are we doing?" I don't really care. In the span of one church service, I've discovered the pleasure of Lee's company.

"A picnic."

Okay, Lord, let's talk. How much for the ruggedly handsome carpenter?

Lee claps his hands together. "Beef or chicken?"

"What?"

"Come on, I'm hungry. Beef or chicken?"

I smirk. "Beef."

"Large or small?"

"Large, naturally."

"Diet or regular?" he asks.

"Regular."

Lee dashes off, hops a low stone wall, crosses busy West End Avenue, and runs into Wendy's. I fall back on the blanket, laughing.

A few minutes later, he jogs back, his church tie askew and his white shirt collar open. He drops to his knees, huffing and puffing.

"You're a nut," I say.

He holds out a food bag. "Your feast."

As I reach for the bag, our hands touch, and I swear it's like a spark of electricity between us. Our eyes meet. Then, as if there's a blip in the time-space continuum, I feel as if Lee and I are the only two people on earth.

He leans. I pucker.

"One Wendy's hamburger, large fry, and a regular Coke." He rattles the bag under my nose. "Here, take it while it's hot."

I unpucker. "Thanks." The world comes back into focus as Lee digs in his bag for his sandwich and fries. I unwrap my burger, feeling like an idiot.

"So, what do you have? A sister? Brother? Couple of dogs?" Since my teeth are stuck in my burger, I nod. "Both," I say after chewing and swallowing. "And you?"

"Two brothers, no dogs." He also tells me he's thirty and a Yankee from New *Joisy*, which I'll overlook for now.

I'm mid chomp on a fry when Lee scoots close and points to my nose. "I like your freckles."

With a gulp, I swallow. "You can have them if you want."

"Great, and I'll keep them right where they are." He smiles with a wink. Every time he does that, my insides melt and run all over. And I have this bizarre urge to kiss him.

"Thanks for coming on my little picnic." He grabs the Wendy's wrappers and stuffs them into the bag, then flops back on the blanket, locking his hands behind his head. "Don't you love days like this?"

"Y-yes, it's a beautiful day." My eyes keep wandering to his lips. Are they as soft as they look? This is nuts. Lord, help. I feel suspended in midair without a net.

He rises up on his elbows. "I know a great place for ice cream. Want to try it out?" He hops up and walks over to the trash barrel with the wadded Wendy's bag.

"Ice cream sounds good." I fall back on the blanket, grasping for my bearings. Lee Rivers and his sultry magic.

"Let's go," he says, tugging on the edge of the blanket. "Ice cream is calling."

"Okay, okay." But before I can smooth my skirt and get up without flashing the Frisbee players, Lee jerks on the blanket's edge and shoots me down a sloping knoll like a human log, rolling over and over. Face down, face up, face down, face up.

I scream, "Leeeeeeeee!" while his laughter trails behind me.

At McDonald's, Lee hands me an ice cream cone without look-
ing me in the eye. "Here you go," he says with a dull snort.

I look at my shoes and force out a thank you.

"Let's go sit on my tailgate."

"Nice ice cream place, Lee," I say, motioning toward
McDonald's while the image of me rolling down the hill yell-
ing, "Leeeeee"—continues to burn in my brain. A snicker leaks
out.

"Thanks." He clears his throat and then adds in a low,
wispy voice, "Leeeeee!"

We fall against the tailgate, hooting, our ice cream melting
down the sides of our cones.

"Man, that was funny." I wipe my eyes.

"I never expected it." He looks down at me. "I like you."

My stomach cartwheels.

We finish our cones and wipe our hands on the Armor
All wipes Lee carries in his truck. "Can you believe it's four
o'clock?"

"Really?" I flip my wrist over to see my watch. Time flies.

"I didn't mean to hijack your day."

Hijack my day? "You made my first Sunday in Nashville
very special."

"I had a great time." He walks with me to my truck.

Every molecule in my body is still curious about the taste
of his kiss. Warm? Sloppy? Firm? Sweet? Or like Ricky, all
about himself?

"Here we are." He pulls me into his arms.

My brain sends a signal to my lips. Pucker up. This is
where my questions are answered. I lift my face. "Here we are."

He picks me up and whirls me around so that my feet fly
behind me like maypole ribbons. "I had a great time."

Oh, swirly whirly. "Me too." He takes my breath away.
"Thanks for inviting me."

He sets me down and backs away without so much as a peck on the cheek. "Thanks for joining me." I watch him head over and open his truck door, then turn.

"Oh, say, Robin," he calls.

"Yeah?" I step forward.

"Do you know how to get to Birdie's from here?"

My shoulders droop. "Over there." I point in the general direction of my new home.

He pats the bed of his truck and waves. "You got it. See you."

When I arrive home, the house is quiet. "Birdie?"

I jog up the stairs, unraveling my thoughts from the dash and smash of Lee Rivers. The afternoon had all the elements of a great love song. Spontaneity. Chemistry. Blue skies. The *almost* kiss.

I pause on the stairs and hunt through my purse for my notebook. *The almost kiss.* Great title. I fumble with a few phrases as I hit the second-floor landing, trying to imagine a story between two new lovers in the park.

Birdie's bedroom door flies open and she jerks me inside.

"Help. He's coming in an hour, and I have no idea what to wear." Her narrow frame is draped with a lacy robe, and her hair is wrapped in a towel.

"He who?" I drop my notebook and purse on her bed.

"Walt. I have a date with Walt."

Grinning, I sit on the edge of the window seat. "I thought he had a thing for you."

Standing at her closet door, Birdie whirls around with two dresses in her hand. "The black or the red?"

"Well, the—"

She claps the hangers together. "What am I thinking? Red is too, you know, take-me-now."

Laughing, I assure her I don't think red is too take-me-now. "Red is bold. Confident."

"Really?" She presses her hand on her forehead. "What am I thinking? I haven't been on a date in eons." She crashes down next to me.

"Relax, it's like riding a bike—you never forget."

Birdie holds out the dresses. "I never learned to ride a bike. It's haunted me ever since."

I make a face. "What kid doesn't—"

"I should wear black. Be conservative." Birdie examines the black dress.

"Birdie, you've known Walt for a long time, right? He's not going to be swayed by the color you wear."

"But we've never gone on a date. We've played gigs, taught songwriting seminars, but never a date." She stuffs the red dress back in the closet. "Oh, I forgot to tell you. Nashville Noise is coming out with the best of the '80s, and I have two songs on the compilation. Two!"

"Good for you."

Birdie hugs the dress to her chest and speaks to the ceiling. "My wallet thanks you, Jim Chastain."

"Say, Birdie. What happened with your Nashville Noise career?"

Birdie hangs her dress on the closet door and unwraps the towel from her head. "Long story." She disappears into the bathroom.

"Is there a condensed version somewhere?"

She pokes her head out. "Let's see. Well, I bet all my chips on a blind bluff and lost."

"What does that mean?"

"I thought you wanted the condensed version."

"That's too condensed."

"Some things happened . . . Jim and I found ourselves in

a long-standing feud. Nashville Noise and I parted ways. I signed with a new label, but they didn't get me or my music. My sales didn't meet expectation, and they dropped me."

"Dang, Birdie, I'm sorry."

She ducks back in the bathroom and fires up her hairdryer. "I'm not," she hollers out. "I stood up for what I thought was right, and I lost. At least I had the moral integrity to speak out."

"I didn't think it would be this complicated."

Birdie comes out with her hair wild and windblown, waving a fat, round brush. "Complicated is the nice word for the music business."

She disappears in the bathroom again. "Where have you been all afternoon? Your face is glowing. By the way, I like what you did with your hair. Tell your friend—"

"Cousin."

"Yeah, her. Good job."

I hop off the bed and lean against the bathroom door. Birdie is flopped over, about to fire up her hairdryer again. "I went on a picnic with Lee Rivers."

She peeks at me through a blonde veil. "Did you now? Interesting."

I bend over to see her face. "Why is it interesting?"

"Well, if I know Lee— Mercy, is that the time? Walt will be here any minute."

14

Daddy is on the phone talking about whittling a new bird-
house for Grandma McAfee as I stand on my deck watching
my own Birdie flutter off into the sunset with Walt.

She wore the red dress. Walt's bright expression said it all.
Propping my feet against the deck rail, I settle back with my
black notebook and pen.

". . . and your momma's garden is growing," Daddy says.
"She plans on winning blue ribbons for canned pickles *and*
tomatoes this year."

"I'm sure she will."

"I'm thinking of kicking licorice cold turkey."

"What? Please, Daddy, how will I recognize you when I
come home if you don't have a licorice whip dangling from
your lips?"

"Now, there's a thought. For your sake, I'll put off quitting."

"I appreciate it."

"Steve called from Iraq. He misses us."

I imagine my sandy-haired brother in combat fatigues
tucking a picture of his pregnant wife in a pocket close to his
heart. "It's hard for him to be so far away."

"I hear it in his voice, but he's proud of what he's doing.

Dawnie is safe with her family and us. And, oh, she invited your momma to go into the delivery room with her."

"Okay, Dawn is the bravest person I know."

"Robin Rae." Daddy snickers.

"Steve's got to hate this . . . missing the birth of his first-born."

"Sure he does, but freedom comes with a price."

"Jesus taught us that, didn't he?" I crack open the black notebook and start to write my thoughts, but tears cloud my eyes. "I miss everybody, Daddy."

"Sure you do. If you didn't, how would you know how much you love us. Give it time."

"I did the right thing, didn't I?" The afternoon with Lee seems far away. "Should I have married Ricky?"

"Did you want to marry Ricky?"

"I miss him, a little. But he doesn't seem very happy with me."

"Of course not. He didn't get what he wanted. But Robin, *did* you want to marry him?"

"Reckon not. I'm in Nashville, aren't I?"

"The Good Book tells us not to be double minded. Besides, you're half Lukeman and half McAfee. Heaven help Nashville. "

I grin and brush away tears. "Guess you're right."

He chuckles. "Of course. I'm your daddy. Now, here's Momma."

"How's the songwriting business?" she asks without a hello.

"I'm going to the Bluebird Café's open-mike tomorrow night."

"I see."

I can't read her tone. Upset? Nervous? Jealous? "I'll be fine, Momma." I say this for myself as much as for her.

"I reckon you will."

When we hang up, I walk inside for my guitar, pausing by the torn picture of Momma and her friends. "You are a mystery, Bit McAfee. And someday, I'm going to sit you down and find out why."

There's a line of songwriters outside the Bluebird Café, and I'm not disappointed. My guess is I'll never make it to the stage tonight.

I forgot all about Blaire's stage fright advice and drank a liter of Pepsi while cleaning the Bennie Dillon lobby and several of the private residence's lofts. Between my nerves and the caffeine, I've got tremors, a dry mouth, and a thin, weak voice. And I swear my left eye won't stop twitching.

"Where have you been?" Black-hat-and-black-duster Graham Young calls out from the front of the line. "I said get here early."

What is he doing here? I walk over with my excuse. "I got waylaid."

"Good thing I came early."

He swaps places with me. Now I'm in line where he once stood. There are only four people in front of me. Count 'em. Four. For a split second, I hate him. "You saved me a place?"

He smiles and chucks me under the chin. "Wanted to make sure you played."

Having a *fear* reputation is the worst.

From the parking lot, a fancy-dressed man calls, "Graham."

"Frank Gruey, as I live and breathe." My new friend wanders off to schmooze, his black duster flapping behind him like a Batman cape. *It's May, Graham. May.*

Midway down the line, a woman stares at me. I smile and make swapping motions with my hands. She snaps her head in the other direction. Hum, guess not. Maybe she's as scared as I am. Staring out at busy Hillsboro Road, I envision myself running away never to be heard from again. Fear is a strange enemy, isn't it? It chokes the life right out of folks.

I meander in the weeds of pretend too long. My foot jerks. My heart races. I wonder for a second if I might go crazy right in front of the Bluebird. I'm a hair's breadth away from running down the road, screaming like a banshee.

No. Steady, Robin. Steady. Calm down. You can do this. You made a Robin McAfee decision.

A drop of peace splashes on my soul, and my foot stops jerking. The panic passes. Drinking from my one ounce of confidence, I pull out my phone. Might as well call in the troops. "What are you doing tonight? Nothing? Good, come to the Bluebird."

"Why?" Skyler asks. "Are you going to sing?"

"I'm in line."

"I'll be right there. Don't leave."

I hang up and notice the late-afternoon sun casts shadows over all the cars and trucks in the parking lot except mine. One thin ray of sunlight shines over Ricky's handiwork like a heavenly spotlight: *Freedom's Song.*

I smile. Tonight, I hope to put a big dent in the old fear caboose. I turn to the guy in front of me and stick out my hand. "Hi, I'm Robin McAfee, and I'm scared."

He scoffs and shakes my hand. "Allen Davis, and I'm not."

Waiting in the crowded Bluebird with thirty other wannabe songwriters, Jeeter's advice skips across my mind: "Sometimes you got to face your fears."

Skyler, Blaire, and I have a table just left of the stage. The Bluebird is stuffed with guitar-hugging folks, waiting for their turn. And in the midst of them, Graham is off yakking with Frank, who, I discovered, is a publisher, song plugger, or producer. I can't remember, but it's something with a *P.*

And lucky me, I'm number five in tonight's lineup. Five. One, two, three, four . . . me.

Skyler taps my shoulder. "How many songs do you get to sing?"

"One." I point over my shoulder to the little sound booth in the back of the room. "The woman over there, Barbara Cloyd, is the open-mike host, and she said there are too many signed up to do more than one."

"Look at you, already a Bluebird expert. So, what song are you singing?"

Was it not a mere week ago that I ran from the Frothy Monkey, terrified? Then braved karaoke? It feels like a month of Sundays.

"Robin," Skyler snaps her fingers in my face. "Focus. What song?"

I bite my lower lip. "I don't know, I hadn't gotten that far."

She rolls her eyes. "You're a mess. Come on, what's your favorite song?"

"Well, I like 'Your Country Princess,' but Graham called it sophomoric."

"Forget him. Sing what feels right to you."

"Last night I wrote a song about Steve being overseas with the Marines while his wife is home, pregnant." I crinkle my brow, waiting for Skyler's approval.

"Sing the princess song. You've worked it longer. Don't sing something you haven't perfected. I hear it from my clients all the time."

"Hadn't thought of that." *What* am I doing in this town?

"Do you have a lyric sheet with you?"

"No." I tap my temple. "In here. Besides, I wasn't planning on being number five and actually having to sing."

"Well, you are." She reaches around for a napkin. "Write it down."

I shove her napkin aside. "I'll remember."

Blaire whispers over the tabletop, "You'll be all right, won't you?"

I whisper back, "Yes." I see in her eyes she's half for me and half against me. If I overcome, does she have to overcome?

Skyler drapes her arm around me. "I've updated my New Year's resolution: get Robin on stage."

"You can't make me your New Year's resolution," I protest, sloughing off her arm.

"Why not? None of mine are working."

"Because your resolutions are stupid, Skyler." Blaire counts off on her fingers. "Meet a man in February. First date in March. Engaged by late August. Married in December. You can't control any of them. Resolutions are about changing *you*."

Skyler twists her lips. "Excuse me, I didn't know there was a resolution law book."

I laugh. Their banter calms me a little and how they cut each other no slack. And if I can't have Arizona and Eliza around, these two are perfect substitutes.

When the fourth songwriter gets up, I smell the rubber burning on the road. This is it. I'm next.

A long-haired, faded blonde with big eyes and a small face sits on a stool before the mike. "I'm number four, Vickie Daniels." Without another word, she starts strumming and singing.

I wince. She's started the song way too fast and is trying to adjust the tempo as her clear, high voice pierces the room—off key.

My heart starts thumping, and I spring to my feet.

Skyler clasps my arm. "Where're you going?"

"Little girls' room." A minute ago I was freezing. Now, sweat trickles down my neck.

"I'm going with you." She stands.

I pull my arm free. "The bathroom is a one-seater." I know she thinks I'm going to bolt, and maybe I am, but for now, I'm going to the girls' room alone.

Unfortunately it's locked and occupied. Two high-pitched female voices giggle and yak behind the door. What is this? Saturday afternoon at the country club?

I knock loud. "Hello, waiting."

The giggles are louder. "Just a minute."

What are they *doing* in there? I bang again. "Got to go."

"All right. Hold your horses." More giggling and yakking.

How rude! I could be sick or dying. And they're laughing. I'm about to kick the door when Skyler bops around the corner. "You're up."

I hear Barbara call from the sound booth, "Number five."

I wring my hands. "I can't."

She grabs me by the elbow and declares, "Yes, you can," and shoves me toward the main room.

I jerk away from her and tug my top straight.

"She's coming," Skyler shouts to Barbara, pointing at me. The front door is obscured by the crowd. Can't run. As I squeeze pass the bar, I hear, "Knock 'em dead, Robin."

I gaze into Lee's strong face. "What are you doing here?"

"Number five." Barbara calls again.

He brushes my shoulder with the tips of his fingers. "I stopped by Birdie's. She told me you were here."

Remember the night at the Hall.

Remember singing karaoke.

Remember the Alamo.

So, I wasn't at the Alamo, but I need a third victory. Fellow Tennesseean Davy Crockett won't mind if I borrow from him.

My legs wobble as I step up to the stage, hugging my guitar like it's a life jacket. The room is a blur. I plug in my guitar with a resounding *thunk!* Moans and *ahhs* float around the room.

"Sorry." I clear my throat. "Hi, everyone." Be cool. Be cool. Look around. Gradually, blurry images come into focus. Skyler and Blaire are smiling, Graham still has his head bent toward Frank. Barbara Cloyd smiles at me with a nod. I like her. And Lee . . . where's Lee?

Just sing, Robin. Sing. I wipe my hands down the sides of my jeans and pull my favorite pick from my hip pocket. "I-I'm number five. Robin McAfee." I sound exactly like a hick from Alabama.

"Robin, move closer to the mike," Barbara calls through cupped hands.

I nod, stepping a little closer. When I do, my pick slips from my stiff fingers into the guitar's hole. *Crap.* I panic and flip my guitar over, crashing into the microphone. It careens off the stage and smacks down on the table right in front. The patrons stumble out of their chairs splashing beer and soda all over.

"I'm sorry, so sorry." *What* am I doing in this town? I'm insane.

The room is deathly silent except for the waitresses cleaning up my mess and the rattle of the pick inside my guitar. Barbara weaves her way through the crowd. "Hold on, folks." She's so calm, so forgiving. A saint. She sets the microphone right, looks me in the eye, and says, "You can do this."

Really? You think so? "Thanks." I think my eyelashes are sweating.

Paranoid I'm going to do a repeat with the mike, I stand a foot away. Skyler watches with her face and shoulders scrunched up. Next to her, Blaire stares at the ceiling, her lips moving silently.

Then I see him. Lee. Standing by the door. He nods his encouragement. Why is he at all of my most embarrassing moments? *Leeeeee!*

A snort escapes my nose. If I'd get over myself, I might just kick butt and take a few names.

I step up to the mike, *carefully.* "Is there a spare pick in the house?"

Laughter rumbles from the crowd, and half a dozen song-writers surge forward offering red, brown, white, gray, and blue picks.

I choose the light-gauge blue one from Vickie and start the opening chords of "Your Country Princess" before I change my mind and run. "In case y'all haven't noticed, I'm scared to death."

A few people applaud. Several shout, "Go for it."

"Go for it," I echo. "Good advice. When God gives you a burning passion that sticks to your soul like warm wax, you have to go for it, right?" I glance around. Blaire's aiming her camera at me.

I give a little intro. "I dedicate this song to my brother, a Marine serving overseas. God bless our troops."

My voice yodels and goes flat on the first line of the verse, but I catch my breath and straighten out. By the time I get to the chorus, I sense the crowd is with me.

Ooo, let me be your country princess . . .

15

My head is spinning. I've officially done the 'Bird. Skyler and Blaire congratulate me with high fives back at the table. I didn't bring the Bluebird crowd to their feet like I did at On the Rocks, but they applauded long and loud. Even heard a few whistles, though I suspect they came from Lee.

"Robin," Blaire holds up a tiny piece of a pill. "This is for you." She drops it on the floor and crushes it with her heel.

I slap her another high five, then catch her eye. "Just be careful, Blaire."

She nods. "I'm talking to my doc and my counselor. Have no fear."

She stops. Her brown eyes bug out. She snorts, then I choke, and all three of us laugh behind our hands, mindful we're in a listening room, not a comedy club.

"Talk about your Freudian slip," Skyler whispers.

We snicker and snort behind our hands again, and I turn my back on them. Otherwise, I'll bust a gut, and Ms. Cloyd will have to kick me out. Besides, songwriter number six is on the stage, belting out a sad, lonesome cowboy number, and I want to listen.

Skyler taps my shoulder and whispers, "We're going to go. I have to get up early."

I nod. "Thanks for being here."

Blaire stretches over for a light hug. "Until next time."

When they leave, Lee slips into Skyler's empty chair. "Hey," he says, his tone rekindling a little of yesterday's longing. My scalp tingles as he drapes his arm over the back of my chair. "You . . . You were great."

The songwriter ends and exits. I focus on applauding for him. "How did you like the mike-knocking-over trick? Smooth, wasn't it?"

He shakes his head. "It was funny and heartbreaking at the same time. But then you started singing and all we remember now is the country princess."

I thump my hand over my heart. "Are you trying to make me fall in love with you?"

His smile fades a little as he sits back in his seat. "Just don't doubt yourself, Robin."

"S-sure." I twist away from him. *Hello, lead balloon?*

Songwriter number seven is up now, wandering through a ballad, but all I can think is how I just crashed and burned with Lee . . . *Trying to make me fall in love with you.* I press my forehead into my hand. Didn't I flunk flirting?

"Robin?" I feel a light tap on my shoulder. Glancing around, I'm face-to-face with Barbara Cloyd.

"Ms. Cloyd."

"Barbara, please. You started out kind of bumpy, didn't you?" She sits in Blaire's chair.

I shake my head. "Sorry about the microphone. I'm not used to—"

Her smile is warm. "You made me look up."

"I know . . . Sorry. I didn't realize I stood so close—"

She shakes her head. "No, Robin. Listen, every once in a great while a new songwriter makes me look up from the sound booth. You did that tonight. I want to see you in here again."

"Really? Thank you. I'll be back. I will." Chalk one up for courage.

Lee gives me the eye after she leaves. "Told you."

For the rest of the evening, the vibes from our picnic lunch linger between Lee and me, though neither of us seems quite sure of what to do about it. I'm aware of how he disrupts my sense of the ordinary, as if one magnifying-glass-like stare could discover all my weaknesses and imperfections. As if he could easily scale the boundaries of my heart.

When he walks me out to my truck at the end of the night, he says, "I had fun." His eyes peer into mine without a blink.

"Thank you for being here."

"My pleasure," he says in such a way that I believe him.

"Robin, you leaving?" Graham struts toward me with his friend, Frank. "Let's do some cowriting. Meet me tomorrow at four. NSAI offices." He stops next to me, giving Lee the once over.

I introduce the men, and instead of shaking hands, Graham tugs on the brim of his hat so his eyes are hidden. "Listen, tomorrow at four, Robin. Don't forget." He strides off with Frank.

"Nice guy," Lee says with a smack of sarcasm. He crosses his arms and settles against my truck.

"He is, under the duster and hat." I unlock the truck door.

Lee steps up. "Here, let me help."

I raise my guitar to slide it over to the passenger side. Lee gives it a little shove. "Oh, wait, Lee, it's stuck." I back up to adjust the guitar case.

Hello! Mars, meet Venus.

Lee's hand collides with my, um, "perkiness." Flames of embarrassment engulf my torso. I don't need a mirror to know my face is every color of red invented.

Lee jerks away. "Robin, I'm sorry." He whips around toward the lights on Hillsboro, his shirttail fluttering, his shoulders shimmying.

Sorry, my eye. He's laughing.

"It's okay. You didn't do it on purpose." I snort-snicker.

He glances back at me. "I'm embarrassed."

"You're embarrassed?" I shove my guitar into the cab and face him, arms crossed. "You know you might have to marry me. Where I come from, touching a girl's breast is practically a proposal."

Lee walks back with a smile on his lips but a scary look in his eye. He props one hand on the truck and hovers over me. "Maybe I will." His dark brown bangs flop forward.

She-doggies. He's confusing me. "I-I w-was kidding." My heart thumps against my ribs.

"Right, I know. Just kidding too."

Oh, shew-wee. For a minute there . . . Dang, is that you, Disappointment? Knocking on my door?

"Hey, Robin . . ." Lee settles against the truck with his hands in his pockets. "I need to tell you something."

"What's up?" I'm struck by how much I feel like his friend already.

He rubs his hand over his hair. "Well, my ex-fiancée came back into my life unexpectedly today."

May fades into June, and I'm busy in the daily routine of cleaning offices, lofts, and lobbies; writing songs; and attending workshops at NSAI and ASCAP. I manage five more open-mike nights—two at the Bluebird, two at the Douglas Corner Café, and one at The French Quarter Café. The freak-out feeling isn't as gripping, but when it's my turn to take the stage, my knees still melt like lumps of clay in the noon sun.

And Skyler tells me I have no stage finesse. "It's like watching Kong tour Manhattan."

Okay, fine, I'll work on finesse. But I do have this—a fan. Not Skyler or Blaire, nor Graham or Birdie. Sadly, not Lee. I've only seen him in church since that night at the Bluebird when he announced his former fiancé came back into his life. We wave hi across the sanctuary, but that's it.

My fan is Mallory Clark. The crazy girl I almost hit while driving to Nashville. I call her when I'm going to an open-mike night, and she shows up.

"I've been doing some singing. Recording demos," she tells me after my last open-mike at the French Quarter.

"So, you're back to singing as a career?" This after a week of sculpting classes and a zealous but short-lived consideration of culinary school.

"Yeah," she says with soft confidence. "My ex messed me up, but I'm back on track."

"Good for you. Never let the ex keep you down." I grin at her and pull out my little notebook. *Never let the ex keep you down . . .*

Besides making open-mike nights, I've been writing songs with Graham, who's become a good friend, and with a woman I met in a NSAI workshop, Kim Flowers. She's a spunky English gal who has helped me a lot with writing melodies.

"You're stuck writing with all the major chords," she told me in her fancy English. "Let's throw in some minors, shall we? Be daring."

I laughed and slapped down a B minor on the song we were writing. "How's that?"

"Excellent, darling."

Being around Kim, hearing her accent, made me think of Eliza, which made me miss her, so I actually sat down at one of the NSAI members' computers and e-mailed her. Not sure, but I think I heard her fainting all the way across the Atlantic. I wrote all about Nashville, songwriter's nights, Skyler, Blaire, Birdie, Graham, and Lee. Doing this miraculously brought my life into focus in my own eyes.

A few days later, she e-mailed me back.

Dear Nashville,

My roommate had to revive me after I got your e-mail. What happened to you? Nashville is truly a city of miracles.

Sounds like all is going well, and I'm proud of you. This is the big sister I know. Oh, by the way, I'm into Keith Urban these days, so if you run into him, hug him for me, 'k? One of my classmates, a girl from Ohio State, has his CD, and if we're not in class, we're listening to Keith.

Summer in Cambridge is beautiful. The days are flying by. I love the course work, Literature— Shakespeare to the Present Day. Am having a jolly good time touring the countryside on the weekends. But I'm homesick for Alabama.

I'm sad to report there's no Greek Tycoon as of yet, but a fellow fellow (little play on words there), Peg, and I are planning a trip to Paris in July.

Momma's e-mailed me a lot. She writes she's worried about you, so Robin, please go home for the Fourth. I know you two struggle, but she does love you, and in her own quirky way, she wants to protect you. She is one strange woman when it comes to you and music, isn't she?

> *Love you and miss you,*
> *Cambridge*

On a cool June afternoon, I sip bottled water on Caffeine's deck while Skyler spends her wise advice on me.

"Don't go with Graham just because Lee is temporarily out of commission."

"We're just friends. Which is more than I can say for Lee and me. We are little more than 'how-do-I'm-fine to each other.'" I shrug. "Maybe he and his fiancée worked things out."

"What's their story anyway?"

"Not sure. Don't even know who she is. All Lee said was that they broke up awhile back, but then she ran into some kind of trouble and needed him for support. Her family is in New York, and her friends are fair weather, apparently."

"Good looking, kind, and a knight in shining armor. Man, I got to get me one of those."

"Don't we all." I sip my water.

"By the way, if you get engaged to Graham, I'll refuse to be a bridesmaid."

I plop my bottle on the tabletop. "You're a loon, Skyler."

She rears back. "Excuse me, I'm merely stating my case."

"I'm not going to marry Graham *or* Lee or anyone, so put your bridesmaid aspirations back in the closet."

She defends herself with her nose in the air. "But let the record show, I warned you."

I laugh. "Let the record show."

"What do you see in Graham as a friend anyway? He's slicker than a bar of soap." Skyler reaches for the remains of *The Tennessean*, folded up on the table next to us.

"He's cocky, but underneath all the garb, he's insecure and sweet. He's taught me a lot about songwriting. He didn't have to take the time to write with me." I glance at my watch. "Between his help and Kim's, I'm braving my first ASCAP pro appointment today at two."

"Well, if you ask me, Graham is riding on your coattails." Skyler drops her nose closer to the paper. Her lips move as she reads. "I can't believe it."

"What?" I look over.

She smashes the pages together. "Oh, Robin."

"Skyler, what?" I yank her hair. "Don't 'Oh, Robin' me and not say why."

She brushes my hand away. "Sit down."

"I am sitting. What did you read?"

She slides the newspaper over to me and points to Brad Schmitt's column, "Brad About You." I read, "Appeared in court . . . Janie Leeds with her fiancé, Nashville contractor Lee Rivers . . . fight with her label over contract conditions."

I snap up the paper and read it again. And again. There's a photo. An adrenaline rush makes my head pound and my hands tremble. "Holy schamoly!" I crumple the pages with a glance at Skyler.

"I remember now Janie was engaged to a local Nashville contractor, but it was some kind of whirlwind romance that burned hot and fizzled fast."

"Lee was engaged to Janie Leeds." I gape at their picture again. My stomach curdles. Janie Leeds is beautiful. The Mary Poppins of country music—practically perfect in every way. From her stylish clothes right down to the tips of her sleek, chestnut-colored hair. In the photo, Lee is holding on to her arm, smiling as if he is in love.

"It's an old picture, Robin. Really. I don't think Janie's hair is brown anymore." Skyler glances at her watch and jumps up. "Shoot, I need to run. Are you going to be okay?"

I stand, folding up the paper. "I need to go too. ASCAP appointment . . ."

"Robin, are you going to be okay?" Skyler presses her hand on my arm.

"Of course. Gee, Sky, I spent a day and an evening with the guy." Lee. Engaged to Janie Leeds. I follow Skyler out and stuff my water bottle, along with the balled-up newspaper, into the trash.

16

Standing in the wide-open, high-arching lobby of the ASCAP building, I grip the handle of my guitar case, trying to calm my jittery nerves.

I feel queasy, like the time I tried out for varsity basketball, knowing I couldn't dribble worth a darn but could sink a three-pointer with my eyes closed.

Why did I think I was ready for this? Lord, if You don't give me peace, I'm leaving.

"Can I help you?" the receptionist asks.

"Yes." I quiver and step forward. "I have an appointment." My trembling hand steadies.

I ride the elevator to Susan West's office and unpack my guitar.

"How long have you been writing songs?" she asks.

"Ten years, maybe twelve," I say, sitting on the edge of a chair, holding my guitar on my knee. "But I've only been in Nashville a month or so."

"Do you have lyric sheets with you?"

"I do."

She smiles as I pass them to her. She reads. I tune. My hands are shaking again.

"Whenever you're ready," she says with a nod.

Ready? That would be never, but I can't sit in her office the rest of my life. "Here goes."

My first song is "Barefoot and Free," the military tribute to my brother.

You always loved to run barefoot and free,
Now you're laying down your life so someone else can be,
And no one loves you for it more than me.

I'm half way through the chorus, settling down a little, giving myself to the lyrics, when Susan holds up her hands.

"Stop."

I think she's kidding, so I keep on singing right into verse two.

She slaps her hand against the top of the guitar. "Stop, Robin. Stop."

Verse two fades away. I gape at her. "What's wrong?"

"Nothing. The song doesn't do anything for me. Go on to the next."

Uh? "O-okay." Hard to go on breathing with a bullet fired into the ole ticker.

I muddle through two more songs, "Rosalie" and "Give My Life," while my confidence leaks all over. Susan stops me halfway through each one.

"Nice melody, but I'm not getting the song. The lyrics seem too simple."

"Perhaps sophomoric?"

"Perhaps."

"Okay." I start to pack up, wrestling with discouragement. Maybe I should've sung "Country Princess." But if Graham called it sophomoric, what would Susan call it? Besides, Graham said, "Try new stuff."

So I did. *Poo to you, Graham.*

"Come back when you have three to five new songs."

"Three to five *new* songs?" Tears threaten to betray me.

Walking out to my truck, I let the waterworks loose. "Who am I kidding?" I mutter. "I can't do this."

*I find Graham in the NSAI meeting room. It's a large, angled-*wall room with low lighting, wood trim, and the same gleaming wood floors as the rest of the building.

He's talking to Frank Gruey and another man dressed in holey jeans (must be a songwriter) and a plaid button-down. He's nice looking, a fiftyish gent with squinty eyes and round cheeks.

Frank looks up. "Can I help you?"

His tone makes me feel small. "I'm here to meet with Graham."

Graham addresses me with his hands in his pockets and one foot jutted forward like he's posing for a picture. "What do you need, Robin?"

"We have an appointment." Don't treat me like I'm a snot-nosed kid.

He turns to the man in the jeans. "Robin's new in town. I'm tutoring her in songwriting." Graham sighs like I'm quite the burden.

Then Frank slaps him on the back. "We're going to grab a bite at Noshville Deli. Why don't you join us?"

Graham nods with a sly smile. "Love to." He looks over at me. "Robin, you remember Frank Gruey? And this is Danny Hayes. He just got a cut with Kristin Waters."

I shake their hands. "Congratulations, Danny."

Frank looks at his watch with an exaggerated swing of his arm. "Better get going, Danny. Graham, you coming?"

"Right behind you." The man in the black duster picks up his guitar and follows Frank and Danny down the hallway.

"Graham?" I catch him before he reaches the door. "You're walking out on me?" Besides writing, I wanted to whine about my ASCAP critique from yesterday.

He stops at the door. "This is important. Very."

"I see."

"So, hang tight, all right?"

I snort my hot breath over him. "Hang tight? I don't like being treated like I'm toilet paper stuck to the bottom of your shoe."

"Toilet paper." He laughs and rolls his eyes. "Don't be so melodramatic."

"My ASCAP appointment didn't go so well," I blurt.

"What'd she say?"

"Come back when I have three to five new songs."

Graham shoves open the door. "Then write three to five new songs." He leans forward and pops a quick kiss on my cheek. "Let's catch up later, okay?"

I rear back and watch him walk away, rubbing his wet kiss from my cheek.

In Writing Room number one, I plop down in an earth-toned chair, stare at the white walls, and dig the heels of my boots in the green carpet. Birdie's right. This business ain't for the weakhearted.

The sting of Graham walking out on me lingers. "I'll show you, Graham Young." I pop open my guitar case. "And Lee Rivers. Dating Janie Leeds. And Miss I-don't-get-your-songs Susan West."

Sitting at the piano, I tune my guitar as my eyes water, wondering if the fallow ground of disappointment and

rejection is where hit songs are reaped. If so, I'm due for
a doozy.

In the midst a good pout, my cell phone rings. I hope it's
Graham with a big fat apology.

"Hey, it's Ricky."

"Hey—" My voice breaks.

"You okay?"

I sink down to the love seat and prop my guitar against the
cushion. "I've had better days."

"You haven't called."

Tears seep from the corners of my eyes. "I'm sorry."

"How's songwriting?"

I shrug and pick at a small hole forming in the knee of my
jeans. "Apparently, I'm not as good as I thought."

"Come home, Robin." His nudge is wrapped with a ribbon
of longing.

Go home? "Today, that sounds pretty good, Rick, but I've
barely started here."

"Come on, I'm sure Chancy would rehire you."

I chuckle through my sniffles. "The Tums people would be
back in business."

He laughs low. "I'd give you another chance too."

My heart thumps. Go home. Marry Ricky. Forget writing
for the Row. What made me think I could fit in here anyway?
"I don't know . . ." I pace back to the piano.

"Please, baby, think about it."

I hit middle C. The single clear tone fills the room.
"Ricky, I—"

"Don't say yes or no. I'm on my way to pick up a car with
Mitch, so just think about it, okay? Pray. I love you."

I press *End* and throw my phone against the chair. Today,
he calls. Of all days. *Lord, did I miss you or something? Take
a wrong turn and end up here?*

Shutting the writing room door, I wonder if Craig Wiseman works up his hit songs this way. Sure feels like I'm living like I was dying. Pieces of me are anyway.

I cry a little, praying, asking for wisdom. Then I hear Granddaddy's voice echoing from the deep recess of my pea brain. "If you go through life looking over your shoulder, you'll wreck for sure."

A small snicker starts in my belly and builds to a laugh. "Thanks, Granddaddy."

For the rest of the afternoon, I sing away my blues, pouring out my soul to the One who holds my destiny in His hand.

In my kitchen I pull hamburger meat from the crisper and mold it into patties. My heart has healed from the stink of the day, but I'm drained.

Between Graham, Ricky, and Susan West; getting up early for work; staying up late for workshops and songwriter's nights; and spending my afternoons digging around the depths of my soul for the next Trisha Yearwood hit, I'm plumb worn out.

Plopping the hamburgers onto a plate, I wonder again if moving to Nashville really was a bad idea. Maybe I should go home and marry Ricky.

My cell phone rings as I mold the last patty. "Shoot." My hands are coated with hamburger meat. But maybe this time it *is* Graham with a fat apology. Or Ricky with a never mind.

I wipe my hands and dig in my purse for my phone.

"Robin, it's Marc."

"What's up, boss?" I cradle the tiny phone against my cheek and open the bottom cupboard for Grandma's old cast-iron frying pan.

"Don't forget Nashville Noise. Five a.m." The offices of the great record label is Marc's newest and biggest account.

"Marc, I know my schedule."

"Marty is assigned to the job too." He has this annoying habit of repeating himself.

"We know." I arrange the hamburgers in the skillet, and it dawns on me—I made too many. I can't eat three hamburgers tonight.

"Be professional." Marc is rushed and hyper. "They're behind on a recording project, so they'll be in the studios at odd hours. Be careful and *be* quiet. Keep a sharp eye out."

"Keep a sharp eye out? For what, an emergency trash emptying?"

"I want you to take this job seriously, Robin."

The sound and smell of sizzling meat rises in the kitchen. "Gee, Marc, and we were planning to toilet paper Mr. Chastain's office."

"What!"

"You know, you have no sense of humor. Why are you so worked up over this job?"

He hesitates. "James Chastain and I hit it off. He might take a listen to some of my songs." His words are jammed together like county fair bumper cars.

"Just like that?" I grab a spatula from the drawer. Marc's story seems rather bizzare. *Hey, Marc, I like your cleaning company. Let me hear a few of your songs.* It doesn't sound like the reputed hard-nosed James Chastain. He once made a songwriter work three years before signing him to a deal, because he thought the guy wasn't ready.

"It's NashVegas, Robin. Anything can happen." Marc's tone has a woo-wee tingle. Like he'd just won a round of Texas Hold 'Em.

I half-decide Marc is dreaming, half-decide I want a sip of whatever he's drinking. "Don't worry, we'll do a good job. And keep a sharp eye out." I can't help it, I had to repeat it.

Marc clears his throat and says, in a low, hurried voice, "Just do the good job you always do."

"Ah, sweet. A left-handed compliment." With a final good-bye, I flip my phone closed and head back to the kitchen.

I'm up to my eyeballs with insults: Susan telling me my songs aren't hits, Graham dumping me for someone he considers more important, and Ricky insinuating I'm crazy for leaving home. But by-gum, Marc, don't challenge my ability to clean a toilet and dump the trash.

I slap the counter with the spatula.

"Robin, you home?" Birdie calls through my door with a light knock.

I whirl around. "Yeah, it's open."

A peaceful feeling washes over me when her pretty face peers around my yellow door. "Smells good in here."

"Please, come in and eat a burger with me."

"If your frying them, I'm eating." She walks over to the counter. "I heard something about you today."

"Me?" I glance up from where I'm pouring frozen fries onto a cookie sheet.

"Walt and I met with Eric Exley to talk about a project he's producing." Birdie comes into the kitchen and starts hunting through the cupboards.

"I assume this is a good thing." I open the freezer and toss the bag of fries back in. "Birdie, what are you looking for?"

"Plates."

I point to the cupboard by the door.

"Well, every time Walt ran into Eric, he'd tease him, 'Put my name on it.'" She laughs.

"I don't get it."

"You know, darling, if Eric wrote a great song, credit Walt as the writer."

"Ah, right." I grin. "Put my name on it. Clever."

"Well, it's just a saying, but Eric finally told Walt, 'Let's put your name on something.'" Birdie finds the plates and pulls down two. "Walt invited me along, and there we are, eating and talking, when this A&R rep Eric knows stops by our table. Honey, if you want to run into someone important, go to the Green Hills Bread & Company."

"I heard Keith Urban goes there."

"The A&R rep has a songwriting son who sang at the Bluebird the same night as you a few weeks ago."

I make a face as I slip the cookie sheet of fries into the oven. "No kidding. Do you remember his name?"

Birdie shook her head. "The dad is Pete Jewel, but can't remember the son's. Pete, of course, went to the 'Bird to hear his boy and found the songs by this vulnerable little redhead very captivating."

I look up at her. "Me?"

"He said you were shaky and uncomfortable, but your songs were so pure, from the heart." Birdie hands me the plates and picks up the spatula. "'Genius' is the word he used."

I gape at her, cradling the plates to my chest. "You're lying."

"Why would I lie?"

While setting the table, I give Birdie the low-down on my week. "Skyler reads in 'Brad About You' that Lee was engaged, or is engaged, to Janie Leeds. Then I go to my ASCAP pro appointment only to be told to come back when I have three to five *new* songs. And today, Graham walks out on me to have lunch with Frank Gruey and Danny Hayes, whoever they are—"

"Not sure about Frank, but Danny is a fabulous song-writer. Been down on his luck though until this recent cut with Kristin Waters."

I pull forks and knives from a drawer. "Right, so there you

go. Graham goes off with them, and while I pout in one of the writer's rooms, my boyfriend, or sorta-boyfriend, calls asking me to come home. I sat in the writing room and cried. Didn't write one *genius* word."

Birdie turns from where she's tending the hamburgers. "Sweetie, it's an afternoon of tears that will yield you the best songs. Don't be afraid of the hard times. It's the only way you'll grow. You have to be thick-skinned. Determined."

I fill two glasses with ice, then shut the freezer door and lean against the refrigerator. "I've been thinking of going home. But how could I hold my head up if I quit after six weeks?"

"Look, Robin Rae, an ASCAP pro didn't like your songs. But an A&R rep saw genius. What does that tell you?"

"One of them is crazy?"

Birdie laughs. "No, it tells me you have some learning to do, but underneath it all is a true gift."

I set the glasses on the table, digesting Birdie's words. "Guess it doesn't make sense to give up so soon."

"No, it doesn't. Give yourself time."

"Say, Birdie, how did you know my middle name was Rae?" I squeeze around her to check the fries.

She lifts her head. "Didn't you tell me?"

"No, don't think so."

Birdie's chuckle is high and weak. "Gee, I don't know. Must have been Jeeter. The burgers are done." She slides the first one onto a bun.

"I reckon. Jeeter's always calling me Robin Rae." Pulling an onion and tomato from the fridge, I confess, "It's hard not to get wrapped around the axel, wondering if I can really make it."

"You'll find your niche as you polish your genius."

"You're not going to let me forget he said 'genius,' are you?"

"Nope." She shakes her hips as she passes me with the

plate of burgers. "But whatever you do, girl, be true to you. What you need to learn from this week is that this town doesn't need any more posers or wannabes. We need true-blue, hard-working songwriters."

"True blue, right." I carry out the mustard, onions, and tomatoes. "Enough about me. How are things between you and Walt?"

Birdie's cheeks redden. "Wonderful. We're going to dinner tomorrow night."

I sing softly. "Walt and Birdie sitting in a tree, k-i-s-s-i-n-g."

She sings along with a pretty high harmony.

17

I wake a few roosters on my way to Nashville Noise at four forty-five in the morning. Marty meets me in the reception area with coffee and crullers from the Donut Den.

"You're not going to believe Mr. Chastain's office. He has his own personal hall of fame."

"I bet." I sip my coffee and munch on my cruller as I follow Marty to the icon's office. The walls are covered with photos, plaques, awards, and platinum albums. I turn in a slow circle. "Holy schamoly."

Marty strolls along the far wall. "If you're the great James Chastain, I suppose everyone wants to know you." She stops to examine one of the pictures. "Who'd you listen to growing up, Robin?"

"Everyone, everything. Granddaddy Lukeman loved all kinds of music. Gospel, contemporary Christian, country, bluegrass, even classical. He talked to me about singer-songwriters Bill Anderson, Jimmy Web, Dolly Parton, Loretta Lynn. Then I found Wayne Kirkpatrick, James Dean Hicks, Victoria Shaw, Diane Warren, and, believe it or not, Avril Lavigne."

I follow Marty down the row of pictures. "Anyway, I read an interview with Anthony Smith, and he said, 'I just pray for

God to help me be creative,' and I thought, 'Dang, he's right. Can't go wrong praying.'"

Marty glances back at me for a second, then moves on, looking at pictures. "I tried to make Delaney Brown something like Heart meets Trisha Yearwood with a dash of Pasty Cline." Marty waves me over. "Look, a young James Chastain."

I look over her shoulder. "He has a nice face." I munch the last of my cruller and check the time. "We'd better get to work. Marc would have a heart attack if he caught us dillydallying in Mr. Chastain's office." I head for the door. "Heart meets Trisha and Patsy, huh? I think it worked."

"Yeah, guess so." Marty's shoulders droop and she motions to the faces on the wall with her coffee cup. "Maybe it could've been me."

I plop my arm on her shoulders. "It still can be you. Get back in the game. Start writing. Go with me to open-mike nights. I could use a buddy."

She shakes her head with a feeble smile. "The passion is gone. I listen to you talk about workshops, spending nights running around town for songwriter nights, trying to meet people so you can set up cowrites, and it gives me one gargantuan headache. All I can think is, I'm glad it's not me." She heads out of the office.

I follow her. "But you don't have to start at the bottom like me. You know folks in the business."

"My stardom ship has sailed, and I fell off the face of the musical earth."

The sad resolve in Marty's voice reminds me of Momma, even Birdie, a little. Women on the verge of achieving their dream only to have life wake them up right before the *really* good part. I want to succeed. For them.

Marty picks up her cleaning gear. "I'll start with the bathrooms, you take the offices."

"Right behind you." I pause to pull my notebook and pen from my hip pocket.

Sad understanding that dreams fade away,
And tomorrow never comes.
She caught a ride on the Ferris wheel,
For the thrill of going 'round.
But found herself still sitting there,
With her feet stuck on the ground.

Nashville Noise has a lot of offices, plus writing rooms and several recording studios. I methodically clean the first floor, humming to myself, dumping trash, vacuuming dirt. Wheeling my little cleaning cart down the hall, I get to the first recording studio. On the other side of the door, I hear muffled voices, followed by footsteps. Then, the click of a door. The voices fade.

I glance to my right down the long hall. Then my left. No one's coming. I drop the vacuum pack and steal inside the studio.

The room is large and square, low lit and painted with warm colors. I close my eyes and breathe in the music.

To my right are two chairs on either side of a large mike. Plus two guitars. One acoustic, the other electric. And to my left is the glass-encased, unmanned control room. I tiptoe over to the chair by the acoustic.

I read somewhere, maybe from *Music Row* magazine, that Nashville Noise is doing more acoustic recordings. Going back to the style of legendary RCA Studio B where greats like Jim Reeves and Eddy Arnold recorded.

I pick up the guitar, a sleek Ovation, and drop the strap over my head. One day, an artist will come in here and lay down tracks to one of my songs. Oh, Lord, please. I don't have a backup plan. If I can't sell songs, I'll be cleaning toilets the rest of my life. Or maybe follow Skyler's lead and study law. I shudder at the sobering realization.

It's songwriting or bust.

I peek over my shoulder at the control room where the computer and console lights reflect in the glass. Still empty. Just to be safe, better make sure the coast is clear. Marc said to keep a sharp eye out. I tiptoe over to the door. Marty is coming down the hall.

"What are you doing?" she whispers as I jerk her inside the studio.

"Pretending." I point to the Fender electric. "Strap it on. Let's play a song."

To my surprise, burned-out, I've-lost-my-passion Marty does not hesitate. She slings the strap over her shoulder and fastens it to the guitar. "We are so fired."

"Shhh, no we're not. We just can't get caught." I pull a pick from my hip pocket and strum. A rich, beautiful G chord sends my heart right over the moon.

Marty snorts. "You carry a pick in your pocket?"

"You weren't at the Bluebird."

"Huh?"

"Never mind. What should we sing?"

Marty smiles. "One of your songs, of course."

I shrug. "I always wanted to hear "Your Country Princess" with an electric. Creep Graham added a sweet lick after the second verse."

"Let's do it. What key?"

"D." I play it through once, showing Marty her part, a tad nervous the recording studio police are going to bust us. But after a few seconds in this danger zone, I settle down. Fear does not define me. Really.

Marty is a skilled musician. She blows me away.

"Let's do this before we get caught." She runs her thumbs over her fingertips. "I have absolutely no calluses."

"Then just come in on the chorus." I ahem a few times to clear my throat and step up to the mike. The coffee I had a few hours ago didn't prime my vocal pump, but I can muddle through. "This song is for . . ." I grin at Marty. "Marc Lewis."

She muffles a chuckle with her pinched lips.

I sing the first verse of "Your Country Princess" with every ounce of my heart and soul, throwing in a few extra guitar riffs for good measure.

Marty cranks it up for the chorus with beautiful lead accents. When I sing the chorus a second time, she comes in with a strong Jennifer Nettles-like voice.

We end the song with a flourish. "Ooooooo . . . Let. Me. Be. Your. Countryyyyyyy. Prince-esss." The electric whines out the last note.

Thump!

Marty and I freeze. "Did you hear something?" she whispers.

Squeak.

"Crap, we're dead." Trembling, I return the Ovation to the guitar stand and scurry out the door with Marty on my heels, shoving me down the hall. We skid around the corner and bust into the ladies' room.

"Do you think Marc is checking up on us?" Marty pokes her head out the door to see if anyone followed us.

At the sink, I splash cold water on my face. "What were we thinking?" My hands shake so bad that I can't grip the paper towels.

Marty laughs. "We, nothing. You. By the way, great song."

I pat my face with a ripped towel. "Really? Graham called it sophomoric."

"Oh brother, don't listen to him. He's—"

Clank!

We shush. "I'm getting out of here," Marty whispers. She cracks the door and recons the hall. "The coast is clear."

Marty dashes left, and I dash right, winding my way back to the studio where, unfortunately, I left my cleaning cart. Returning to the scene of the crime can't be wise. But I find the studio is still abandoned. *Shew.*

Must have been the pipes. Old buildings have a song of their own. I start to wheel away, then stop, back up, crack the door, and slither my hand inside and grab the trash.

After I finish at Nashville Noise and run a few errands, I call Skyler for an early lunch.

"Meet me at Bread & Company."

"Good idea."

The restaurant is packed. I maneuver my way through the crowd, secretly scanning for famous faces. A trick I learned from Blaire. And Birdie said important people come here. But after a few minutes, I feel sorta stupid. Unless a major artist walks through those doors, I wouldn't recognize a Music Row powerhouse if my life depended on it.

Skyler calls. "I'm running late. Order me a turkey on whole grain, no mayo, and a large Diet Coke. I'm dying for something fizzy to drink. "

I pull a ten-dollar bill from my pocket. "Turkey, no mayo." She keeps forgetting Marc doesn't pay lawyer wages.

Meanwhile, I can't figure out which Pay Here register also takes orders, so I shift lines one too many times, and after ten minutes, I'm still at the end.

"You have to pick a line and commit."

"Yeah, I guess so." I glance around. "Oh my gosh, you're him."

He smiles, and the fingers of my soul pluck my heart strings. "I am."

"Aren't you supposed to be on tour?" The line can move all it wants. I'm not moving unless he does. What a great face.

"I'm home for a few days."

Remembering my Billy Currington bungle, I gather my few wits, pretend I'm cool, and stick out my hand. "Robin McAfee. Songwriter."

He laughs low. "Keith Urban. Songwriter too. Nice to meet you."

We meander through the line, chatting about the biz. Keith is personable with an air of humility, as if he understands fame is fleeting but character endures. "Keep writing," he tells me. "You'll find your place." His order is to go, so when they hand him a package, he heads toward the door.

"Can I ask a small, itty-bitty favor?" My insides shimmy. This is ridiculous, but the words are out there.

He grins and yanks a napkin from the dispenser. "It's not illegal, is it?"

I grin. "No, it's not illegal. My sister is a huge fan. She said to hug you if I ever . . . you know . . . ran . . . into . . ." Oh my gosh, this is the stupidest thing I've ever done.

Without a word, or making me feel like a twelve-year-old, Keith embraces me in a light and polite hug. "For your sister," he says.

"For Eliza." I grin, holding it together. Barely. Shaking all over. Maybe he doesn't totally believe it's for my sister, but who cares? I just got hugged by Keith Urban! Man, I love this town.

By the time Skyler shows up, Keith is long gone, and I've eaten half her turkey on whole grain, no mayo.

She sits at my table with a huff. "Can any man talk more than my boss? I'm sorry I'm late."

"No worries, mate," I say in my best Aussie accent. "Keith and I chatted."

She makes a face as she drops her purse on the spare chair. "Keith who? Did you eat half my sandwich?"

"Yes, I only had enough money for one sandwich and a drink. You forget I'm not made of money. Urban."

"I'll pay you back—" She stops, and her eyes bug out. "You talked with Keith Urban? He was here? Oh my gosh." She whips her head around, looking.

"Save yourself the whiplash. He's gone."

"Oh my gosh . . . You're lying. No, you're not lying. You talked with Keith Urban?" Skyler picks up the other half of the sandwich. "I'm gonna kill my boss."

I grin. "He hugged me too."

She slaps the table. "He did not."

"He did. For Eliza, you know."

Skyler laughs, then pounds the table. "You have the best luck. First Billy, then Keith. You've got to e-mail Eliza today. She'll die."

Since I'd planned to write at NSAI in the afternoon anyway, it's no bother to take a few minutes to e-mail my sister.

> *Cambridge,*
> *Three words for you. Hugged. Keith. Urban.*
>   *NashVegas*

I run into Graham at The Frothy Monkey on the Wednesday before the Fourth of July. I'd finished cleaning the Pagadigm Group offices, picked up my paycheck from Marc, and decided to treat myself to an iced mocha.

"Graham." I tip up my nose.

"Short stuff." He gazes down at me as he steps up to order. "Large black coffee."

I squint at the menu on the wall. "Do they even sell black coffee?"

Graham laughs, fishing a fistful of coins from his pocket. "You still mad at me?"

"Should I be?" The girl hands over my iced mocha.

"No. It was business, Robin."

"Then your business isn't very nice."

Graham laughs and winks at the girl as if they know something I don't. "Have to work deals, girl, or your career goes nowhere."

"Does that include dissing your friends?"

He looks away. "Like I said, it was business, Robin. Just business."

We walk outside and chat for a few minutes on the deck. He must have looked at his watch ten times in ten minutes.

"You in a rush, dude?"

"Well, I do need to get going." He steps down to the sidewalk. "I'll call you."

"I'll hold my breath."

18

Momma calls around dinnertime. "*Are you coming this* weekend?"

"I might."

"Jeeter's going around telling folks you're singing in the Fourth Fest, to which I say, 'Don't count on it, Jeeter.' So Daddy insisted I give you a call."

"Your support overwhelms me, Momma."

She huffs. "Sorry, Robin, but I've been around this mountain too many times."

She's thrown down the gauntlet. "I'm coming and—" here goes nothing "—I'm singing."

"You say that now. But wait 'til Jeeter calls your name."

I see all the years of false starts have messed with her confidence as much as my own. I pick up the gauntlet. "Momma, I'll sing. I promise."

"Are you telling me you're over your stage fright?"

I sigh. "I'm still terrified, but I'm learning to let God's love be my strength and song."

"Guess I'll stop contradicting Jeeter." The pitch in her tone tells me she's still a doubter.

We say good-bye, and I toss the phone on the coffee table.

Guess I'd better pack and let Birdie know I'll be gone. It occurs to me I could use some Nashville courage in Freedom, especially if I'm singing in the Fourth Fest. Especially if Ricky is going to be around.

I dial Skyler. "Want to go see Grandpa and Grandma McAfee this weekend?"

She hesitates. "Normally, yes."

"But . . ." I collapse over the arm of the couch.

"I have a date." The business quality of her voice drifts into a goofy lilt.

"With who?"

"A guy I met at your last open-mike night. He said he liked your voice. I said I was your cousin. He asked for my number, and now we're going out."

"He likes my voice and you get the date? How's that work?" My attempt at indignance fails.

"Hey, don't mess with my system. You get the applause, I get the guys."

"So, who is the lucky schmo?"

We talk about Trey Phillips, his kind demeanor and easy smile. Their first date is dinner and a movie.

Skyler asks for an update on Ricky. "I called him a few days ago just to talk. Told him I wanted to give Nashville a chance."

"What'd he say?"

"'Do what you gotta do' and hung up."

"Robin, end it with him. It's not fair to keep his hopes up when you're not really planning on marrying him. Besides, what if Lee becomes available?"

"I'm not holding on for Lee. We're still just waving across the pews."

"I haven't heard any more about Janie and her court case."

I stuff one of the throw pillows under my head. "Here's a

bit of good news you'll like." I pause for effect. "Graham and I made up. Sorta."

"You call that good news?"

"What's your problem with him?"

"I don't like how he treated you."

I flop my arm over my eyes. "He's just inconsiderate."

We argue the point for a second, but I can't convince her Graham is a good guy underneath his duster of ambition and hat of conceit.

After talking with Skyler, I call Blaire to see if she wants to go to Freedom, but she reminds me she's on her way to Hilton Head with her parents.

Looks like I'm traveling to Freedom alone. I slip off the couch and take my guitar out to the deck. The night is thick and dark. In the distance, the orange hue of downtown lights arch over the city, and firecrackers explode on the next block over. Screams and laughter float over the rooftops and settle on me.

I love the Fourth of July. In Freedom, half the town gathers at Granddaddy's the night before, and we sing and play well into the night. Momma bakes a half dozen of her famous Red, White, and Blue cake. Game and food booths line the streets.

Going home will be good. I can redraw my emotional boundaries and shake the lost feeling of being a newcomer to Nashville. My recent journey may not be *at all* about becoming a published songwriter, but about connecting with the perfect Love that overcomes fear.

The first breeze of the night ruffles through the maple, and for a long time, I sing and talk to my Father.

My old truck, Freedom's Song, whizzes by the town limits around noon. The smell of pine whooshes through the open windows.

Graham cranes around to read the *Let Freedom Sing* sign. "I love it," he says, jutting his elbow out the window. The wind tugs at the brim of his hat.

I glance over at him. He called last night, to my surprise, just before I crawled into bed. After our Frothy Monkey meeting, I didn't really believe he'd call anytime soon.

"Short stuff, what you got going for the Fourth?" he asked.

"Actually, I'm—"

"Let's grill out. Go down to the Cumberland and watch the fireworks. Maybe do some writing. What do you say?"

"I have plans, Graham."

The disappointment in his "Oh" killed me. I suggested he call his other friends, but it didn't take much hemming-n-hawing before I realized I was his other friend.

"Why don't you come down to Freedom with me?" The invitation tumbled out before I could consider all the ramifications. Like . . . Ricky.

Graham didn't hesitate. Not one second. "Great," he said. Something in his voice told me I couldn't take back my invite, even though he tossed me aside like an old shoe a few weeks ago.

After we hung up, I clicked off the light and lay on top of the covers for awhile, asking myself, "Can I trust him?"

In the end, the idea of him sitting home alone, watching NASCAR, eating take-out, convinced me. Besides, I think it's what Jesus would do.

"Freedom seems like a nice place to grow up." Graham breaks into my thoughts.

"It was . . . is." I wave at folks coming out of the downtown shops. "Where did you grow up, Graham?"

"Everywhere. California to Maine. Army brat."

Those two words, "Army brat," paint a whole new picture of my songwriting friend.

He chuckles. "I made a lot of money moving around."

I grin. "Doing what? Singing songs?"

"No." He hesitates. "Let's just say I had the ability to help out in the test-taking department."

"Really? What kind of ability?"

He taps his temple. "God-given."

The conversation ends as I turn into my parents' driveway. Mo and Curly explode across the yard, barking, chasing the truck as the tires crunch and crackle over the gravel toward the house. A mess of colors and darks hang on the line, snapping in the breeze. The porch is loaded with folks waiting on us.

Graham whistles. "It's a Rockwell painting."

My emotions swirl as I step out of the truck. "Yep, it is." Mo and Curly jam their wet noses against my hands. I stoop to bury my face in their manes.

"There's my girl." Daddy grabs me and whirls me around. The smell of his aftershave stirs up memories. "Land sakes, it ain't been the same around here without you."

"It's good to be home." I kiss his cheek.

I hug the grandparents, Uncle Dave and Aunt Ginger, and Dawnie.

"It's a boy," she says, patting her round belly. "Steve is thrilled."

"Me too. We need some more boys around here."

Moving through the family on the porch, I hug Aunt Lynette and Uncle Roland, surprised to see them. Momma, Aunt Lynette, and their older sister, Aunt Carol, patched up a long-standing feud when I was a teen, but the love between them remained a little lean. They typically only gather in one place for the major holidays—Thanksgiving and Christmas. Granddaddy insists.

Besides the family, there's the Bluegrass Boys, Jeeter, Grip, and Paul. They hug me as if I were their own and tell me Nashville looks good on me.

"By the way, the triplets are going to the national clogging championships," Paul says after a hug and kiss hello.

"You think they'll win?" I ask with a wink.

He pops his suspenders. "I reckon they will. They always do."

Momma waits by the kitchen door like the Queen Bee.

"Hey, Momma." I fall into her embrace. She smells like home—fresh baked bread, vanilla and spice, and her staple Suave herbal shampoo.

She wipes her cheeks when I step away. "Well, you look happy and healthy." For Bit McAfee, the confession is huge. "Mercy, what'd you do to your hair?" She brushes my short locks.

"Skyler. She thought I needed a new look."

Momma pinches her lips. "Louise never did have control of that girl."

"Momma, stop. She didn't do the cutting. Besides, I like it."

While the porch crowd chimes in about my hair, "Looks good, Robin Rae," Graham butts in with an, "Ahem."

Oh, right. Graham. "Everyone, this is my friend"—I stress friend—"Graham Young. A very talented guitarist and song-writer."

He's greeted with a chorus of how-dos, welcomes, and good-to-meet-yous.

"Guess we can sign you both up for Fourth Fest." Jeeter's words tie an instant knot in my gut. Is it too late to change my mind? I shoot a glance at Momma. Her face is pinched.

Yeah, it's too late.

"I'd be happy to play," Graham says, slinging his arm around my shoulders, hugging me into his side. "Robin's looking forward to it too."

"I saved the best for last, Robin Rae." Jeeter winks.

Yippee. All that fear I conquered in Nashville? It's back.

On Saturday evening I stand behind the outdoor stage in Pete Hadley's green field waiting to go on. The fragrance of cut grass and hay lingers in the air, along with the thick aroma of barbecuing meat.

Seems the whole county has turned out, and half of the next, for this Fourth Fest. More like Torture Fest. Here I am with my family and friends, the silky evening breeze in my face, and I can't enjoy one minute of it.

The Dixie Dos have already performed, with a new clogging platform, so I can't count on them to crash and burn. But, man, it would've really helped me out.

Graham strums a soft song as I pace under the oak tree. Its ancient branches shade the stage while my old nemesis, fear, conquers all my courage. All the strength of my past victories has vanished. Gone. Hightailed it like hungry hounds at the clang of the dinner bell.

Smiley Canyon strolls toward me from the other side of the generator that powers the lights and sound system. "You going on?"

Graham answers for me. "She is." He shakes Smiley's hand. "Graham Young."

Smiley yucks it up. "She is, is she? Wouldn't be the first time she ran out on a show." I lurch at him with a growl, and he scoots away knowing darn well I could put a choke hold on him.

"A friend of yours?" Graham asks, tugging his hat down around his eyebrows.

"Sorta. Look, Graham, you go on without me. I don't know what to sing, and even if I did, I'd forget all the lyrics."

"Robin, you can't pull a Frothy Monkey on me now." Graham's expression is shadowed by the brim of his hat.

"She's been like this since I've known her." Arizona floats toward us with a plate of barbecue. Graham's shoulders square, and his gaze zeros in on my gazellelike friend.

"Graham Young." He bows low, tapping the brim of his hat.

Oh, brother. "Graham, this is Arizona, who's taken, so knock off the Don Juan routine."

She greets Graham with her bright smile, then offers me a rib. "I thought I should check on you."

I refuse the rib. Too full of anxiety. "Can't do it, Arizona."

She shakes the meaty bone at me. "Yes, you can."

Graham smirks and falls against the tree trunk. "What's the big deal? This is home folks. The best audience anywhere."

Home folks? That's it. I freak and run across the field, aiming at nothing, ending up on the other side of the port-a-potties.

Graham follows me. "Is this where you hide? Smells like a barnyard."

"We are in a *cow* pasture." I thump my hand against one of the traveling bathrooms. "And these are Porta Potties."

Graham takes my hand and leads me out to the open field where the wind is clean and white wispy clouds float between the red and gold fingers of the lazy, setting sun.

I whisper, "I thought I had this beat."

"You do. In Nashville. Time to beat it here."

"Don't you ever get afraid?"

"Of being on stage? No. Of failing? Yes."

"Guess I'm afraid of failing too." I half-laugh, bending down to dab my eyes with the hem of my shirt.

"Robin, you can get up there with the best of them." Graham wraps his arm around me. I glean courage from his comfort. "With some songwriters, you wonder how long they'll hang around before realizing they don't have it. With other songwriters, you wonder how long it will be before the world sees they're a cut above the rest of us. You are one of those. A cut above the rest."

I tip my face up to him. "I thought my song was sophomoric."

He laughs. "You're graduating, slowly."

"So, which cut are you?"

"Ah, see, that's *my* fear. I'm afraid I'm in the first."

I hug his waist. Guess we're encouraging each other this weekend. "If I have to get over my fear, so do you. Look, Danny Hayes wouldn't write with you if you didn't have something special. And Frank Gruey wouldn't give you the time of day, right?"

He shrugs. "Danny Hayes is an old-school—" He stops and whips me off the ground with a yee-haw. "You ready to blow this gig up?"

I raise my arms. "Yee-haw."

He sets me down like we're in a slow-motion movie scene. Our eyes lock, and I peel off his hat. Long blond hair tumbles over his forehead.

Graham swipes his hair away from his face. "Hat head."

I swallow hard. "Your hair's beautiful." Out from under his hat, Graham's brown eyes appear ten times brighter. He has strong, even features that go with his strong chin.

I hold up the hat. "Now why do you want to be Kenny Chesney when you can be Keith Urban?" I run my fingers over his hair. "Better yet, why be anyone else when you can be Graham Young?"

He tries to snatch back his hat. "Graham Young ain't much to brag about."

"Graham, I'm serious. Why do you hide?"

"I'm not hiding. The hat is just me." He lunges for the hat again, but I twist away, giving him a stern, schoolmarm face.

"It is *not* you. And if I have to find the courage to go out there tonight, so do you. Sing without your hat and that ridiculous duster, Graham. It's July, for crying out loud. You're not Montgomery Gentry."

He tips his head and gazes down at me, then snatches for the hat again, or so I think. Instead, he grips my arms and pulls me to him. Then, right there in Pete Hadley's field with stinky old Rocky watching, Graham Young kisses me.

19

Shoot fire. He turns me loose with a swanky smile. If he intended for his kiss to weaken my knees, it didn't. It tickled my funny bone.

I snicker behind my hand and toss his hat to him.

"That bad, short stuff?" he asks, settling his hat on his head.

I squeeze my lips together. They're actually buzzing a little. "It was a nice kiss." Linking my arm through his, I start back toward the stage.

"Do I need more sex appeal?" He stops, juts one foot forward, and tips the brim of his hat down. "How about now? It's my best Tim McGraw."

I double over, laughing. "Would you stop? Be you, Graham." I stretch to jerk his hat off again.

"Robin, come on, give me the hat."

"Go on without it." I run from his outstretched hand while Rocky cheers me on from his pen with a loud bellow.

Graham chases me. "See, even the bull is on my side."

"Your side? He's rooting for me." I skip out of Graham's reach, waving the hat over my head, taunting him.

He crushes my game with one quick stride. My short

limbs are no match for his long ones. He literally tucks me under his arm and carries me toward the stage. I laugh and squirm.

Jeeter is center stage, emceeing, announcing the next act.

"We're up next," Graham says at the oak tree, strapping on his guitar. He holds out his hand for his hat.

"Sing without it," I say, reaching for my guitar, plopping the hat on my head.

"Can't." Graham snatches the hat and walks off to tune.

Can't lingers in my ears and sinks down in my soul. With cold fingers, I drop my guitar strap over my head. My heart races alongside my thoughts. *I can do this. I. Can.*

"Robin, were you planning on ignoring me all weekend?"

I whirl around. "Ricky, hello."

With his chin tucked to his chest, he swoops me into his arms and kisses me, hard and determined. When he lets me go, I step back, brushing my lips with the back of my hand.

"You didn't come over to the house," I say.

"I could say the same."

We stare at each other for one long, hairy second. Sweet mercy, don't tell me he wants to have it out now.

"Robin, come on, we're next." Graham bursts into the middle of my stare down with Ricky.

"Who's he?" Ricky fires.

"Graham Young, a friend from Nashville," I say. "Graham, this is Ricky Holden."

Ricky shuns Graham's handshake and peers down at me. "You brought a guy home?"

"Hey, take it easy, man." Graham steps between us.

"Did I ask you?" Ricky slaps his palms against Graham's chest.

Graham stumbles back, holding onto his guitar, a string of blue words spilling out. Getting a foothold, he whips off his guitar and shoves it at me. "You want a fight, homeboy?" He goes nose-to-nose with Ricky.

"'Homeboy'? Were you raised in the 'hood?" Ricky balls his fist. Graham circles.

"All right," I say. "Come on, this is ridiculous. You're not fighting."

One flashing right hook and Ricky knocks Graham to the ground. Okay, I guess they *are* fighting.

Faster than a mad rattlesnake, Graham wraps up Ricky's knees and drops him to the dirt with a thud.

"No, no, this is not happening." I try to get Graham's attention, or Ricky's, but there I am, holding two guitars, helpless.

So I do what any redneck girl would do. Kick them. "Stop it, stop it." My boot cracks Ricky in the ribs, then Graham, then Ricky again.

But they don't give it up, rolling over my foot and almost getting me tangled up in their mess. I hate to do it, but I've got to bring out the big guns.

Screaming.

"Help! Fight!"

A herd of men working the stage scramble out at my plea and break the two idiots apart.

"What's going on here?" Jeeter asks, standing in the middle of them, hands on his belt. He's a good two or three inches shorter than both of them, but clearly in command.

Ricky wipes the blood from his lip, breathing hard. "You're a smart man, Jeeter. You figure it out." He walks off with a backward glance at me.

Tears burn in my eyes. Dang, Ricky. "You couldn't leave well enough alone," I yell after him.

Graham yanks his guitar from me, beating the dirt from his duster with the brim of his hat. "What a son-of-a-gun. You need new friends, Robin."

I peer up at him, hand on my hip, chin jutted out. "Yeah, I do."

I'd like to walk off, get in my truck, and drive back to Nashville, leaving all this crap behind me and Graham to hitchhike home. But I can't.

Why? Because Jeeter is center stage, announcing us. "We got us a real treat tonight, folks. A couple of up-and-coming songwriters from Nashville."

"I need a second," I mutter to Graham, walking off. "Oh, Lord please, peace." My legs tremble as I circle the oak. "And Ricky, calm him down. Help me know what to do about us." I circle the oak again, praying, listening for a still, small voice.

"And now," Jeeter calls, "please welcome our own Robin Rae McAfee and Nashville's Graham Young."

The crowd's applause is light, as if they're unsure. They know: *Robin's not coming out, is she? Bless her heart. And who in the world is Graham Young?*

Graham leaps onto the stage with starlike zeal. I creep up the steps with my head down, feeling like the ugly girl in a beauty contest. My knees are knocking, I can't catch my breath. And why did Ricky and Graham have to puff out their chests like barnyard roosters. I ain't their hen.

Graham walks up to the mike with a big how-do smile. "Hello, Freedom!" Multicolored lights swing over us as the crowd answers with a cheer. There must be a gazillion people out there.

Graham starts one of his songs. He shouts to me, "It's in E!"

Come on, Robin. Focus. How big is your God? You know he's got you.

Graham gets the crowd clapping and swaying, and—forgetting he's in a cow pasture singing to a bunch of rednecks and hillbillies—he busts a move right in the middle of his song. He grabs the mike from the stand and flails across the stage.

Great day in the morning. No wonder he needs the hat.

"Take it away, Robin." He jukes and skips across the stage, whirling the mike over his head.

I gape at him. Take it away? To where? Graham sways in front of the crowd, "Oh, oh. Oh, oh." He glances back at me. Play!

Play what? A guitar solo? Strumming, I stand like a cardboard cutout, plunking and twanging. It's awful. Weak. What does he want from me? He's not helping my anxiety one iota.

"Whoooo!" Graham slaps the mike back in the stand and starts playing again.

Good grief.

He sings through the chorus of his song a few times, and I manage a little backup harmony but I still feel pretty much like an elephant tiptoeing through the tulips.

I work out my jitters on another of his songs, peeking out over the audience from time to time. Arizona's front and center with her arm linked through Ty Ledbetter's. Her eye catches mine. She winks. Looky there, she's in love.

Stage right is Daddy and Momma with Dawnie. Daddy looks proud as punch, clapping his white-boy clap. He has no rhythm. Dawnie is snickering at Graham, and standing next to her, Momma looks constipated.

Graham strides across stage, pumping his guitar, acting like he's bucking for Entertainer of the Year. "Take it away, Robin Rae."

Again? His music fades, so I figure he wants me to play one of my songs. My fingers fumble up and down the fret, and my pick slips around in my sweaty fingers. But I hang on.

This must be what it feels like to be the third-string quarterback on fourth-and-goal with the championship at stake. Who can take that kind of pressure? I want off. I want to run. Graham sidles up next to me.

"If you don't sing, I'll kiss you right now in front of all these people."

I press my lips against the mike. They should be safe from him there. "This is a song I wrote a few weeks ago called 'Let Go.'"

So, I do.

Momma's Sunday dinner is more crowded than a one-cent sale at the flea market. We can't fit everyone inside, so Daddy, Grandpa McAfee, and Uncle Dave set up tables under the trees for a picnic.

"All right, Robin Rae, tell us about Nashville." Grip pulls up next to me and Graham, stirring his coleslaw into his baked beans. "I remember those days, singing in honky-tonks, fairs, churches, festivals." He looks out beyond the trees. "Any place to get your song heard, tell your story."

"Well, Grip, mostly I've been cleaning toilets."

"Don't let her yank your chain," Graham interrupts. "She's writing songs, singing around town. She's a mighty fine songwriter."

I narrow my eyes at Graham. "'Mighty fine'? Since when do you say 'mighty fine'?"

"Never you mind what I say. You're good."

"'Never you mind'?" I've got to get him back to Nashville, quick. He's a country chameleon.

Daddy and Momma sit across from Graham and me. "Shew, it's warm out here," Momma says, fanning her pink face with an extra paper plate.

"You and Loralee outdid yourself, Bit." Grip holds up his plate. "Mighty fine spread."

"How's it going at Birdie's place? You liking it around Music Row?" Jeeter wants to know, tapping my foot with his.

"It's going great, Jeeter." From the corner of my eye, I see Momma shifting in her chair, chomping on a cream cheese-filled celery stick. "Birdie's been dating someone you know—Walt Henry."

Momma moans and stuffs another whole celery stick into her mouth. She looks like she swallowed a pair of oars.

Jeeter slaps his knee. "Walt Henry. That fox. You tell Birdie I said watch out, now." Jeeter wags his finger in the air with a high *tee-hee*.

I prop my elbows on my knees, holding my plate in my hand. "Tell me, Jeeter, do you know why Birdie parted ways with Nashville Noise?"

"Good question, Robin Rae. Good question."

An eerie hush hangs over us. Then . . .

"Good beans, Bit."

"What you got for dessert? I'd better save room."

"Best coleslaw I had in a long time. Um-um."

Odd, quick change of the topic. Weird.

Graham jumps in with, "Y'all have to come up to hear Robin at the Bluebird. She's singing at a songwriter's night in November."

"Robin, you singing at the Bluebird?" Granddaddy Lukeman asks. "Why don't you tell some folks?"

My eyes meet Momma's. "Yeah, Granddaddy, I tried out and got a spot the first Sunday in November."

A chorus of "We'll be there" rises.

"Save room for Jenny and me," Reverend Miller says.

I grin. "I really appreciate everyone's support, but I'm not sure I can invite the whole town. Gotta save room for the other songwriters' friends and family, you know."

We talk about the Bluebird for a few minutes until Graham gets up for seconds. I follow him. "Can I talk to you about last night? The thing with Ricky . . ."

"Guys like that only know one thing." He scoops beans onto his plate.

"He's not like that, and you sorta provoked him."

Graham reaches for a large fried chicken wing. "Who is he anyway?"

"My boyfriend."

He doesn't flinch, but reaches for more chicken. "You can do better."

"With who? You?" I pick up a biscuit, but I'm not hungry.

"I'm just saying you could do better."

With a sigh, I walk off. Not so much as an apology. I didn't expect one to Ricky, but to me, at least.

20

By evening the house is quiet. Graham dozes on the couch with
Daddy. I toss grapes at Daddy's open mouth until Momma
makes me quit.

"You're getting grapes under the couch, Robin Rae. The
ants will move in."

"I'll get them." Crawling on my belly, I fish blindly under
the sofa skirt for wild grapes and find all of them. Okay, most
of them. On my way to the trash, I tell Momma, "I'm going to
go find Ricky."

Her knitting needles stop clicking as I pass by, and she
touches my hand. "All right."

Her tenderness surprises me a little. She's been so tense and
terse all weekend. "Momma, do you want to tell me something?"

She shakes her head. "Did you have a nice time this
weekend?"

Glancing back at Graham, I smile and nod. "Outside of the
fight, I did."

"Boys will be boys."

I take my keys from the hook by the back door. "If you
mean acting stupid, yeah, boys will be boys."

"And Graham? Is he . . ."

"A friend. Only a friend."

Momma nods. "Dawnie says Steve might come home the month the baby is due. So say your prayers. Can you believe he's going to be a daddy?"

I glance back at Momma. "He's a Marine. I reckon he can handle fatherhood."

"I don't know—a stinky diaper can bring the bravest man to his knees." She laughs.

"I suppose so."

Her knitting needles start clicking again. "Go on, now. I'll see to Graham if he wakes up."

*If not fishing, Ricky is at Mitch's Body Shop. Goes without say-*ing. I cruise by his folks' house just in case, but like I figured, find him in a paint-stained T-shirt, working on a rusted-out Dodge Charger with Mitch. Alan Jackson is singing from a vintage '80s, grease-streaked boom box. Makes me grin. Ricky, for all of his quirks, knows good music.

Just an old plywood boat
With a '75 Johnson . . .

"What do you want?" He glares at me from around the hood, wiping grease from his hands.

His tone smacks at my confidence. "To talk to you, if I could. Hey, Mitch." I slip my hands in to my pockets and rock back on my heels.

"Hey, Robin. You did good last night. The guy in the duster was a character, though."

I grin. "He is quite the character."

Mitch tosses his wrench onto the workbench. "I guess I'll go out for a Pepsi."

The side garage door bangs shut, and I gather my thoughts, staring at faded posters of Dale Earnhardt and Richard Petty while Ricky stays hidden behind a faded red hood.

"Why'd you hit him?" I ask.

"Because I can't stand smart alecks." He reaches around for the wrench Mitch tossed aside.

"Hello, pot. I'm the kettle, and you're black."

He looks around the edge of the hood. "What's that supposed to mean?"

"You're just as much a smart aleck as Graham. Geez, Rick." I walk around the car. "Where'd you guys find this?"

"Out in front of Carter Benson's place. Been sitting there for twenty years."

I laugh. "Didn't recognize it without the weeds and grass growing underneath."

Ricky doesn't so much as crack a smile. "He wouldn't sell until Mitch agreed to cut the grass after we hauled off the car."

"Despite popular opinion, no flies on Carter." I kick away a clump of mud from the deflated front tire. "What are you going to do once you fix it up?"

"We've got a 440 four-barrel to drop in. Mitch wants to do some road racing."

"Look out, Bo and Luke Duke." I slap the peeling, white-vinyl roof. "The Dukes of Freedom are hitting the dirt."

No smile yet. Dern, Ricky, be hard nosed, why don't you. I prop my elbows on the side of the car under the hood. "I'm not coming home."

He reaches down and works a bolt with the wrench. "Is it because of him?"

"No, it's because of me. I'm writing songs, singing at open-mike nights, overcoming my fears . . ."

"Lost your fears in NashVegas?"

I like his insight. "Yeah, I suppose. Working on it, anyway." A soft sensation of accomplishment moves over me.

The wrench slips from his hands, clattering against the cement floor. "I guess we should end it, then."

I stretch my foot under the car and draw the tool out with the tip of my boot. "Maybe it would be best."

He doesn't move, just hangs over the side of the car.

"I'm sorry, Ricky."

His arm constricts as he works the bolt again. "For what?"

"For not being what you wanted me to be. But I can't—"

"Ricky, honey, I brought over some dinner." The side garage door squeaks open, then claps shut.

He freezes as Mary Lu Martin peeps her brunette head under the hood. "Well, hey there, Robin." Her gaze flits from me to Ricky.

"Hi, Mary Lu, I was . . . just . . . leaving." I run my fingers down Ricky's back. "See you."

Ricky moves out from under the hood and touches my arm. "I'm sorry for hitting your friend."

I nod, chewing on my lip, fighting the tears. "I'll tell him."

"Mary Lu, can you give us a moment?" Ricky's eyes never leave mine.

"S-sure, Ricky, honey." She heads back out the door.

Tenderly, Ricky pulls me to him and touches his forehead to mine. "I guess we'll never make love on the banks of the Tennessee."

"No," I whisper, my voice caught, my vision blurring.

He wraps me in his arms and lifts me up. Our eyes meet, and then he touches his lips to mine. It's a soft, tender good-bye. "You're not going to be easy to get over."

I run my hand through his hair. "Give Mary Lu a real chance. Stop messing with her heart. She's a nice girl. And you know I'd never bring you dinner on a Sunday night."

He laughs, despite the moment, and lowers my feet to the dusty garage floor.

"Kick butt and take names in Nashville." He leans against the car, legs crossed at the ankle.

"I'll do my best."

"Hey, guess what we're going to name her?" He smiles.

"I have no idea."

"*The Robin.* Classic and powerful, but needs a lot of work."

I make a face. "Am I supposed to honored or insulted?"

"Honored," he says.

I turn to go. "See you, Ricky."

His juts out his chin. "See you."

When I show up for work Tuesday morning, Marc meets me instead of Marty.

"She called in sick," he says. "I'm filling in for her."

"Lucky me." Shoot, now there's no coffee, no Danish, and no how-was-your-weekend girl talk?

I'd wanted to talk through the events of the past few days. After my talk with Ricky, I went to Arizona's to cry it out before going home. Knowing I did the right thing doesn't make it easier. About the time my well of tears ran dry, Ty came over, so Arizona baked a cake, and we played a couple of rounds of three-handed Spades.

Graham didn't try to kiss me again but he gave his attention to talking music with the Bluegrass Boys and learning some banjo from Granddaddy. By the time we drove home Monday evening, I longed for my bed at Birdie's.

Marc breaks into my thoughts. "Where's your cleaning chart?"

"We don't have one, Marc. We just clean."

"What? Robin, you and Marty *must* follow procedure."

I flash my palm. "Talk to the hand, Marc. I'm in no mood to argue procedure at five a.m. We get the job done. Here's our routine."

After giving him the breakdown, he follows me to the executive offices. "I want to check out what you're doing. I set up procedures for a reason, Robin."

"Marc, I promise you, we do a fantastic job. You would be *so* proud."

In James Chastain's office, I break out my feather duster and attack the pictures and awards. Marty normally cleans his office, so I'm taking my time, studying the wall of fame.

"This is amazing." Marc leans in to examine each frame.

"Careful, my boss doesn't want anything messed up in here."

Marc snarls at me. "You should do stand-up comedy instead of songwriting. Be a great outlet for your sarcasm."

"Naw, then I wouldn't have anything left for you."

He ignores me. "James Chastain is quite a legend. Look at all these platinum and gold records."

"Didn't you see this when you met with him?"

He shakes his head. "We met at LongHorn Steakhouse."

I continue with my dusting while Marc reads the inscriptions aloud.

"Nashville Noise CMA winners, 1980 . . . There's Grace Harding." He looks at me. "My mom played all her records. What an incredible voice, Grace Harding."

"Yeah, my granddaddy and grandma liked her too."

"There's one of James cutting the ribbon at the Nashville Noise opening, 1980. Hey, there's Birdie."

I walk over to see. Marc points to a picture of James Chastain's first nobodies. "Nashville Noise. First signed artist."

They all look so young, dressed in bell bottoms, sporting long hair. "Sure enough, Birdie is standing next to Grace Harding and Tuck Wilder."

Mr. Chastain's smile is brilliant, like he knows he's created something great. His arm is around a pretty woman with swooping hair. I don't recognize her. "Wonder what happened to her?" I say to Marc as I take a closer look.

I jerk upright and stumble backward. *Holy shamoly. Oh. My. Gosh.* The air is sucked out of my lungs and . . . *Oh my gosh, oh my gosh, oh my gosh.*

I can't breathe. Is this hyperventilating? I glance at the photo again.

Oh my gosh. I see spots. Purple ones. Blue ones. Big black ones. I sit in Mr. Chastain's chair and tuck my head between my knees.

Marc touches my shoulder. "Robin, are you all right?"

I nod. *Breathe. Calm down.* After a few seconds, when my heart stops wigging out, I look up, gulping for air. The spots fade away, but I'm still shaking. I glance at the picture one more time.

I do *not* believe it. Without a thought, I jerk the picture off the wall and run out with Marc calling after me.

Birdie is asleep when I pound on her bedroom door. "Wake up. It's me. Robin."

I hear a light switch and shuffling feet across the hardwood floor. Birdie opens the door with her eyes half shut, her blonde bombshell hair exploding all over her head. "Where's the fire?"

"In my belly." I barge into her room.

Birdie cinches her robe. "Hey, Robin, why don't you come on in?" She yawns and scratches her lopsided head.

I pace around her bed. "I found this picture on James Chastain's wall." I hold it out for her to see, but when she tries to look, I jerk it away. "I can't believe it."

Birdie snatches the picture from me and bends into the lamp light. "Did you steal this?" She hands it back to me.

"No, I borrowed it. It's almost like the . . ." I bolt out of her room and up to my apartment.

"Robin." Birdie shuffles up the stairs after me.

On the bookshelf, I pick up the ripped picture of Momma with her bell-bottomed, big-haired friends. Three of the faces are in James's picture. Two I don't know. But one, I do.

I hold both photos up for Birdie to see. "You wanna tell me what's going on?"

Bleary eyed, she turns for the stairs. "I'll make coffee."

At six in the morning, Birdie scoots about the kitchen in silence, brewing coffee, toasting bread.

"Birdie, talk to me."

She opens the cupboard for the butter, then yawns. "I'll be right back."

"Is she the reason you left Nashville Noise?" I holler after her. "Birdie, were you and my Momma rivals?"

I slump over the center island, staring at the pictures. Good grief. How in the world did the hounds of Freedom keep this bone buried? Between Jeeter, Grip, Paul, and all the family, surely someone would have slipped.

But no. Not one word about Momma being a Nashville Noise artist. It blows my mind.

Surely this is the core of her feud with Aunt Lynette and Aunt Carol. She signed on at Nashville Noise without them. And maybe it's why she bristles at the sound of Birdie's name. Maybe it's why we never had any music in our house growing up except when Granddaddy came over.

Birdie returns with my toiletries bag. "I packed your toothbrush and face soap. You don't wear contacts, do you?"

"No." I take the bag. "What's this for?"

Birdie hunts through her cupboards. "Well . . . Ah, here it is." She pulls out a 1960s-green thermos and fills it with coffee. Then she butters the toast and wraps it with a paper towel. "Off you go."

"To where?"

She shoves me off the stool. "Grab your bag." At the front door, she hands me the thermos, the toast, my keys, and my purse. "Go home. Talk to your momma."

I jerk away from her touch. "No, Birdie, I want you to tell me. She's been lying to me for twenty-five years."

Birdie taps the picture with her spearlike fingernail. "She won't now."

21

I barrel down Main Street toward Whisper Hollow Road a few minutes before eight a.m. Careening into our driveway, I skid to a stop just shy of the willow tree.

Jacked up on a thermos of coffee, I've had two highway hours to mull this over. I'm good and mad.

With Mr. Chastain's picture in one hand, my guitar in the other, I stride toward the porch, muttering, "Lord, Momma, better tell me the truth."

The kitchen screen slams behind me as I enter. Momma whirls around, hand over her heart. "Oh, Robin Rae, you scared me. Land sakes, girl, what are you doing here?" She takes a step toward me, her forehead wrinkled.

Daddy rises from the table where he's nursing a cup of coffee. "Everything all right?"

My boot heels thud against the hardwood. I drop my guitar case on the kitchen table and snap open the buckles.

"Play." I thrust my old Taylor at Momma, trembling so bad the guitar shimmies.

"For crying out loud, Robin. Get that out of my face. What on earth?"

Daddy sips his coffee, watching.

I grit my teeth. "Play it, Momma."

Momma stares me down with one hand on her waist and the other resting on the edge of the sink. Suds drip from her wrist onto the floor. "I don't know what kind of foolishness you're up to, Robin, but I know this—" She turns to the sink and starts washing the skillet.

"Momma!" I screech from the core of my being. "Play it." I stomp my heel against the floor.

"Dean, are you going to let her talk to me this way?"

Daddy looks between us. "Robin, watch your tone. Your momma deserves respect. I don't care if you are grown—mind yourself."

"Yes, Daddy." A sudden drop in my adrenaline leaves me weak and wobbly.

"Bit, I reckon you'd better do as she asks. *If* she asks you nicely."

"Dean!" Momma whips around, splattering water all over. The old skillet clatters to the floor.

Daddy tips up his coffee cup for the last drop. "This don't concern me, Bit." He puts his cup in the suds, then stoops to pick up the skillet.

"It does so concern you, Dean." Momma's eyes narrow and her lips pale.

I back away, feeling like I've jerked a tiger by the tail and am about to lose my arm.

"Bit," Daddy says softly, "she asked you to play a little guitar. That ain't so bad, is it?"

"Momma." I walk closer. "Please play."

The tip of her nose and the high angles of her cheeks redden. She wipes her hands on a faded dishtowel and takes the guitar.

Without a word of excuse or explanation, she balances the instrument on her knee, and with ease and beauty, she plays the most haunting melody I've ever heard.

My mind is stirred with an image of young lovers torn apart. Her fingers move up and down the fret as if she'd played every day of her life.

When she finishes, she hands me the guitar. "You happy?"

"No, I'm not. Why didn't you tell me you could play? That was beautiful."

"You knew your granddaddy taught me. For pity sake, he taught you. And you knew about the Lukeman Sisters."

"But, I didn't *know*, Momma. What's the big secret? How come you never played for us kids? How come we never had music in the house?"

"Bit, go on. Tell her."

Momma nails Daddy to the wall with a hard look. "Dean, please . . ."

"Tell her," he urges with his gentle voice, smoothing his big hands along her slight shoulders.

"Will this help to get things started?" I hand Momma the photo from Mr. Chastain's wall.

With a fleeting glance, she rolls her head back and lifts her hands. "Oh, heaven help us, Robin, where did you get this? Did Birdie give this to you? I knew it, I knew it."

"No, in fact, she didn't. I saw it when I was cleaning Mr. Chastain's office. Nashville Noise is one of Marc's customers."

"Of all things . . . Dean?" Momma's eyes seem to plead with him to get her out of this situation.

"Go on, Bit."

"I found this too." I bring out the torn photo from the attic. "It was sticking out of the side of your old trunk. I'm sorry, it tore."

She pinches the edges between her finger and thumb, and a very slight smile plays across her lips. "I was looking in the trunk before you left. I always liked this picture. Remember Burt Michaels, Dean?"

"I do."

I pull up a chair. "Do you want to tell me what happened?"

Momma pieces the torn photo together. "I dropped out of high school at seventeen and ran off to Nashville with my head full of dreams. Your granddaddy was madder than a hornet and demanded I come home, but I refused. Lynette and Carol were angry because I left them. We were about to sign a gospel deal with a producer over in Muscle Shoals."

"Thus the silent feud."

Momma smoothes her hands down her hips. "The lure of fame makes people crazy."

"Did it make you crazy?"

"In a manner of speaking. I'd met Birdie during a fair tour. We became instant friends. She was older, wiser—a star. I wanted to go where she was going. So, I left the Lukeman Sisters and moved to Nashville. Birdie had a nice place in Forrest Hills in those days."

"Why didn't you tell me any of this?"

"It was a long time ago . . ."

"In a land far, far away?"

"Don't be fresh." Momma pats her curls into place.

"Is this why you were so against me moving to Nashville?"

Momma doesn't answer at first, then mutters, "I reckon so."

Daddy moves to the wall phone by the door. "Gary, it's Dean. I'm gonna be a while . . . Not sure . . . Be along soon as I can . . . Thanks."

"Why would you get in my way? Because things didn't work out for you?"

Momma jerks a chair away from the table and plops down. "Good heavens, no. I want you to do what your heart tells you to do."

"Is it me? Or are we talking in circles? You want me to fol-low my heart, but you want me to stay home at the same time?"

Daddy pours another cup of coffee. "Your momma did make it in Nashville, Robin. In fact, she sang backup on one of Grace Harding's albums. She's the beautiful echo on 'Living Without You.'"

My mouth drops. The song is a cover band classic. "*You're* the famous echo?"

Her lips twitch, and she folds her fingers together so tight the tips turn white. "Guilty."

I can't believe it. I just can't believe it.

"Nashville Noise planned on releasing her solo album in 1981." Daddy stirs in his sugar.

Momma cradles her chin in her hand. "I thought I owned the world."

"So, where's this album?"

Momma glances away. "I didn't finish recording it. My heart got broken, and I came home." She smiles weakly. "Ain't that a country classic?"

"Who broke your heart, Momma? Did you and Birdie fight over someone?"

"No, no. Birdie was a good friend. The best, but . . ." She gazes toward the door. "It was a long time ago and not important now."

"Not important?" I peek at Daddy, hoping he'll spill more of the beans, but he doesn't. "So a guy broke your heart? Why did you quit?"

"You know there's no accounting for actions of the broken hearted."

I sit back. This is amazing. My momma, a James Chastain protégé. How different my life as a songwriter would be if Momma's broken heart hadn't driven her home. "Why didn't you go back? I'm sure Nashville Noise would've—"

"I fell in love with your daddy," Momma says. "We got married, had you, then Eliza and Steve. Next thing I know, you're all grown, trotting off to chase your own dreams."

I edge around the table and kneel beside her. "Momma, thank you for telling me."

She kisses my forehead gently. "You're welcome. Don't let no sweet-talking man break your heart, hear me?"

"I won't. I promise."

Daddy sets his coffee cup in the sink. "I'm going on to the plant." He kisses Momma, then me.

We watch him drive off, standing shoulder to shoulder on the back porch. Slate gray clouds weep a gentle rain. The grass is wet and green, the air fresh and sweet.

"Did you have breakfast?" Momma asks in the next minute.

"No, and I'm starved. Eggs sound good."

"Come on, then."

Momma retrieves the skillet from the dish drain and scrambles up some eggs while I perk another pot of coffee. At this rate, I won't sleep for a week.

"What happened between you and Birdie?" I sit at the table and reach for the *Freedom Rings* front page.

"Oh, she went on with her life, me with mine. I don't have to tell you people drift apart."

I look up from the headline: "Target Store To Break Ground." "Drift? You act like you never knew each other. She saw that torn picture of you and never said a word."

"Leave it be, Robin."

I suppose we've done all the soul bearing we're going to do for today. When Momma hands me my breakfast, I offer up the wisdom of twenty-five years. "Everyone makes mistakes."

She jerks open the silverware drawer for a fork. "Some mistakes hurt innocent people, and no matter how hard you pray, they can't be undone."

While I eat, Momma washes the skillet and starts a load of laundry, giving me an update on the town, telling stories about her friends.

"And, Robin, I like to have died when Henna talked prim and proper Sissy into riding a horse for the Founder's Day parade." Momma laughs with her hand on her middle. "She sat atop the horse wearing white gloves, her back as stiff as Custer's at the last stand."

Momma is light hearted, almost floating. I do believe the Nashville Noise confession cut a weight from her soul.

"But the horse trotted off the parade route, and Sissy couldn't get him back in line. The whole time, she's bouncing and listing to one side, hollering, 'Henna, you crazy woman, putting me on this crazy horse.'" Momma wipes her eyes. "Oh, my."

I laugh with her. "Only in Freedom."

By now the rain has stopped, and Momma hurries out to tend her garden before the next rain cloud bursts. I wash my dishes, watching out the window as a thick water droplet stretches down from the porch eaves. Now that the dust has settled, I'm wore out.

In my old room, I crash face-first into a pile of pillows. Birdie must have anticipated an emotional meltdown or something. Otherwise, why pack my overnight bag? She underestimated the stamina of the McAfee-Lukeman women. I'll go home after dinner and, if I'm not fired, go to work in the morning.

Dialing Marc, I leave a voice message apologizing for my abrupt exit, promising to explain later—and return the picture. Pressing *End*, I toss my cell onto the nightstand and flop over on my back, staring at the ceiling. My room is layered with memories. The walls are privy to my dreams and tears, laughter and songs.

Momma. An original Nashville Noise artist. Who'd have thought? Mercy almighty. What else you got in your bag of tricks, Momma?

Words form in my head, so I reach for my notebook, the idea of a song sparking energy.

She left her daddy's world, barely seventeen,
With dreams in her heart, to a place she'd never been . . .

Grabbing my guitar, I decide to work out the song on the front porch. An hour later, I'm frustrated, and my notebook is filling up with scratched out lyrics.

Momma comes out with the prettiest Gibson I've ever seen and trades me for my old Taylor.

"Your tempo feels a little too fast for the lyrics. It's bumping going to the chorus from the verse." She settles in the rocker next to me with my guitar on her knee.

"Momma, where did you get this?" I run my fingertips along the smooth, polished red grain of the Gibson.

"Gibson gave them to all the Nashville Noise artists our first year."

"You hid this away for twenty-six years?"

She flashes a sly grin. "I parted with Nashville Noise, but not that guitar." Her smile is like the one in the torn picture. Carefree. "Once in awhile, I'd get it out and sing to your daddy."

I start strumming. "Liza used to tell me she heard music at night. I told her ghosts lived in the attic."

Momma pops my knee with her fingers and laughs a hearty, feel-good laugh. *Hello, who are you, and what have you done with my mother?* "Do you know how many nights she came crawling into bed with Daddy and me, scared half to death?"

"Oops, sorry." I point at my song notebook. "So, what's wrong with my melody?"

As white clouds float across the blue afternoon, Momma and I write a song about a girl who followed her dream and found life didn't turn out as she'd planned. But God was still in control. The song is part her and part me.

Momma's got some pipes. A little bit of diva going on. We sing so loud, and with so much soul, Mo and Curly point their noses north and howl. I about fall out of the rocker, guffawing, as Mo shifts his brown eyes at me as if to ask, "Is this right?"

Momma slaps her palm on the arm of the rocker. "Put to shame by a hound. Don't that beat all?" She stands and swaps my Taylor back for her Gibson. Guess if she didn't part with it twenty-six years ago, she isn't parting with it now. "I'll take the howling as my cue to quit and get to fixing supper."

"I'm heading out afterward."

"I figured as much." She pauses at the screen door. "I hope you can forgive me, Robin."

"For hiding a broke heart? Of course. I only wish I'd known sooner."

"Well—" She hesitates, gazing at me, her lips quivering. "Better get to supper." The screen door claps shut behind her.

22

Skyler, Blaire, and I finally have movie night at my place around mid-August. The goal? Introduce Blaire to hick chick movies like *Jeremiah Johnson* and *Outlaw Josey Wales*. She wanted to rent *In Her Shoes*, to which I said, "Over my dead body."

"Still no update on Lee Rivers?" Skyler tosses a bag of popcorn in my microwave.

"You tell me. Any more 'Brad About You' blurbs?"

Skyler shakes her head. "Nope, but I heard from a lawyer friend that Janie settled her dispute with her record label."

"Really?" I decide we need more pillows. "When?"

"Two weeks ago, maybe?"

I open the closet and pull out the pillows Momma sent with me in May. "Guess I won't be having coffee with Lee after all."

"Sorry, cousin."

I shrug. "We had one date and a lot of chemistry. No big deal. Easy come, easy go." But deep down, my heart accuses my lips of lying. I wanted more than one afternoon with Lee Rivers.

"What's up with you and Graham?" Blaire asks from her spot on the floor where she's setting up to polish her nails.

"Nothing. He's been acting weird ever since we came back from Freedom." I hand a pillow to Blaire and she stuffs it behind her back.

"Maybe it's because you laughed at his kiss," Skyler suggests. "Which, by the way, was wise of you."

I plump a pillow on the sofa for myself. "No, it's not the kiss. We've met a few times to work on songs, but we ended up arguing about lyrics and melodies. Honestly, if he's working with Frank and Danny, why does he need me?"

"Have you written any new songs?" Blaire pops open a Diet Pepsi.

"As a matter of fact . . . Kim Flowers helped me fine-tune the one I wrote with Momma, She Was Seventeen. I think I'm ready to brave Susan West at ASCAP again."

Blaire scoops her dark hair back from her face. "'She Was Seventeen'? How very Janis Ian of you."

"I think so." I hold up the DVDs. "Which one first? Redford or Eastwood?"

"Redford," Blaire says, with Skyler agreeing.

I pop in *Jeremiah Johnson.* "You're gonna love this movie, Blaire."

"What if I don't?"

Ten minutes into the movie, Blaire admits the scenery is breathtaking, but she hates that Jeremiah is a trapper, "It's so cruel." Then she screams when he comes up on a frozen man.

"If you can't watch like a grown-up, I'm going to have to put you in the other room," Skyler declares, arching a piece of popcorn over my head toward Blaire.

"There is no other room," Blaire says with a laugh, ducking the popcorn.

"If I met a mountain man who looked like Robert Redford, I'd follow him to the highest peaks," I decide, dumping a handful of popcorn in my mouth.

"I'd *so* be a mountain woman," Skyler agrees.

Blaire strokes dark red polish on her toenails. "You're crazy. He'd probably smell like horse manure on a hot day. His teeth would be rotten and his fingernails caked with dried blood and dirt." She wrinkles her nose as if she actually smells the manure. "Look at the old bear-hunting man Jeremiah ran into. Trust me, it takes a skilled stylist to make Redford look so messy, yet astoundingly sexy."

Skyler points at Blaire. "She makes a good case."

Blaire taps my leg. "Robin, I found this great Bible verse the other day. 'Perfect love casts out all fear.' Isn't that great?"

I grin. "Very excellent verse, Blaire."

"Shhh, we missed the beginning of the wedding scene." Skyler jerks the remote from my hand and rewinds.

Blaire whispers, "Her last date with Trey didn't go so well."

"Quiet, Redford is talking." Skyler gestures with the remote.

"Sorry about Trey," I say in her ear.

She shrugs. "No biggy. He likes quieter women."

I choke on my popcorn.

When *Jeremiah Johnson* is over, Skyler stretches and suggests, "Let's get ice cream, then watch *Josey Wales*."

I hop up. "You drive."

Blaire runs her hands over her face with a muffled moan. "I don't know how much of this I can take. Jeremiah ends up alone. This is not even close to a chick movie. Not even a hick chick."

Skyler stands by the door. "*Josey Wales* is even better."

"I bet." Blaire pushes off the sofa. "I'm getting my own carton of Ben & Jerry's."

We thunder downstairs, carrying on like a bunch of high school girls at a slumber party night.

"What's all the commotion?" Birdie meets us in the foyer.

"Going to Harris Teeter for ice cream. Wanna come?" I sling my arm over her shoulders.

"Let me grab my wallet." She hurries up the stairs with her elbows cranking up and down.

By the time we pull into the parking lot, we're all riled up. Birdie sent us over the edge with a Robert Redford story.

"He kissed my cheek the first year I went to the Sundance Festival."

"No way," Skyler says with a gasp of air. "Which cheek? What was it like? Soft? Tender? Take-me-I'm-yours? What?"

Birdie views Skyler through narrowed eyes. "Simmer down, girl. It was a peck on the cheek. Pity sakes. He was married." She looks at me. "Are you sure you want her hanging around?"

I shrug. "She's family. What can I do?"

"I suppose. We all have our weird ones."

We clump through the front doors around eleven p.m. No one is milling about, and our voices seem like explosions in the quiet atmosphere.

Birdie grabs a shopping buggy. "Get in." She motions to me.

"What?" *Get in?*

"Get in." She points to the empty basket.

"I'm not getting in there."

"Skyler, Blaire," Birdie calls. "Get a buggy."

"Why? What are we doing?" Blaire yanks one free from the row.

Birdie bugs out her eyes and leans over the handle. "Buggy races. Used to have them all the time when I worked at Kroger."

The three of us gawk at her. She's crazy.

"Get in," she orders.

I grab the buggy and whirl it around. "If we're going to do this, you get in. I'll race."

"Nothing doing. I'm driving," Birdie insists, motioning for Skyler to climb into her buggy too. Which she does, tucking her knees under her chin.

I glance at Blaire's long, muscular legs. We don't stand a chance. "This isn't fair . . . Got an old woman as my runner . . ." I mutter.

Birdie whacks me on the back of my head. "I'll have you know I ran the 440 in fifty-six seconds flat in high school." She and Blaire push us through the produce department.

"That was thirty-five years ago," I counter. "You've aged some."

"Blaire, you and Skyler race the back aisle. Robin and I'll race down the front. First one to the ice cream wins. Losers buy."

Why do I even bother talking?

"Can you get down lower, Robin? Less wind resistance."

I grip the sides of the buggy and duck down. "Gee whiz, how fast you planning on running?"

"Just hang on."

Gazing down aisle three to the back of the store, I see Blaire, in her shorts and flip flops, bent over her buggy. Like me, Skyler is folded below the top of the cart. Birdie raises her arm to signal the start.

My heartbeat thumps in my ears. "Come on, Birdie," I say with gritted teeth. "Let's smoke 'em." I glance around to give her the thumbs up. She's beaming, and she looks so young in her skirt and . . . *Whoa.* I stand in the cart. "Birdie, you can*not* run in those shoes."

"Time out," she hollers to Blaire, lowering her arm, gazing down at her feet. "Why not?"

"They're, they're . . . What are they? Big, thick, wooden clunky things."

"They're called mules. Now sit down."

I sit. "You can't run in those."

"Watch me."

Help. The woman is crazy. I thread my fingers through the thin rods of the buggy's frame. A song flits through my head:

Steppenwolf's "Born to Be Wild." Not sure the songwriter had buggy racing in mind.

"Ready," Birdie calls, raising her arm again.

"Ready," Blaire echoes.

Birdie drops her arm with a "Go!" and charges forward. Her foot slips, jerking the cart to the right. My chin crashes against a jagged edge.

"Ouch." I touch my chin and blood dots my fingertips. But no time for doctoring. "Come on, Birdie. They're ahead."

Behind me, Birdie huffs and puffs as she races down the aisle. The heels of her mules beat against the tile floor with a rapid *clump-clank-clump-clank*.

Around aisle ten, we nose ahead and then finally round the corner toward dairy and frozen foods. Next thing I know, *wham!* Birdie crashes smack dab into . . . Lee Rivers.

"Whoa!" He doubles over the cart with an *oomph*. The contents of his little basket fly in the air and scatter down the aisle. His nose stops a millimeter from mine.

"Well, look at what's on sale this week," I say, even though my heart is about to leap out of my chest and smack him on the lips.

"Hang on, kids," Birdie hollers as she *clump-clanks* around the corner. "That rascal Blaire has such long legs." Birdie's mules flip through the air. One to the right, one to the left. She puts her nose down and, with a war cry, forges ahead with Lee and me riding along.

"How're you?" Lee asks, all serious, like riding bent over a grocery cart is an everyday event.

"F-fine." Dern, he makes my toes tingle.

He looks over his shoulder. "Come on, Birdie, you're almost there."

"I'd be there if I didn't have you hanging onto my buggy, you big lug."

She's so intent on winning and Lee is so . . . bent over the buggy. I can't help it; I laugh. He could've hopped off, but he hung on for the ride.

He peers at me through squinted eyes. "You think this is funny?"

My skin prickles. "Yeah, I do."

He touches my bleeding chin. "You're wounded."

We whiz past the yogurt and cottage cheese, but not before Skyler and Blaire arrive at the ice cream.

"Well, Robin, I did what I could." Birdie hunches over, winded and gasping. "But we didn't win."

Lee climbs off the cart and helps me out. He doesn't let go when my feet hit the floor.

Didn't win? Wanna bet?

While Blaire charms the Harris Teeter manager, begging forgiveness—the Entenmann's display was in an awkward spot—Lee lends me his handkerchief for my chin.

"Won't even notice it tomorrow," he says.

At the checkout, Birdie pays for the ice cream and promises the manager to never, ever race a buggy again.

"Scouts' honor," she says, but I see her crossed fingers behind her back.

I whisper over her shoulder. "I'm on to you."

Lee walks with me to Skyler's car. "Can I drive you home?"

"Lee's bringing me home," I call to my girls. As far as I'm concerned, girl's night is over. Skyler waves to me like she'd expect nothing less and would give me the dickens if I didn't go off with him.

Blaire, meanwhile, asks Birdie, "How'd you get so freakishly fast?"

On the drive home, Lee and I chitchat. *How are you? Fine,*

and you? But once we pull into Birdie's, we hang back while the girls *flip-flop* and *clump-clank* up the porch steps.

"So . . ." I say, moving slowly up the walk. My insides shimmy, and my bones rattle like I'm cold.

"So," Lee echoes. "I'm glad I ran into you."

"I think we ran into you." I brush my fingers through my bangs and wonder for the first time all night if I look all right. Hope there's no popcorn stuck in my teeth.

He laughs. "Guess you did."

"Do you want to sit?" I ask, taking one of Birdie's big rockers.

Lee settles in the rocker next to mine, his clean fragrance reminding me of summer nights up in the hills after a slow rain.

"I thought about you a lot," he mutters, putting his chair into motion.

"Yeah? I always look for you at church. You've missed a few Sundays."

He reaches over and grabs my rocker, sliding it across the porch, closer to him. "My ex found a new church, so I went with her until she felt comfortable."

"Must be some ex-fiancé to get this much attention from you."

He slips his fingers through mine. "You know it's Janie Leeds, don't you?"

I look him in the eye. "I read about her in Brad Schmitt's column."

"I figured." He starts the rocker swaying, back and forth, his fingers still gripping mine. "I didn't want to make a big deal about it, Robin."

"Too late—dating Janie Leeds is a big deal."

He rests his head on the back of the rocker. "From the outside, I guess it might seem like a big deal."

"How'd you meet?"

"I built her manager's new house. She'd just come off a

world tour and wanted to settle down. I'd finally gotten my business to a place where it didn't consume me 24/7. We met, hit it off. It seemed like providence at first."

"She's beautiful, isn't she?" My words catch.

"Yes." He glances over at me. "But why does it matter?"

"Because she captured your heart."

"She did, for awhile."

"You asked her to marry you." For the first time, I feel the weight of those words, *Will you marry me?*

"Janie's a lyrical, magical person. She has this unique ability to make people love her. It's one of the reasons she's so popular with the public."

I slide out of the rocker and prop my shoulder against the stone porch post. "Lyrical? Magical? Those are powerful words. Are you sure you're over her?"

"Long over her. Before I met you." Lee leans forward and gazes beyond me into the night. "We said our final good-bye two weeks ago."

"I see." I can't look at him, because all my senses are going crazy trying to figure out what to think, how to feel, how to be.

"I didn't call," he starts, "because I wanted to clear my head, make sure *she* had finally moved on."

"Oh."

He gets up and walks over to me. "I can't change the fact that we were engaged, Robin. But what about you? Have you moved on? What about your guy back home?"

"We ended things Fourth of July. But Lee, when Ricky asked me to marry him, I said no. He's not lyrical and magical. More like kind but ornery. And he has a unique ability to draw people close and then irritate the crap out of them."

He laughs and leans against the porch rail, arms crossed. "Lyrical, magical people can be irritating, too. There's no denying I fell for Janie, but Robin, we weren't meant to be."

Well, I'm stubborn, but not stupid. I scoot over and rest lightly against him. "I'm glad you're here."

"Me too. Glad I needed toilet paper and dish soap."

Skyler pokes her head out the door. "You two want some ice cream?"

"No," we answer, arms still touching.

"Robin, it's over between Janie and me."

"How do I know she won't suddenly need you again?" Without actually saying it, I want him to get how it feels to be me after he's dated the beautiful, talented, *lyrical* artist Janie.

He slips his arm around my waist. My heart beats faster. "You don't. You have to trust me."

Smoothing my hands down the soft cotton of his shirt, I remind him, "Trust is earned."

"I suppose it is." He pulls me closer so my cheek rests against his chest. We hold each other for a few minutes, but too soon, Lee says, "I should get going. It's late."

I swallow. "Yeah, I suppose."

He stops at the edge of the porch steps. "So, are you available for coffee?"

I cross my arms and twist my lips into a sly grin. He remembered. "Yeah, I'm available for coffee."

23

Lee and I join Skyler, Blaire, Walt, and Birdie at the Green Hills Grille for after-church lunch the second Sunday in September.

"Hey, everyone." I reach for the chair next to Blaire, but she blocks me.

"I'm saving this for Ezra." She blushes.

"Well, well, excuse me." Turns out the Harris Teeter manager, Ezra Longoria, is a good man who charmed Blaire's heart. Why else would she switch from being a Methodist to a Baptist? They've been dating ever since our buggy race.

The server takes our drink order, and the lunch conversation is lively and fun. Birdie and Walt have signed a deal to write songs with Eric Exley for a new pop-country singer he's producing, Juli Love.

"No guarantees, you know," Birdie tells us, minimizing her newfound success, "but we're having fun."

Lee drapes his arm around the back of my chair, stroking my arm with his thumb as if to remind me he's there. I settle against him and listen as Walt asks about renovating a room in his home for a recording studio.

The second table conversation is Skyler rattling on about her latest client, who signed a mega-deal with Curb Records.

"Speaking of singing," Birdie jumps in, nudging me, "are you ready for your writer's night debut at the Bluebird? I know it's not until November, but . . ."

I reach for the ketchup bottle, trying to ignore the spazzing butterflies in my middle. "I'm ready, I think. Maybe." I pound the bottom of the bottle with the heel of my hand. "How will I know? Fear is so unpredictable."

Walt chuckles with a light shake of his head. "I remember the first time I heard Birdie singing."

In one accord, we all angle toward Walt. "Do tell," I say.

"Hush, Walt," Birdie protests, patting him on the hand. "They don't need to know ancient history—"

"A bunch of us had gone out to Kris Kristofferson's place for fun and food. Guess it was around '71. Ain't that right, Birdie?"

"This is your story, Walt. Now don't be asking me."

I catch her eye. Yeah, it was '71.

"Anyway, Guy Clark, Johnny Cash, Ray Price, Harlan Howard, and Willie Nelson were there. Lots of other friends and folks. Naturally, we get to pulling guitars, sitting around playing and singing. Willie does his own version of 'Crazy.'" He nudges Birdie with a wink.

"I love that song," Skyler says.

"Apparently, so did Birdie," Walt says, his grey eyes snapping playfully.

Birdie props her chin in her hand. "Do tell, Walt Henry, if you know so much."

Walt kisses her cheek, then goes on with his story. "Well, we played and hummed along with Willie, then out of nowhere came this *voice*." Walt holds his hands apart. "This giant voice."

"Oh, please, now you're exaggerating." Birdie drums her fingers on the tabletop.

"We started craning our necks, you know," Walt says, "Who's brought the pipes to the party? It was this little blonde girl with eyes the size of golf balls."

Birdie slaps his shoulder. "Golf balls?"

"We stopped playing, but she just kept on singing. When she realized she was the show, her face turned all beet red, but we gave her a standing ovation." Walt laughs. "Saw her again about two years later. She'd just signed with RCA."

Something about the story ignites my courage. An inkling, but courage none the less. "Must have been an incredible night, Birdie. How'd you get invited?"

"A songwriter friend of mine. He left town the next year, but his invitation changed my life. Through folks at that barbecue, I met the legendary Chet Atkins, who was then running RCA Nashville."

"Studio B," I mutter, "when did you switch to Nashville Noise?"

"When James formed the company, I'd ended my deal with RCA, was looking for something new, and he convinced me I needed to go with him. He produced my first platinum album."

In one accord, we all sit back. *Shew.*

"Robin," Walt starts, reaching for his tea, "you keep fighting. Dig deep for that song only you can write. Tell a great story in a unique way, then wrap it all up with a sweet melody. You'll be begging to get up on that stage."

I wince. "Gee, Walt, is that all?"

"Mark my words. And listen, cowriting is great, but don't stop working it out on your own. Develop your writing. Believe me, you'll get there."

From his lips to God's ears.

Lee pulls in behind me at Birdie's and waves me over to his
rolled-down window. "Let's go downtown."

"Why?" Lunch at the Green Hill Grille was good, but now
I'm sleepy, ready for my Sunday afternoon nap.

"I want to show you something."

I grin and prop my arm on the door. "Can I trust you?"

Lee brushes my cheek with the back of his hand. "I think
you can."

"Okay, but be warned, I know ka-ra-tay." I jump back and
hold my hands like Jackie Chan.

He laughs. "Get in."

We cruise down Demonbreun in the easy, Sunday-afternoon
traffic and park behind the Country Music Hall of Fame.

"This is my surprise? A trip to the Hall of Fame?" I ask,
walking along the side of the great building.

"Yep, this is it. Your destiny."

I bump him with my shoulder. "Right." A quote etched
in one of the foundation stones stops me. "'A good country
song takes a page out of somebody's life and puts it to music.
Conway Twitty.'"

Lee wraps his arms around me and reads another quote
over my shoulder. "'Country music isn't a guitar, it isn't a banjo,
it isn't a melody, it isn't a lyric. It's a feeling. Waylon Jennings.'"

"Those are the types of songs I want to write, adding in a
dash of God's true love and hope."

"You will," Lee says, and leads me inside the Hall, where
he buys two tickets. Together we journey through the history
of the world's best music.

"Imagine how it must feel to play music of your heart and
soul," I say, reading an exhibit about the Carter family. "Then
have it shape a generation."

"Pretty amazing." Lee gazes down at me. "Just think—one
day, it'll be you."

I peer into his eyes to see if he's teasing, figuring a man might say sweet-nothings to a girl he's wooing. "Do you know something I don't know?"

"Yes, you're special." Lee takes my hand. "After being around Janie and people in the business, I can recognize the will-bes from the wannabes."

"And I'm a will-be?"

He nods. "The day I met you at Birdie's, I knew you were different."

"Like a freak-of-nature different, or what?"

"No." He laughs and shuffles me off to the next display. "You're like a cool breeze in a stale, hot room. A budding rose in the desert."

"Budding rose in the desert. Very nice." I tug my notebook from my pocket. *Cool breeze . . . budding rose . . .* "Maybe *you* should be the songwriter."

"Can't sing, can't rhyme, can't play." He bends down as if he's going to kiss me, but doesn't. Since the night on Birdie's porch, we've hung out a dozen times, But still no taste of his lips.

"I sure hope you're right." I slip my notebook back into my pocket, then wrap my arm around his waist and lean against him as we walk past the black-and-white exhibit of the early Opry days.

"Do you want to be in the Hall someday?"

I glance around. "I thought I *was* in the Hall."

"Ha, funny girl, you know what I mean."

Facing a picture of DeFord Bailey posing with his harmonica, I confess. "I reckon none of these folks played music with the idea of being famous in mind. They just did what they loved. That's what I want to do—and stand before God confident I used the gift He gave me. If I go on to do something grand like impacting a generation with my songs, that's His business."

"See, that's why you're different. Fame is not important

to you," Lee says, adding a whistle as we come up on a gold Cadillac. "Can you picture Elvis behind the wheel?" He stoops to see inside the legend's gold-plated car.

"Too *rico* for me." My eye catches the display of well-played, well-worn guitars, and I move on.

We finish the early-history side and mosey around to the present-day side. There's a whole showcase devoted to Nashville Noise and the legendary James Chastain.

"Lee, here's a picture of Birdie. And my momma." I tap the Plexiglas, squinting. Momma will faint when I tell her the original photo of the Nashville Noise artists is in the Hall.

Lee props his hands on his knees. He looks at me, then back at the picture. "Who's this, now?" He wrinkles his forehead.

"See the woman with the dark curls and enormous smile? Right there next to James Chastain? That's my momma."

Lee stares at the infamous image, glances back at me, then at the photo again. "That's your mom next to James Chastain?"

"Yep."

"Have you met him?" Lee straightens up and rests his elbow on my head.

I squirm out from under the weight of his arm. "Oh, sure, I stop in his office every morning for tea and cakes right after I clean his toilets."

"He strikes me as more of a coffee-and-donuts kind of guy." Lee ganders at the picture one more time. Then, I don't know, loses his mind or something because he sticks his wet finger in my ear.

I yelp and jerk away. "What are you doing? You can't give me a wet willy." I rub my ear, then snatch his hand and bend back his wrist. "What's wrong with you?"

His expression is one of *Who, me?*

I release him. "Wipe that look off your face, you don't fool me. Let's move on, and keep your hands to yourself."

Next is the Dolly Parton and Porter Wagner exhibit. One of Dolly's original outfits hangs behind the glass. "Lee, look how tiny she was."

"Yeah, tiny. Not the word I'd use, but hey . . ." He attempts another wet willy.

I slap his hand away. "Stop." I hunch up my shoulders to protect my ears and hurry to the next exhibit.

Lee saunters up behind me. "What's this Chastain guy's relationship to your family?"

I feel his hand slip over my shoulder. I walk away. "He discovered Momma and signed her as one of his new artists." A wet finger touches my ear.

I whirl around and pop him on the arm. "Did you treat Janie this way? Sheez."

"She's less of a sport than you."

"Cut it out or I'll take you down."

He gawks at me. "You and who else?"

In one smooth move, I swing my foot around with all the weight of my five-foot-four body (it's my one ka-ra-tay move) and cut Lee off at the ankles. He hits the floor right on his sass. I stand over him. "Don't need anyone else."

He guffaws and hops up. "Oh, it's on now, missy."

"Ack!" I skedaddle toward the stairs and jigger down to the main floor with Lee skeddaddling after me.

Once we're outside in the September sun, Lee swoops me up and tosses me over his shoulder, smacking my rump.

"Help!" I scream and kick. "Help!"

"Quiet down. People will think you're serious."

"I am serious." I pinch his derriere.

He leaps forward as if he can actually get away from my pinchers. But where he goes, I go, dangling down his back like a sack of feed.

"Hey, no touching that . . . area."

"You slapped mine."

He jogs across Broadway at the light and heads up Fifth. "All right, new rule: hands off." He sets me down and wags his finger at me. "No touching . . . for any reason."

I stick out my hand. "Deal."

He shakes. "Deal." But he doesn't let go of my hand. "Robin, I do want to kiss you." His voice is husky.

All the noise of downtown Nashville fades. I can only hear, see, think, feel one word: *kiss.* "Who's stopping you?"

He dips his head and kisses me, intensely and passionately, wrapping his arms around my back. It's not a Ricky-kiss where I feel part wanted and part slimed.

When he releases me an "Oh, man," rushes from my soul. His lips taste like I'd hoped. Firm but sweet.

"Oh, man?" He brushes his hand over my hair. "Is that good?"

"It ain't bad." I rest my forehead against his broad chest, catching my breath.

Without asking this time, he kisses me again. "You really are amazing, Robin. And beautiful." The sun is behind him, casting his shadow over me.

Holy molie. Can't. Breathe. Lee is the best thing that's happened to me in a long time in the man department, but his actions . . . today . . . in downtown Nashville knock me off kilter.

He chuckles and steps back. "I've been trying to figure out how and when to kiss you and—"

"I liked the kiss. And what better place than across from the Hall of Fame?"

He laughs. "How about ice cream to seal the deal?"

"Not McDonald's again."

"Nope, something better."

Dubious of his ice cream expertise, I follow Lee to Dixieland Delights, where he buys a couple of cones with two scoops of chocolate.

"Now this is good ice cream," I say, wandering downtown with him. We look in shop windows, sharing our favorite summertime memories.

I pause outside Gruhn Guitars and peer through the window. "One of these days, I'm going to walk in there and say, 'Give me the best you got.'"

"I'm sure you will." Lee bites into his cone.

Walking on, we stop in at Tootsie's for a short listen to the band while I finish my ice cream.

The sun is sinking beneath the skyline as we walk back to Lee's truck. I decide we need a song. About Lee. I hum a little tune. "Lee, Lee with your eyes so green . . ."

"They're blue." He pops his eyes open wide.

"Is this your song?" I continue my impromptu lyrics. "You've got the biggest teeth I've ever seen."

"Ah, now, that's plain evil." He stretches his lips to cover his teeth.

I laugh and fish for my next line while walking backward in front of him. He steers out of the path of a couple pushing a stroller. "And I'm the luckiest girl, to have you in my world."

He nods. "I like it. Keep singing."

We round the corner of the Hall and head for the parking lot. "So, I'll keep you around, just for awhile, as long as you buy me ice-cream cones from Dixieland Delights."

He tips back his head and laughs. "Ladies and gentleman, you heard it here. Nashville's next hit song. Call the publishers. Call Martina, Faith, Trisha, and Carrie."

I walk on without him. "You're overworking it, Rivers."

He jogs up behind me, still laughing. We laugh a lot, Lee and I.

"So, what happened to your mom's deal with Nashville Noise?" he asks after we climb in the truck and buckle up.

"Apparently some guy broke her heart, and she went back home." I wipe my hands with an Armor All wipe.

"Who broke her heart?"

I shrug. "She didn't tell me."

"Robin," Lee starts, making his way toward home, his expression pinched, his tone serious, "do you think—"

My cell rings. "Hold that thought." I answer.

"Are you listening to Big 98?" Skyler blurts when I answer.

"No." I turn on Lee's radio. "Why are you screaming?"

"Robin, they're playing 'Your Country Princess.'"

24

We gather in Birdie's living room. Skyler, Walt, Lee, and me.
I'm trembling, pacing, fretting. Great day in the morning. A
veteran country artist, Emma Rice, recorded "Your Country
Princess." How? When? Who?

"Robin, who's heard 'Your Country Princess'?" Birdie asks.
"Anyone for some iced tea?"

When in crisis, please, serve up some sweet cold tea.

"I don't know, Birdie, I mean, I've sung it at a few open-
mike nights. But it's been awhile."

"Did you give a work tape to anyone? A lyric sheet?" Walt
takes over the questioning while Birdie runs to the kitchen.

"No, I haven't made a work tape, and the lyric sheet is in
my guitar case. Graham helped me rework the song a little
back in May when I first came to town, but—" Ah, hold it. I
wince. "Marty and I sang the song in Studio A at Nashville
Noise. Just goofing around, you know."

Walt stood, his eyebrows crinkled together. "Were they in
session?"

I crack my knuckles. "Yes, sorta. I think they'd taken a
break."

Walt lowers his chin. "Robin, your goofing-off could've been recorded."

"Are you serious? There wasn't anyone around. Well, we did hear a noise . . ."

Skyler walks in the middle of us, waving her hands. "This is pointless. You can't sue. It would be your word against the songwriter and all of the Emma Rice camp. She's making a comeback with SongTunes, and they aren't going to take a challenge lightly. I've butted with their lawyers before. Not pretty."

"But I am the songwriter, Skyler," I wail.

"Correction," Walt says. "Were the songwriter."

I sink to the ottoman. "You're right." My mouth is dryer than dirt. "Lee, do you know anything about this?"

He stiffens. "How would I know?"

"Well, you know Music Row people. Did you tell Janie—"

"No, Robin. I can't believe you'd even think such a thing. I heard the song once. Until today, I didn't even remember it." His stance is stiff.

"Stop." Skyler steps between us. "We can find out who the writer is without accusing people." She looks at me and whispers, "What's wrong with you?"

Walt suggests buying Emma's CD. "That'd answer our question of who wrote the song."

"We could run down to Davis-Kidd and buy it." I jump up with a glance around the room.

Skyler shakes her head. "Her CD's not out yet. I read in *Music Row* that it comes out next month. This song is her first single release."

Birdie hustles in with a tray of teas. "Here we go."

Walt pats my shoulder. "We'll find the writer before then, Robin. Enough of us in this room have Music Row connections. Right, Birdie? Robin?" He takes a glass of tea from Birdie, but doesn't take a sip.

"Right."

"Sure, shug, we'll find out." Birdie hands me a tall tea.

I smile at Walt. He's trying to be the calm, fatherly one. "Guess you're right, Walt. Thanks."

"Don't let this get you down now," he says, sitting next to me on the ottoman, patting my arm. "It ain't the end of the world."

"Right, just my first country cut and no one knows it." Who betrayed me? Marc Lewis? If the song did get recorded in the Nashville Noise studio, did James Chastain get a hold of it? Did they think it was a demo for one of Marc's songs?

Then there's the mysterious disappearance of one Marty Shultz, who says she was too old and too tired for a comeback. But perhaps it was all a ruse.

And not to be forgotten, the charming and schmoozing Graham Young, working deals with Frank Gruey and Danny Hayes. But he doesn't need my song, and I seriously doubt he's a backstabbing, low-down, song-stealing kind of guy.

I drop my head to my hands. Perhaps it was the butler in the kitchen with the candlestick. I'm clueless.

Skyler addresses Walt. "Do you know anyone in Emma's camp?"

He juts out his chin. "I have connections with SongTunes. I could give them a call tomorrow, ask around."

"Be careful, Walt. Don't let on it was stolen. They'll—" Skyler pops her hands together. "The Internet. Robin, we can look on Emma's Web site. Maybe there's a blurb about the songs, why she recorded them, who wrote it, blah, blah."

"Great idea." Birdie leads the way to her little office off the living room.

In no time, Skyler finds Emma's Web site. Sure enough, there's a whole gob of stuff dedicated to her new release, *Gentlemen Beware.*

The six of us hover around Birdie's twelve-inch laptop. Lee stands off to the side, watching and waiting. I gaze over at him. He arches his brows at me.

Skyler clicks through the web pages. "At least the thief had presence of mind to retitle the song. Emma's cut is 'I Wanna Be.'" She sighs and falls against the back of the chair. "You can listen to an MP3, but no lyrics or songwriters."

Can I cry? Better yet, can I punch someone? Emma Rice is singing my song, and she doesn't even know I'm alive.

I barge into the NSAI offices Monday afternoon and knock on the membership manager's door. "Jack, do you know who wrote Emma's new cut, 'I Wanna Be'?"

He frowns. "No. Why?"

"My song, 'Your Country Princess'—" Oh forget it. It's too tall a tale for even me to believe.

In the meeting room, several songwriters gather for a morning conference. Most of them are from out of town, so fifty bucks says they don't know who wrote Emma's new single either.

This is crazy. Who tossed a lasso at the moon with my song and landed an Emma Rice cut?

Skyler buzzes me on my cell. "I've called around. Left messages. So far, nothing. I checked with Chris Oglesby at Oglesby Songwriting Management. He said he'll get back to me."

I sigh. "Thanks, Sky."

"How are you?"

I pause. Yeah, how am I? Frustrated. Angry. "I'm fine. Call if you get any news." I flip my phone shut and wander into the computer room.

Is this situation really all that bad? So Emma Rice is belting out my song and doesn't know it. The Lord knows I'm the writer, and isn't that all that matters? It should be.

Right. Tell it to my pride. And my pocketbook. I plop my forehead down on the table. "This is rotten." But my cell rings again before I can swim too far out in the pity pool. When I go to answer, I see it's Arizona.

She screams. "The whole town is going nuts. Buttons popping all over the place."

"W-what are you talking about?" I can feel the blood draining from my face.

"Emma Rice recorded 'Your Country Princess.'" She screams again.

Oh my gosh.

"So, how'd it happen? Brilliant plan to surprise us. Scaredy-cat Robin McAfee moves to Nashville and sells her first song before the summer is out. Oh girl, you showed those naysayers. Sounds like Emma changed the chorus a lot, but I suppose they do that sort of thing. But, what a fabulous voice. A great comeback song. She's going to owe you big. Did you go to the studio when she recorded it? Robin, I'm shaking, and it's not even my song. How'd you keep it a secret—"

"Arizona, stop. I didn't sell the song."

"Huh? What do you mean? Emma wrote a song like yours?"

"No, someone sold it to her without my permission."

"You've got to be kidding. Who in all God's creation would stoop so low?"

"You tell me."

She sucks in a deep breath. "Oh, Robin . . ."

"Arizona, please, I'm begging you, do what you can to squelch the town celebration. Please."

"I'll do what I can, but gee, Robin, if I act like it's no big deal, they'll think I've gone over to the Dark Side. I'm your best friend. And the whole town remembers the night you finally made it center stage with 'Your Country Princess.'"

Trapped in my own triumph. "You think Jude Perry will print a big headline in *Freedom Rings!* above the fold?"

"Probably."

We hang up, and I scurry into the computer room to send Jude an e-mail. I roam around on the web until I find the *Freedom Rings!* web page and an e-mail link to Jude.

Dear Jude,

Please, please don't print a story or a headline or even a one-sentence congrats on the "Around Town" page about "Your Country Princess" being on the radio. It's a long, long story, and some day I promise to give you the scoop. But please, not one word. I'm begging you!!! Please.

Your friend, Robin McAfee

When I click *Send*, my stomach goes kerplunk. "Lord, let Jude get this before press time."

As Jude's e-mail zips through cyberspace, I see several messages from Eliza. It's been awhile since I checked e-mail, apparently. Her first one is from August.

I click on the subject line: Keith Urban. Smiling, I read.

NashVegas,

You dog! I can't believe it. You actually talked to him? And hugged him? For me? I'm moving to Nashville when I graduate.

I love Shakespeare, but our professor is v. boring.

Love you,

Cambridge.

There's a second one, dated the first week of September. The subject line reads: Sweet Home, Alabama.

Dear NashVegas,

I'm so glad to be home! The Alabama air never smelled sweeter. Europe was great, Cambridge a blast, but there's no place like the hills of Freedom. Or Auburn's campus.

I hope you're sitting down for this, but my friend Chelle talked me into getting football tickets, so guess what I'm doing every Saturday? Yep, sitting in the stands, watching football. It's fun if you're into really cute frat men sloshing beer all over you.

We've been in class for a few weeks already. I got home from Cambridge and hit the ground running, though I managed a short weekend home. Momma told me about Nashville Noise. I fell out. Our Momma, a signed artist with Nashville Noise? No way. You must've freaked when you saw her picture. And, she's the background voice on Grace Harding's biggest hit? Unbelievable. But ya know, it explains her pinched face when it came to you and music, doesn't it?

I'm not into school this semester after the summer of studying, but I'm so close to graduating, I grit my teeth and forge ahead.

Oh, guess what, I'm tutoring one of the football players, Joel Hawk. Knowing him makes the games a little more exciting. He's one of those big muscle guys who tackles or runs around behind the quarterback. He's cute in a no-neck, obtuse sort of way. And oddly enough, more interesting than my Shakespeare prof when he talks football. Thees and thous versus x's and o's? I like x's and o's.

Paris rendered no Greek Tycoon, or any man remotely close. I'd have settled for a handsome Englishman with a lot of credit on his MasterCard, but alas, 'twas not meant to be.

I miss you! Momma tells me you're singing at a
Bluebird Songwriter's Night, so I'll be there.
                    Love,
                    Back at Auburn
                    P.S. Anymore K.U. sightings?
                    Think he'll be at the Bluebird
                    when you're there?

I laugh out loud at her P.S. Yeah, Liza, Keith will be there.
We're tight now, you know. Best buds.

But Eliza's insight on her summer of Shakespeare reminds
me life doesn't always turn out like we expect, but we go on
living anyway. As long as Jude gets my e-mail and complies, I
can live with Freedom folks thinking my song is a hit. Right?
Right.

I click *Reply* and type Eliza a short note.

Back at Auburn,
    I'm glad you're home, safe. I've missed you. Lots
going on around here. I'll have to call you. Great for
Chelle to get your nose out of the books and have fun
with life. Sorry about Shakespeare and the Greek
tycoon.
    No more run-ins with K.U. And are you crazy? He
will NOT be at my Bluebird night. Even if hell froze
over. If he wanted to come, I would beg him to stay
away. I'll be nervous enough as it is with you guys in
the audience.
                    See you soon. Love you,
                    Nashville

I click *Send* and am ready to exit Yahoo when a new e-mail
arrives from Eliza. Subject line reads: !!!!!!!!!!!!

*Ahhhhhhh!!! I just heard Emma Rice's new single.
Oh my gosh! Why didn't you tell us? Details. I'm on my
way to class, but call me or e-mail or something. I can't
believe it!*

So, the frenzy has started. I click out of Yahoo. I don't
have the energy to respond. Walking out to the foyer, I hear
Graham at the front desk, talking to Ella.

"We can grab a bite to eat, maybe—" He looks over at me
and stands straight.

He seems guarded, but he's been that way all summer.

"Robin. What's up?" He winks at Ella though he's talking
to me. What is wrong with him these days?

"Did you hear Emma Rice's new cut?"

He props his elbow on the top shelf of the reception desk
and leans toward Ella. "I've been busy. What's up with her
new cut?"

"She's singing 'Your Country Princess,' although she titled
it 'I Wanna Be.'"

He drops his chin to his chest and tugs his hat over his
eyes. "She's singing your 'Your Country Princess'?"

"Do you know of another? Yes, my 'Your Country Princess.'
Graham, I didn't sell the song to Emma." I slap my hands on
my hips, waiting for him to turn livid. "Someone stole it."

He laughs and fiddles with the NSAI newsletter on Ella's
desk. "Sure, someone stole it. Robin, come on. Who would steal
your song?"

"That's what I'd like to know, Graham." I moan. "Emma Rice
doesn't even know I'm alive, and she's belting out my song.
The chorus is different, but the rest is exactly my lyrics and
melody."

Graham stoops to pick up his guitar. "You mean to tell me
someone sold her a song exactly like yours." He makes a kissy

face at Ella. "Well, they say there's nothing new under the sun. Like ideas are all over the place. Hanging in the air."

"Are you saying someone had the same idea as me?"

Graham throws his arm around me and walks me to the basement stairs. "It's possible."

"That's insane."

"Stranger things have happened." He stops outside Writers Room number two. "Listen, I have an appointment with a new writer in a few minutes."

Crossing my arms, I lean against the doorframe. "Do you know who wrote the song? Or, who's credited with writing the song?"

He tunes his guitar. "Robin, if I were you, I'd put the button on saying Emma Rice is singing your stolen song. Ain't no better way to make an enemy."

Crud. I flop down on the love seat and cover my eyes with my arm. "What should I do?"

Graham tunes his guitar. "Move on, Robin. Forget about the song. It's too late."

"Easy for you to say. Emma Rice is not making a comeback singing your sophomoric lyrics over the airwaves."

"She's not singing yours either. Better decide that right now." He stays focused on retuning the top E string.

"You're right—" Outside the door is a light knock.

"Phoebe, come in." Graham greets her with a blinding smile.

Phoebe's hips sway as she enters. "Thank you for meeting with me. I'm sooo excited."

"Phoebe, this is Robin McAfee."

"Nice to meet you," she gushes, her contact-lens blue eyes stuck on Graham.

"See ya, Robin." Graham pulls me off the sofa and shoves me out the door.

Skyler calls later for an emergency latté at Caffeine's.
"Did you talk to Marc?" she asks, digging in her Prada bag for change. "I haven't had time to get anywhere with your song."

Not finding another quarter to pay for her mocha, Skyler dumps her purse contents on the counter. Dollar bills hit the counter and float to the floor.

"Good grief, it's a Prada junkyard," I say, stooping to pick up two fifties. "Granddaddy always said you can find valuable things at a junkyard."

"I was in such a rush when I stopped by the bank."

"I hope you don't organize your cases like you do your purse, Sky."

"My cases are *why* my purse is like this. So, did you talk to Marc?" She hands Reuben, the guy behind the counter, a fifty.

"He laughed and said if he was going to steal a song, it wouldn't be from me."

"Smart aleck." Skyler scrapes the junk back in her purse.

"Hi, Robin," Reuben says, "what'll it be?"

"A White Chocolate Symphony, please." I help Skyler lighten her load by scooping up all the loose change. "You still owe me ten dollars."

"Fine, here, take this too." She flips me one of the fifties. "Happy—" She glances at her watch. "Happy September twelfth."

"And to you, cuz." I wave the bill at her. "I'm not too proud to take it."

"Robin, when do you play here again?" Reuben asks. "We have a lot of requests for the nervous songwriter chick."

Great, I'm getting a rep. "I'm on the schedule for sometime in November, after my songwriter's night at the Bluebird."

He takes the mountain of change from my hand and pops open the register. "It's sorta nerve-racking, isn't it?"

"Sorta?"

"Say, Reuben," Skyler says, "have you heard about Emma Rice's new single? Maybe who wrote it?"

He looks over from where he's blending my Symphony. "No, why?"

Skyler shrugs. "Just wondering. Her new release is really good—'I Wanna Be.'"

Reuben passes over my drink. "Not really into Emma Rice. She's more like my mom's generation."

"Fine." Skyler rolls her eyes and snatches a couple of napkins from the dispenser.

I laugh. "Thanks, Reuben."

We sit outside for a few minutes in the warm September sun.

"I saw Graham in the NSAI office a half hour ago. He advised me to let it go. Don't sully my name accusing Emma Rice."

Skyler sips her latté. "I hate to agree with him, but he's right. By the way, how'd he seem? Nervous? Suspicious?"

"Neither. He flirted with the receptionist, Ella, then shoved me out the door when his cowrite showed up. A cute chick with big blue eyes. I bet she's never written a song before today."

Skyler smirks. "Probably not even today." She closes her eyes and turns her face into the breeze. Her sleek dark hair flutters over her shoulders. "When I get back to the office, I'll dig around some more." With a sigh, she shoves out of her chair. "I need to run. No time for leisurely coffee breaks these days."

"Thanks for all you're doing to help."

"You'd do the same for me," she calls over her shoulder as she walks toward her car. "Besides, you'll get my bill."

25

"So, you're back." Susan West motions for me to take a seat.

"I am." I perch on the edge of her sofa, my confidence already leaking.

She leans forward with her elbows on her knees. "Do you like what you've written?"

I look up from tuning my guitar. "Y-yes." If I can't feel confident, it'd be nice to at least sound confident. But no.

It's been a week since I heard my song on the Big 98. I've worked hard to put it behind me, go on with my songwriting, forgetting I could've been accredited with a hit. But the irony of sitting in Susan's office for a pro critique while *my* song has Music Row buzzing burns my buns.

Susan says, "Whenever you're ready."

"Okay." With my hands trembling, my mouth dry, and my hopes on hiatus, I start my first song, "She Was Seventeen." To my surprise, Susan lets me sing it all the way through.

"Better," she says, smiling and nodding. "Much better. Sort of has a '70s folk sound to it."

"Janis Ian," I say.

"Exactly. Janis Ian."

I wait. She stares. So, are you going to tell me it's good enough to take to a publisher or . . .

"Do you have another song?" she asks, reaching for her bottle of water.

"Right, next song."

Susan stops me in the middle of "Let Go" and "Desert Rose." "You're getting there, Robin. I'm starting to feel the emotion. But . . ." She launches into a lecture about commercially appealing and high-concept songs, reminding me to pay attention to the hits, attend ASCAP workshops and as many songwriter's nights as I can.

I want to say, "What do you think I've been doing?" but I button it up. She's trying to help, really.

"Have you heard Emma Rice's new song, 'I Wanna Be'?"

My head snaps up. "Yes, I have. Do you like it?"

"Love it. Fantastic song. Now, there's a hit song to study, Robin. The lyrics and the melody have perfect commercial appeal. Then, with a diva like Emma singing . . . mega-hit song."

I lower my guitar in its case. My heart thumps when I ask, "You don't happen to know who wrote 'I Wanna Be,' do you? Maybe I can look them up and get a few pointers."

Susan slaps her hands together. "As a matter of fact, I do know who wrote the song. We were just talking about him this morning. He's long overdue. I'm so happy for him."

I leave Susan West's office with steam whistling from my ears. Graham Young. That low-down, lying, sneaking snake. I whip out my cell and dial him up. He doesn't answer—go figure—so I leave a message.

"Hey, it's Robin. Give me a call. Now!"

Climbing in my truck, I barrel up 17th Avenue South,

getting madder by the minute. Darn it, what is he up to? I decide not to wait for his call; I'm hunting him down.

This makes no sense. Sure Graham's ambitious, but a thief? A liar? My legs jitter involuntarily as I wait at the stoplight, my mind racing. Why? When? How?

"My song. My sophomoric song." With a low growl, I slam the heel of my hand against the steering wheel. Stealing any of my songs would've been bad, but "Your Country Princess" is special to me. Didn't he know that?

When the light turns green, I gun the gas and head east on Wedgewood Avenue. At Graham's apartment, I pound on the door. "Graham. Open up."

His neighbor peeks out. "He's gone, honey. Moved out about three weeks ago."

"Where?" I demand.

She shrugs. "Didn't say. I ain't his keeper."

My shoulders droop. "Guess not."

My anger is morphing into tears. Talking to God and half muttering to myself, I work my way back to Music Row and the NSAI office. Surely Ella has seen him.

"Not since the day you were here," she says with a pout. "Robin, you two don't have a thing, do you?"

"No, Ella, he's all yours. If there's anything left when I'm done with him."

"What?"

"If you see him, tell him I'm looking for him."

No word from Graham? Lee asks, tossing a DVD on the coffee table while I spread out a Tennessee Titans blanket. Winter temperatures are descending on our October days.

"Not one. And I've called him every day for the last two weeks."

He captures me and pulls me down to the couch with him. The leather crunches and squeaks as we land.

"What are you doing?" I laugh.

"We never talked about this, but did you really think I would give your song to Janie, or to anyone, without talking to you?" His eyes lock onto mine and hold on.

Squirming, I plead, "Insanity."

He doesn't let me off so easy. "Trust works both ways, Robin."

"Again, insanity." Slipping my arms around his neck, I kiss him. "Forgive me?"

He brushes my hair away from my eyes. It's gotten long again since my May shearing, and my bangs touch the tip of my nose. "Absolutely." His kiss reminds me why I love being a woman.

With that issue resolved, Lee cuts me loose and pops in the movie. He aims the remote and hits *Play*, then snuggles under the blanket next to me. Just when we're warm and cozy, and in the middle of Will Smith running from aliens, Momma calls.

"Can we bring fifty people?"

"To where, the Bluebird?"

"No, I'm calling about the state fair. Of course, the Bluebird."

"My songwriter's night isn't until November, Momma."

"We're planning ahead."

I push myself forward. Lee runs his hand gently over my back. "Well, I guess y'all are. No, you can't bring fifty people. There won't be room for the other guests."

"Well, shug, who do I tell no? The aunts and uncles, grandparents, your granddaddy's bluegrass boys? They're all just dying to see you sing in Nashville."

Lee kisses my check and whispers, "I'll be back."

"I already have Lee, Skyler, Blaire, Birdie, Walt, Arizona, and my one nonfamily, nonfriend fan, Mallory Clark. Plus you, Daddy, Eliza, and the grandparents."

Momma's silence is thick. "I gotta tell Henna and the girls they can't come?"

Tough task. "Sorry, Momma."

"Henna already made T-shirts: 'What happens in NashVegas stays in NashVegas.'"

I laugh. "What are they planning to do, run naked down Broadway?"

"For heaven's sake, no. You know Henna; she has to have a hat or T-shirt for every occasion."

"Momma, tell them I'm sorry, but when I sing at the GEC, they can have front-row seats."

The sound and smell of popping popcorn fills the apartment. "The GEC?"

"The Gaylord Entertainment Center. Big place downtown."

"Well, I'll tell them, but they won't be happy. Robin," she hesitates, " they all bought Emma's new CD."

My heart thuds. "You're kidding?"

"They want to know why Graham Young's name is on your song."

I draw the blanket over my head. What a nightmare. "Momma, just tell them it's business."

"All right. How are you doing with this?" Her voice is like an embrace. She and Daddy were spitting mad when I called to break the news about Graham stealing my song. But more than Daddy, or anyone else in the family, I believe Momma shoulders the load of my disappointment. She's walked a mile in my shoes, and then some.

"I'm okay. Everyone's been so great—Lee, Skyler, Birdie, Walt. But no clues as to where I can find Graham. I've asked everyone I know. He's disappeared."

Lee yanks the blanket off my head and slips in next to me with a big bowl of popcorn.

"Well, the Lord sees and knows."

"He does." Momma's a good one with "the-Lord-knows" or "the-Lord's-will" Band-Aid of truth. "Listen, Lee's here and we're watching a movie. Talk to you later."

"Good night, my songbird."

"G-good night." I hang up. Songbird? Momma's never used affectionate nicknames before. I don't know about the rest of the world, but Robin and Bit McAfee are experiencing their own global warming.

When the movie credits roll, Lee clicks off the TV and kisses me with powerful, electric lips. Clearing that last bit of Janie dust from our air has turned up the heat. *Shew-wee.*

"I'm really proud of you," he says.

"Well, thank you. You're a good kisser too." I fall against his chest.

His laugh rumbles in my ear. "I mean how you're handling this song business."

"What choice do I have? Deal with it or run home. And I'm not running." I sit up. "I keep telling myself that at the core of this, my song is a hit. Even Susan West thinks so."

"I don't know how Graham stole your song. If he saw in you what I see—" Lee shakes his head. "He'd have never done it."

"You're trying to melt my heart, aren't you?"

He kisses me. "Maybe." A light knock echoes on my door. "You expecting company?"

"No." I shove my hair from my eyes, thinking I need to make an appointment at Bishop's tomorrow, and skid across the floor in my stocking feet. Birdie and Walt are on the other side of the door.

"Hey, you two, come in."

Lee calls from the kitchen, "Y'all want something to drink?"

Walt raises his hand. A thick gold ring is wrapped around his middle finger. "We're good, Lee, thanks."

"And what are you two lovebirds up to this evening?" I fold the blanket to make room on the couch.

Walt holds Birdie's hand as she sits. I perch on the arm of the club chair. "Is everything okay?"

Birdie gushes. "We're getting married."

"Holy cow, you're getting married." I crush Birdie with a hug. "Congratulations."

"Yeah, we're getting hitched," Walt says with a raspy chuckle.

Lee comes in with two glasses of Pepsi. "What brought this on?" He stoops to kiss Birdie's cheek. "Congratulations."

Walt gazes at Birdie when he says, "We've known each other a long time. And once you know, why wait?"

"Sounds good to me." Lee's tone makes me go *ah-o.*

"There's more," Birdie says. "I have—"

"May have," Walt interrupts.

"May have cancer."

I set my drink down and drop to my knees in front of her. "Cancer? Birdie . . ."

"Crazy cigarettes."

"You smoked?"

"For years. I quit awhile back, but the doctor found some spots on my lungs."

I slip my hand under hers. "When did you find out?"

Birdie squeezes my hand. "A few days ago. It's just a few odd-looking cells, but the doc wants to take a closer look." Her blue eyes fill with tears.

Walt wraps both of his arms around her. "I don't want her going through this alone."

Birdie laughs softly. "I refused his first proposal. I can't see putting this kind of burden on a new marriage, but he insisted." Birdie flashes her ring finger under my nose.

"Sakes alive, Walt." Birdie's diamond blinds me. Like the time I tried to look directly into the sun on a dare. "It's beautiful."

She squishes up her shoulders with a sigh. "He did good, didn't he?"

Walt nudges her cheek. "I'll be hunting for your false teeth when you're ninety, pet."

Love believes all things.

"We're not really church people, you know," Birdie says, "but do you think your pastor, Shawn, would marry us? In a few weeks?"

Lee nods. "Ask him."

"And, Robin, will you be my bridesmaid? I never had a daughter and—"

"Sweet Birdie!" I throw my arms around her. "I'd be honored."

Walt stands and hooks his thumbs in his waistband. His wide belt buckle holds up his blue jeans. "This calls for a toast." He scurries down three flights of stairs for a bottle of wine. When he returns, we toast love, life, and health.

"And to friends," Birdie says with her gaze fixed on me.

I raise my goblet. "To friends."

When Birdie and Walt leave, Lee lures me out on the deck, into the chilly night. He wraps me in his arms for warmth.

"Look how bright the stars are," I say, hooking my hands around his arms. "Like they know Birdie is in love."

"What about you?" He tightens his arms.

"What about me?"

"Are you in love?" he asks.

"Are you?" I counter, suddenly nervous.

"Is this Twenty Questions?"

"I don't know, is it?"

Lee looks down at me. "Robin, be serious for a moment."

"I am."

He turns me to face him. "I want to talk to your dad."

"About what?"

"About us."

I can't see his face very well in the dim light, but his tone tells me he's talking serious. "Y-y-you mean like, like Birdie and Walt?"

"What do you think?" His breath is warm on my hair.

"After two months?" I break away. "We haven't even said I love you yet."

"I love you, Robin."

Okay, there's that. "Lee," I smooth my hand down his strong arm, "you're the most amazing man I've ever met. When I'm with you, I feel like I can buy the world with Lucky Charms and Cracker Jacks."

He holds my face in his hands and kisses me.

This ain't helping. I flounder to express myself. Darn, I hate this. I want to move forward with this relationship but not straight to the altar. Seems as if Lee's already pulled into the station and called "All aboard."

"I'm meeting people around Nashville, learning the business, and with the Lord's grace, beating stage fright. For the first time, I don't feel quite like an alien."

"What are you saying?"

"I've bit off all I can chew right now. I know God is able to handle everything, but I'm only one bitty woman." I hold my hands to my shoulders. "See, narrow shoulders."

Lee doesn't so much as smile.

"I'm not ready for you to talk to my daddy." There, I said it. Not in a smooth, country ballad kind of way, but I said it.

Lee's chest rises and falls. "I understand, but Robin, I do want to mar—"

"Don't say it." I stick my fingers in my ears. *La, la, la, la.* "I don't want to hear it. I've already said no to one proposal this year."

Sheesh, if I say no twice in one year, Skyler would flat kill me.

Lee crawls back inside. I crawl in after him. "Lee, I'm sorry. I reckon I'm just not—"

"Do you love me?" He grabs his jacket.

I wring my hands. *Do I love him?* "Lee, you are incredible. In every way. I can't believe I met a man like you so soon. You're becoming my best friend, but I'm just not ready to say things like 'I love you' or 'I'll marry you.'"

He jerks open the door. "I'd better go. It's late."

"It's nine o'clock."

"I've got an early breakfast meeting."

"On Saturday?" I drop to the sofa. "Are you mad?"

"No, just disappointed." He opens the door.

"Call me?"

"Sure." He closes the door without so much as a smile or see ya later.

Ah, crud.

26

Saturday morning, Skyler calls. "Get up and come down here!"

I push my eyes open. "Come down where?" I glance at my clock. Seven a.m. Is she crazy?

"Pancake Pantry. I had a hankering for pancakes. Then we're going to my place to bake goodies for my church's youth fund-raiser." I hear her car door slam.

"I don't bake," I say, untangling my feet from the sheets. See how I'm not ready for marriage? I don't bake. And I'm a bed hog. All the covers are mine. Mine.

"You can stir the batter, crack eggs, measure sugar."

"Isn't that baking? I may be half asleep, but I'm not stupid."

"Fine, sing to me while I slave away."

"Skyler, do tell, how do you get into an emergency baking situation?"

"Mrs. Gillaspy called last night desperate for more baked goods for the October Fest fund-raiser."

"Well, since it's for October Fest . . ." I fumble my way to the bathroom unable to open my eyes. They're glued shut with dried tears.

"Great. And this afternoon, we're boot shopping. I want to go to the Boot Corral."

"Boot shopping? My dear lawyer cousin, once again, I'm flat broke."

"I'll buy you a pair. Merry early Christmas. You've got to see this place, Robin. Every boot imaginable, and the walls are lined with pictures of country stars. Besides, every songwriter needs a good pair of boots. Red ones."

"We do? Says who?"

"Me. I'm in a shopping mood. You in the car yet?"

"No, but I'm in the bathroom."

"That's a start."

When I pull up to the red-brick Pancake Pantry, the waiting line wraps around the block. With an awkward, "I'm looking for my cousin," to those who think I'm cutting in line, I spot Skyler along the row of windows, waving from a table in the corner.

"This place is packed," I say, dropping my keys on the table. "By the way, I left the house without my purse, which means no wallet, no driver's license, no money." A waitress fills my coffee cup.

"What happened to you?" Skyler wrinkles her nose at me while motioning for the waitress to hold up. "Give us two orders of the original pancakes and two sides of bacon."

"Lee told me he loved me last night. He wants to talk to Daddy—"

"Oh my gosh, Robin, I've got goose bumps. I'm so jealous. Look at you, a hit song, a very handsome contractor fiancé—"

I stop her verbal skip down the rose-trimmed path. "I didn't say it back. And it's Graham's hit, not mine."

"You didn't say it back? What's wrong with you? And it is your song, just no one knows it."

I unroll the silverware from my napkin. "We've only known each other for five months. Dated for two. I'm only twenty-five."

"Oh my gosh, cry me a river. You've had two marriage pro-
posals in a year. I haven't had one in twenty-six."

"Technically, he didn't ask. He's only hinted."

"You're scared, aren't you?" Skyler motions to the waitress
for more coffee.

"Maybe. Some. Not much. Come on, marriage is a serious
commitment."

She shakes her head. "You beat all, you know?"

I don't want to talk about it anymore, so I change the subject. "How's Kip?" Skyler went on a blind date last week with
a friend of Blaire's steady, Ezra.

She grins. "Good. He's called a few times." Kip turned out
to be exactly Skyler's type—a good-looking athletic physician's
assistant.

"He's coming to church with me tomorrow."

Our waitress brings breakfast, and my stomach, if not my
brain, wakes up, and, for the moment, my problems disappear
with a pat of butter and swirl of maple syrup.

Tuesday morning Marty Schultz shows up at Nashville Noise.

"Beat me with an ugly stick. Where've you been?" I throw
my arms around her.

She looks happy. Happy for Marty. Her hair is dyed a rich
brown, and her blue eyes are no longer streaked with red. Her
jeans and baggy T-shirt are the same but a might neater than
in the past.

"I'm moving back to Arkansas."

"Why?"

She reaches in a Starbuck's bag and hands me a coffee.
"For old time's sake," she says with a confident smile. "The
coffee, not the move."

I walk to the reception area and perch on the sofa.

"I decided to go to college," Marty says, sitting next to me. I choke on my coffee. She shouldn't drop bombs on me without a shrill whistle or a "Bombs away."

"College? Really?"

She laughs softly. "I know it's out of the blue, but I always wanted to go to college and study music, maybe teach. You gave me courage to face my fears."

"How George Bailey of me." I wink at my friend. "But, I have to ask, what fears?"

She fiddles with her coffee cup lid. "I barely graduated high school. By seventeen, I was already playing gigs, traveling weekends. What did I need with school? After the Delaney Brown fiasco, I took a close look at my life and decided school actually sounded fun, but I was afraid of bombing out again. If I failed school, what did I have left but cleaning toilets the rest of my life? Then I met you, fighting for your dreams, overcoming fears, and I thought, 'Why not me?'"

I hug her again. "I'm proud of you. College is a lot of work."

She wrinkles her nose, but her eyes are lit up. "I know. I would've been a terrible student at eighteen. But I know what I want now. Mom is paying my way, so I don't have to work unless I want to."

"So, why'd you disappear on Marc?" I check my watch. Almost nine. "Sorry, Marty, but I need to finish up here. Marc left early to meet with a client, and he's got me scheduled for jobs all day."

Marty wads up the paper bag. "I understand. Listen, I didn't disappear on Marc. I called in sick so I could extend my Fourth weekend and visit the college admissions office. The same day, I e-mailed him with my plan, but he never checks his e-mail. He's a phone man. I got a response from him a month later."

"He never told me."

"I'm sorry I didn't call you." Marty rises, and I walk her to the front door.

"It's okay," I say, adding with a chuckle, "it figured you needed a break from this town." I laugh. "But I did wonder if you stole 'Your Country Princess.'"

Marty gasps softly, tipping her head sideways. "Someone stole your song? I've been out of touch . . . Oh my gosh." Then she narrows her eyes. "I would never steal someone else's song. I know what that feels like."

"I came to the same conclusion." I give her the sixty-second sound bite of how I discovered Emma Rice singing my song. And Graham Young's name is on it."

She moans and grips my arms. "Don't get bitter, just get better. Write another hit song. Be more careful in the future." She's intense, like she's willing me to not suffer her plight. We stop by the front door.

"I will. Marty, I'm going to miss you."

She sniffles. "I already miss you. But not Marc. Not this job. Not this town. Only you. Thanks for being a light when I needed one."

"Any time." We hug good-bye. I hope this is not the last I see of Marty Shultz.

My last chore at Nashville Noise is to toss the garbage in the dumpster. But Marty's surprise visit made me skip Mr. Chastain's office, so I run back to check his trash.

His light is not on. Good. I'm running behind and don't want him to catch me. Marc would have a cow. I untie the Hefty bag and reach under the desk for his trash can.

The picture I borrowed is back on the wall, safe and sound. And praise be, I never heard a word from Marc about it.

Looking back, that whole ordeal gives me the willies. "What a shocker," I mutter as I dump Mr. Chastain's trash.

"What's a shocker?" The overhead lights flicker on.

I snap around, dropping the trash can and ramming my hand into the side of the desk. *Ow.* "M-Mr. Chastain."

"Good morning." He's dressed casually in khakis and a white button-down. His graying hair is still wet from the shower. He looks different than the picture on the wall. Older, wiser.

"I'll be right out of your way, sir." I slide his trash can under the credenza.

"No, not until I hear about the shocker." He sets his laptop case on his desk.

I fudge since I don't want to tell him about the picture. "Well . . . sir . . . "

"Did you take my picture?" He points to the very one.

Aha, James Chastain's elves hold my feet to the fire. "Yes, sir. But I brought it back, unharmed."

He walks over to the wall of fame, hands in his pockets. "I tried to sell this picture on eBay when Gilly Stone put out his two-CD set of golden hits."

"You did?"

He swirls his big leather desk chair around and sits. "Didn't get one bid."

"I don't believe it."

"Well, okay, one. My friend Wynn bid on it for me."

A snort escapes my nose. Can't help it. His expression is funny.

He stares at me, and I drop my gaze to my Nikes. The Hefty bag dangles from my hand. "You didn't want to sell it anyway, did you?"

He unsnaps his laptop case. "I have about fifty of those in the storage closet."

"Still a rare find. At least this one is signed, and Casey Jones just passed away." I walk over for a closer look, not so shocked anymore to see Bit Lukeman's face. "I saw this picture in the Hall."

"Why'd you take it?" he asks, booting up his laptop.

I tap the glass. "That woman is my—"

My confession is interrupted by his ringing phone. He answers with a "Hullo," then yuks it up with the person on the other end with phrases like "you devil," and "Yeah, he hit number one."

I feel rather silly waiting around with a garbage bag in my hand, so I tiptoe to the door.

Mr. Chastain's voice chases after me. "Don't go." I stop short. "Grant, hold on a sec. No, let me call you back." He drops the phone to the cradle and fishes something out of his laptop case.

"I believe this is yours." He hands me a clear jewel case with an unmarked CD inside.

My pulse races. "I don't think so."

"You didn't record a song in my studio with Marty Shultz?"

Oh, crap. See, this is what daredevil actions get me. Purple spots float before my eyes. And fat, arctic-blast goose bumps shiver down my arms and legs. "I'm sorry, we were just—"

"Goofing around?"

How many little elves does he have? I lift my chin. "How did you get this?"

"A recording engineer was dozing in the booth when you snuck in. You seem adept in stealth."

"I grew up in the hills." He doesn't laugh or even smile. "I apologize, sir. We overstepped our place. I'd be happy to pay for—"

"Did you write the song?" His tone warns, "Don't lie to me, girl."

Ain't no flies on James Chastain. I blurt, "Yes, sir."

He rubs his chin. "Did you sell it to Emma Rice?"

"No, sir."

His phone rings again. At the same time, a fancy-dressed woman knocks on his door. "James?"

"Merrillee." He looks at his watch. "Come in."

I hoist the Hefty bag and slip away to the dumpster.

Lee calls Monday five minutes after I arrive home. "How are you?"

"Missing you," I confess.

"I miss you too," he says. "I took yesterday to think and pray."

"I understand." Leaning against the kitchen counter, I wrap my arm around my waist, shaking from the cold apartment, but more from anticipation.

"I'm sorry I sprung the idea of marriage on you so soon."

I shake my head. "No, Lee, please . . . I'm the one who should be sorry. Look, I'm not ready for love and marriage talk but I don't want to lose you."

"You won't. But how will I know you're ready?"

I sigh. "Good question."

"Got an answer?"

I think for a moment. "I'll tell you I love you."

27

The second Sunday in November, I'm sick. Really. My stomach churns, my head pounds, and my toenails ache. True, all true.

Momma calls from Daddy's cell. "We're on our way. We'll see you at the Bluebird. Did you get snacks for people when we go back to your place?"

"Turn around, Momma, I'm sick."

"For crying out loud, Robin, you are not sick. Are you in bed? Get out of bed—" Her voice trails off and Daddy's comes on.

"Robbie, we're all rooting for you."

"But I'm sick."

"Tell the truth—are you really?"

Drat. The old tell-the-truth trick. "No."

"Come on, get out of bed, get cleaned up, you'll feel better. Spend some time in prayer."

"You're gonna knock 'em dead!" Arizona and Eliza cheer from the back of Momma's van.

Daddy hangs up, and I crawl out of bed. The clock reads two-thirty, and I've successfully spent the day in bed, fretting.

Over in the corner of my tiny living room, the afternoon light shines on the polished wood of my guitar. My fingers are sore and calloused from practicing all week. I stayed up until two a.m. rehearsing each number, jotting down what I should say between songs, working up smooth transitions from one song to the next. The floor around the kitchen table is littered with all my crumpled up notes.

I stare at the pile and burrow back under the covers.

Stand on my head, naked, in Freedom's town square.

Eat warm fish guts on *Fear Factor*.

Wear baby blue eye shadow.

Three things I'd rather do than sing at the Bluebird tonight. I feel like one of Granddaddy's old scratched 78 records when the needle gets stuck. You're afraid . . . You're afraid . . . You're afraid . . .

Open-mike nights I learned to manage because the expectation is zilch. They expect you to suck. But this is a performance. The audience wants to be entertained and uplifted. I have to be smooth and charming and on key.

The Bluebird will be packed. Standing-room only. And Sunday night won't thin out like open-mike nights. I'm dead. So dead. Jesus, help me.

I sit up with a sudden thought. *Maybe, by some miracle, Nashville's been hit with a natural disaster.* Wouldn't that be great? The Bluebird would be closed.

I throw on some clothes and run down to Birdie's.

The winter of my junior year, I had a huge geometry midterm. I'd studied and studied, but in the end, I couldn't make myself care one whit about the volume of a cube with a side length of 6 centimeters. I went to bed that night begging God for a favor. "Just a few inches of snow, Lord. Please."

Don't you know? Freedom woke under a half inch of snow. Very rare event. No school for two days. I hung around with friends, ate cookies, drank hot chocolate, and waged a snow-mudball war against the boys that is still legend in northern Alabama.

So maybe, just maybe . . .

Birdie and Walt are in the kitchen fixing sandwiches. "Well, good afternoon, Princess Robin."

"Did Nashville have an earthquake or tornado?"

Birdie laughs. What nerve.

"I'm serious."

"Just anticipation," Walt says, pointing his mayo knife at me. "You'll feel better once you get up on stage."

"Right. No natural disaster?"

"No, songbird, all's well in Music City."

I whirl around to go upstairs, then stop, one foot down the hall. "Did you call me songbird?"

Birdie thinks for a second. "I suppose I did."

"Momma called me that for the first time the other day."

"Did she?" Birdie pours me a cup of coffee, but I refuse. I'm hyper enough. "Isn't that interesting," she says. "You remind me of a flitting, fluttering, occasionally lost and frightened, but always beautiful songbird."

I sneer. "You make me sound like a flake."

"I mean it with heartfelt tenderness." Birdie turns me toward the stairs. "Get ready."

Momma slaps her hand on my leg. "Stop jiggling. It'll only make it worse."

I remove her hand by lifting her pinky. "You got your ways, I got mine."

So here I am, seated up front as if on the edge of the world, terrified I might fall off. But it's time to cowgirl up. Just like the night at the Hall when the triplets tumbled.

On the other side of Momma, Daddy looks amused. "This is a neat place, Robbie," he says.

"There must be a bazillion people in here, sucking up all the oxygen. A girl can't draw a deep breath."

Next to me, Lee slips his arm around my shoulders.

"This place wasn't here when you came to town, was it, Bit?" Granddaddy asks from the table behind ours.

Momma's face tightens so her eyes bug out a little. "No, Daddy, it wasn't."

Grandma and Grandpa McAfee, overdressed in their Sunday best, carry on with Birdie and Walt.

Arizona and Eliza are two tables over, saving chairs for Skyler and Blaire. And in the back by the wall is Mallory and her new man, Liam somebody. When I catch her eye, she gives me a thumbs up.

My gaze shifts to the door. Can I get out? I'd have to crash over five tables and knock over ten standing guests, but I think I could do it. I plop my forehead down on the table. I'm a mess.

A hand runs up and down my back. Lee's deep whisper comforts me a little. "You can do this, Robin."

"Old habits die hard."

"Robin, maybe what you're feeling is anticipation, not anxiety."

I lift my head. "Walt said the same thing."

He lifts my chin with his finger. "There you go."

"Robin." Momma nudges me. "Reverend Miller and Jenny said they'd be praying for you tonight. He said, 'Remember Columbia,' whatever that means."

His exhortation makes me feel warm. Facing the Bluebird is way easier than facing guerillas. This is way easier than *that*.

What are three things I'd rather do than sing at the Bluebird's Songwriter's Night?

I take a deep breath.

Well, I'd . . . No that's gross. Um . . . I'd rather be . . . No, too ridiculous. Well, doggies, my mind is actually blank on this one. Now that I'm here, I can't think of anything I'd rather do.

The Bluebird's Sunday-night host, Jeff Pearson, takes the stage. My stomach turns a cartwheel. It's on now.

"We have a great show for you all tonight. Remember, this is a listening room, so please no talking while the songwriters perform, and let's cut off those cell phones."

"Robin," Blaire whispers over my shoulder, "tonight I'm tossing a whole pill." She winks at me.

Jeff calls out the order of singers. I'm number ten of twenty. But he'll do a little intro before each one.

"We'll get started here in a few minutes." Jeff hurries off the stage.

My stomach churns. Lee's right. It's anticipation. I know I can do this.

Then Momma's gasp draws my attention. I look over to see James Chastain standing by Walt and Birdie.

"Good evening everyone," he says.

I rise slowly. "Mr. Chastain."

"Hello, Robin." He maneuvers around the tables to shake my hand. "I heard a talented new songwriter was performing here tonight."

I shoot a fiery glance at Birdie. She turns her head and rolls her eyes up to the ceiling.

"Nice to see you again, Bit." James says.

"Jim." Momma doesn't look at him. She must be embarrassed for running out on her record deal all those years ago.

Daddy stands. "Dean McAfee. Nice to meet you."

James grips Daddy's hand firmly. "The honor is all mine, believe me."

Jeff is back onstage, starting the show, so there's no time for chitchat. No time to decipher what in Sam Hill brought James Chastain out to hear me sing.

Momma mutters something to Daddy about how she can't believe Birdie invited *that man* . . .

Lee taps my shoulder and gently nudges me close. "I think he's the one who broke your mom's heart."

I sneak a peek at Mr. Chastain. Then Momma. "You think?"

"Good chance."

"Sheesh, the way our lives have been going, I wouldn't be surprised."

The first songwriter takes the stage. I anticipate being sick-to-my-stomach nervous, but with each singer-songwriter, my excitement grows.

Something else sticks out to me. These other songwriters are folks made of flesh and blood just like me. Their voices warble and crack. Their legs shake a little. They start songs too fast or too slow.

After the first few singers perform, a buzz starts about Mr. Chastain being in the room, and several of the songwriters are visibly anxious. A few others show off. It isn't every night one of the pit bulls of Music Row wanders in to an amateur songwriters night.

I peek over at him. He really came because Birdie called? What about her blind bluff and losing it all?

No time to ponder, because Jeff is up at the mike and introducing the next singer. Me.

Here goes nothing. I run my hands down the sides of my jeans. Granddaddy passes over my guitar and taps over his heart. "Remember, you got it right here."

Arizona gives me a thumbs up. Do I peek at James Chastain? Oh, mercy, he has the same amused look as Daddy.

"This next performer has performed several times at the Bluebird open-mike night." Jeff smiles at me. "Y'all are gonna love this woman's music. Put your hands together for Robin McAfee."

To the applause and the family's hoots and whistles (thank you, Arizona), I step up as Jeff steps off. So far, so good.

All eyes are on me. Pinching my pick, I start strumming on "She Was Only Seventeen."

"It's been a journey to get here. I won't bore you with the details, but let me just say, whatever you're facing in life, God is bigger." I look over at my table. "I wrote this song with my momma."

She wipes her eyes.

The melodies pour out of me and the peace washes over me. And for the first time in twenty-five years, I sincerely exhale.

28

Plastic cups and empty chip bags are stacked on the table and kitchen pass-through. Grandma Lukeman starts to clean up, but I stop her.

"It's late, and y'all have a long drive. I appreciate you being here."

"All right, if you're sure. I know your granddaddy would like to get on the road."

So, a little after midnight the last of the Freedom caravan starts for home. Arizona and Eliza bum a ride back with Grandma and Grandpa McAfee, so only Momma and Daddy are left.

Momma commences the clean-up detail, but Daddy tells her to stop. "Come sit."

"I should help Robin clean," she says, fidgeting with the wild curl that always falls over her forehead.

"Leave it, Momma. I'll get it tomorrow." I collapse in the club chair, wide awake and over-the-rainbow with my Bluebird triumph. "Isn't the Bluebird great?" I look at Daddy. "There are other great places in town to play, too, but the Bluebird is—"

"Robbie, your Momma has something to tell you." Daddy gestures again for her to come and sit.

She does, hugging a wadded-up chip bag.

"Go on, Bit."

Momma crushes the bag between her hands. "Don't push me, Dean. I'll get to it."

I've seen terror, I've felt terror. Momma is truly terrified. "What's going on?"

"Does he have to be here?" Momma hops up from the couch.

"He who?" I look around. "Lee?"

"Well, I don't mean your daddy."

"This looks like a private matter, Robin. I'll just go on home." Lee takes his jacket from the back of the couch and kisses my cheek. "I'll call you in the morning. You were magic tonight."

When the door closes behind him, I feel agitated. "Why'd you drive Lee out, Momma?"

"Bit?" Daddy urges.

"Well, I need to tell you something, Robin, and it ain't easy. You're just gonna hate me." She drops the chip bag onto the coffee table.

I walk over to her. "I'm not going to hate you. I can't count the number of times you irritated me, but hate? Never."

"She didn't tell you the whole story about Nashville," Daddy says.

Momma gets up with a moan and circles around to the back of the couch.

"Does this have to do with Mr. Chastain? He's the one who broke your heart, isn't he?" I ease down on the edge of the coffee table and face my parents.

"Yes." Momma's voice is liquid with emotion.

"But it's been over twenty-five years."

"It's not that simple."

"So the man broke your heart, Momma. Lots of girls get

their hearts broke. But it worked out. You married Daddy, had me, Liza, and Steve—"

"He's your father." Momma presses her hands to her cheeks.

"What?" I look over at Daddy.

Momma blows her nose on a napkin. "I ran away to Nashville to marry Jim. Two months later I told him I was pregnant, and he walked out."

All images in the room fade to black, and there's only Momma and me. "Y-y-you married James Chastain? H-he's my father?"

"Yes, Robin Rae, James Chastain is your father."

My old Chevy flies down the highway. The speedometer bobs around the ninety mark. My knuckles ache from gripping the wheel, and my eyes burn.

James Chastain is my biological father? Not kind, gentle, loving Dean McAfee? Bile stings the base of my throat, and I lean a little harder on the gas.

Freedom's Song's chassis rocks and rolls as the engine whines. The sight of James shaking Daddy's hand flashes through my mind. *The honor is all mine, believe me.* Translation: *thanks for raising my kid.*

I fly around a car going slow in the left lane. How do I digest this? How do I reckon my life now? I'm not a McAfee. I'm a Chastain.

Great day in the morning.

Momma's scattered explanation rattles around in my brain. *Children weren't on his agenda . . . Apparently, long-term commitment wasn't either. Birdie was furious . . . gave Jim a piece of her mind . . . made him so angry . . . She walked out—cost her a record deal. I ran home . . . Marriage was annulled . . . My heart broken into a million pieces . . . so embarrassed and lost . . . I married your daddy when I was eight months pregnant . . . Birdie tried to keep in touch, but I didn't want anything to do with memories of Nashville. It hurt too much . . . Never showed anyone our marriage license . . . I really loved Daddy, Robin . . . He was my knight.*

I shake the muddle from my mind. *Momma, Momma, Momma.* No wonder she's been tighter than a drum all her life. Pretty, dark-haired, dark-eyed Bit Lukeman grabbed the tiger by the tail and captured a little bird named Robin.

Enter hero, Dean McAfee, in a '69 Shelby. "I always loved your mother," Daddy assured me while I stood there trembling, mumbling unintelligible questions. "You were my daughter from the moment I put eyes on you. So tiny and pretty with hair the color of Alabama clay."

My eyes fill with tears, blurring the highway lines. I lift off the gas when I pass the fifty-five speed-limit sign, and the speedometer drifts down to the sixty-five tick. I crack the wheel with my fist. *I am the daughter of a man who can't carry a tune in a bucket. I am Dean McAfee's.*

Birdie told Jim about you. He knew who you were that day in his office . . . You pointed to a picture and said something about "that woman."

So, all the secrets are out, right? Let the universe continue. The stars are in place. The moon is glowing, and I'm the unwanted child of James Chastain. I feel sick.

I gun the gas again and barrel toward an I-440 exit. Within a minute, blue lights flash in my rearview mirror. A trooper. Doesn't he have a donut waiting on him somewhere? I pull over. He has me dead to rights, which burns me even more.

"License and registration, please." A deep voice comes from a dark silhouette standing just behind my door.

I hand them over and start the groveling process. "I'm sorry, officer. I received some bad news . . . Well, not bad news. Disturbing news. More like mind-blowing news. You know, the kind that knocks your socks off and fries the ends of your hair?" I touch my hair. "Well, actually, my hair's not fried, but I do need a cut, you know . . ." I glance back at him. "My hair's red . . . like . . . my . . ."

I stretch to see my face in the mirror. Now I see it. I'm the spitting image of Mr. Chastain. Red hair, green eyes, square chin, high brow, narrow nose. "It's red like my father's."

I drop my forehead to the wheel.

"Do you know how fast you were going?" the trooper asks.

"Seventy or something." Do I cry now? It would really be no problem. My eyes are brewing fresh tears.

He passes back my license and registration. "Seventy-two. But, I'm gonna let you go."

Let the water works begin.

The officer clears his throat. "Please be safe and drive the speed limit. And next time you get disturbing news, take a walk or ride your bike. Stay off the highway." He steps away. "Be careful."

"Thank you," I blubber, unable to stop the tears.

I creep along the berm until I'm off the exit ramp, and park at an abandoned gas station. With the emotion of my journey collapsing on my shoulders, I fall over on the seat and weep. Fighting fear; braving open-mike nights; falling in like with Lee, but not being ready for more; someone stealing my song; my first songwriter's night . . . and Momma's news . . . Momma's news . . . Momma's news.

I cry so long my face hurts. There are no napkins or tissues in the truck, so I wipe my eyes on my sleeve and blow my nose on the edge of my top. (It's going straight into the trash.)

I'm weary and want to sleep. Maybe stay here forever. Hide.

Yeah, hide for awhile. Jesus, you and me, right? I don't need all
this mess. Stupid Momma. Stupid James Chastain.

Tap, tap, tap.

   Who's there? Come in.

   Tap, tap, tap. "Miss? Are you all right?"

   I bolt straight up, knocking my funny bone on the gear
shift. Gripping my elbow, I glance at my watch. Six a.m. I'm
late for work.

   "Miss, are you all right?" The trooper who pulled me over
last night peers through the passenger-side window.

   I stretch to crank it open. A cool Tennessee breeze licks my
face. "I'm fine. Guess I fell asleep."

   "Your family is looking for you."

   My family. Suddenly my senses are awake with the reality
of the last eight hours. I crank the engine. "Thank you, officer."

   He taps the side of my truck. "Drive safe."

   I watch him walk back to his car. *Drive safe.* Is anything
in life safe?

Lee raps on my door around dinnertime. I shuffle over to
answer it.

   When he steps inside, I fall into his arms. "Birdie told me
what happened."

   Thank you, Birdie. "I still can't believe it. But for my first
mind-blowing, I'm hanging in there."

   He laughs and walks me over to the couch. Good. I haven't
lost all my wits. I curl up under his arm.

   "You want to talk about it?"

   He's so much better than a girlfriend, isn't he?

   "James Chastain is my biological father." I shrug. "What

else is there to say?" I am surprisingly practical about this now that my tears have been shed. I had a strange dream, too, where I saw the eyes of Jesus. They were so peaceful and full of love. I tried to remember my fears or why my soul felt so troubled, but as long as I looked in his eyes, I couldn't remember.

Lee smoothes his hand over my hair and kisses my forehead. "The day we toured the Hall of Fame, you looked so much like his picture, I wondered . . ."

"That's what you were trying to ask me . . . when we were leaving and Skyler called. I'm so dense."

"Dense? Robin, why would you even suspect such a thing? I just thought it was odd you have the same face as he does." Lee rests his head on the back of the couch. "Man, I'm tired. I quoted five new jobs today, started a new home construction, and finished a remodel."

"Do you want to order pizza?"

He *hum-ums*, drifting away. I slip out of his arms and spread Grandma's old afghan over him. He looks so cute sleeping under pink and yellow yarn.

"Sleep tight, my prince."

I call in our pizza order and take a hot shower. As the water runs over me, I see the eyes from my dream.

Yeah, everything is going to be all right.

The Saturday after Thanksgiving, in a candlelight service at Woodmont Baptist Church, a hundred or so black-tie guests watch as Birdie Griffin strolls down the aisle on the arm of her eighty-year-old daddy.

Mr. Griffin escorts Birdie slowly, letting her have her bridal moment in the spotlight. Her cancer test came back benign. She broke the good news to Walt by giving him a cup of plastic dentures soaking in blue water.

Walt can't keep his brown eyes off of her. His two-toned hair is slicked back and his goatee trimmed. The man has found love again, and it's written all over his face.

I stand at the altar, holding my shivers together, trying not to look like I feel. Terrified. Blaire dressed me up in a sage-green bridesmaid's dress we bought from a secondhand store. She assured me it was the way to go. And for the first time in my life, I'm wearing pumps. Taupe, toe-pinching, pumps. I didn't even know taupe was a color.

Among the guests in the pews, Lee sits with my parents. When I peek at him, his wink makes my heart go *kerplunk*. He said he needed to ask me something at the reception. Oh, please, he's not going to push the marriage thing, is he? It's been almost two months since he told me he loved me, but I have yet to confess the same. I'm still not ready.

Shew, is it hot in here? Where's the door?

Steady, Robbie, steady.

Until now, I've been doing fine. I'm happy to be Birdie's maid of honor. But as I watch her glide down the aisle, I feel trapped. Such a solemn moment . . .

My chest rises as my lungs gasp for air. Need. More. Air. My skin is hot and prickly.

Run . . .

My heart races. I don't want to be here. I want to be outside in the cold night air, running as fast as I can. Pumps or no pumps.

My foot jerks. My leg quivers. I scan for an escape route. In the pew behind Lee, Blaire clings to Ezra. Next to her, a bored-looking Skyler sits with Kip, who's talking, oh brother, on his cell phone. And the only exit sign I see is way at the end of the sanctuary. The best way out is the way I came in—down the main aisle.

Walt takes Birdie's hand when Mr. Griffin stops at the first pew. The old man kisses his daughter's cheek then releases her into Walt's care. His wrinkled cheeks are wet with tears.

Birdie hands me her bouquet. "How're you doing?" she whispers.

With a vigorous nod, I squeak, "Good."

"Welcome, beloved," Pastor Shawn says, commencing the ceremony.

I hear a subtle creak from the back of the sanctuary, and from the corner of my eye, I see him.

Holy Toledo. My eye starts to twitch. My pulse races, and is it me, or are the walls moving in?

". . . join in marriage, before God and men, until death . . ."

Mr. Chastain slips into a back pew. The white and gold lights of the sanctuary fade to browns and blacks.

Why is he here? What does he want? Please don't make a scene.

I glance at Lee for a dose of courage. Nothing. He looks at me like, "What?"

Fear spews all over me. I close my eyes and try to conjure up the picture of Jesus' eyes from my dream. But all I see is James Chastain sitting in the back of the church.

I ditch the bouquets and run, down the altar steps and up the main aisle, the heels of my pumps clicking every step of the way.

29

A block away, it's clear I didn't think this thing through. I don't have my truck since I rode with Lee, and my purse is in the church's bridal room. But I can't go back, so I press forward, pitifully limping and waddling down the narrow side of a busy Hillsboro Road.

I glance over my shoulder a few times to see if Lee or Daddy is coming after me, but they aren't. Good. I don't want everyone to ruin Birdie's big day—

I stop, jamming my toe into the grass. *Crud.* I'm the one who ruined Birdie's big day. Her maid of honor. Oh, Birdie, I'm so, so sorry. How could I have been so selfish? How could I have surrendered to my enemy—fear—once again?

Salty tears gather in the corners of my lips. I wipe them away with the back of my hand. How will I ever be able to make it up to her?

I wander for awhile, crying, until I see the Bluebird Café. Ah, my harbor in this storm. I dash inside. The early songwriter's session is going on.

"I just came from a wedding," I explain to Zoë, the hostess at the door. "Are there any seats?"

She smiles. "Sure, you can sit at the bar."

I give her a soft smile. "Thanks, Zoë." Cold, drained, and weary, I make my way to the bar, and without asking, Trevor slides me a Coke. I let the pumps drop from my feet to the floor.

"I don't have any money," I say.

"Don't worry, we'll make you sing for it."

For a long time, I sip my drink and dry my tears. How could I have given up the fight so easily? I'd made such progress. Dern, I owe Blaire a whole bottle of Lexapro.

The familiar atmosphere of the Bluebird is comforting. And as I ponder my plight, I see His eyes again, and peace fills me once again.

"Hey, Trevor, another?" I motion to my empty glass.

"I'll have what she's having." I turn to see the square-jawed face of Mr. Chastain.

"What are you doing here?"

"Looking for you." His voice is deep and steady, like that day in his office.

"It only took you twenty-five years, but hey, pull up a stool."

He sits. "Better late than never."

"According to whom?" I'm mad at myself; might as well take it out on him.

Trevor refills my Coke and serves one to Mr. Chastain.

"Why'd you come to the wedding?" I ask.

He twirls his glass between his hands. "Birdie invited me. We've made our peace."

"Guess there's a lot of that going around."

"I'd like to make my peace with you."

I look him square in the eye. "Why?"

He doesn't flinch. "Because I shouldn't have abandoned you and your mother. I'm sorry, Robin. I was a selfish, arrogant bastard. I can't change the past, but I'd like to change the future."

My eyes well up. Mr. Chastain is trying. He's asking for forgiveness. "Why did it take you so long?"

He adjusts his suit jacket and holds up his glass for a refill. "Actually, I tried to get in touch with you about ten years ago, but your mom thought it best to leave things alone."

Figures. "I didn't know."

When Trevor hands him a refill, he lifts his glass to me. "What do you say? Friends?"

I hesitate. Friends? With James Chastain. It could make my life in Nashville a whole lot easier. Momma didn't raise no dummy. I hoist my glass too. "Maybe. Friends."

We listen to the last few songs of the early in-the-round show. Two of the songwriters come over to Mr. Chastain to say hello. One of them writes for Nashville Noise Publishing, the other for Wrensong.

Quickly, the Bluebird clears out and Mr. Chastain drops a bill on the table, offering me his arm. "Care to be my date to a wedding reception?"

"You think they'll let me in?" I work my feet back into those cruel pumps.

"I think so."

"I'd love to go, Mr. Chastain."

"Jim. Please call me Jim."

He escorts me to his silver Mercedes. "Thank you for finding me."

"What are friends for?"

Walt and Birdie dash away from the reception after a smash of cake and gulp of punch.

"We waited to . . . you know . . ." Birdie giggles as she sets her punch glass on the linen covered table. "For our honeymoon."

I blush. She's said nothing about my abandonment. When I came in with Jim, she hugged me and said, "Welcome back."

But I can't let it go that easily. "Birdie, I'm sorry I ran out. It was rude. I was only thinking of myself."

She presses her finger to her lips. "Shush. All's well that ends well." She wraps me in a bosomy hug. "We'll have supper and talk when we get back."

I smile. "The Caribbean will never be the same."

She wiggles her tush as she turns to find her groom. "I certainly hope not."

Driving home from the reception with Lee is chilly and stuffed with inane chatter like:

"Looks like the leaves are all gone."

"Yep."

"They're saying winter is going to be harsh."

"I heard."

"Better check your tires in case it snows."

"Oh, good thinking."

He parks in Birdie's drive and walks me to the front door.

"Aren't you coming up?" I reach for his hand. It's like holding a dead fish.

"No, I'd better run."

"Lee." I lean into him. "Don't go. I just sorta freaked out is all."

He peers down at me. "Does it really scare you that much? Commitment?"

"No. Well, just a little, but today was about everything. Momma and Jim, my song, getting up early, staying up late, the rush of helping Birdie with wedding plans, you wanting to ask me a question—"

"What question?"

"You said you wanted to ask me something during the reception."

He grins. "Freaked you out, did I?"

I pop him. "This is not funny." Truth is, I've been freaking myself out for years."

"One of my clients is having a house-warming party. I was going to ask you to go with me. Next Friday."

"Oh."

He sighs. "Robin, we agreed to wait for your signal. I'm not going to pressure you."

"My bad. I'm sorry."

He snickers. "I wish we had video of you running down the aisle in those shoes. It's about the funniest thing I've ever seen."

"Be nice or I won't go to your silly house warming."

He snatches me up for a hearty kiss. "You're going to be the death of me."

"Lee, I'm sorry. You picked a weird girl to love."

"I know. But when a guy falls in love . . ."

I kiss him with all the passion my heart contains.

Wednesday afternoon the following week, Jim calls. "Robin," he says in a chairman-of-the-board sort of voice.

"Jim," I say in my cleaning-woman voice.

Since our Bluebird Café heart-to-heart, I'm at peace with him. I figure I have the best of both worlds. A Father in heaven who loves me without condition, an earthly Daddy who thinks the stars get their light from my eyes, and this new friend-father who told me during Birdie's reception that I'm one of the most promising songwriters he's heard in a decade. No lie.

"I'm having a meeting with . . ." He pauses. "Graham Young."

My heart drums against my ribs. "You're kidding. He's the one who—"

"I know."

"How'd you find him?"

"Arrogance always uncovers itself. I put the word out I was looking for him. Next thing you know, his publisher is calling."

"Do you think his publisher knows?"

"No. It's a new company, LightLyric, and though the owner's been around the Row for awhile, he's not as scrupulous as he could be."

"What are you going to do?"

"Care to join me?"

"I'd love to."

"Come to my office around five after eleven. Follow my lead."

"What's the plan?" I ask, loving the cloak-and-dagger approach. Jim is a crafty guy. Go figure.

"Get your song back."

A feathery feeling tickles my insides all the way down to my heels. "See you tomorrow."

The cleaning job I have on Thursday morning is at a tech company at One Lakeview Place. But the TechCom gang must have thrown a party or something, because the place is trashed. Cake icing is smeared on every door handle.

I call Marc. "This is going to take longer than two hours."

"Do the best you can. I'll get Laura to cover the Pagadigm Group."

When the staff staggers in, I'm still cleaning. Every once in a while, I hear, "Oh, gag!" and I know it's an office I haven't cleaned yet.

At ten fifteen, I ring Marc. "I'm still at TechCom, but I have to leave for an eleven o'clock meeting. I've cleaned 80 percent of the place. Bathrooms and lunch room are left."

"You can't leave."

"Marc, I've been here for over four hours. I'm sorry, but I have a super-duper, cherry-on-top important meeting." I crinkle my nose when I reach for the trash in the senior vice president's office. I've smelled sweeter pig pens.

"With who?" he demands.

"It's personal." I cradle the phone over my shoulder and wrinkle my nose while the contents of the trash slips into my Hefty bag.

"Finish the job. If you leave, you're fired."

"What? You can't fire me. I'm you're best employee and one of the few you have left." You wanna play chicken with me, Marc?

"Robin, I'm serious."

"Then do it. Fire me." Heading toward each other at a hundred miles per hour, neither I nor Marc Lewis flinch.

"Robin . . ."

"Marc . . ."

"How important is it?"

"Very."

He hesitates. "No, finish the job. Arnold Hancock is a big client. He'll bill *me* if you leave."

"Marc, I'm going to this meeting, but I promise I'll come back and finish."

"Then I guess you're fired."

Ooo, good for him, he didn't flinch. "Okay. I'll pick up my check tomorrow."

Ooo, good for me, I didn't flinch.

At precisely four minutes after eleven, I knock lightly on Jim's door.

"Come in," he beckons.

I shove the slightly ajar door the rest of the way open. Jim is propped against his desk, his legs stretched in front of him. He's laughing and talking, using his muckity-muck voice and words like "drive-time song" and "multialbum deal."

"Hi," I say a little too girly. I'm not sure of my role here yet.

Jim waves for me to come in. "Robin, welcome. Glad you could make it."

First, I see Frank Gruey then the back of Graham's head. I know it well. He's hiding under his hat and the long leather duster. He stiffens when Jim says my name.

"Frank Gruey, Graham Young, I'd like you to meet a really good friend of mine, Robin McAfee." Jim motions for me to come on in.

Graham jerks forward but doesn't get up or look around. He flips up the duster's collar and tugs his hat lower.

Shaking, I walk across the room.

Frank shakes my hand. "Hello, nice to meet you."

"Again. We've met. Several times."

Jim walks around his desk to his chair. "Robin's a new songwriter in town, an excellent new songwriter. Ever seen her around, Graham?"

Graham rises slowly and turns to me with his chest puffed out. "Good to see you, Robin."

All right. Forget the sting, forget Jim's plan. "You stole my song." I ball my fist and pow! Right on his big square chin.

Graham topples over Frank's chair, thudding to the floor like a sack of dirt.

"You stole my song, you lying, yellow-bellied river rat."

Frank rushes to Graham's aid, shoving me aside. "Jim, what is going on? Who is this crazy girl?"

Jim shakes his head. "I hate to tell you, Frank, but your boy stole her song."

"What? That's impossible. I checked it out."

I face the stupid Frank Gruey with my hands on my hips. "Well, get better sources."

Graham gets up, rubbing his jaw. "It's my song, Robin. Tell the truth."

Oh my stars. He's crazy. Plumb crazy.

"We have the original work tape." Frank rages. Apparently he wasn't paying attention the night I sang it at the Bluebird.

Jim drops a CD into a player behind his desk. "This was recorded in my studio around June twenty-ninth."

Graham scoffs. "Why would I steal from her? I'm the published songwriter."

Jim presses a button. My voice billows from his stereo. Graham snorts and steams like a mad bull. "Frank, you've had my work tape since May."

"May?" I kick him in the shin. "You stole my song in May?"

Graham stares me down. "I don't have to stand here and take this." He kicks the chairs and strides out of the office.

Why that arrogant son of a gun. I bolt after him.

As he pushes through the Nashville Noise doors, I dive for the edge of his duster. He trips and hits the ground face-first.

"You stole my song." I grit my teeth and mash his face in the grass and dirt. "And you lied to me the day I saw you at NSAI."

"Get off."

"No wonder you didn't return my calls."

"What calls?"

I lean my elbow on the base of his neck. "The hundred I've made since Susan West told me you wrote 'I Wanna Be.' Why'd you do it? How'd you get a work tape?"

"Get off." Six-foot Graham doesn't have to work hard to knock me off his back. Once he catches his wind, he pushes off the ground with a wild roar.

"Get off, you monkey."

I clasp my hands against his Adam's apple. "I trusted you. I took you home to Freedom. You kissed me!"

He gags as he tries to wrench free. "Get off me." A couple on the sidewalk stops to gawk.

I press harder against his throat. "Why? Tell me why? I thought we were friends."

He flails around, trying to get me off, refusing to answer. Then it hits me. This is ridiculous. I'm ridiculous. If the man under the hat had an ounce of character, he wouldn't have stolen my song in the first place. He's not going to tell me *why* or *how*. And since I'm not going to choke him to death, I don't have any other recourse except to ride around on his back all day hoping he'll confess. But he won't.

I let go.

Graham stumbles forward, coughing, rubbing his throat. "I can't believe you. Accusing me like that in front of Mr. Chastain. You may have ruined my chance with him."

I swat the dirt and grass from my jeans. "No," I shake my head with sadness. "You did it all by yourself." I turn to go.

"Robin."

"What?" I catch a flicker of something in his eyes. Regret? Sorrow? His slumped demeanor zaps my heart and makes my eyes water.

"I—" He hesitates, then drops his gaze and walks off.

30

The receptionist busies herself with sharpening pencils when I go back inside. Jim is reading Frank the riot act.

"... make it right."

"I wouldn't pull this kind of stunt on purpose. He brought me the song months ago. Emma loved it, we checked it out ... He claimed he wrote it. He's brilliant, you know. Photographic memory."

"Brilliant? He's a thief. Get him to sign at least half of the rights over to Robin."

Frank sighs. His first hard lesson in the business, and it's a doozey. "I'll do what I can. But like it or not, Graham Young and LightLyrics own the song. It's Robin's word against ours."

Jim gives him a stern look. "Do what you can."

Frank leaves, and Jim closes the door behind him. "Are you all right?" he asks me.

I bite my lip and stare thoughtfully at my hands. "I'm sorry for Graham." I sink down into one of the chairs, feeling weak.

"He's finished in this town, you know." He sits next to me.

"That's why I'm sad. He's better than this."

Jim touches my hand. "You sound like my mother."

I look at him. "How so?"

"She's tenderhearted, but spunky. She would have done exactly what you did today. Socked him right on the chin, then pined over his plight."

"I sang at the Bluebird for the first time because of him." My stomach feels like I swallowed a rock.

"We'll see if Frank can't get you part ownership of the song."

I slide down in the chair. "I don't want half the song. I'm sick of this whole mess. And I guess, technically, he did rework the chorus, and that's the best part of the song."

Jim perches on the edge of his desk. "Songs get reworked all the time. It doesn't take away from the fact it's your song. This is a huge hit for Emma, Robin. It'll be on her greatest hits album coming out next year. You're looking at a couple hundred grand. But, if you don't need half of that, then I'll tell Frank to forget it."

I jerk forward. "A couple hundred thousand dollars?"

"At least." A smile tips his lips.

"Well, I did get fired today."

He frowns. "Marc fired you?"

"Yeah, but technically I walked out on a job."

He laughs and stands. "Come on, I'll buy you lunch. Maybe we can find something for you to do here at Nashville Noise."

"Well, I don't want nepotism or anything. I'd like to earn my way."

"Nepotism?" Jim holds the door open for me. "What nepotism? I need someone to clean the toilets and empty the trash."

"Ah, well, then I'm your girl."

On December twenty-third, Lee's F350 flies across the Freedom County line. I wave at the *Let Freedom Ring* sign. Home for the holidays.

The past month has been fantabulous. Is that a word? It is

now. Jim hired me to work in the Nashville Noise office, so I'm learning the business side of Music Row. I do a lot of flunky work, but my days of inhaling Clorox are over.

Marc begged me to come back to work for him. I refused, but he was a good boss, and I reminded Jim about his promise to look at Marc's songs. They have a meeting set for early in the New Year.

Despite what he did to Momma and me, Jim Chastain is a kind, good man. He's not my daddy, but I respect the fact that he owned up to his mistakes and is trying to make it right.

Lee slams on the brakes to do a little rubbernecking. "Is that snow?"

"Fake snow. Thank you, Henna Bliss."

"What's a Henna Bliss?"

"Friend of Momma's. Town busybody and decorator."

"Babe, how did they get all this fake snow here?" He strokes my fingers absently with his thumb. Makes my brain buzz.

"Big trucks. Eighteen wheelers."

He laughs. "This is amazing."

I twist his class ring around his finger. "Hey," I blurt. "Can I wear this?"

He lifts his hand. "My ring? Why, you want to go steady?"

I make an "aw" face. "I've never gone steady before." I yank that ring off his finger.

"Robin, forget going steady. Let's get engaged."

"Let's go steady." With my foot, I unlatch the glove box. I thought I saw some duct tape in here . . . Yep. I dig my pocket knife from my purse and slice a ribbon of tape to wrap around the ring.

"Perfect." I wiggle my fingers in his face.

He guffaws. "There's more tape than ring." Then he slams on the brakes again. "What in the world?"

I look where he's pointing. "It's the candy-cane field."

In the open lot between the drugstore and the library, giant red-and-white candy canes dance in the breeze above a layer of fake snow.

"This is incredible. Where do you buy this stuff?"

"Phil Beautner knows someone who knows someone. Fake snow is actually a line item in the county budget."

A minute later, Lee almost wrecks when we pass Santa's Toy Shop. "This I gotta see."

Outside, he tromps through plastic flakes to see the craftsmanship of the Toy Shop. "Unbelievable." He turns a circle. "All of Main Street is the North Pole."

"Yep." I tip my head and squint in the sunlight. "I told you Christmas ain't Christmas until you've been to Freedom, Alabama."

"What about the Nativity? Don't you tell me Freedom's gone PC."

"Has hell froze over? It's on the other side of the town."

Lee opens his door for me. "You should drive. I might wreck otherwise."

On the back side of the town square, between the new Wal-Mart and Libby Dankin's bookstore, The Book Worm and Café (yeah, Mayor Bedford warned her people not to associate worms with lattés, but Libby already had the sign hung), is the Living Nativity.

"Real people?" Lee asks, stepping out of the truck.

I join him, slipping my arm around his waist. "Yep, real people."

"If it weren't for the Wal-Mart, I'd swear I was in old Bethlehem."

The baby Jesus starts to cry, so Mary picks him up and thumps him on the back. Then she sniffs the little guy's rear. Her nose wrinkles.

Before we can say "O Holy Night," she rips off his Huggies, wipes him with a wet wipe, rediapers, reswaddles, and just like that, baby Jesus is happy and back in character.

Lee laughs. "Just like Mary did two thousand years ago."

I elbow him in the ribs, "shhh, the actors are doing their best to portray one of the greatest days in human history."

"I'm sorry," he whispers. "This *is* amazing."

"Every night at dusk, the Shepherds come, then at midnight, the Wise Men come."

Lee shakes his head. "People come from all over the state to see this?"

I pat him on the back. "Honey child, they come from all over the world."

He kisses the top of my head and softly whispers, "I wish I could've been there for the real thing."

I lean against him. "Me too. Me too."

Momma kills the fatted calf and half of the family getting ready for Christmas. She has Lee toting firewood and polishing silver while Dawnie, Eliza, and I wrap presents for the needy families in the community. Steve's presents were shipped weeks ago, and we're talking to him tomorrow at noon.

"So, Momma told me," Eliza says, sticking a big bow on a small package.

"About Jim Chastain?" It still feels sort of surreal.

"I couldn't believe it," Dawnie says. "I haven't even told Steve yet."

"I still can't get my mind around it. God's peace does surpass all understanding."

I cut a square of wrapping paper from a large roll. The scissors are dull, so the end rips a little.

"You'll always be my sister," Eliza says. "I can't imagine Daddy not being your daddy."

"What do you mean I'll always be your sister?" I toss aside the wrapping paper roll. "Daddy is my daddy. And you are my sister. There's no statue of limitations."

Dawnie snickers.

"I just mean nothing has changed for me."

I tear off a large strip of clear tape. "Nothing's changed for me either, Eliza, except I have this new man in my life who is responsible for my red hair and green eyes."

She laughs with a shake of her dark head. "Sure explains Momma all those years, doesn't it. No wonder she looked like she sucked on a lemon for lunch."

"She smiles a lot more now." Dawnie reaches for the tape.

"I've noticed," Eliza says, reaching over and yanking the bow off my package.

"What gives?"

"The bow doesn't match the paper." She searches in the bow bag for another bow. "Here."

I shake my head, laughing. "How can you ever doubt being my sister. You've been doing this to me for twenty-two years." I press the bow on to the box. "Really, Eliza, do you actually think some little boy is going to care if his box had a purple bow on blue paper?"

"Yes."

"You're a pain, you know that?"

"But you love me."

A wave of sentiment crashes over me, and I croak, "Yeah, I do."

In the midst of the Christmas frenzy, Momma corners me in the kitchen.

"You know, your daddy's never heard me play or sing in public. So, I want to sign up for the Spring Sing."

I notice the dishes piling up, so I plug the sink and squirt soap under a stream of hot water. "Good for you."

She grabs me by the shoulders. "I want you to sing with me."

"Me? Why?"

"It's been awhile, Robin. Besides, it'll be fun. Can you just see your granddaddy and daddy? They'll be bustin' all their buttons."

I've never seen Bit McAfee so energized. "I guess we could, Momma." But a duet adds a new level of complication to my anxieties. Will we get the timing right? Hit the right harmony?

"I've been working on a song. You can learn it easy enough."

I gaze into her excited blue eyes and realize I cannot deny this woman. She's breaking my heart. At forty-three, Momma still has a dream.

"Okay, Momma, I'll do it."

"Oh, good." She claps her hands and does a little jig. "I asked Winnie Engledow to sew us some costumes."

"Say you didn't." I laugh.

She winces. "Sorry, but I did."

I shake my head. "All right. For Winnie's sake."

Winnie Engledow is the town seamstress. She's sewn school and church costumes, bride and bridesmaids' dresses since Jefferson Davis ruled the South. She's probably the sweetest southern lady ever born.

"Thank you, Robbie." Momma kisses my cheek and skips—yes, I said skips—out of the kitchen. "By the way," she says from the hallway, "check the refrigerator door. Then come on up to the attic. There's some stuff in the old trunk I want to show you."

I twist around to check the fridge door. "I'd love to go through the—" I frown and shake the soap from my hands. The waterlogged, faded *Lose 25 lbs* note is gone. In its place is a new note. *Lose 18 lbs.*

My eyes well up. Good for you, Momma. Good for you.

On the drive home the day after Christmas, Lee is quiet.
"What's on your mind, big guy?"

He reaches for my hand. "Just thinking."

"About what?"

"If you're ever gonna say it."

"I'm gonna say it," I whisper.

He looks over at me for a split second, then back to the road. "I suppose I have to believe you, but, babe, it's been almost three months since I told you. Things are becoming a little lopsided."

I twist his duct-taped ring around my finger. Why is this so hard for me? In late November I knew I was falling in love with him. I remember the first time I felt it. The night before Thanksgiving. He was out back helping Walt smoke a turkey. I played guitar on the stoop, watching, listening to the even, sure sounds of Lee's voice. When he looked over at me, brushing aside his bangs, it made me weakkneed, and I flubbed the next chord.

The family *loooves* him. Daddy almost cornered Lee about his "plans." I saw it coming and threw a wrench in the works with a quick, "Who wants cake?"

Okay, it's time for a ride to Honest Town. "I'm afraid, Lee. Afraid of being consumed and smothered. And losing the joy of my life, losing sight of songwriting."

"Consumed and smothered? By me?"

"Well, by marriage in general."

"You can't be serious." He shifts in his seat and grips the wheel so his knuckles bulge.

"I am." I gaze out the window. "Lee, what if I want to sing at a songwriter's night or go out to hear other songwriters? Will you get mad? Will you expect dinner on the table at six? In case you haven't noticed, I'm not a dinner-on-the-table-at-six kind of girl."

"I'm not a dinner-on-the-table-at-six kind of guy, either. More like seven."

"You're making fun of me."

"Look, Robin, marriage is about two people merging their lives, adjusting to each one's gifts and callings. I would do everything in my power to help your dream of being a songwriter."

Well, just melt my heart and pour a little warm caramel over it. "Lee, one more thing. I've never really been—"

I'm cut short when my cell phone rings. "Hey, Sky— What? . . . No way. Please say you're kidding . . . Right . . . Absolutely. Eight o'clock."

I flip my phone closed. "Blaire and Ezra broke up. Skyler's called an intervention at their place tonight."

When we arrive home, Lee carries up my presents. "Put them there." I point to the tiny dining table and toss my suitcase behind the bedroom divider.

We have some time before I have to meet Blaire and Skyler, so I walk over and give him a soft kiss, expecting him to swoop me up in his big arms for a cuddle on the couch. But he barely kisses me back. A cold chill runs over me.

Lee sighs. I don't like the echo of sadness. "Do you want me?"

I swallow. So, we're back to this? "Y-yes."

"Then I need to hear you say you love me. This is getting ridiculous."

I square off with him. "I will, when I'm ready."

He walks to the door. "I'm pretty sure you love me, Robin, but for the life of me, I can't figure out why you won't tell me."

"You can't force me to say something I don't . . . am not ready to say."

He raises his hands in surrender. "I see. Maybe I'm wrong. You don't love me." He turns the knob.

"Where are you going?" I'm trapped in my own paradox.

He pauses, facing away from me. Six foot two, confident, kind, successful, lover of Jesus, Lee whispers, "This is starting to hurt too much."

"Lee, please, I'm just not ready for marriage." Say it, Robin, you egghead. Tell him. "I'm only asking for a little more time."

"You got it." The door clicks closed, and his footsteps resound on the stairs.

I bite back a blue word and kick the wall. Merry end of Christmas.

31

Skyler and Blaire share a swanky refurbished condo in Green Hills, not far from Lee's place. He's on my mind as I drive down Hillsboro Road.

I'm sad he's sad. I hurt because he hurts, and I am really wondering why I can't force those three little words out of my mouth: "I love you."

No, that's not true. I know why. I've never been in love before. Infatuated, intrigued, in like, but not in love. Not even with Ricky.

My reasons for holding back are unfounded. Lee embodies my courage. He shows up at the Bluebird without being asked and tells me I ruined the audience for all the other song-writers. He supports my career.

Can't I trust him with my heart?

By the time I swing into a parking space in front of Blaire and Skyler's, my mental debate comes to an end. I love him, and I'm gonna tell him. Soon. Really soon.

A melody forms in my head, and I scramble in my purse for my black notebook. Gum wrappers, pens, wallet, hair tie, pocketknife—shoot fire, everything but the kitchen sink is in here. Where's my notebook?

I check my hip pocket. Ah, there it is. Finding a pen, I jot down a few lyrics.

> *For the first time, I feel it,*
> *Like a warm breeze after a winter rain.*
> *For the first time, I know it,*
> *Like the haunting call of a distant train.*
> *I'm in love with you,*
> *I'm in love, it's true*
> *For the first time in my life*
> *And it's with you.*

Skyler swings the door open and jerks me inside. "Praise God, you're here. I'm running low on sympathy."

"I told you to keep a reserve supply." I dump my new suede Christmas jacket on her head.

"I can't do comfort. I can't do hand holding." She tugs the jacket off and drops it on the couch. Her hair stands up with static electricity. She looks like Young Frankenstein's bride.

"Where is she?"

"In her room."

I take the stairs two at a time, rap twice on her door, then barge in. Blaire's room is pitch black. When I flip on the light, she screams and slithers under a mountain of blankets.

"Come on, Blaire, let's go. Up and at 'em." I strip back the first layer of covers.

"No. Go away. I want to hibernate until 2010." Her muffled voice is buried in the pillow.

I peel back another layer. "Starting to smell like an onion in there."

Blaire pops out like a jack-in-the-box. Her dark hair is tangled and wild, and her eyes are ringed and red. "Smell like an onion? Girl . . ." She plants both feet on the floor, wraps the top blanket around her neck, and struts toward the bathroom, tugging the covers to the ground. "I'm heartbroken, not insane. I showered this morning."

"When did you eat last?" Skyler asks, crossing her arms and leaning against the doorframe.

"Yesterday," Blaire responds with no conviction whatsoever. "I think."

I start bossing in my big-sister voice, "Blaire, get dressed, comb your hair, put on deodorant—"

"I told you I showered," Blaire hollers as she and all her bedding disappear behind the bathroom door. "And I'm not going out."

"All right, Blaire, you leave me no choice. I'm calling Ezra."

I whip around to Skyler. "Whoa, bringing out the big guns." The bathroom door flies open. "You wouldn't dare."

Skyler narrows her eyes. "Watch me. I'm gonna tell him how devastated and distraught you are, crying over him."

Blaire's presses her lips into a tight line. "Two minutes. I'll be ready."

"Good." Skyler motions for me to follow her downstairs. "My father gave me an iPod for Christmas. I downloaded 'I Wanna Be.'"

Two minutes later Blaire comes down looking like death warmed over. Her ratty hair is out of her face, bunched up in a half ponytail, but stray wisps fly about her face and neck. Baggy sweats hang from her slender frame, and her porcelain skin looks blotchy and pasty.

I clap my hands and smile. "Great. You look—"

"Horrible." Skyler steps up. "You're actually going out like that?"

Blaire smoothes her hand over the university letters of her sweatshirt. "Ezra used to wear this when he played football in the park." She flops forward over the brown chair. "I want Ezra," she wails. "Why? Why did he break up with me?"

I grab her shoulders and push her upright. "Blaire, get a hold of yourself. Why do you even want a man who's stupid enough to let a beautiful, wonderful woman like you get away?"

"Robin, I'm not as strong as you."

Skyler sighs from where she waits by the door. "Good grief, it's the pot calling the kettle black. You're doing the same thing to Lee, Robin."

"I am *not* doing the same thing to Lee. Do you write your own fairy tales or get them from the Soap Network?"

"What? You are so doing the same thing to Lee."

I argue with Skyler while trying to steer Blaire out the door. It's like trying to grasp a flopping fish.

Skyler tosses Blaire's coat over her shoulder. "We'll take the Beamer. I have child locks in the back."

Once we get Blaire in the car and buckled up, she starts crying. "He said he loved me, y'all. Love. You don't just say it if you don't mean it."

Skyler turns left out of the complex. "Let's go to the Mellow Mushroom for pizza."

Blaire slaps the back of my seat. "He said he *loved* me. Creepasoid liar."

Skyler brakes for a red light. "Then be glad you're no longer tied to a creepasoid liar. He did you a favor."

"But he's a Christian man. Why'd he lie?"

A high-pitched, fake, "Ha, ha," peals from Skyler. "How're those rose-colored glasses fitting, Blaire?"

"See, this is exactly why I haven't told Lee I love him. I don't want to utter idle words."

Blaire flops back against her seat. "How could I be so blind and stupid?"

I stretch over the seat and grab her arm. "Blaire, stop. He charmed all of us."

"I'm afraid I'll always be alone."

Skyler swerves into the parking lot across from the Mellow Mushroom. "You will not be alone, Blaire. And Robin, good grief, you love Lee and you know it."

"You can't let him get away, Robin," Blaire whispers.

"Lord?" Skyler addresses the roof of her car. "What'll you give me for these two loons?"

"Speak for yourself, I-get-bored-with-a-guy-after-two-dates." I shove open my door.

"I do not. More like five dates."

We banter about relationships as we walk into the restaurant. Finally, Skyler sums it up. "Blaire, you always toss your heart out like it's a two-dollar Frisbee. Why don't you just be happy being you? Blaire Kirby, fantastic photographer, lover of God, beautiful woman. Why do you need a man?" She puffs the paper from her straw. "And you, on the other hand." She points to me. "Stop being stubborn and afraid. It's getting old. Seal the deal with Lee. Please."

I stick my tongue out at her. "I'll say it when I'm ready."

"Nothing wrong with waiting until you're ready," Blaire says, reaching for a napkin.

"Fine," Skyler says. "Then, let's talk about me."

"Oh, yeah," Blaire says with her first genuine laugh of the night. "We *never* talk about you."

Jim picks me up for dinner two days before New Year's Eve. He wants to take me to his favorite steak place, The Stock-Yard Restaurant, over on 2nd Avenue North. "The owners renovated the old Nashville Union Stock-Yard building. Livestock was traded down here for about fifty years, but when they closed down, the buyers couldn't believe the marble and cherry wood décor of the offices. Made for a great renovation."

"I love this town."

Jim chuckles. "This town has had everything. Gospel to rock music, sports, the Grand Ole Opry, and some of the finest dining anywhere."

"Nashville is starting to feel like home."

He cuts a glance at me. "I'm glad. And I hope you like steak. The Stock-Yard serves the best Angus Beef."

"I never turn down a good steak," I say as we head down Broadway.

The Stock-Yard is amazing. The atmosphere is Victorian with rich wood trim and a shiny marble floor. A heavy chandelier hangs from a domed skylight and illuminates the entrance. The ambiance is rich and classy.

A burly cowboy of a man greets us with open arms, "Jim, good to see you."

I choke back a laugh, unprepared for the big man to have a high, squeaky voice.

Jim motions to me. "Robin, this is the manager, Rusty Allender. Rusty, this is my, well—"

I offer my hand. "Daughter. Robin McAfee."

Rusty shakes my hand. "Very nice to meet you." Then he pounds Jim on the back. "Good heavens, man. Known you ten years and never knew you had a kid."

"Actually, we just met." This is hard for him. A chink in his armor. But he's swallowing his pride with dignity.

"Congratulations, then." With much pomp for a small circumstance, Rusty escorts us to a nice booth in the back.

"Pick an appetizer, you two. On the house." Rusty pats his broad, hairy hands together. "Rooster fries?"

Jim looks at me, grinning.

I squirm. "No, please. No."

"Give us a couple of shrimp cocktails and iced teas please," Jim says.

Rusty's big laugh billows behind him as he barrels toward the kitchen.

"He asked on purpose. He likes to mess with people," Jim says, reaching for his silverware, unrolling the napkin.

"Rooster fries." I shiver.

"So, tell me about Robin McAfee," Jim says, as a server comes with our teas, promising our appetizer will be out in a moment.

"Not much to tell." I give him the lowdown on growing up in Freedom, my short-lived college career, and the four jobs since then, singing on the porch with Granddaddy and the Bluegrass Boys, the family.

"So, are you married?" I ask Jim. "Any other kids?"

Jim shakes a packet of sweetener then dumps it in his tea. "I almost got married a few years ago, but we called it off. And, you're my only . . ."

A different server brings our shrimp. "Ready to order?"

"Oh, no, I haven't even looked." I reach for a menu, but Jim cuts in.

"Care if I order for you?"

I pause mid-reach. "Okay, yeah, sure."

He orders a prime rib with baked potato, fixings on the side, and a salad with ranch dressing, on the side. And a porterhouse for himself.

"How'd I do?" He leans toward me.

"Freakishly well." I grin. "I like blue cheese more than ranch, but it's good."

"I'll remember next time."

"Next time, I'll order for you."

He laughs. "Now you sound like my kid."

It's weird, but I don't mind him saying I'm like him. Sort

of puts some of my quirks into perspective. "Why'd you start Nashville Noise?"

Jim spears a few shrimp for his plate. "I wanted to be an artist."

I take a big gulp of tea. Shrimp isn't my favorite. "So you started your own label?"

"Not at first. I was going around town with my guitar, pretending to be Glen Campbell mixed with a little Roy Orbison, but I never made it to the stage."

"Why?" Boldly, I take a few shrimp and spoon some cocktail sauce. Don't want him to eat them alone.

"Stage fright."

I freeze, mid-cocktail sauce dip. "You? I got it from you? All these years, feeling like an alien, writing songs without the guts to sing them, and it was *you* all along."

"Certainly not your momma. She wasn't afraid of the stage." He stares me straight in the eye. "I admire you."

"This is unbelievable. I feel like I'm seeing myself for the first time."

Jim chuckles. "I'm sorry, I should've—"

I hold up my hand. We've covered this territory already. "So, anyway, you wanted to be an artist."

"Yeah, so one night, I was backstage at the Ryman with some songwriters I'd done some arrangements for, and this young woman with a big voice hits the stage."

"Momma?" I asked.

"No, Grace Harding. She was engaged to Tuck Wilder, and they were fighting like cats and dogs before the show. Hitting and spitting."

I laugh. "You're kidding."

"The stage director comes back, tells them to knock it off, they're on in five minutes."

"What'd they do?"

Jim chuckles. "Grace stood up and said, 'Help me get ready.' And Tuck trotted off after her, telling her to wear her blue-sequined dress. Grace came out and sang like a pro, left the stage, and went back to fighting with Tuck. I pulled them aside and said, 'We have to work together.' Two people with that much passion had to make some great music. I formed Nashville Noise and signed Grace and Tuck the next month."

"Unbelievable." Our server comes around with our steaks. My stomach rumbles. "You know, I saw something in Graham Young when he talked music with Granddaddy and the boys back home. I think he has a knack for recognizing talent and trends. Too bad he's—"

"The boy is arrogant."

"Too bad he's afraid of failure," I say.

By the time our food arrives, the conversation flowed from the music biz to Jim's family. Over thick juicy steaks and buttery potatoes, I learned he has three sisters and two brothers. And more nieces and nephews than I care to count.

The idea of a whole new family makes my head swim. "If it's all the same to you, I'd like to keep our relationship between me and you for now."

He saws off a large chunk of steak. "Your choice." His gaze shifts to my face. "But I have to tell you, my mother's been praying for you for a long time."

His confession catches me off guard, and my eyes well up. She watched over me without ever laying eyes on me. "I'd like to meet her . . . someday."

"She'd like that a lot. You say when."

By the time dinner is over and dessert consumed, I'm stuffed and sleepy, but content. Discovering Jim Chastain has been the best part of the night.

While Rusty and Jim haggle over who's picking up the check, I excuse myself to the ladies' room. As I round the corner, humming a melody, I hear, "Hold this for me, Lee, darling, I'll be right back."

I look toward the lobby. Standing there, holding a woman's purse, is Lee I-love-you-Robin Rivers. He's dressed up, looking darn handsome in a brown suede jacket and jeans. His hair has been trimmed since he dropped me off at home, and apparently he's acquired a tall, leggy blonde.

"All set?" she asks, returning. She's gorgeous.

"Sure," Lee says, shining his suave smile on her.

I start to shake all over. Lee?

"Robin, is everything okay?" Jim's hand touches my shoulder.

"Fine." I watch Lee and the blonde follow the hostess to a table on the other side of the restaurant.

Jim hands me my coat lovingly. "He's not the two-timing kind, Robin."

I look up at him. "Thanks for dinner."

I feel ill.

32

"*Okay, here's what you do,*" *Skyler says over the phone while*
I lay on my bed. "Write him a song."

"Write him a song?" My face itches from the dried tears.

"And sing it to him at the Bluebird."

"Sheesh, like that'd be comfy. Hello, strange people, please
join me in this very intimate moment while I tell my boyfriend
I love him for the fist time. Hold your applause until I'm done
baring my soul."

"Are you PMSing?"

"No. You're ridiculous." I sit up and stuff my feet into my
Nikes. "You know what? Forget strategy. I'm going over to his
house and tell him." Seeing Lee with another woman did what
nothing else could do—give me the courage to tell him."

"That-a-girl. Take action."

I slip on my jacket. "What if *she's* there?"

"She who? Didn't we decide Lee's a one-woman kind of
guy. Look what he did with you when his ex needed him."

"Right. Here I go." It's eleven o'clock, but I don't care. Lee
Rivers is going to hear "I love you" tonight. Preferably from me
and not the leggy blonde.

Hidden among maple and hickory trees and one weeping willow, Lee's house on Sharondale Drive is pitch black. Not so much as a porch light glowing. I park my truck next to his garage and cut the engine.

Now what? I drum my fingers against the steering wheel. I've never done this before. Made a move on a man. Ricky chased me for over a year before I let him catch me. When he said he loved me, I asked him if he wanted ketchup or mustard on his hotdog.

But my life is all about change and discovery these days. Who knew I'd move to Music City and discover my red hair is not from cousin Mickey O'Dell, four times removed? Who knew I'd find out the blood of a Music Row tycoon flows through my veins? Who knew I'd have compassion for the man who stole my song? Who knew I'd figure out that being found comes only after being lost?

And who knew I'd fall in love for the first time? Not me. Yet here I am.

Cold air seeps into the truck cab. The tip of my nose is getting numb. I figure I'd better do something or go back home. Glancing up at Lee's window, I rub my hands together for warmth, thinking, and stalling.

Get out and knock on his door. The night ain't getting any younger.

I shove the door open, then slam it shut again. Wait. What am I going to say? "Hey, Lee. Did I wake you?"

Or, "Hey, about you and that blonde? I'm not jealous, but by the way, I love you."

There. The three platinum words. "I love you." Here goes. Knock on his door, and when he opens, fall at his feet and grovel.

Wait, that's a terrible plan. What if he's still upset with me? What if he doesn't love me anymore? What if the blonde really is the other woman? I chew on the tip of my thumbnail.

Mountain of indecision? Meet valley of regret. I'm para-
lyzed by my own ability to see both sides.

The passenger door creaks open. I scream.

"Robin. Hey, hey, shhhh. It's me. What are you doing?"

"Lee! Great day, are you trying to give me a heart attack?"

He slams the passenger door shut and walks around to
my side. My legs wobble as I step out. He shines his flashlight
down on me.

I pop his arm. "You scared me."

"What'd you want me to do, leave you sitting in the driveway all night?"

"You knew I was here?"

"I saw you pull in."

"Well, why didn't you come out?"

"I just did!"

"Oh, forget—" I glance at Lee in the glow of his flashlight.
He's wearing a pair of baseball pants (no lie), old-man slippers,
and a long, Darth Vader-like robe that hangs open. She-doggies.
I whirl around. What is it with me and guys with six- packs.

"Robin?" His hand touches my shoulder.

"I love you, Lee Rivers. There. I said it. I love you."

"Gee, Robin, you sure?" Sarcasm oozes. "I'd hate to force you."

Six-pack or not, I whirl back around and kiss Lee Rivers
like he ain't been kissed ever before. At least not from me.
When I let go, he stumbles back.

"Wow!"

Every fiber of my five-four being pulsates. "Are you in love
with that blonde chick?"

"W-what blonde chick?" He takes a deep breath and clears
his throat.

"The one you were with at The Stock-Yard."

"You were there?"

"With Jim. Please, don't love her."

He shakes his head. "Valerie's a client."

I exhale my last anxiety. "She's not the other woman?"

"There is no other woman. Just you." He grips my collar. "I love you, Robin." He kisses me as if he wants to permanently seal the deal.

I lay my head against his bare chest. The night is cold, but Lee is warm. So very warm.

"I know you're not ready to talk marriage, Robin, but it feels great to hear you love me."

"Lee," I whisper, "I've never been in love before."

His heartbeat quickens. "Oh, I see." He rests his chin on my head. "How do you like it so far?"

"I like it."

Then, there's a rumble in his chest. "So, you were jealous of Valerie Floyd?"

I push away. "No."

"You just happen to decide to tell me you love me at eleven o'clock at night after seeing me with Valerie?"

"Well . . ." I lift my chin. "I'd already decided, but seeing you with her made me realize I shouldn't wait."

"You wanted to make sure I didn't run off with another woman." He slips his arm around me and walks toward the house. "I see how it is. But what you don't know is that Jim and I worked out this big plot to trick you."

I laugh. "Liar."

He laughs. "How about some hot chocolate?"

"I'd love some."

The night wind whistles through the trees. It's cold and crisp. Love is in the air, and I'm taking a deep, deep breath.

The third Thursday night of February, I'm ready for Pitch-to-
Publishers night at NSAI. Jim and I agreed it's good for me
to go through the steps of becoming a published songwriter.

He calls it grooming.

I call it agony.

But I don't want to be a one-hit wonder, which I would've
been with "Your Country Princess." I still have some things
to learn about writing lyrics and melodies that strike a chord
with folks.

I have a new song, "He's Not the Two-Timing Kind." Got
the idea after seeing Lee with the leggy blonde. I've polished
the song at open-mike nights and even endured another song
critique with Susan West and one with Walt and Birdie.
(Which, by the way, were brutal. Bru-*tal*.) But their input
inspired me to make it a better song.

Jim met with Marc too. Liked his stuff and suggested we
get together. We have an appointment to write next week. I'm
going to like songwriter Marc Lewis way more than boss Marc
Lewis.

Just before the workshop, a fellow songwriter named
Quinn Damon catches me in the foyer. "Hey, Robin, Mallory
Clark was looking for you."

I make a face. "Mallory Clark? Really? How do you know
Mallory Clark?"

Quinn scoffs like I'm an idiot or something. "You gotta keep
up with the news if you're going to make it in this industry."

I sigh. "Right, Quinn. Anyway, Mallory?"

"Mallory just signed with Curb Records as an artist."

"Mallory Clark? Petite chick with soulful eyes?"

"She's the one."

"What'd she want with me?"

He shrugs. "She didn't say."

I dig my cell phone out of my purse and make the call.

"Hey, it's Robin . . . Fine, how are you? . . . I know, I just heard. Fantastic . . . I'd be blown away too . . . Oh? Really? . . . Sure . . . Right, I understand." I check my watch. "Noshville Deli in thirty minutes."

I press *End*. Well, what do you know? How far a little kindness goes.

Quinn passes by again. "What'd Mallory want?"

A big grins splits my face. "Have a nice evening, Quinn."

"Robin, aren't you staying for the workshop?"

"Not tonight." I dial another number. "Hi, are you in the office?"

A few minutes later I meet Jim at Nashville Noise. "What's on your mind?" He rocks back in his big leather chair.

I start to sit across from him but notice something new on his credenza. "Where did you get those?"

Jim glances over his shoulder. "Your mom sent them."

I walk around his desk. "Oh, for crying out loud. She sent you these?"

There's a shot of me when I was three holding onto a big plastic guitar. Another one when I was ten with Granddaddy's Taylor guitar. It's as big as I am. Then pictures of my high school graduation and one of the whole family.

"She said your brother serves over in Iraq."

"Yes."

"I hope you don't mind . . . about the pictures."

"No, no." Watching Jim catch up on being a father, reconciling his past with his present and future, is sorta cool in an odd, quirky way. "I have more pictures if you want."

He turns to his desk. "That'd be great." His voice is gruff and low. "Maybe we could get one of, you know," (*cough, sputter*), "us. Me, and you."

"I'd like that."

He nods, then chuckles as I tell him how six of us toilet papered the school courtyard the night before graduation. When the principal handed me my diploma case, I opened it up to find a square of toilet paper. Scribbled on it was "See me."

He laughs.

"I liked to have died, right there."

He asks about the other pictures, and I give him little anecdotes, sitting on the edge of his desk.

"I'm glad you had a nice life."

I grin. "It's getting better. Mallory Clark called me. She wants to cut some of my songs for her new CD."

Jim smiles. "I heard about her deal. Let's sign you to Nashville Noise Publishing before this ball gets too far down the lane." He's in command now.

"Are you sure?" I hop off the desk. "I'm sure SongTunes or—"

"Funny, very funny. Remind me to thank your mom for raising a sarcastic kid."

I sit across from him. "Jim, seriously, do you think I'm ready?"

He stands. "Not entirely, but Mallory has a unique sound, and a few of your songs might work well with her." He clicks off his desk lamp and closes the lid to his laptop. "But even if you weren't my daughter, I'd want to sign you. So, let's do it."

"Thank you." I stand. "I'm supposed to meet Mallory and her producer at Noshville in ten minutes. Will you come with me?"

He walks over to the coat tree and picks up his jacket. "What are fathers for?"

33

Run across Pete Hadley's field with one leg in a cast while his bull, Rocky, chases me.

Smack a baseball through Old Man Crumley's window while he watches from his front porch.

Bump into Freddie Krueger on a dark and stormy night.

Three things I'd rather *not* do than stand backstage at the Freedom Music Hall waiting to go on with Momma wearing look-alike outfits.

It's the first of May, springtime in the hills. They're ready to sing.

And so am I. As we wait, I confess, I'm a little nervous. Maybe a lot nervous, but it's anticipation, not anxiety. God's brought me a long way. I'm not turning back now.

Smiley Canyon saunters over. "You ready to go on?" He nudges me in the ribs with his pointy elbow.

"You bet." I nudge him back.

Smiley cackles. "Can't believe a year in Music City and you're cured."

"Let's just say, I lost my fears in NashVegas."

"All righty, I'll buy that. I'll buy that."

When I look Smiley in the eye, I see what I never thought I'd see. Respect.

"I'm proud of you, gal. Plumb proud."

"That means a lot, Smiley." I sniffle and clear my throat.

"Get ready, Robin. You and Bit are up next." Jeeter grins as he straightens his bolo tie. "Hey now, those are some red boots. Where'd you get them?"

I slide my foot out to show them off. "Boot Corral. A gift from my cousin." I glance at him. "Have you seen Momma?"

"Nope." The old emcee shakes his head with one eye on center stage. The Blues Street Boys are singing again. "Shewwee, somebody's gotta tell them fellows that harmonies are supposed to be, you know, harmonious."

I nudge him forward. "Go ahead, tell them."

He steps away. "You tell them."

"Not me. I'm just a freebird singing her songs. If The Blues Street Boys have courage enough to get up there and sing, who am I to tell them different?"

Jeeter jerks his thumb over his shoulder. "Go find your momma. This is their last song."

I set my guitar down just as Arizona and Eliza come up the backstage steps. "You seen Momma?"

"No," Arizona says, her big round diamond sparkling on her hand. Ty just asked her last week. I'm a maid of honor again. "We came to make sure *you* were going on."

I push past them. "Please. The fear stuff was so last year."

Eliza laughs. "You think Momma caught it from you?"

"I don't know, but we need to find her."

Arizona says that she'll check outside, and Eliza heads off for the dressing rooms. I make a bee line for the ladies' room.

The door is locked. "Momma?"

"She's not in here."

I press my lips on the crack between the door and the metal frame. "Sure sounds like she is."

Momma opens the door and jerks me inside. A wad of wet paper towels drips from her hand.

"I can't go on. It's been twenty-six years since I sang on stage. What was I thinking? I'm not young, cute, adorable Bit Lukeman anymore."

Fear blows over me, but only briefly. "You're going out there, Momma."

"I'm not going nowhere."

"Yes, you are."

"No, I'm not."

We do another round of this before I get an idea. "I'll be right back."

Scurrying out to the stage where the Blue's Street Boys are bowing to mild applause, I catch Jeeter's attention. "Pssst. Come here.

He shakes his head and waves me onto the stage. Oh, brother. I scuttle out, the heels of my boots thumping against the ancient hardwood. I whisper in Jeeter's ear.

He nods and announces, "Would Carol Honey and Lynette Good please meet Robin backstage? Quickly."

"Be right back," I murmur to Jeeter.

"What am I supposed to do?" he asks.

"Sing a song."

"We're ready."

Jeeter stops singing immediately. "Ladies and gentlemen, I'm pleased as punch to introduce the highly anticipated Robin Rae and Bit Lukeman McAfee."

Shoving against the applause, Momma and I rush out on stage with Aunt Carol and Aunt Lynette. Daddy's all smiles

from the front row, with Lee next to him. They talked out on
the porch last night, in cahoots with the crickets who sang
over their conversation. My stomach knots when I think of
Lee, down on one knee, asking, but I know my answer will
be yes.

Next to Lee, Granddaddy and Grandma Lukeman beam.
Then there's Grandpa and Grandma McAfee, Lee, Eliza, and
her new man, a rodeo clown named Rascal, and my brother,
Steve, home on leave. He's holding his son, Burch, while
Dawnie leans against him.

One row back, Arizona and Ty snuggle together, and next
to them is Jim Chastain. Momma invited him down and one
Miss Henna Bliss latched on to him. By the smile on his face,
I do believe Jim Chastain has a fondness for Freedom women.

I plug in my guitar. "Good evening, Freedom."

Freedom answers with shouts and whistles.

For one second, the bottom of my stomach drops out, but
my courage reaches down for the save.

"Many of y'all remember the Lukeman Sisters." Applause
ricochets around the room. "For the first time in twenty-six
years, they're going to sing one of their favorite hymns together."

I start "Just a Closer Walk with Thee." At first, the
Lukeman sisters are spread across the stage, stiff as doorknobs.
But their voices are sleek and blended, their harmonies perfect.

When they belt, "Grant it Jesus is my plea," Momma
walks over and slips her arm around Carol who then gathers
in Lynette. When the song is done, so is the healing.

Momma is warmed up now and in the groove. She gives
me the signal, and I start the song she wrote for Daddy.
He whips out his hanky when Momma's velvet voice sings,
"You're the melody of my life."

The place goes nuts when she finishes, and Momma is still
the darling of the stage.

When the applause dies down, I start my latest song, "Midnight Blue."

"I wrote this with a friend of mine, Marc Lewis. We almost got a cut on a CD by new artist Mallory Clark, but . . ." I peer at Jim, "better luck next time."

Momma sings backup while Aunt Carol and Aunt Lynette sway in the corner just out of the spotlight.

My voice soars above the thousand pairs of watching eyes. God's pleasure washes down. I know beyond all doubt He's my strength and song.

And this, I will do for the rest of my life.

Acknowledgments

My motto would be "Lost in Palm Bay" if it hadn't been for the amazing support and advice of so many people. Every ounce of me screams thank you, thank you, thank you to everyone who encouraged me with this manuscript . . .

Jesus, my Friend—Your love delivered me from all my fears.

My husband and best friend, Tony—you travel the journey of each book with me. Blessings upon you for not caring about piddly stuff like food and wrinkled laundry. I love you very much.

My agent, Karen Solem—you called me one day with an idea, and lo these many months later, here it is. This book began with you.

Christine Lynxwiler—you read one version after another. Thank you for your critique and loving this manuscript once we got it off the ground.

Tracey Bateman, Susie Warren, and Susan Downs—thank you for the encouragement. Susie, the "three things" are dedicated to you.

Colleen Coble—thank you for helping to open doors. May the Lord return to you a hundredfold what you pour out.

Allison Wilson—Thank you for brainstorming and lunching at Atlanta Bread.

My editor, Ami McConnell—your stellar reputation precedes you. I'm so honored to work with you. Thank you for your friendship.

My other editor, Leslie Peterson—thank you for your encouragement, insights, and edits.

Lisa Young—my songwriting soulmate. Your company made my nights at the Bluebird and learning the songwriting business a blast.

Vicky Beeching—thank you for the chat at Starbucks. And hugs to Cassie Campbell for introducing us.

Chris Oglesby of Oglesby Writer Management—thank you for taking the time to help me understand the music business. It was fun!

Ree Guyer Buchanan of Wrensong Publishing—thank you for sharing your expertise and insight on the journey of a songwriter.

All the songwriters who aided me—Jeff Pearson, Sheryl Olquin, Karen Staley, Barry Dean, Craig Monday, Lorna Flowers, James Dean Hicks, and the songwriters who played at the Bluebird Café—I knew nothing about this business until you guys shined your light. Also, thanks to Dave Petrelli at NSAI for pointing me in the right direction.

Ted Travers—thank you for funding my research trip.

Eric Exley, my "son"—thank you for making me write my own lyrics.

Kaye Dacus and Rebecca Seitz—for showing me Nashville.

READING GROUP GUIDE QUESTIONS

1. Robin is a dedicated employee at Willaby's even though she knows she should be doing something else. Have there been times in your life where you struggled between being comfortable and being ambitious enough to go after your dreams? (p. 16)

2. Reverend Eli mentions that he had to pray hard to love his captors in South America. Do you grapple with loving your enemies? (p. 35)

4. Robin made many outward changes (haircut, manicure, pedicure), but remained the same person on the inside. When have you tried to mask the inside by recreating your outward appearance? (p. 112)

5. Robin wonders if Blaire is "for or against her". "If I overcome, does she have to overcome?" Are there times in your life when you felt like you had to be the example to help someone else stay on track? (p. 137)

6. Robin knows she is still terrified to sing in front of people, but decides "to let God's love be my strength." When have you taken a stand and made a true leap of faith? (p. 170)

7. There is a passage where Robin has an epiphany about why she moved to Nashville. Have you had times in your life when you realized there was a greater purpose to the things you were doing? (p. 171)

8. After meeting Robin and seeing how she faced her fears, Marty decides to face her own fear and go to college. When have your actions had an impact on the life of someone else? How did that make you feel? (p. 250)